The Good The Bad And The Undead

The Good, The Bad and The Undead

An Interactive Novel by

Ashton MacSaylor and Jamie Thomson

Art by Callie MacSaylor

Published by Fabled Lands LLP
2018

Story by Jamie Thomson and Ashton MacSaylor
Writing by Ashton MacSaylor
Art by Callie MacSaylor
Edited by Richard Hetley

Published by Fabled Lands LLP

Fabled Lands LLP
Cambridge House
16 High Street
Saffron Walden
Essex
CB10 1AX

Printed by Ingram Spark
www.ingramspark.com

This novel is interactive. You will be asked to make choices as you read. If you start at the beginning and read through all pages in order, it will make little sense.

For Eddy, Jackie, Andrew, Matthew, Natalia (pronounced Natalie), and the other students from Prospect High School during the spring of 2015, who helped me develop this story by joining my weird after-school roleplaying game. I only had to bribe them with a little bit of extra credit.

Yet thence his lustful Orgies he enlarg'd
Even to that Hill of scandal, by the Grove
Of Moloch homicide, lust hard by hate;
Till good Josiah drove them thence to Hell.

—Milton, *Paradise Lost*

Josiah da Silva
Former U. S. Marshal
Kansas City, Missouri 1866

Walter Korse
The "Killing Angel"
Duluth, Minnesota 1867

Diana James
Independent Trader
Richmond, Virginia 1863

Affliction, Texas
1870

The Good The Bad And The Undead
Ghost Canyon
Mining Camp
Field of Rocks
The Devil's Anvil
Juniper Grove
Red Bluff
Abandoned Mill
Church
Saloon
SALOON
Hangman's Hill
Undertaker
General Store
Stables
Affliction TEXAS
Manor
Jail

The Good, The Bad, and the Undead

The last sliver of sun, now red and dark, vanished beneath the horizon, and the long shadows that had been growing across the desert swallowed the town.

Day Three

Sun baked the cracked dirt roads. The wooden buildings that lined the street were half-burned and bone dry as year-old wasp hive. A lone figure, barely alive, stumbled out into that heat. A fine layer of dust caked him from head to foot, dulling his tailored grey suit and long moustache.

He lifted one hand to squint at the horizon. The sun burned, low and huge and red, shimmering in the heat waves coming off the desert.

Marshal Josiah da Silva slumped against a post in the shade and took a deep breath. After a moment, he tilted his head down to look at the golden marshal's star pinned to his breast, its gleam obscured by a layer of dust and charcoal. He unpinned it and rubbed it on his jacket, but the dust simply smeared.

Gritting his teeth against the pain, he spat upon the star and laboriously wiped it until it shone when he held it out in the sun. Satisfied, he pinned it back on his chest. The fingers of his left hand were swollen and moved unevenly, barely able to grip the pin. It took him four tries.

The sun was touching the horizon now, half of its great, burning bulk gone beneath the rim of the world. Taking a deep breath, Marshal da Silva staggered to the middle of the street and drew himself up to his full height.

The fire from the night before had ravaged the street, leaving nothing but a burnt out husk of the town he had once helped build. Yet he knew the ruins would hide their approach. Any minute now…

Planting his feet, he pulled back his jacket, revealing the ivory handle of a long Colt pistol. This he drew, holding it in his one good hand while he rolled his shoulders.

He watched the sun sink. "The Lord is my shepherd…" he murmured.

The shadows began to move. First it was simply a stirring behind a dark window, something that could have been mistaken for wind touching an unlatched shutter. Then came the groans.

A door burst off its hinges partway down the street. Josiah settled his grip on his pistol, feeling the familiar weight of it in his palm.

A human shape slouched out of the building, silhouetted against the last light of the dying sun. Smoke began to rise from the dark form, and it let out an inhuman keening sound, its large head rolling from side to side until its eyes fell on him. Dark lips peeled back in a grin of sadistic pleasure.

That's when the marshal fired, blowing the creature back off its feet to land in the dust. It did not move again. The marshal whispered, "Thy rod and thy staff, they comfort me."

The last sliver of sun, now red and dark, vanished beneath the horizon, and the long shadows that had been growing across the desert swallowed the town.

A cacophonous howling rose from the surrounding buildings, and one door after another burst open. Shadows slunk into the street, snuffling and searching, drawn to his rich, red scent by the strength of their thirst.

He fired, knocking another off its feet. He fired again, blasting a third to the ground.

The others turned to look at him with one motion, their large, bright eyes blinking in the growing darkness. His next shot blew a grinning head clean off.

The monsters rushed toward him, hopping and sliding and howling.

He fired again, blowing out the leg of one, taking off the arm of another. His clumsy, swollen left hand couldn't reload the pistol, so instead of trying, he fired one last time and discarded the ivory-handled treasure, drawing another identical pistol from his other hip.

The first shot took a woman between the eyes, dropping her. His next hit an old man who gibbered madly, running his tongue along bloodstained teeth. The marshal fired with precision and speed, killing them almost as quickly as they could come. Almost.

He gritted his teeth as he said, "Goodness and mercy shall follow me all the days of my life." But the street was filled with them now, and after he dropped one just a few steps from him, only three bullets remained. He whispered, "And I will dwell in the house of the Lord forever."

Two bullets.

"Amen."

One bullet.

Marshal Josiah da Silva examined his face in the small wash-mirror. Turn to 1.

1

Day One

Marshal Josiah da Silva examined his face in the small wash-mirror. It was a broad, lined face, with clear grey eyes looking out from above a bushy moustache. The moustache was in the Portuguese style, with great drooping ends, the only thing left to him by his conquistador ancestors.

Using quick, precise motions, he wet his cheeks and began to shave the night's stubble clean, working around the carefully-groomed moustache. The train rocked as he did so, causing his blade to bite briefly into the soft skin below his jaw. A drop of blood welled up from the tiny cut.

"Careful," the man behind him said in a slow, mocking drawl.

With an irritated glance, Josiah looked at the man who shared his small room on the train. The fellow was built like a knife, tall and lean, with muscles like whipcords and a face hard and cold as death itself. He was chained hand and foot.

Josiah's eyes flicked to the manacles restraining the man's wrists and ankles, quickly checking their sureness before he returned to his grooming. The sun was rising through the window to the east, and rays of golden light shot into the cabin briefly as the train came around a curve. Outside the window, the sunburnt lands of the west stretched out wide and open before them.

Josiah used a handkerchief to mop up the dot of blood, inspecting the cut. It was a tiny thing, already done bleeding. He mopped it one more time and returned to his shaving.

As he opened his mouth to respond, the train rocked again—this time his blade was safely in the washbasin—and the door to the tiny bedroom compartment opened.

"Fairfield, next stop," the conductor said, smiling in the doorway. His face fell as his eyes landed on the man in chains. The prisoner leered up at him, his jackknife face split in a wide, mirthless grin. With a quick motion the prisoner lurched forward slightly, shaking his chains.

The conductor scowled, taking an involuntary step back. To the marshal, he said, "Here now, you sure this one's gonna be arright?"

"Don't worry. He'll hang soon enough," the marshal said in a cultured, southern accent, wiping his now-bare chin clean.

The conductor closed the door, grumbling, and Josiah could feel the train slowing as it approached its next stop. He shrugged on his suit jacket and smoothed the fine, grey cloth, looking at himself in the mirror.

He turned to his prisoner.

"Time to go. You have one chance to come along peaceably," Josiah said. Turn to 25.

Josiah grabbed the prisoner's chains and hefted him to his feet. Turn to 13.

2

The cold morning air greeted them as they stepped down from the train. The conductor called, "Here now, watch yer step. Fairfield, this stop Fairfield!"

Josiah stopped to take in his surroundings, jerking the prisoner to a halt next to him. He looked around at the town, blinking in the early morning sunlight. Numerous tall, freshly painted buildings lined a broad main avenue already bustling with finely dressed people.

"A fine town, ain't it?" The conductor remarked, following Josiah's gaze. Without giving him a chance to answer, he continued, "Founded 1845, same year as the Texas annex. But you wouldn't a' believed it's the same place. Why, the first time the train came through here, I swear this town was no more than a couple hovels and a dozen head of cattle."

The conductor laughed jovially at his own observation. He patted the side of the train, "And it's all thanks to this marvelous machine."

"I know," Josiah said.

"Sorry?" The conductor blinked into the rising sun.

"I was here when this town was founded. I know what year it was," Josiah said. He tugged on the prisoner's chain and led the lean man into town.

"Fairfield, this stop!" The conductor called behind him.

Josiah wanted to look around a bit before anything else. Turn to 30.

Josiah took his prisoner to the Bad Dog Saloon. Turn to 9.

3

Josiah grabbed the boy's arm. "Listen son," Josiah said, "Sometimes things ain't all what they seem to be."

"Yes sir," the lad said. He kept listening, as though expecting words of wisdom to drop like rain from the older man's lips.

Josiah seemed about to say more, but instead he just released the young man's arm. The fellow nodded again, vigorously, and put his hat on. A shadow of perplexity crossed his face.

Josiah took his second shot of whisky without a word. Turn to 12.

4

Diana tipped her hat without smiling. She swung the rifle off her back and leaned it against the bar within easy reach.

"Welcome to the Bad Dog Saloon. You new in town?" The bartender asked. Her gaze lingered, not on Diana herself, but on the weapon she had brought with her into the bar.

Diana nodded shortly.

"Well, I'm Mama Nell, and this here's my bar." The woman gestured at the establishment.

"The name's Diana," she said. She glanced over at some of the patrons who were still staring at her. They quickly looked away as soon as she met their eyes.

Mama Nell said, "Don't mind them. What can I get for you?"

"Information," Diana said. Turn to 29.

5

Josiah jerked a thumb at the prisoner. Nell whistled. "Finally caught the bastard, huh?"

"He gave me a run for it, that's for damn sure. I'll say this about the man: he knows the wild like no one else."

"How'd you get 'im, in the end?" She asked.

He shook his head, rotating the whisky glass between his fingers. "Got lucky. I managed to clip his leg while he was ridin' away. He rode that horse to death, but once it was gone, he couldn't walk far. Cornered him on a little farm up in Dakota Territory." He shrugged. "Could have gone better, but here he is, ain't he?"

"You did good, Joe. Not many could'a done what you pulled off. He goin' to hang?" She asked.

"Sure as God's green earth. He'll hang back where it all started." He held up the shot glass, looking at the golden fluid in the light.

"Affliction…" she said softly.

Josiah nodded. He took the shot with the swiftness of experience. The whiskey burned going down, but the pain satisfied him.

"It ain't good news from those parts, Joe," Nell said.

He slid the empty glass back across to her. She picked it up absently and started cleaning it. "What's the word?" he asked.

Nell shook her head. "Nothin'. That's the problem. We've had folk go that way, and they jes' don't come back. Used to be a little cattle rustlin' was the worst of it… now, I just don't know anymore."

Josiah let out a big breath, hooking his thumbs on his belt. "I got to go, Nell. Ain't no choice about it."

"I'd consider those words…" she said, shaking her head.

"He gave me a hell of a run, Nell, but I caught him. He's going to hang in Affliction."

A hint of a mischievous grin tugged at Nell's lips. Her eyes sparkled as she said, "Same old Joe."

"You seem to be doing well for yourself," Josiah said. Turn to 19.

6

"You can sleep here, so long as you don't bother me," Diana said.

The marshal nodded and strode away towards his animal. Diana cocked her head, watching him go. He wasn't like other men she'd met on the frontier. They were simple creatures, driven by spirits, food and women. There was something different that drove him.

She went about her business, and let him go about his. As he set up for the night—there was enough room for each to claim their own building—she noticed that he had another man with him, a prisoner tied and bound something fierce.

Later that evening, she found the marshal setting up a fire in a spot sheltered from the wind between two of the ranch buildings. He looked up at her, his craggy face illuminated from below in the firelight.

"Think we'll run into outlaws on the road?" She asked, joining him by the fire. "Some people say the Killing Angel's still loose in these parts."

The marshal grunted. "Unlikely."

"Why are you so sure?"

He gave her a level look, then jerked his thumb at the prisoner and went back to tending the fire. "Because that there's Walter Korse, the man they call the 'Killing Angel.'"

Diana's eyes widened, and she gave the bound man another look. There was something sinister about him, lean and devilish. She'd heard of the Killing Angel.

Folks said he had murdered dozens of folks up and down the frontier. Didn't matter who they were, women, children, he sent them all to meet their maker.

The prisoner noticed her looking and met her gaze. He had striking, light blue eyes in an Indian face. She almost caught her breath. She'd never seen a face like his before, the mixing of white and red features, the long, straight black hair falling down around those blue eyes.

He grinned without humor, showing teeth that gleamed in the firelight. He stuck out his tongue and waggled it at her in a lewd gesture. She narrowed her eyes, then looked away with studied indifference.

The marshal just stirred the fire.

"What are you bringin' him to Affliction for?" Diana asked.

Josiah wasn't in the mood to talk about it. Turn to 14.

"That's where it all started," Josiah said. Turn to 26.

7

"What sort of things was he buyin'?" Diana asked casually.

"Everything," Mr. Hastings growled. "The man damn near cleared me out. And he hired help too, a dozen men. Said they would be digging somewhere, up in them mountains." He waved a hand toward the west.

"You know where?" Diana asked, her heart suddenly pounding very hard.

"Nah, I make it a practice not to ask questions if I don't need to," he answered, dashing her brief hopes. Of course it wouldn't be so easy.

"What did he buy, specifically?" She asked.

The man gave her a quizzical look. "Picks and shovels, mostly. Food. Water. Dynamite. Lotta the same things yer gettin', truth be told. But he weren't planning on sellin', that's for damn sure. He had an aim to use it all. Don't know for what. Didn't ask." He grunted. "I do wish he'd paid, though."

Diana sighed. It figured she would follow him halfway across the country and still be cleaning up after him.

"How much did he leave owin' you? Could be I might cover some of it," Diana said. Turn to 15.

"Thank you, Mr. Hastings. You've been very helpful," Diana said. Turn to 11.

8

Josiah nodded, listening as the Sheriff described the attack. Sheriff McCann was a stout Irishman with a broken nose and a flair for the dramatic, and his story of the outlaws' assault framed himself and his deputies in the best possible light.

"You say they laid down arms, then?" Josiah asked.

"Yup! Once they saw me and my boys, they gave it up for a bad job. These mongrels have been troublin' us for years, harryin' the roads down south. 'Bout time someone brought 'em to justice. That leader of theirs, mind, he's a piece of work." The sheriff leaned in confidentially and said in a hearty whisper, "Some say he's even the Killin' Angel himself, incognito."

"That so?" Josiah said in a deadpan tone.

The sheriff nodded with slow, self-important confidence. "But never you fear. We got him locked up tight. If that man is Walter Korse, I'll beat it out of him. He ain't escapin' justice this time."

"I see," Josiah said. Looking to the door to the cells, he asked, "Mind if I have a word with him? I have a certain interest in the, ah, 'Killing Angel,' myself."

"Oh, sure," Sheriff McCann said, puffing up with self-importance that a Federal Marshal was taking an interest in his business. "Right this way."

The keyring jangled as the sheriff let Josiah into the back room where several cells lined the walls. Only one of them was occupied.

"Where are the others?" Josiah asked.

"Oh, we sent 'em on to the county jail. We just kept this one for questionin'. I don't think he's told us all yet."

"I see," Josiah nodded. He stepped up to the cell. The man inside wore black clothes that once had been fine, but were now caked with dust and dried blood. He looked up, meeting Josiah's eye without fear, and gave a roguish grin that flashed gold teeth. "Another to poke and prod at the misfortune of others? Or do you actually have intelligent questions for me this time?"

"You shut yer mouth, ye hear?" Sheriff McCann shook his baton threateningly, and the outlaw leader lifted his palms in mocking surrender.

"Give us a few moments. Would you mind, Sheriff?" Josiah said.

The sheriff nodded and went out, saying, "Be careful with this one. He's smooth as glass, and 'e's killed more'n we can count."

The imprisoned man looked up from where he sat on the floor. With a mocking smile, he asked, "Here to discover the truth? 'Am I the 'Killing Angel.''" His voice had an incongruously upper-crust accent. It took Josiah a moment to place it. Virginian, probably.

He waved a hand dismissively. "I just have a few questions."

The man coughed painfully, then gave a rueful smile. "Very well. Ask your questions."

Josiah gave him a hard look. He said, "I understand your gang usually works the roads south of here. What brought you to Fairfield? Didn't you know it was a risk to hit a town this large?"

"Of course we knew it was a risk. Insult my ability, but do not insult my intelligence, sir."

"So what happened?" Josiah asked, tucking a thumb into his belt loop.

The man coughed again and shifted. "The roads south of here have not a thing to offer any longer. The pickings are just no good."

"Why not?" Josiah asked.

The outlaw shook his head. "Who can say? No one travels those roads anymore. Going into Affliction was too dangerous, so we came north."

Josiah narrowed his eyes. He repeated, "Affliction was too dangerous? Why?"

"You don't know?" The man cocked an eyebrow.

"Just tell me," Josiah growled.

The outlaw shook his head, as if struggling to find words. "Something is not right in that town. More than usual. The outlying ranches are abandoned. No one goes in or out. We see their lights at night, but never a soul in the day. When I sent some of my men to go raid the town..." he paused for a coughing fit.

When he could speak again he finished, "They never came back."

"You don't know what happened to 'em?" Josiah asked.

The outlaw sighed, "No, and I don't aim to find out. That's when my men and I decided to head north. We hit Fairfield. We figured either we'd be rich or we'd be in jail. Either way, it's better than being dead." He shrugged. "We took our chances and we lost, fair and square."

Josiah nodded grimly, and his expression as he left the jail was dour. A man like that, someone who had been preying on roads for years… he didn't give himself up easily. He knew attacking Fairfield was a lost cause. He almost seemed relieved to be caught. What had put the fear of God like that into him?

Josiah rode out of Fairfield with his prisoner in tow. Turn to 10.

9

Josiah took his prisoner to the Bad Dog Saloon. He was pleased to see the place still stood at the center of town, as mean and stubborn as the last time he saw it. It was a solid, familiar knot of wood, surrounded by flowery new growth.

He walked up the stairs to the saloon doors. The sign swinging above the front porch bore the same mark of a snarling dog, its only concession to the changing times being a coat of fresh paint. He pushed his way through the double doors, dragging the prisoner in behind him.

The rush of remembrance came hard and thick when he saw the bartender. Nell stood behind the counter, entirely the same, yet entirely different. Her arms were set against the bar—they looked stronger than he remembered—as she squared off against a drunkard who must have been up boozing all night long. Josiah tied his prisoner to one of the support beams while she sent the drunkard off to bed with a string of foul language.

"Woman, you could peel paint off walls with that tongue," Josiah said.

Nell turned to him with a glower, but her face transformed with recognition. "Josiah! By God, I never thought I'd see the day! Come here, you old bastard!" she called, coming out from behind the bar and spreading her arms to embrace him in a huge hug.

"Let me get a look at you," she said, grabbing him by the shoulders and looking him up and down. He looked back at her; her hips, like her arms, were wider than he remembered, but her smile was exactly the same.

"You went and grew old on me!" she said, then she laughed and slapped his shoulder hard enough to make him stagger.

Josiah smiled and allowed her to settle him into a stool by the bar. She poured him a drink and slid it across to him, then gave him a steady look. "It's been twenty-two years, Joe. What brings you back this way now?"

"Never one to mince words, were you, Pretty Nell?"

She barked a laugh. "It's Mama Nell now, you old dog. Ain't nobody called me 'pretty' in a long time!"

"Mama Nell?" Josiah asked, raising an eyebrow. Turn to 24.

Josiah jerked a thumb at the prisoner. Turn to 5.

Josiah rode out of Fairfield with his prisoner in tow. He hadn't made as good of time as he'd hoped, but the sun was still high; with any luck, he could cover plenty of ground before nightfall.

His thoughts drifted back to Nell. For a woman her age, it was a sign of God's blessing how good she still looked. Perhaps a bit of the "pretty" shine had rubbed off in the years since he'd seen her last, but that same good cheer animated her. He was glad to have seen her, if only briefly. He'd have to make a point of stopping in for another visit on the way back.

Who else would he run into, coming back to Affliction? After his wife passed on… well, there just hadn't seemed to be much left to hold him there. But he had helped build that town, and surely they hadn't all forgotten him.

The sun crawled across the sky, and the landscape changed slowly, the way it does. The green earth around Fairfield faded to brown, then to tan as the vegetation died off. This was dry land, land he knew.

The prisoner made no fuss as they travelled. If he thought anything at all, he didn't speak his mind.

As the sky darkened into evening, the road took them by an abandoned ranch house. Josiah tugged on the reigns, pulling his horse to a stop. Korse's mule came up short, nearly bumping into the horse, and shook its head, grunting its annoyance.

"Whoa, boy!" Josiah reined in his horse to prevent a fight. Once the animals were disentangled, he swung off and tied both to a fencepost. He smacked the wood with one hand. The fence needed repair in more than one place, but it would hold.

He looked up at the quiet ranch. If it truly was abandoned, it could be a good place to pass the night. No lights glowed in the four or five buildings. No cows lowed or chickens pecked. Yet there was no sign of violence or disturbance. Josiah frowned. What had happened to the people who lived here? Where were they now?

He pushed his way in the gate, keeping his hand close to the holster at his hip. The place had several buildings: a house, a barn, and a couple sheds. As he crossed the yard to the main house, he noted a month or longer of growth in the weeds.

The steps creaked as he ascended them to the front door of the main building, which was already standing unlatched and ajar. He pushed, and it swung inward with a groan of annoyance, revealing the dark interior.

"Hands where I can see 'em," a voice came from behind him. Josiah stiffened. He raised his hands and turned slowly. A woman held a rifle pointed at his chest.

It was the woman he had nearly bumped into leaving Nell's place. He could see in her eyes she recognized him too. Her gaze flicked to the marshal's badge on his chest, and she raised her gun high, taking the aim off him. "I saw you in town," she said.

Josiah touched the brim of his hat. "Marshal Josiah da Silva, at your service."

She nodded. "Diana. Diana James," she introduced herself. Diana had the look of the road upon her, the dust of long miles travelled alone. She wore riding leathers, and her hair was pulled back in a ponytail which blew in the wind.

From this vantage point, he could now see a covered wagon that must be hers, half-hid behind one of the buildings. "That yours?" he asked, gesturing as he lowered his hands.

"Closest to a home I got," she said. "That barkeep said you might be headed this way. Didn't figure I'd run into you."

Josiah hooked his thumbs into his belt loops. "Well, any friend of Nell is a friend of mine. What brings you out this way?"

"Lookin' for someone," she said. Then she glanced over at her wagon. "And doin' a bit of trading. A girl's gotta eat."

Josiah frowned. He weighed his words, then carefully said, "Don't you think it's a mite dangerous to be travelling out here without a man to protect you? There's outlaws on these roads. Some of them just raided Fairfield itself not a few days ago."

The woman hefted her rifle in one hand. With the other, she drew a shotgun out from near the driver's seat in her wagon. "I got two men to protect me right here, Winchester and Remington."

She laughed at the expression on his face and turned to put away both guns.

"You can sleep here, so long as you don't bother me," Diana said. Turn to 6.
"I hope you ain't planning on staying here," Diana said. Turn to 22.

"Thank you, Mr. Hastings. You've been very helpful," Diana said. "Just one more question. Anyone else around here who might have had dealings with Professor Enfield?"

He nodded. "Aye, take yerself over to the Bad Dog Saloon. Mama Nell is the proprietor, and she's the other one sold him some goods. Food, spirits and the like, I think. Got herself just as taken as I was. She'll have some words for you about him, and they'll be hot too!"

He gave her directions to the saloon, and Diana thanked him again before turning to go. He waved it off and returned to his list, saying, "Good luck to you, Ma'am. I got most of what yer lookin' for. You stop on by a little later and I'll have that wagon all loaded and ready to go. Just be sure to pay before you leave and all." He flashed her a quick grin, showing more than one missing tooth, and she tipped her hat with a smile.

A dusty wind blew down the main street of Fairfield. The sun was getting higher in the sky now; soon the heat would become oppressive. She looked up at the purple mountains, low on the horizon to the west. Enfield could be up in those mountains somewhere right now, toiling away with his men to dig at... God knows what.

She sighed. She couldn't find him by thinking. Besides, her nausea was starting to come back. Best to find some shade and a place to sit down, and maybe she could learn a little more at that saloon...

She found the Bad Dog Saloon exactly where Mr. Hastings had said it would be. Turn to 27.

Josiah took his second shot of whisky without a word. The boy hovered, looking about to say something else.

"Shoo now!" Mama Nell barked. As the boy made his exit, she watched Josiah's face closely.

"You're something of a hero around these parts," Nell said softly.

"Ain't no fault of mine what people think," he said, looking at his glass.

"Joe... it ain't your fault. None of it..." Nell said.

Josiah shrugged. "Don't worry about it."

Nell leaned both arms on the bar and said, "Before you hare off toward Affliction, you ought to know how bad the roads are. There's bandits and outlaws a plenty. It's gettin' so bad, a gang of 'em came ridin' in right here in Fairfield the other day."

Josiah frowned. "Strange they'd come for such a big town."

She laughed. "Strange, and stupid. They got themselves plumb locked up 'fore you could say, 'lickety split.' Didn't even seem too sour about it, neither. A hungry lot they were. I think they was just happy to have a warm bed and a spot o' food, even if it were in jail."

"I'd like to have a word with these men," Josiah said, standing.

"You know where to find the jail," Nell said.

Josiah made a face. "Mind watching Korse here for me for a few? He won't be no trouble, tussed up as he is. Oh, and I'll need some horses on my way out."

Nell nodded. "I ain't got but one horse to spare, but I got a mule you can have for the prisoner. Just put him in back for now. Don't want him scarin' away my customers."

Josiah dragged the prisoner to a back room and tied him there. "Don't cause no trouble, you hear?" The man simply stared, a disturbing lack of fear in those bottomless blue eyes.

"Thanks, Nell. I won't be long," Josiah said. He tipped his hat on the way out the door.

Diana James stood in the morning sun, directing the movement of boxes. Turn to 28.

13

Josiah grabbed the prisoner's chains and hefted him to his feet. "Let's go," he said calmly, flexing his strong arms to lift the prisoner's long body and slam him against the wall. Holding him with one hand, he opened the compartment door with the other.

The prisoner bucked and twisted in his grip like an angry bronco, nearly throwing Josiah back. It took all his strength to subdue the man, even chained as he was. When the prisoner was finally held tightly, he stared at Josiah gasping, sweat on his brow and hatred in his eyes. Then, that slow, mocking grin returned to his face. He spat at his captor.

A large, wet glob of spittle landed on Josiah's cheek, spraying his face and eyes with flecks of saliva only a moment after he reflexively closed them. His mouth turned slightly in repressed disgust.

Josiah calmly wiped his face. Turn to 23.
Josiah struck the prisoner, hard. Turn to 16.

14

Josiah wasn't in the mood to talk about it. "I don't see as how that's any of yer business," he said. "No offense intended, Ma'am." He tipped his hat.

To her credit, the woman didn't ask any more questions that night. They ate their respective meals and retreated to their respective cabins. He didn't expect he would see much more of her after this, and that didn't really bother him.

When Diana rose at dawn, the marshal was already up. Turn to 18.

15

"How much did he leave owin' you? Could be I might cover some of it," Diana said.

The store owner brightened, saying, "Well now!" Then his face fell. Sourly, he said, "Naw, 'twouldn't be right to ask a lady to pay a man's debts. Unless he's your family 'n all?" he looked at her hopefully.

Diana hesitated for the briefest moment before shaking her head. "No," she said firmly.

Mr. Hastings sighed. "Yer a sweet one, Miss, but 'tain't yer problem. He'll come back through, sooner or later, and he'll settle with me then if he's any man of honor. And if he don't, well, I got only me own fool self to blame."

"Thank you, Mr. Hastings. You've been very helpful," Diana said. Turn to 11.

16

Josiah struck the prisoner, hard. The man buckled in pain, sagging against the wall. Josiah pulled his handkerchief out, snapped it open, and neatly wiped his face. "Gentlemen," he said with a nod to a couple of travelers passing by, as they eyed the scene with discomfort.

The prisoner shook himself like a dog shaking off water, then stood back up to his full height. A small, mocking smile pulled at the corner of his swollen lips as he met Josiah's eyes. Josiah clenched his jaw, grabbed the chain, and forced the prisoner sharply ahead of him. "Move," he ground out.

The train was slowing to a stop now, as the tidy houses of bustling Fairfield rolled into view through the small window. Josiah guided the prisoner down the walkway between rows of finely dressed passengers, who looked away as they passed.

The cold morning air greeted them. Turn to 2.

17

"Last letter I got from him was addressed from Affliction. Fairfield's as close as the train'll take me. So here I am. Know anything about how that place stands today?"

The bartender furrowed her brow. "Honestly, not much. As far as I know it's a ghost town by now."

"What do you mean?" Diana's chest contracted in worry. If anything had happened to him...

"The town ain't so far away, they just never were folk who got out much. But recently, we ain't had no word at all. The town could have burned to the ground for all we know. And considerin' their luck, it just might have."

Diana chewed her lip, considering these words. It wasn't good news. She fought down a sense of queasiness.

The bartender gave her a keen look. "If he was headed to Affliction, then that makes him the last man we saw headin' that direction." She leaned in. "Listen, miss, I wouldn't recommend followin' him. You don't know what kinda trouble he might have got himself into down there, or even if he's still alive."

Diana settled her hat back on her head and dropped a few coins on the bar. "Afraid I don't have much choice. Thanks for the drink."

"Suit yourself," Mama Nell said. "But a word of advice before you go. There's a man 'round here somewhere, Marshal Josiah da Silva. He's a good man, and he's goin' that way too. You'd do best to look him up. Ain't no sense in travelin' those roads alone."

Diana gave a wry smile. "Thanks, but no thanks. I suit my own company best." She tipped her hat and went out into the morning sun.

Josiah nodded, listening as the Sheriff described the attack. Turn to 8.

18

When Diana rose at dawn, the marshal was already up. The wind was even worse this morning, whipping between the ranch buildings with so much force that twice she almost lost her hat. She groomed the cart horses and hitched them to the wagon that carried her trade goods. By the time she was finished, Josiah had both himself and his prisoner in their respective saddles.

He waited on his horse while she led her wagon back to the road. Once she was close enough, he called to her, "I ain't waitin' for that cart. The road should be safe, just go on up till you get to the Devil's Anvil. Across it you'll find Affliction."

She nodded. "I got a map," she called back.

He hesitated only briefly, then spurred his horse and started down the road. She quelled the pang she felt to see him go. Really, it was for the best. He'd seemed like a solid sort, but she preferred to be on her own. Maybe she would run into him again in Affliction.

Her regular nausea got the better of her about midmorning, and she had to stop the cart to throw up by the side of the road.

"Are you well?" a male voice called.

She looked up, instinctively reaching for her rifle even as another retch threatened to rise. She fought it back down—adrenaline lending her strength—but relaxed when she recognized the marshal.

"I thought you weren't waiting," she said, wiping her mouth with the back of her hand.

He scowled. "The road forks up ahead. Stay to the right." And he turned and rode on once more.

Diana sighed as she climbed back into the wagon. Thankfully, her nausea receded as the sun rose higher in the sky. It had been getting better lately. Either that, or she was just getting used to it. The shade over the driver's bench on the wagon was barely enough to hide under. It was hotter here than she was used to, farther north or east, and the heat affected both herself and the wagon horses.

The marshal's advice turned out to be sound. She took the right fork, and after another few hours' travel, she crested a hill to see a vast, white plain stretch out before her. That must be the Devil's Anvil.

Not far away, the broad-shouldered form of Josiah da Silva was waiting. He tipped his hat to her, and Diana tried not to smile. "You must be worried about me after all," she called.

Ignoring her, or pretending not to have heard, he said, "There's a good spot here to fill up on water and take a breather 'fore you ride ahead. Last water for a few miles, so take as much as you need." He pointed to a small stone well set back from the road a ways. It was surrounded by greenery, some of the last Diana could see.

With that, he turned from her and walked over to the well. His legs had the stiff look of someone who had spent long hours in the saddle.

She found a good place to stop the wagon and breathed a sigh of relief. There was a bit of shade here, one of the few trees she had seen all day.

As she approached the well, Josiah pulled up a clanking bucket. He passed some water to her, then used the rest to water himself and his horse. Taking off his hat, he splashed the cool liquid over his face and hair, breathing deeply.

Diana did the same when he was done, gasping in delight as the cold water hit her face. She met Josiah's eyes and grinned. He let a smile touch his lips before turning away.

As she watered her horse, she noticed the prisoner, still chained on his mule. The man sat so still he could have been part of the landscape itself. "What about him?" she asked.

The marshal nodded. He pulled a little tin cup from his pack. Filling it, he brought it over to the prisoner. "Take some water," he said. "There won't be water in that desert, and I can't have you dyin' before I get to hang you."

The prisoner did not respond as Josiah lifted the cup to him, so he slapped the man in the leg. Walter Korse slowly lifted his face. Something made Diana shudder when she saw the look in that face. It was long and weathered, with blue eyes that glittered beneath his lids. Those eyes settled on the cup of water.

For a long moment, nothing happened, and she wasn't sure if the man was well enough to understand. Then, slowly, Korse began to move. He took the water from the marshal's hand and held it, watching sunlight glitter off the shifting surface.

With slow deliberation, he turned the cup and poured it out. Diana stared. The water glistened in a tiny waterfall as it splashed to the ground. It pooled briefly, then vanished into the thirsty dust.

Walter Korse looked up and smiled with cracking lips, a grin that had no humor in it at all.

Josiah shook his head in disgust as he turned away. "Ain't no more where that came from." To her, he said, "Finish with the animals. We won't break again 'till we get there. It's a hot road ahead."

Walter quickly regretted rejecting the water. Turn to 31.
Walter did not regret pouring out the water. Turn to 39.

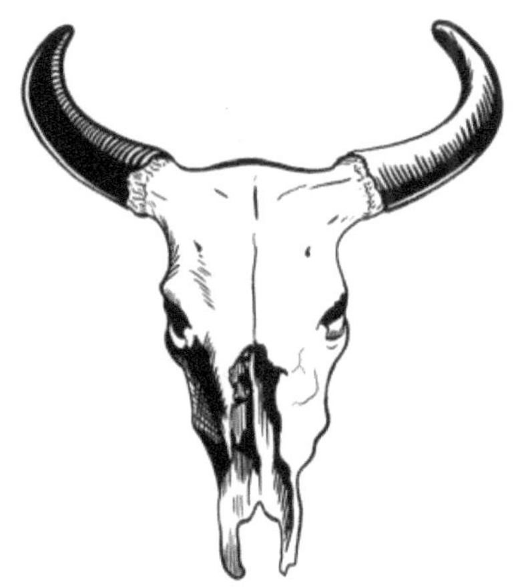

19

"You seem to be doing well for yourself," Josiah said.

Nell laughed, reddening. "This town, it just took off I guess. After you and them boys cleared out the Injuns around these parts, well… folk never stopped comin'! Ever since Red Bluff, we can't chase 'em off!"

Josiah grunted. "Glad I got out when I did. Too many folk for me."

"Say," a young man at the bar had been listening, and now he spoke up. "Did she just say you fought at Red Bluff?"

Josiah sighed. "That I did, boy. What's it to you?"

"What's it to me?" The lad clutched his hat. "Why, you're a goddam hero, that's what! Which one are ya? Hobfield? McCann?"

"He's Josiah da Silva. That's Marshal da Silva to you," Nell said, as she refilled the marshal's drink. She slid it across to him without asking if he wanted another.

"Josiah da Silva," the young man breathed, a note of reverence in his voice, "Why, you're one of the damn Band of Brothers yourself! You made it all happen! You're a hero!" The boy could hardly stay in his seat, fairly bursting with excitement

Nell smiled indulgently at the antics of youth, but catching the look on Josiah's face caused the smile to vanish. "Come on now, don't bother the man! Don't you have work to get to?" She shooed the young man away.

"Yes Ma'am, I do, and I got to be going, too." Despite this, he kept hovering over Josiah for a moment, nearly dancing in excitement.

Josiah grabbed the boy's arm. Turn to 3.
Josiah took his second shot of whisky without a word. Turn to 12.

20

Diana smiled. She swung the rifle off her back and leaned it against the bar within easy reach.

"Welcome to the Bad Dog Saloon," the barkeep said. "You new in town?"

"You could say that," Diana replied.

"Folk call me Mama Nell, and this here's my bar," she gestured at the establishment.

"Diana. A pleasure," Diana replied, looking around. Two men who'd been staring were still looking at her. She smiled knives at them and touched her rifle. The men swallowed hard and turned away. Diana, amused, turned her attention back to Mama Nell.

"What can I get ya, miss?" The woman was asking.

"Information," Diana said. Turn to 29.

21

Diana grimaced. "I'm sorry to hear that. He was… well, he may have made some mistakes along the way."

"What's your interest in this man?" Mama Nell asked.

Diana sighed and looked at the portrait. She folded it up and put it back away. "That's personal."

Nell grunted. "Any idea what brought him out here?"

Diana said, "He calls himself a scholar of natural philosophy. He said he was onto something big, but he weren't supposed to be gone this long. I can't wait for him any longer."

Nell considered this. "What makes you think he headed to Affliction?"

"Last letter I got from him was addressed from Affliction." Turn to 17.

22

"I hope you ain't planning on staying here," Diana said. She cinched some of the knots tight on her wagon, to keep everything secure even if the wind picked up overnight.

She wasn't sure what to make of this stern marshal. A U.S. Marshal, he was likely harmless enough, but she'd been on her own long enough to know that men were unpredictable, even the supposedly good ones. She didn't want any trouble.

Except for Garland, or, as she had first met him, Professor Enfield. She smiled at the memories that flickered quickly through her mind. He never would have made the first move. In order to get him into her bed, she'd practically had to…

But never mind all that. Now was no time to be thinking about that.

The marshal was talking, and she hadn't missed much. "…of a mind to," he finished. He wasn't leaving.

She turned back to him, opening her mouth to tell him off, but something in his appearance stopped her. His jaw had a certain set to it; he would do what he chose for himself and nothing else. She instinctively changed tactics.

"You can sleep here, so long as you don't bother me," Diana said. Turn to 6.

23

Josiah calmly wiped his face. Once he'd gotten the bulk of the spittle off, he used his handkerchief to clean the rest. All the while, he leaned into his hold on the prisoner, keeping the man pinned to the train wall with his off hand.

Josiah nodded to a couple of other passengers walking by, who stared at his wet face in surprise and disgust. When they passed, he grimaced and said, "If you're finished, we have an appointment to keep." He yanked, moving his prisoner by sheer force ahead of him and out into the walkway.

The train was slowing to a full stop now, and the tidy houses of bustling Fairfield rolled into view through the small window. Josiah carefully guided the prisoner down the narrow aisle between rows of finely dressed travelers, nodding with tight smiles to the onlookers. The prisoner continued to struggle in small, convulsive bursts, startling some of the passengers, but Josiah held him tightly until they reached the exit.

The cold morning air greeted them. Turn to 2.

24

"Mama Nell?" Josiah asked, raising an eyebrow.

She laughed. "I got me two boys now. One of 'em's run off to California to find his fortune in gold. The other," her eyes narrowed as she looked around. "Why he's around here someplace, gettin' in trouble, most like."

"The world never stops turning… I suppose it has been a long time." Josiah turned his whiskey, looking at the amber liquid.

"Joe…" Nell hesitated, then said softly, "I was sorry to hear 'bout yours…"

Josiah's eye twitched. "I don't much care to discuss it." He took his whiskey in one swift swallow.

Nell nodded, not meeting his gaze.

Josiah licked his lips, set down the whiskey glass, and jerked his thumb at the prisoner. "Anyway, I got my man. Took me five years, but I got 'im."

Nell's eyes shifted to the prisoner, tied up not far away. "That why you're in town?"

Josiah grunted. "Taking him to be hanged where it all started."

"Affliction…" Nell said.

Josiah nodded and slid the empty whiskey glass back across the bar.

"You seem to be doing well for yourself," Josiah said. Turn to 19.

25

"Time to go. You have one chance to come along peaceably," Josiah said.

The prisoner leaned back, stretched, and made himself comfortable, a grin tugging at the edges of his mouth. "I do believe I feel satisfied right here," he drawled.

Josiah's moustache twitched. "Yer goin' to hang either way. Might as well make it easy on yerself on the way there." The train rocked, coming around the last bend, and the horn bellowed into the sky, announcing its arrival in Fairfield.

The prisoner put his hands behind his head. "You sure know how to win over a fella," he said, closing his eyes.

Josiah grabbed the prisoner's chains and hefted him to his feet. Turn to 13.

26

"That's where it all started," Josiah said.

She gave him an inquiring look, and he found himself examining her face. At first glance, she was rough, travel-worn, a denizen of the open road. But her face had a prettiness to it at odds with her rugged appearance. Something about those clear eyes…

He cleared his throat. "I did some things I ain't proud of, back when Affliction was gettin' started. Before it was called Affliction and all." He nodded at the prisoner. "You could say that man is a direct result of those choices. I made him."

He paused. He had to choose how much to say.

"And he made me," he added. "Five years ago, he killed someone very close to me."

The woman listened without speaking. At least she had the good sense to avoid any silly, sentimental comment. Josiah clenched his jaw and took in a deep breath.

"That's all there is to it. He's gonna hang."

Sensing that he was done talking, she let him eat in silence. After a time she fetched some food of her own. He was grateful that she didn't push the issue any more than she already had, and his respect for her went up a notch.

"G'night, Marshal," she said, before retiring for the night.

"Goodnight." He tipped his hat to her.

When Diana rose at dawn, the marshal was already up. Turn to 18.

27

She found the Bad Dog Saloon exactly where Mr. Hastings had said it would be. The building seemed out of place somehow. It was low, squat, and old, a far cry from the tall, brightly painted facades all around it. Nevertheless, it didn't seem to lack for clientele.

As she stepped up to the door, a square-shouldered man came out, nearly colliding with her. Each came up short, and their eyes met briefly. He had grey eyes and a long, finely groomed moustache, yet for all that he seemed as out of place as the saloon itself. He touched the brim of his hat by way of apology and moved on.

She let her eyes follow the man for a moment, indulging an idle curiosity, then went into the saloon. The interior was dark and smelled of fresh beer. It was early enough that only the most sodden or desperate of drinkers could be found here, and yet there was no shortage of them. Several looked up, their eyes lingering in the way she'd grown to expect from men on the frontier. But none of these seemed the type to cause trouble, so she ignored them.

She took a seat on a stool near the bar, where a thick armed woman bartender was cleaning glasses. The woman looked up as she approached. "Howdy Miss."

Diana tipped her hat without smiling. Turn to 4.
Diana smiled. Turn to 20.

28

Diana James stood in the morning sun, directing the movement of boxes. Half a dozen laborers were working on bringing supplies from the train platform over to the warehouse behind the general store.

The store owner, Mr. Don Hastings, came up to stand beside her. He said, "That seems to be the last of them. Thank you, Ma'am. You got me a better deal than if I'd gone through the standard company."

The train whistle let out it's long cry. The platform was only a few blocks away, and Diana watched as the massive iron beast began to pull away. "Nothing to thank me for, Mr. Hastings. You paid a fair price."

"What's next for you? Staying in Fairfield for a few days?" he asked.

She shook her head. "Actually, I'll be moving on. In fact, I need to buy some supplies for my next stop."

Mr. Hastings looked at her with a new gleam in his eye. "Ah, what can I get for you?"

"Mining supplies, I think. Dynamite, picks, and some general goods. Anything a little miner's town might need. A wagon and horses to move it, and some food and water for the road."

He nodded slowly as she spoke. "Certainly, certainly. I can provide all that. There's a few minin' towns 'round these parts you could make a good sale on those goods. If you don't mind wand'rin' the desert alone, that is." He peered at her curiously.

"I'm used to travelin' alone," she said.

He shrugged and led her back inside, where they started the work of settling exactly what she would purchase and for how much. As they did so, her mind drifted back to the real reason she was here: a certain man with more brains than he knew what to do with. Too many brains, and not enough good sense.

She turned to the store owner, interrupting their work. "You get anyone else passing through here recently, loading up like this? Maybe a professor, a young man, goes by Garland Enfield."

Mr. Hastings turned to her with a slow look. "I sure did. Few months back. Mebbe two? He a friend of yours?"

Diana wasn't quite ready to tell everyone in the world what she was doing. She shrugged. "I know him. He owes me some money," she lied.

Mr. Hastings barked a laugh. "You and every other damn person in this town. Yeah, I sold him some goods a while back. He came through all fire and brimstone, and ain't never paid. Left a note sayin' he'd pay with dividends once his ship came in. Whatever the hell that means." He spat to show his contempt.

It didn't seem as though the good professor had changed his ways, despite all her hard work. She sighed.

"What sort of things was he buyin'?" Diana asked casually. Turn to 7.
"Thank you, Mr. Hastings. You've been very helpful," Diana said. Turn to 11.

29

"Information," Diana said.

Nell raised an eyebrow. "Nothin' to drink?"

Diana shook her head. "My stomach ain't itself this mornin'."

"How about some heated water, then? Just the thing for a soft stomach."

"Sure," Diana said. This woman was alright. She looked like she could break a man in half with her bare hands, but she hovered like a mama hen when she thought she could help.

"What brings you to Fairfield?" Mama Nell asked as she set the kettle on a hot, wood-burning stove.

Diana hesitated. "Trade, mostly. Got some mining picks and dynamite I was thinking to unload."

Nell shook her head, "You'll have a hard time sellin' that around here. Not much mining, 'less you plan on goin' on some hard ridin' round these parts."

"Well, I ain't aimin' to stay in Fairfield. I'm headed toward Affliction town, sellin' there. Think you could answer a few questions?"

"Affliction?" Nell said, her eyebrows shooting up. "That's no place most folk like to go. There's a reason it's called 'Affliction.'"

"Why is that?" Diana asked.

Mama Nell gave her head a shake. "A place has enough bad luck, it earns a bad name. The town started out just fine, why… near on thirty years ago. Same time as us, really. They jus' never took off the way some other towns did. I guess after enough illness, death and mishap, most folk just steered clear. After a time, the town named itself. Why'd you want to go there anyway?"

Diana sighed. She reached under her jacket and took out a sketched portrait. "I'm bringing goods to sell just to make the trip worth my while. If there's one thing my daddy taught me, it's never to pass up a chance to turn a coin."

It was his bad example taught her that, but no need to go spilling her whole life story.

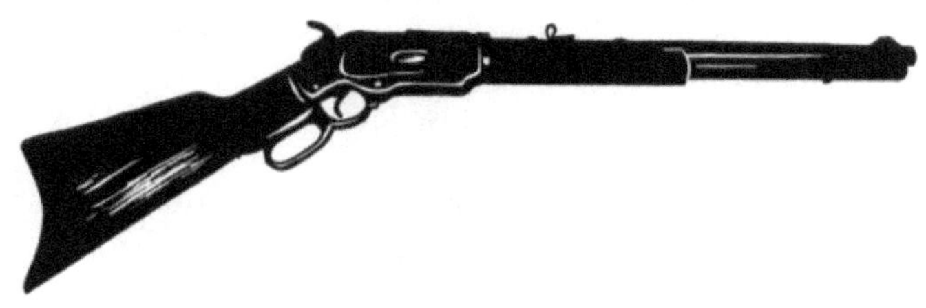

She flipped the portrait around to show it to the bartender, saying, "The real reason I'm goin' all that way is this man. Professor Enfield. Garland Enfield. I understand you've met him?"

Mama Nell leaned in. The portrait was a young man of breeding and money, his hair well-groomed, with a tidy, mutton chop beard, and a pair of spectacles perched on his nose.

The bartender gave a sort of laugh. It was not a nice sound. "Yeah, I seen him. Came through a few months back and cleaned us all out. Took a wagon and supplies, then just skipped town without payin' a dime for it all. Never said where he was going."

Diana grimaced. Turn to 21.

"Last letter I got from him was addressed from Affliction." Turn to 17.

30

Josiah wanted to look around a bit before anything else. Even at this early hour, with the sun barely above the horizon, the streets were busy, with gentlemen farmers and finely dressed ladies going to and from the various buildings. As he walked down the main street, he passed several shops, a post office, and a tall bank. All had freshly painted signs.

Still dragging his prisoner, he stopped at a small street cart, where a trader offered pots and pans at low prices. "Awful busy round these parts," Josiah commented, idly picking up a pot.

The shopkeep, a thin, sallow man, grunted. "Yep. This town has more folk than it knows what to do with. They jes' swarm in like locusts off that train. But they bring their money, don't they? Cain't complain," he finished with a grin.

"What's goin' on around town?" Josiah asked. "Anything a man should know about?"

The trader scratched his beard. "Had a gang of outlaws shoot up the place a few days ago. They didn't get far though. Laid down arms once they saw they was outnumbered. We ain't gonna put up with no nonsense like that here in Fairfield." The man was watching Josiah's prisoner as he spoke, his eyes curious. Finally, he burst out, "Say, who's that fella' anyway?"

The prisoner knew he was being talked about. He stuck out his tongue and waggled it at the shopkeep, making the man recoil.

Ignoring the prisoner, Josiah asked, "Was anyone hurt?"

"Two of them outlaws was shot, but Doc says they'll pull through. They didn't have much fight in 'em, truth be told."

Josiah asked, "Where are the prisoners now?"

"Sheriff McCann's holdin' 'em. Talk to him in the jailhouse. Can't miss the place, sir." The main pointed. Josiah nodded without looking. He knew the town.

He tipped his hat and said, "Thank you, sir." Hand firmly on the prisoner's chains, he kept moving down the street. He'd want to talk to those men later, and the sheriff too. But for now, he had an old friend to look up.

Josiah took his prisoner to the Bad Dog Saloon. Turn to 9.

Walter quickly regretted rejecting the water. The heat grew as they rode out into the endless white expanse of salt called the Devil's Anvil. Mirages shimmered up off the white flats, and the sun seemed to beat upon him from all sides, not just above.

As they rode, his mind treaded familiar paths, grievances both old and new gnawing at him. For the thousandth time, he cursed the injury which had laid him up in that cabin, where the marshal had at last caught him. But there was a blessing in that curse, a silver lining in the dark clouds. The marshal was taking him back to Affliction—and he thought it was a punishment. Walter would have laughed if his mouth weren't so dry.

The litany of names ran through his mind: Abe Korse, Roy Johnson, Curtis Leney, called 'the Rustler,' Bo Bansen, Toby McCann, Dave Hayes, who fell from his horse and died before Walter could ever reach him, and William Masters.

William Masters. The greatest and oldest. The only one still living. He lived in Affliction. Walter tried to lick his lips, but found his tongue was as dusty as the sand dunes in the distance.

"That was stupid, boy. You let your emotions get the better of you." A voice—familiar, painfully familiar—startled him awake. Walter's head snapped up. What was this? Was he hearing voices? Had his mind gone so far already?

Yet there, standing in the shimmering air of the Devil's Anvil, was a figure from his earliest memories.

The shaman looked as though he had hardly changed. Turn to 37.

32

"Leave her alone," Josiah said sharply. He could barely see in the dim light of the hallway, but he saw enough to recognize the body language, and he didn't like what he saw.

The man in the darkness turned with a sneer. "Oh? Why should I?"

Josiah smiled. He brushed back his coat to show his gun and said again, more quietly, "Leave her alone."

"Who the hell are you to tell me my business?" The man snarled, turning toward Josiah. As he moved, he no longer blocked Josiah's view of the woman. It was Diana. She rubbed her wrist where it had been grabbed, then knelt and picked up her rifle from the floor. Her eyes flashed hard as she leveled the weapon at the man's back.

"Just a U.S. Marshal, is all," Josiah said, touching the brim of his hat.

The man stopped in his tracks, and a slow grin spread across his face. "Well, well, well. Aren't we fancy today! Our very own U.S. Marshal. Say Marshal, don't you recognize me?" He spread his arms. Josiah squinted. He had one of those half-familiar faces. It had just been too long.

"Dan? 'Course, I was a boy then, just Little Dan. Remember how I followed at your boot heels? I wanted to be just like you. Remember how you never had the time of day for me?"

Josiah sighed. "Guess I still don't. Stand down, son."

Dan snarled. For a moment, Josiah thought he would back off. Instead, he leaped straight at Josiah, extending his hands like claws.

Josiah drew with practiced speed and fired. The shot took Dan in the throat, mid-leap. Surprise etched on his face, he collapsed, writhing on the floor.

Silence stretched across the hall, and Josiah turned, expecting the faces of the crowd to be shocked, horrified… anything but smiling.

It was the same smile on each face. Turn to 46.

33

"I'm going to ask a few more people," Diana said.

As Josiah vanished into the crowd, she sighed and looked at the letter she'd received from Garland, re-reading it one more time. It was so vague. Just a few lines about the exciting progress his excavation was making. Nothing about her or them at all. He didn't even say he missed her.

She hoped he would be happy to see her, and happy to hear the news she brought…

Bringing her thoughts back to the present, she surveyed the bar, wondering who she could approach. They all looked the same to her, hard frontier folk, of a kind with those she had seen in dozens of other towns. Why had Garland come here, of all places? What was so special that was up in those mountains?

Turning away from the pounding feet and lively bodies, Diana lifted her glass of whiskey and considered it. It glowed, golden and smoky in the glass. Her father had always drunk cognac, when he could afford it. It had been a long time since that had happened. Cognac was Garland's favorite drink too. She shook her head with a self-mocking smile.

When would she see him again? Was he here somewhere, or had he vanished, haring off in some new direction and leaving her to carry the fruits of their mistakes?

She turned to the barkeeper. "Otto, right?" The balding man glanced up at her without smiling.

"Know anyone else I could ask, who might have seen Professor Enfield?" she asked hopefully.

The man didn't respond, just looked at her. Just as she was starting to wonder if he'd even understood, he shook his head and went back to polishing his glass.

Diana bit back a grimace of annoyance. She turned in her seat to look out at the crowd. Who else could she ask? That last letter had been postmarked from Affliction. He had to be here.

Cursing his poor choice of hobbies, she turned back to the bar. But as she did, one person caught her eye. A little girl, not more than nine years of age, sat on the end of the counter. She wore a plain red dress, and golden curls framed her pretty face. She was kicking her feet in the air, watching the dancers with no expression.

After considering for a moment, Diana left her unsipped drink behind and moved to sit next to the child.

"Hi there," Diana said. The little girl turned to face her. Still without changing her expression, she said, "My name's Ruby. What's yours?"

"I'm Diana. Are your parents around?"

Ruby said nothing at all. At that moment, Otto moved up from the other side of the bar, his large presence suddenly there. He said quietly, "Ruby got no parents. Her brother looks for her now."

"Dan looks for me now," Ruby repeated.

"I see... Is Dan here?"

"Yes. He's right there." Ruby pointed to a tall young man currently dancing a jig with a pretty girl. Looking back at Diana, Ruby asked, "Would you like to play dolls with me?"

Diana hesitated for only a moment. "Sure, why not?" She gave the little girl a smile.

Ruby lifted her arms for Diana to help her down. When she picked up the girl, Diana couldn't help but notice how light the little girl was. Barely more than a feather. She made a mental note to give Dan a few words on the importance of feeding his sister.

"Our room is this way." Ruby pointed, then grabbed Diana's hand and pulled her in that direction. The glint of excitement in her eyes was the first emotion Diana had yet seen, and she had to laugh at the childish enthusiasm.

"We're going to play dolls," Ruby said in a childish burble. "I have one that looks just like you! You can be the mommy."

Diana felt a tightening in her chest. The little girl was so precious. She thought of Enfield... had he met this girl? If—when—she found him, they would have so much to talk about... she had no idea how he would take it all.

Behind the dance hall was a low, poorly lit hallway. Ruby opened a door and entered a dark room. For a moment, as the door swung shut, the room was plunged entirely into darkness. Diana blinked, taken aback. Then a match was struck, and she could see the girl's small face in the light of the match.

Diana took a deep breath. Her heart was racing. The girl used the match to light the wick of a glass lantern, then she turned up the wick so that the lantern would cast a light strong enough to fill the room.

Diana, fighting to quiet the strange rush of adrenaline she felt, found a cushion to sit on, while Ruby opened a drawer to pull out two dolls. "These are the parents," she said. "Do you want to be the mommy or the daddy?"

"I… I'll take this one." Diana reached for the closest doll, which happened to be female. It wore a faded pink dress, and in the lamplight, it reminded her of her own mother. "Ruby, I wanted to ask you a few questions."

"Oh?" The little girl turned her angelic little face up toward Diana.

Diana's gaze was caught by those perfect blue eyes. She almost lost her train of thought. "I… was just wondering what's been going on around the town lately."

Ruby looked uncertain. "I'm not sure I should tell you. I think it's a secret."

Diana blinked. "Secret? I mean, you can tell me. I won't tell anyone."

Ruby looked down, troubled, then looked up through her eyelashes at Diana and smiled a secret smile. "Okay, but you have to lean in close so I can whisper it in your ear."

Diana leaned in close, pulling her hair back to expose one ear. Turn to 54.
Diana shook her head, saying, "There's no one else around." Turn to 49.

34

Walter crouched in his cell. He knelt with his back to one wall, arms curled around his legs. His eyes glittered in the growing darkness. He thought.

William Masters was here. He had seen him. He was so close now… He could nearly taste the man's blood. Soon it would be over. Soon…

After a long spell of stillness, he stood. The marshal had removed the heaviest of his chains, leaving him bound at only the wrists and ankles. He prowled around the room, examining every inch of the cell. His fingers ached for the grip of his revolvers, two long, gleaming guns he could use to shoot a spider at twenty paces. He longed for his whip. He longed for the open sky and a strong horse under him.

He'd gotten the marshal to transport him to Affliction, to William Masters. But if he died here in the morning, before finishing it, then he would have failed. He needed a plan.

The walls and floor were all of solid stone, impossible to burn or break through, not without dynamite. Only the interior wall of the cell was not stone, but bars, each bar implanted deep within the stone both above and below. He went down the line and tested each one, but could find no frailties.

In the south wall a tiny window showed sky, punctuated by the bars that covered it. The sky was purpling from dusk into evening, and stars were beginning to show. Over the buildings to the south and east he could see the gallows outlined against the twilight sky. The single noose still twisted in the wind.

An image came to his mind of his own body dangling there. Idly, he noted that the thought didn't cause any particular reaction. Living past this had never been part of the plan.

An opportunity would appear. He just had to be ready; he would have his chance. He turned back to the cell. Inside with him was nothing except a mat of crushed straw and a low, wooden table, half-rotted with age and disuse.

Moving to the table, he knelt beside it. It was a small, low thing, perhaps more of a stool than a table. A pointless thing. He turned it over and over in his hands. The wood was so old and dry that he could have split it with a single blow.

Instead, he picked a spot from one leg and measured a length, tracing his finger along a seam of the grain that was already starting to separate.

Taking one of the links of his chain firmly in one hand, he struck the table leg a blow. Then another. The crunch of metal against wood seemed loud to his ears, but no alarm was raised. He struck a third and final time, breaking off a sliver of wood almost as long as his forearm.

Turning it over in his hand, he decided it would suffice. He replaced the table in the far corner of the room, the injured leg facing the corner. Then he sat down on the stone floor with the sliver of wood and proceeded to use his chains to polish and sharpen it.

The Blood returns.

Diana joined Josiah as he went down to the saloon. Turn to 43.

35

"I understand," Diana said, her face pale. There was only so much they could do against those numbers. Yet whatever happened, whatever it took, she would get Garland out of their grasp.

"You hear me, you bastards!" She screamed at the blank wall. "I'm coming back for him! I'm coming back for you, Garland!"

"Diana!" the muffled voice came from inside, barely audible over the tumult.

"Garland!" She cried.

"Diana, just run! Go away! Hear me? Run and don't ever come back!"

"No!" She shouted, starting toward the sound of his voice. Josiah grabbed her arm.

One of the other prisoners was trying to crawl out of the opening now, but even as they watched, his eyes went wide in pain and surprise. Then his body jerked back in, pulled by someone inside.

"We've got to go," Josiah said.

Diana nodded. It took everything she had to force herself to turn her steps away from the man she loved, the man she had come here to find, and run for safety. She would be back.

Josiah stopped once to shoot at something behind them, but she simply jogged on, head down. The streets were still empty, and he reached the jailhouse ahead of them.

"Inside, quick!" Josiah called.

She put on a final burst of speed to make it there.

Josiah held the door open as Diana pounded inside. Turn to 56.

Diana reloaded her rifle and headed for the door. She turned the knob carefully, not wanting to attract any more attention than she already had. The hallway was dark, except for the light spilling down this way from the main room.

Heart pounding, she looked toward the bar, where the sounds of revelry continued unabated. Had anyone heard her gunshot? The music was faltering, and she could hear sounds of confusion and questioning. Any second now, someone would appear to investigate.

She couldn't go that way. Not with a dead little girl left in the room behind her. How could she explain it? The memory of pain and sharp teeth flashed through her mind, and she turned the other way.

She moved quickly and quietly down the hall. On the left she came to another door—this one crudely locked by means of a railway spike jammed through the handle. Curiosity piqued, she tugged at the spike. It came out easily.

"Can I help you with something, missy?" A man had appeared at the end of the hall. Dan. His voice had dangerous undertones as he slid toward her, his silhouette blocking half the light coming from the main room.

Diana froze. She thought of Ruby, lying cold and dead where he had seen them together just moments ago. She thought of the blood on her neck. Her words stammered as they came out. "Lookin' around. Thought I heard somethin' down this way is all."

"So did I." He moved closer. "Where's my sister?"

"What do you all keep behind this door?" Diana countered a question with a question, jerking her thumb at that door.

Dan took another step closer. In the darkness, she could see a strange smile spread across his face. "You'll stay away from that door if you know what's good for you."

Diana started to lift her rifle to keep Dan at bay, but he pounced as soon as the muzzle twitched. Before she could get it in position, he wrapped his fingers around the barrel and ripped it from her grasp, tossing it to the floor.

"I asked you a question," Dan hissed, grabbing her wrist. Diana gasped with pain.

A few other people were gathering now at the end of the hall, Josiah among them. The marshal stepped forward from the crowd and planted his feet.

"Leave her alone," Josiah said sharply. Turn to 32.

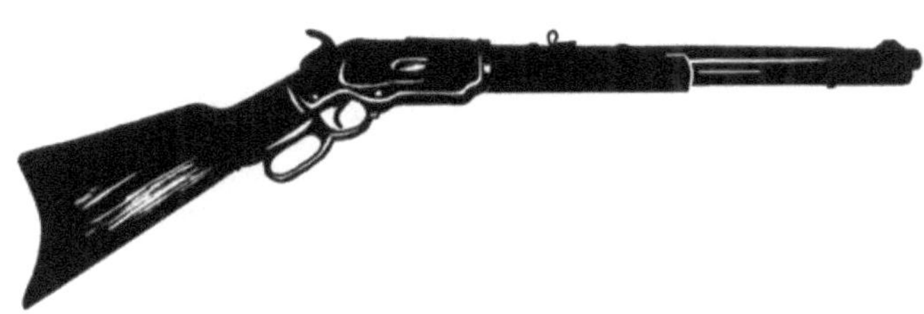

The shaman looked as though he had hardly changed. Dry River was Walter's mother's uncle, and a shaman of the Arahoca. He had the distinctive angular features of his people... Walter's people. A gold piercing ran so high and deep through his nose that it went through bone.

"How...?" Walter struggled with the words. He tasted blood on his cracked lips.

His grand-uncle had survived the massacre, though no one knew it except Walter and his mother. Yet to see him now, so many years later... The shaman had been ancient even when Walter was a child, yet in the years since Walter had seen him last, he didn't look to have aged a day.

Dry River patted his cheek. "Little Wolf, you look not so good."

Walter tried to move to touch the older man's hand, and in his heat-blurred state, he found himself surprised that his hands were still tied.

"I got most of them, kioma." He used the Arahoca term of respect. "All except Masters." He gasped, "All except William Masters."

"Shhhh... shhh... it's not over yet. There is just one left. You are the last of us, and you must carry it home."

"But it cost..." Walter laughed without humor. His dry lips cracked, and he tasted blood. "She... she jumped in the way... I didn't..." his mind was blurring. He couldn't think straight.

"Bring it home. That's all that matters. Here, have some water." The shaman unclasped his own water skin and held it to Walter's lips. He drank greedily.

After a few gulps, Walter pulled away and shook his head violently. "What do you mean? I thought you were dead! What do I need to do?"

"The Blood returns," the shaman said cryptically.

The heat was too much. Walter closed his eyes. He just needed a moment. The salt flat shifted beneath the feet of his horse, the rhythm lulling him into a stupor.

When he jerked himself awake, he didn't know how much later, his grand-uncle was gone.

"The Blood returns," Walter whispered through dry lips.

It took them the rest of the day to reach Affliction. Turn to 44.

"It was a mistake," Josiah said, turning away. It had all been a mistake, and coming back here was too. He didn't need this. Didn't need complications, entanglements. He was here for one purpose, and that purpose had nothing to do with pretty dancers.

Marie flounced in disappointment. She tried to pull him up to dance again, but he turned her down, as gently as he could. "I just want to sit for a spell, you go have fun." She reluctantly let him be, but not before giving him a glare that Josiah found surprisingly malevolent. As she left, he thought of that look in her eye, and it made him uneasy. This way was definitely for the best.

He was starting to nurse his next glass of whisky, sipping this time, and lost in memories, when he heard the gunshot.

He leaped to his feet. "What was that?" He demanded, but no one else at the bar seemed to have heard it. It had come from deeper in the building, down that hall where he had seen Diana go. As he watched, another man disappeared into the hallway, probably following the same sound.

The whisky had gone to his head, but not so much that he forgot he was a marshal. He loosened his guns in their holsters and made his way to the back hall. The hall was dim and he blinked until he could see.

There at the end of the hall, a man was leaning threateningly over a woman. He couldn't recognize them from here, but he didn't need to.

"Leave her alone," Josiah said sharply. Turn to 32.

39

Walter did not regret pouring out the water. It had been worth it to see the look on da Silva's face. He would have laughed if his mouth weren't so dry. And if he did die from it, what of it? He would be dead soon enough anyway.

Yet... he had to carry on a little longer. His task was not yet done. One still lived.

The litany of names ran through his mind, as it had so many times before: Abe Korse, Roy Johnson, Curtis Leney, called 'the Rustler,' Bo Bansen, Toby McCann, Dave Hayes, who fell from his horse and died before Walter could ever reach him, and William Masters.

William Masters. The greatest and oldest. The only one still living.

William Masters waited in Affliction, unaware that his judgement was riding in upon him this very day.

Korse's lips twitched in a wry, self-mocking smile. What a vision of judgement he made, chained and dying. Nonetheless, he would make it work. He had to. He would kill Masters. Only then could he rest.

The heat grew as they rode out into the endless white expanse of salt called the Devil's Anvil. Mirages shimmered up off the white flats, and the sun seemed to beat upon him from all sides, not just above.

Walter's lips cracked. His tongue grew swollen and thick. Yet it was only discomfort. It did not matter. None of it mattered. Nothing except Masters.

What was that, he saw there? A man? How could a man be standing in the blistering heat of the Devil's Anvil? The figure became sharper, clearer, appearing as if in a vision through the shimmering heatwaves.

He did not recognize the one that stood there, until he heard his voice. "You're a fool, boy. You've let yourself be captured."

Walter mumbled something, but his mouth wasn't working properly. He tried again. "Dry River?" he asked.

The shaman looked as though he had hardly changed. Turn to 37.

"I can't leave without him!" Diana cried. She wrestled against Josiah's grip, and he had to use all his strength to hold her back.

"Garland!" She shouted.

One of the other prisoners was trying to crawl out the opening now, a man gaunt from weeks of little food. His eyes widened in pain and surprise, and his body suddenly vanished, jerked back by someone inside.

"Garland!" Diana shouted again.

"We have to go!" Josiah hissed. "We'll come back for him!"

"No!" It was a choked sob. The strength sagged out of Diana, and she fell against Josiah's weight. He held her for the briefest of moments, then shoved her toward the jailhouse.

Stumbling, she broke into a slow, painful run.

Josiah tried to stay with her as they ran, at first, not letting her fall behind. Teofilo was slow too, the wound in his arm taking its toll.

As Josiah looked back, he saw someone crawling out of the opening. It was one of their pursuers; he could tell by the mad grin on the man's face. Josiah stopped long enough to aim his pistol. He fired without hesitation, blowing out the man's brains. His body sagged, blocking the opening. That would buy them the time they needed, but his heart sank. That was two dead, at least.

Then he ran ahead through the empty town, stopping only when he reached the jailhouse.

"Come on!" he shouted, and Diana put on an extra burst of speed, the other two not far behind.

Josiah held the door open as Diana pounded inside. Turn to 56.

"I'm going to take a look around," Josiah said.

Diana nodded. "Go on. I'll be here."

The marshal stood, tucking his hat back on his head. He paced around the room, making small talk as needed, but a nagging sense that he was missing something kept him moving. He paused by the door, watching the dancers. When a moment came where no one was looking, he slipped out the front.

The night air was clean and fresh, and he felt his head clearing just standing in it. The stars were bright. Too bright. Why weren't there no lights to shine 'em down?

Taking the few steps down to the dirt of the main road, he looked around. Darkness and silence was all that met him. No matter where he looked, he couldn't find another light in the whole damn town, not even a candle.

Maybe the people were asleep, all those who weren't dancin'? No, that didn't make sense. Not all of 'em.

He strolled down the block a ways, looking between buildings and in windows. All had the appearance of a thoroughly abandoned town: window shutters swung on broken hinges, doors were smashed in, houses looted and covered in dust. The more he saw, the more his gnawing sense of unease grew from intuition to certainty.

Something wasn't right in this town, and it wasn't just memories.

There was only one place to get answers. Besides, his travelling companion was still in that bar.

He turned his feet with purpose back toward the bar. His fingers brushed the reassuringly heavy handles of his pistols. Never knew what trouble might arise.

When he pushed his way back through the swinging doors, the scene seemed unchanged. Dancers whirled to the tune of a half-broken down piano in the corner. He narrowed his eyes, looking for the clue that would make it all make sense.

Then, a gunshot.

The sound could only be faintly heard over the clamor of the dance, but there was no mistake. It came from somewhere deeper in the building. And as he looked, he saw another man vanishing down a hallway, presumably following the same sound.

Josiah shoved past dancers—in no mood for politely navigating the moving bodies—until he stood at the entrance of the hallway. It was dark, but not so dark that he couldn't see a man down the hall leaning threateningly over a woman.

"Leave her alone," Josiah said sharply. Turn to 32.

42

Diana slapped the man she had come here to find. He stepped back, his hand going to his cheek, his eyes wide with surprise. "What?" he murmured.

"I thought I'd never see you again," Diana said. Tears stood in her eyes.

Garland mumbled something.

"Damn you, you can't even apologize properly," she said.

"I'm sorry," Garland said.

Diana rolled her eyes. "Come on, we've got to get you out of here. Time for stories later."

"You got a way out I don't know about?" Josiah asked. Turn to 48.

43

Diana joined Josiah as he went down to the saloon. The stars were beginning to show in the sky above them, and with the infectious jig of the piano floating across the town, the streets took on a totally different character.

They walked in silence, listening to the music, until Marshal da Silva turned to her and asked, "Does the lady dance?"

"Does the marshal?" Diana shot back.

He grunted—was that a laugh under his moustache?—and said, "You've been nodding to the beat since we heard that music."

Diana smiled wryly. "It takes me back, is all. My family had money once; I grew up dancing." That was before her Daddy had run the family fortune into the ground. She felt the marshal's eyes on her, but said no more. This was it. She didn't have time for nostalgia now. After all the worry and hard decisions and travel, she was here. Garland could be inside that bar.

The saloon loomed large on the northern side of the street, the music growing stronger as they approached it. Through the half-shuttered windows, they could see warm light and figures whirling.

Marshal da Silva ascended the steps before her and turned to offer her his hand. Diana inclined her head and graciously accepted. In the simple gesture, she saw a shadow of her old life, a life of gowns and social calls, of tall white houses and proud men and women. It was all a long time ago.

As she came up the steps, the marshal's eye fell on the rifle strapped across her back. "Bringing your gun?" he asked, lifting one bushy eyebrow.

"You got yours," she pointed out.

"I'm a marshal," he said.

"Well I'm a pragmatist, and I like to keep it on me. 'Specially in these frontier towns." She quirked a smile and elbowed past him.

When she pushed through the swinging doors and into the saloon, her senses were assaulted by smoke and heat and the sound of feet pounding the wooden floors in rapid time to the music of a noisy piano.

At first no one noticed them, until a greying, paunchy man sitting at the bar looked up and his eyes grew wide. "Joe? Hell, da Silva? Is that really you!?"

As the marshal went to greet his old friend, Diana scanned the crowd. She didn't see Garland here, but that would have been too much to hope for. Surely someone here would have seen him, though.

"Diana! Get over here, Tom's treating us to drinks," Josiah called her to a spot at the bar with a big wave of his hand. Diana tipped her hat to the strangers.

He shouted, "Get me some of that coffin varnish, Otto! And for the lady too. She's my guest. Diana, I'd like you to meet Otto. I knew him when he was a wee lad." The tall, balding man behind the bar nodded at her as he poured two shots of whiskey.

Gesturing to the next man, da Silva said, "And this here's Tom O'Day, best trapper in the west. Tom, this is Diana James, my traveling companion."

"Howdy do, miss?" The potbellied old man smiled at her and took her hand with rough exuberance. His mountain accent was so thick she could barely understand him. There was a twinkle in his eye as he asked, "How long have you been with Joe here? He treating you right?"

"We've been travelling together for less than a day," she said. "And so far, he's been a perfect gentleman. We'll see if that holds." She raised an eyebrow archly at da Silva, who blustered, much to Tom's amusement. Otto slid each of them a shot of golden amber whiskey.

Josiah met Diana's eye and together they lifted their drinks. Turn to 47.
Josiah met Diana's eye, and neither touched their drinks. Turn to 45.

44

It took them the rest of the day to reach Affliction. Diana drove her wagon under a covered canopy which kept out the worst of the heat, but the prisoner and the marshal both rode exposed to the sun. The marshal had a hat; Walter Korse didn't even have that much protection, and it wouldn't have stayed on his head if he had.

The prisoner swayed and sagged in his saddle, his face occasionally waxing expressive for no apparent reason. He mouthed words, even grinned a few times. But mostly, he rode in a half-daze, his eyes lidded, head lolling. If he hadn't been tied to his saddle, he likely would have fallen.

Far ahead, low, purple mountains beckoned them. Eventually, the white salt changed to brown earth and dust. As the sun lowered, hanging heavy and red in the sky directly before them, they approached a gentle incline: the first hill they had seen in miles. At the crest of the hill stood a gallows, a single fresh noose swaying in the wind.

"There she is," Josiah said as they rode up the slope, coming to a pause so close to the gallows that Diana could hear the creaking of the rope as it spun in the breeze.

From the crest of the hill they could look down on a little frontier town. A few dozen wooden buildings lined a main road with few side streets. She could make out a general store, saloon, and the only stone building: a jailhouse. It spoke to the character of the town that a settlement so small had need for a sturdy jail.

At the far end of the main street rose a church, dominating the little town the same way the pastor dominates small town life. The shadow of the steeple in the evening sun stretched long and straight down the street, its black, cut edges engulfing the town as the sun lowered.

Up in the mountains, to the north, the hills were crisscrossed with mining trails. An abandoned mining camp slowly moldered in the sun near several dark openings of mine shafts. Halfway up to it, beside a dry stream bed, squatted an empty mill building. There were no sounds at all, save the low moaning of wind through a gap in the rocky hills somewhere above them.

"Lively place, isn't it?" Diana asked. Her lips felt strange after so many hours' silence.

The marshal grunted and said, "Wait here." He nudged his big grey into a walk down the hill and into town.

"Like hell," Diana said. With a flick of her reins, she urged the wagon horses to follow the marshal.

Nothing stirred as they descended into the town. No welcome committee rode out to greet them. No challenge rose from a darkened window.

As Josiah reached the main street, he slid off his horse and looped the reins over the fence outside the stable. He took a few steps down the street, his ears keen. He swept back the sides of his coat, putting his guns within easy reach.

A lone tumbleweed blew gently across the dusty street. When it came into sight, one of the horses stamped uneasily. The sun was a tiny sliver of reddish gold on the horizon. A fly buzzed near him, fairly glowing in the red light of the dying day. A wooden shutter flapped in the wind, a lonely sound.

As the last burning sunlight vanished across the town, Josiah heard a click of a boot-heel. He whirled, his gun leaping into his hand—to see a tall man standing on the balcony of the general store.

"Easy, cowboy," a familiar voice said.

For a moment, the two men stared at each other, motionless. Then Josiah laughed, recognizing his opposite. He slipped his half-drawn gun back into its sheath. "Bill Masters," he said. "You still in this one-horse town?"

Masters stepped down to the street, waving away a big, summer fly that buzzed around his head. His spurs clinked with each step. He was tall and lean, aging, but still muscular, the picture of a border cowboy. He fingered a bright star on his chest and said, "Hell, Joe, they made me Sheriff. Couldn't very well walk out on 'em then, could I? It's good to see you!"

He grabbed Josiah's hand in a fierce shake and the two men patted each other on the shoulders, grinning like long lost army buddies. "When's the last time?" Masters asked, "Was it when we cleaned out those Injuns?"

Josiah took off his hat and ran a hand over his thinning hair. "Yeah, I reckon it was."

"You skipped out on us after that! And we all had such a good time of it too. Had the run of the place once the savages were taken care of. Gold has been good, Joe. The town's prospering."

The marshal glanced back at Diana, who watched without expression. He raised an eyebrow meaningfully and looked around the still, silent town. "I can tell," he said dryly. "Say, Bill, where the hell is everyone?"

"At worship," Masters said, with a short laugh. He cleared his throat. "Sorry, my little joke. Damn near the whole town's in the saloon, celebratin' a good haul today. Can't you hear them?"

Josiah cocked his ear. Drifting across the silence that pervaded the town, sure enough, he could hear the strains of a reedy piano floating down the street.

"Well, now, who's this?" The sheriff drifted toward the horses, eying the chained and ragged prisoner. "You bring us a head for gold, Joe? I didn't know you were in the bounty business."

"That's no bounty. Leastwise, not just a bounty. Take a closer look, Bill. You'll know 'im when you see 'im."

Masters stepped closer to the prisoner and almost reached out a hand to lift the man's chin, when suddenly Korse opened his eyes and looked directly at the sheriff.

The transformation that came over the prisoner was sudden and absolute. For a moment, his eyes simply stared, dilating as they adjusted to the light. Then, recognition flashed across his face, followed quickly by a hate so pure and absolute that the man vanished, replaced by raw savagery.

Korse leaped forward with a cry of rage, and the sheriff stepped back nimbly or he would have had his throat ripped out. Korse's chains brought him up short—causing him to nearly slip from the mule's back. Korse let out a snarl, straining himself blue in the face by pulling even against the chain round his neck.

Josiah grabbed the sheriff and pulled him back another step with a forced chuckle. "I don't think he likes you, old man. Do you have keys to the jailhouse? I'd like to lock him up somewhere safe. He's got an appointment with the rope tomorrow morning that I wouldn't want him to miss."

Masters whistled. "You actually caught the sonuvabitch. I never thought we'd see Abe's boy again. His daddy was a good man. Saved my life up at Red Bluff. Shame this is what his son turned into. Sure, here, lock him up good and tight, then come say hi to the boys at the saloon."

The sheriff handed Josiah the keys and said, "Oh, and put on your best bib and tucker. There's dancin' on." He grinned and sauntered off without looking back.

Korse had not stopped straining against his bonds. His eyes were like twin daggers of murderous hate, following William Masters with unrelenting precision until the man was out of sight.

"Come on Korse, you can stare from your cell," Josiah said. As soon as Masters disappeared back into the general store, the strength seemed to leave the prisoner. The tall, lean man folded in on himself, and the marshal was easily able to drag him into the jailhouse, where he tossed the murderer into a cell and locked the door.

"You stay put now, hear?" he said. Korse did not reply.

When Josiah stepped back out into the main street, Diana was waiting for him with troubled eyes. "I ain't never seen a man look like that."

"Like what?"

"Evil," Diana said. Josiah helped her finish grooming and feeding the animals, neither of them speaking.

Walter crouched in his cell. Turn to 34.
Diana joined Josiah as he went down to the saloon. Turn to 43.

45

Josiah met Diana's eye, and neither touched their drinks. Josiah said, "Say, Tom, I've heard some strange rumors comin' out of Affliction lately. You know anything about all that?"

The trapper rolled his eyes and took a quaff of his drink. "What's it this time?" he asked, rubbing the froth from his lip. "Cattle thieves, disease, death? It's always somethin'. If it ain't real, it's made up."

Josiah furrowed his brow. "Up in Fairfield they say they haven't seen hide nor hair from no one down this way in nigh on two months now."

Tom shrugged. "Could be that's so. I ain't been up that way. Don't got much call to go. Probably the same goes for the rest of the folk here. Hey Joe, why you so determined to have a bad time, anyway? Why don't ya loosen up and have a drink?"

"I like to savor my drinks, Tom. You know that," Josiah said. He smelled his whiskey, but still did not sip it.

Diana leaned in to ask, "You seen a young professor come this way? Name of Enfield. Garland Enfield."

Tom shook his head. "Can't say that I have," he frowned. "You want professors, look in the city. Here all's we got is ore and miners." He laughed without humor.

Diana unfolded a paper and spread it out on the bar. "See, the thing is, I got a letter from this man—he's a friend of mine—and it was addressed from here in Affliction." She pointed to the address. "Seems he must have stayed here in this saloon."

Tom just shrugged and took another drink. "Well I ain't seen him. Listen, Joe, I got things to do. See you around, right?" He stood up and gathered his things, making for the door.

Diana let out a small sigh of frustration. "Otto, have you seen a Professor Garland Enfield?" She called to the barkeep. The man silently shook his head.

"Don't worry, we'll find him," Josiah said. He turned in his seat to look out over the room. The chairs and tables had all been pushed to the sides to open the floor for dancing, and the janky piano on the far wall was incessant in letting out its raucous dancing tune.

He stood and put on his hat.

"I'm going to take a look around," Josiah said. Turn to 41.
"I'm going to ask a few more people," Diana said. Turn to 33.

46

It was the same smile on each face. Eyes slitted, lips turned up in sadistic pleasure. Josiah backed up, his heart skipping a beat. "Now then, everything's all right. I'm a U.S. Marshal in the execution of my duties. This man was a threat to innocent civilians, and to myself."

The crowd took a step forward. Not a soul among them spoke or reacted. Josiah took another step back, and with a collective shuffle, the mass of them moved forward again.

"If you have any questions, you can take them up at the courthouse in…" Josiah started to say, but the words trailed off. There was something indefinably eerie about that mirrored look in each of their eyes.

"Josiah," Diana said, a warning in her tone.

"Right," he said, and he bolted down the hall toward her.

His rapid movement seemed to break whatever invisible bond had been holding the crowd back. They pounced like cats, fighting each other to be the first into the hallway.

Diana held open the door and shouted, "Get in!"

The two of them tumbled through the door and Diana closed it after them—just as the frontrunners of the crowd came within reach.

Josiah threw his weight against the door to hold it closed. A fist pounded on the door, the thumps impacting his back. He grimaced. Then fingers clawed at the door. A body slammed against it, almost knocking him forward. Still, no words of parley were spoken.

"Here!" Diana hissed. She was shoving a heavy box toward the door. Josiah helped her pull it into place, bracing the door with his foot as he did so. His heart was pounding.

"Stand down!" he called through the door. "I am a U.S. Marshal!"

There was no response. Voices could be heard chattering quickly, but not loud enough to make out distinctly. Then one rose above the others. "Just leave them in there! Why not keep all the food in one place?" This was followed by a chorus of laughs.

"What the hell is wrong with them?" he demanded.

"I don't know!" She said, grabbing another box and passing it to him. They seemed to be in a pantry or store-room of some kind. As his eyes adjusted, Josiah looked into the shadowy corners of the room—he saw dozens of pairs of eyes looking back at him, glinting in the faint light coming through cracks in the door.

He grabbed Diana's arm as she reached for a third box to block the door.

Diana turned. "Who's there?" she hissed.

"We're prisoners here!" a soft voice came. Then another, "Who are you?" And another, "Please, you have to help us!" People were moving near the walls, hands outstretched.

"Wait, wait, wait!" Josiah said, holding his hand out, palm forward. "Tell me what's been going on here."

Suddenly a heavy impact struck the door, nearly tumbling the top box down. Diana threw herself against the box, shoving it back into place.

"Yooohooo," a singsong voice came from outside the door. Another voice mockingly said, "Did you think it would save you to lock yourselves in there?" This brought renewed, raucous laughter. Then the door banged again as something—or someone—hit it heavily. Diana grunted. But another impact was not forthcoming. Instead, the people outside seemed to be discussing amongst themselves.

Josiah turned to the people locked in the pantry with them. "What happened here?" he demanded in a low hiss. "Speak quickly!"

An olive-skinned young woman stepped forward from the rest. She was wearing the tattered remains of what had once been a very nice dress. With a hint of a Spanish accent, she said, "It all started one month ago. People went missing. First a few, and then more, and more."

"Then they returned," a young man said darkly, in the same accent.

The girl nodded, the gesture stiff and weak. "All at once. They… they took the town. Dragged many away, and locked the rest of us up here."

"Who are you?" Josiah demanded.

"I'm Beatriz," the young woman said, "And this is my brother Teofilo." She gestured to the young man sitting next to her. They were dressed in the elaborate finery of Californios, but their clothes, his especially, were worn and filthy now, and both appeared starved.

"How long have you been in here?" Diana asked.

"We shouldn't even be here! We were simply visiting!" Beatriz wailed.

"We are from California," Teofilo said. "We should have been home by now."

"We have been locked up for weeks," Beatriz said bitterly. "Every few days they come and take one. Soon…" Her voice caught, and she laid a hand on her brother's arm. "Soon it will be one of us."

While they were talking, another of the prisoners was creeping forward. Now, the newcomer spoke in a soft voice. "Diana?" he asked. Her name hung in the silence, and all eyes turned to the speaker.

He was young man in a vest with muttonchops and spectacles. "Diana is that you?" he asked, his voice more puzzled than interested.

A low moan escaped Diana's lips and she threw herself at the man. "Garland!" She cried.

Diana slapped the man she had come here to find. Turn to 42.
Diana wrapped her arms around the man she had come here to find. Turn to 53.

47

Josiah met Diana's eye and together they lifted their drinks. Diana sipped hers and made a face—it was not a drink made for sipping. Josiah exhaled, slamming his down on the bar. "Terrible!" he said.

"I know!" Diana agreed with a grin. Otto raised an eyebrow at her, lifting the bottle, and she waved him away. "One's enough for me," she said. Josiah, however, nodded, and held out his shot glass for a refill.

As Otto refilled the marshal's glass, Tom volubly filled him in on twenty years of town gossip. Other folk came by, some of whom recognized Josiah, and others who treated them both as newcomers. She hadn't been drinking as much recently as she once had, and the whisky went quickly to her head. The world seemed to take on a golden tinge, and she faded onto the sidelines as people crowded around Josiah.

"So what brings you to town?" one kindly woman asked, sitting herself next to Diana.

Diana shook her head. "A mistake!" she said wryly.

"Ain't that the truth!" the woman said. "I'm Marie, by the way." She stuck out a hand, which Diana shook.

"Diana," she said.

"Did this mistake take the form of a man?" Marie asked with a wink.

Diana smiled ruefully. "How'd you guess?"

"Most mistakes do…" Marie sighed.

Diana burped, making it as unladylike as she could. "I'm looking for this lazy, no-good scoundrel. You seen him? One Garland Enfield. Calls himself a professor."

The woman shook her head, frowning slightly. "I don't recall. Otto, you seen a man named Garland Enfield round these parts?"

"Nope, not here," Otto said, but at almost the same moment, another passing man paused to ask, "Enfield? You mean the professor?"

"Oh yes, I do recall now!" Marie said quickly. "Yes, we had a professor come through here a while back. Didn't stay long, though."

"Didn't stay long," Otto said, glowering at the passing man until the fellow moved on.

"Which way did he go?" Diana asked, not sure which of them she should be listening to.

"Oh I couldn't say for sure—" Marie said.

"Up into the mountains," Otto said, talking over her. "Ain't seen him since, neither. Don't expect he'll be coming back."

"Where up in the mountains?" Diana pushed.

Otto shrugged. "Nothin' up there. You'd have to be crazy to think there was. Who knows what he was after? But it's hot and dry up there, and if he ain't back by now, he's likely killed."

Diana bit her tongue on a sharp answer. She turned away, anxiety threatening to turn into despair. For all of his good qualities, Garland had never been a shining example of sanity and good sense. She could all-too-easily imagine him lost and alone in the desert mountains, no food, no water, no map to get home.

"Diana," a calm voice said. It was Josiah, looking at her. "I don't know what this man is to you, but I'll help you look for him if that's what you want. Tomorrow, once this business with Korse is complete."

Diana nodded. "Thank you."

"Well, enough o' sad talk!" Marie hooted, "Let's dance!" She grabbed Josiah's arm and pulled him away, despite his humorously pained expression. Turning back to Diana, she hollered, "You coming?"

Diana shook her head with a smile.

"I'm going to ask a few more people," Diana said. Turn to 33.
Josiah allowed himself to be swept out onto the dance floor. Turn to 50.

48

"You got a way out I don't know about?" Josiah asked.

Diana looked around the room. There had to be something. She couldn't have come this far and found Garland, only to be trapped now. The room had no windows and only one door.

An old man said, "Yer in trouble miss. We been here a spell already. All they gotta do is lock that door. Ain't no other way out."

Diana moved to one wall. "All it is is wood walls. That's at least one way out." She unslung her rifle.

Before she could get any further, a weight hit the door. "Come on out and let's have dinner!" A voice called from the other side. A chill went down Josiah's spine. He knew that voice: Marie.

"Whatever you're going to do, do it!" Josiah snapped to Diana as he stepped up to the door. He threw his weight against the boxes holding the door shut. As he did so, a terrible impact slammed against it, jarring him down to his teeth. The door wouldn't hold long...

Behind him, Diana's rifle sounded, leaving his ears ringing. But it would take more than one shot to bust out a section of wall. The next impact on the door knocked it open a crack and, despite Josiah's efforts, the next knocked it open still more.

Then the boy, Teofilo, was by his side, throwing his weight into the battle. Josiah could hear the jangling of gold decorations running down his sleeves—those that hadn't been torn off or tangled in the weeks of neglect.

With a heave, they forced the door closed once more, but not before a hand reached through the opening, feeling and grasping as though it had a life of its own.

"Again! Push!" Josiah called to the young Californio. With a cry of effort, they shoved with all their might. The door closed with a sickening crunch on the wrist of whoever was reaching through.

Josiah expected a cry of pain, but there was none—only another raucous laugh. The hand, hanging at a grotesque angle from broken bones, continued to reach and writhe, making rude gestures when it failed to find anything to grab.

His blood ran cold, but he did the only thing he could do: he shoved again. The door slammed into the already injured wrist with the force of a guillotine, severing flesh and skin, and the disembodied hand tumbled to the ground.

On the far side of the door, he heard a voice, more annoyed than anguished, "He took my hand!"

The skin on Josiah's wrist tingled in sympathetic discomfort. Why was the man not screaming in pain?

"Well get that damn door open! We'll get him for this. We'll get all of them," another voice said. It was Marie again. How… how could she?

"Marie! What are you doing?" he bellowed. He had known the woman for over twenty years—why would she do this?

She laughed, and her voice came clearly through the wooden door. "Why don't you open on up and let me show you?"

"Like hell!" Josiah shouted. He turned forward. "Diana?"

Diana's rifle flared and he heard the sound of wood splintering. The people outside started banging against the door, and he threw his back against it. Across the room, Diana beat at a broken section of wood with the butt of her rifle.

"Get out, Beatriz!" Teofilo shouted. White-faced, the young woman nodded and crawled out the opening, while other prisoners tore at wood planks, widening the hole. Diana's friend, Garland, looked back and forth nervously between both sides of the room.

There was a moment's rest on the door—then an impact so hard it shocked Josiah into staggering several steps away from the door. He shook his head to clear it.

Behind him, a person was shoving his way in through the partially open door. His head and shoulder were in now, and he met Josiah's eyes, leering.

"Come on!" Teofilo shouted. He grabbed at Josiah and ushered him to the hole in the wall. There was no time for hesitation. Josiah threw himself into the opening and forced his way through, tearing clothes and skin on the unforgiving edges. Then he was under the bright moon, breathing fresh air.

He turned to offer a hand to Diana, who was coming through next. Her clothes became stuck on a splinter of wood, and Josiah jerked, tearing the wood, the clothes, or both, and she came tumbling out.

Behind her, he could see the door fly all the way open. Mad townspeople poured through as prisoners screamed.

"Garland!" Diana cried, reaching out her hand. He came toward the opening, kneeling to crawl out. He was almost touching Diana's hand when one of the townsfolk grabbed him by the other arm and yanked him back. "Where do you think you're going?" the crazy man snarled. Garland stared with wide eyes.

"No!" Diana screamed. Josiah had to grab her to keep her from flinging herself back into the room.

Teofilo crawled through the opening now, but a painful scream tore from his lips before he made it all the way through. Beatriz grabbed him and helped him out. His arm was bleeding, his face pale.

"Come on!" Josiah snapped at the two of them. "We have to get somewhere safe!"

"Where?" Beatriz asked.

"The jailhouse. It's the only stone building in town," Josiah said.

"I can't leave without him!" Diana cried. Turn to 40.
"I understand," Diana said, her face pale. Turn to 35.

49

Diana shook her head, saying, "There's no one else around. I think it's safe for you to tell me your secret."

The girl gave her a withering look and said in a hoarse, loud whisper, "Secrets have to be whispered!"

"You're whispering right now," Diana pointed out. There was really no reason not to humor the girl, but it did a child no good to give in to every whim. Even children not your own.

Ruby rolled her eyes in exaggerated exasperation. She stood up and walked over to the door. She opened it and looked out.

Something tickled at the back of Diana's mind. Some alarm bell she couldn't place. Without fully understanding why, she stood up. "Ruby, I'm afraid I have to go," she said.

"Shh!" The little girl said with an imperious air. She leaned into the open door and called, "Dan!" into the hallway.

Diana's brow furrowed. He wouldn't think she had done anything to hurt the girl, right? She shook her head and took a step toward the door. "I've got to go, Ruby. I'm sorry I can't play dolls with you."

"Just a second," Ruby said, holding her finger up.

Flustered, Diana didn't know what to do. And then Dan was standing in the doorway, his figure a shadow at first, resolving into the masculine outline of a young cowboy. He pushed open the door with a broad smile. As if he shared some secret joke with his little sister. "What do you need, Sweet Potato?" he asked.

"I'm sorry to bother you and your sister. I was just going," Diana apologized.

"Hold her for me!" Ruby commanded, pointing at Diana.

"What do you say?" Dan asked, still smirking.

Ruby put on her best polite face and said, "Dan, would you hold her for me please?"

"Now wait, just a moment—" but Diana was too late. A grin flashed across Dan's face, and he moved with startling speed. Suddenly he was upon her, clasping both hands on her wrists with terrible strength.

Pain shot up from Diana's wrists. "You're hurting me!" She cried, but even as she did so she knew that he would not let her go. Her mind flashed to the gun hanging uselessly over her back. She wrenched, grunting with the exertion, but his grip was like iron. No matter how she struggled, she couldn't even budge.

Ruby was stepping closer now, a vision in the lamplight, with her red dress and curls. The same gleam of excitement she had seen in the girl's eyes earlier was back, with a hint of a smile. That smile… it was a smile of anticipation, a predatory smile.

Strong arms forced Diana to her knees. She gasped and considered screaming, but some fool pride inside her wouldn't let her give them the satisfaction.

Ruby stepped forward and wrapped her arms around Diana's neck. She turned her face upward, bringing her lips close to Diana's ear. Diana could feel the brush of the girl's golden, curled locks against her neck.

A tiny voice whispered, "You smell like sunshine." Pain blossomed in Diana's neck.

She gasped, but before she could react, the pain turned to a strange sensation of delightful, torturous pleasure. Her gasp changed character, mid-breath. She tried to fight it, but she wanted nothing more than for this sensation to go on and on.

"Are you… biting…?" Diana tried to force the words out, but a terrible lassitude was spreading across her limbs.

Ruby pulled away. Diana's vision swam as that little golden angel filled her vision. An angel with bright red blood on her lips. Was that her blood? Diana's hands had become free at some point, and she lifted one to her neck. It came away wet.

"Dan, look!" a voice said. "I have a new doll! Isn't she perfect? I'll call her Mommy." Turn to 52.

Josiah allowed himself to be swept out onto the dance floor. At first he felt as though he had two left feet, but he was in whiskey up to his moustache now, the piano was right, and he held a soft woman in his arms. Some of the moves came back to him.

"Is it really you, Joe?" Marie asked. "I never thought we all'd see you again, after you ran off."

"It's me," he said gruffly.

She laughed as he spun her in a daring move, and as he pulled her back close to him, she said, "You always were such a dancer!"

"We had some good times, didn't we? 'Course, I was married then, and so were you."

"Not anymore," she said, looking up at him with a thirst in her eyes for something he couldn't quite identify.

The music came to an end, and Josiah was panting. Marie didn't seem winded, but her hand as he took it was cold.

"Lord, woman, you're cold as ice! Let's get another drink in you."

Laughing, she allowed herself to be pulled back to the bar. As they went, Josiah noticed Diana leaving the room with a little girl in a red dress. He made a mental note of it and called to Otto for another round for him and Marie.

As they sat, Marie asked, "What are y'all gonna do after this?"

Josiah shrugged with one shoulder and said, "I 'spect I'll move on." Otto brought them their drinks, and he slid one to Marie and tossed the other back himself. Soon he'd be up to his eyeballs, and then it would really be a good night.

He eyed Marie. She had been a pretty woman then, and still was now. If she was a bit older, well, so was he. She had been such a dancer when they were young. If he hadn't a been a married man when the two had first met… but that was a disservice to his wife, may she rest in peace.

Marie put her hand on his knee and said, "Why don'tcha stay, Joe? We could use a man like you 'round here. Someone to get the work done, when these boys don't want'do it." She took in the company at the bar with one sweep of her eyes.

Josiah shook his head. "There was reasons I left," he said simply. It had all been so long ago. He couldn't go back… could he?

"Hell, Joe, this town wouldn't be what it is without you. You practically built this town with your own two hands. This is where you belong!"

He looked into her thirsty green eyes.

"It was a mistake," Josiah said, turning away. Turn to 38.
"Maybe yer right," Josiah said, gazing into her eyes. Turn to 51.

"Maybe yer right," Josiah said, gazing into her eyes. He moved toward her, and her arm slipped around his. Her lips looked bright red in the lamp light, her skin pale and soft. He touched her cheek. It was so cold... he felt the urge to warm it, and had a suspicion he would kiss those lips before the night was over.

They laughed and had two more shots, dancing forgotten in the pleasure of each other's company. They spoke of old times, people they had known, events they both remembered. He found it was good to talk to someone who had been there, to remember things that weren't the sad stories. And slowly, a warm, pleasant fuzziness grew in his head.

When she wrapped her arms around his waist, he exclaimed, "You're still so cold!"

"What are you going to do about it?" She asked with a smirk.

He let out a sigh. "Hmmm, a nice, quiet room with a fire. A private room," he said, with an emphasis on the word private.

She giggled, and looked up at him. "You really do belong here with us. Think of what we could do together."

"Nonsense! I'm a U.S."—he interrupted himself with a hiccup—"Marshal! My place is on the road."

"What if I could offer you more?" she asked, her eyes gleaming.

He chuckled, letting his hands roam. "You don't mean to say…"

She gave a throaty laugh, but knocked his hand away. "Not that! That ain't somethin' you can buy, 'cept with sweet words, and you're a real good talker." She paused, and her lips looked so kissable, if they hadn't a been in public… Then she went on, in a different voice, a voice weighted with promise. "I'm talking about something else. Something powerful." Her eyes gleamed.

"What the devil do you mean?" he demanded. A note he didn't recognize had been added to this song.

"I'll tell you," she said in a tantalizing tone, "But it's a secret." She crooked a finger, the teasing look on her face beckoning him close, as if for a kiss.

Her eyes were dancing and eager, and he found himself leaning down. She brought her lips to his ear—and that's when he heard the gunshot.

His instincts kicked in immediately. He stood up, nearly knocking Marie over in his haste. "Where'd that come from?" he demanded, but no one else at the bar seemed to have heard it.

Marie glared at him, but he could soothe her pride later. Now, there was work to do. A few people were gathering at the hallway to the back of the building, the one he'd seen Diana go down earlier with that little girl. One man went down the hall, vanishing into the dimly lit passageway.

"Come on back here!" Marie said in a voice that was half whining, half angry.

"Sorry. Duty calls." He straightened his hat and checked that his guns were in their holsters, and only wobbled slightly as he raised a hand and hollered, "Make way! U.S. Marshal!"

Josiah elbowed his way through the crowd toward where the shot had come from. Turn to 55.

"Dan, look!" a voice said. "I have a new doll! Isn't she perfect? I'll call her Mommy."

A male voice laughed warmly. Dan, Diana realized. Her thoughts were so sluggish. He asked, "Are you going to keep her?"

Ruby giggled. "I'd rather drink her all up. May I, Dan?"

Diana tried to force herself to stand. No. No. No. She had to move—do something!

"You can drink as much as you like, Sweet Potato. As much as you like," he said fondly, tousling the girl's golden hair.

Ruby turned to Diana, bouncing with excitement. "You hear that Mommy? I can drink as much as I like!"

Dan laughed and let himself out of the room, closing the door behind him. His laugh lingered in the air after he was gone.

The little girl was sitting now, picking up the dolls. "Do you want to play with the dolls more, before I drink you up?" She asked, holding out a doll for Diana to take.

Diana reached for it, but the world spun. She sank to the wood floor, feeling the grain of the wood and the curled knots of the one simple rug under her cheek and finger, as though she had never felt such things before. Was that her own hand, so large and lifeless?

Ruby giggled and reached out to brush back Diana's hair with tiny fingers. "Does it hurt?" her beautiful little voice asked. "Let me kiss it and make it all better."

The little girl leaned in slowly, eyes gleaming with hunger. Her angelic curls fell across Diana's face as she drew closer.

Diana fumbled with something, her motions clumsy. Her fingers felt packed with cotton. She was reaching for... no—she couldn't even think it, or she would stop. A choked sob threatened to rip its way out of her chest.

"Shhhh," the little girl said, putting a finger to Diana's lips. "It's time to go to sleep." The girl's perfect face moved out of her field of vision as she brought her lips to Diana's neck.

The shot rang out, loud and clear in the small, quiet room. The little girl tumbled backward and landed sitting up against the leg of a chair. She looked down in stunned amazement at the red wound which blossomed in her abdomen.

"What?" Ruby said in a small voice. "What did you do?" She coughed, and blood rose to her lips. Her eyes widened in confusion and pain.

A terrible wave of exhaustion and terror came over Diana. Her rifle felt like a snake in her hands; she dropped it as if it would bite her. What had she done!? She started to leap for the child, to cradle her, to offer her anything if it would heal her—but a part of her mind screamed at her to fight, to hold on.

Her hands flew to her head, gripping at her hair, trying to use pain to bring some sanity. She just had to keep control for a few more moments while the beast died.

A hiss of pure hatred emerged from the tiny figure of the golden-locked girl. Her eyes pierced Diana, black as pitch. Then the hiss turned to a cough, and her body slumped, the life gone from it. Diana felt a moment of panic as she looked down on that fallen angel. Then the little bloodstained teeth loomed in her memory, and a shudder of revulsion went down her spine.

Slowly, she felt her own strength returning; whatever effect it was that smothered her thoughts like a blanket was now gone. In the new clarity, her mind spun. What had just happened? Could this be real? Where was Garland, and where was Josiah? She swallowed hard. Had she imagined this whole episode? But there was the little girl, dead on the ground.

Heart pounding, she picked up her rifle and got to her feet, gripping it like a lifeline. Whatever was going on, she needed to get out of here.

Diana reloaded her rifle and headed for the door. Turn to 36.

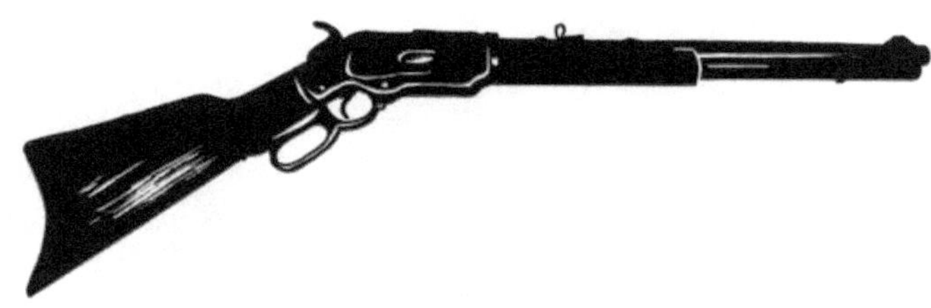

53

Diana wrapped her arms around the man she had come here to find. He accepted the hug wide-eyed, until Diana pulled away. "What are you even doing here?" She demanded. "Do you know how far I had to come to find you?"

"I—" he said.

"Three months you've been gone! You were supposed to write! To come home!"

"Uh…"

Diana shook her head. "I want to know everything later. Right now, we have to get you out of here."

"You got a way out I don't know about?" Josiah asked. Turn to 48.

54

Diana leaned in close, pulling her hair back to expose one ear. The girl was so small that Diana had to get off her cushion and kneel to get close to her. The little girl wrapped her arms around Diana's neck and pulled herself close in a hug that left Diana's heart melting. How could such a tiny creature be left alone with nothing but a brother to care for her?

Ruby turned her face upward, bringing her lips close to Diana's ear. Diana could feel the brush of the girl's golden, curled locks against her neck.

A tiny voice whispered, "You smell like sunshine." And pain blossomed in Diana's neck.

She gasped, but before she could react, the pain turned to a strange sensation of delightful, torturous pleasure. Her gasp changed character, mid-breath. She tried to fight it, but she wanted nothing more than for this sensation to go on and on.

"Are you… biting…?" Diana tried to force the words out, but a terrible lassitude was spreading across her limbs.

Behind her, somewhere in another world, she vaguely heard the sound of the door opening and clicking closed again. Diana tried to look, but her body wasn't behaving properly.

Ruby pulled away. Diana's vision swam as that little golden angel filled her vision. An angel with bright red blood on her lips. Was that her blood? Diana lifted a hand to her neck. It came away wet.

"Dan, look!" a voice said. "I have a new doll! Isn't she perfect? I'll call her Mommy." Turn to 52.

55

Josiah elbowed his way through the crowd toward where the shot had come from. Pushing past the people who were gathering in that direction, he found himself looking down a dark hallway.

At the far end of the hallway, a man was leaning in a threatening manner over a woman. Josiah barked, "Hey! Get away from her!" He started down the hall.

The man turned, and his face split wide in a grin. "Well, look who it is. If it ain't the high and mighty marshal, beloved of all Affliction."

Josiah hesitated. The man had another of those familiar faces, probably known years ago but no longer truly remembered.

"What, you don't recognize me?" the man asked, stepping forward. "Dan! Little Dan! I used to follow you wherever you went when I was a kid. I wanted to be just like you. Now look at you!" He held his hands out and scoffed. "Drunk and weak. I don't know why anyone wants you here."

Now, Josiah saw that the woman he had been threatening was Diana. She rubbed her wrist as though it hurt, then bent to pick up her rifle. Her eyes flashed hard when she stood back up with it pointed at Dan's back.

Josiah fumbled at his coat, revealing the hilt of one pistol. "I wouldn't come no closer if I was you, Dan."

Dan barked a laugh. "You think I'm afraid of you, old man?" He leaped forward, so quickly that even Josiah's trained reflexes had no time to react. Before Josiah could clutch for the hilt of his pistol, Dan swung in and hit his arm with a backhand so strong that it numbed his arm from the elbow down. Another punch took him in the gut, knocking the wind out of him.

"What do you think of him now?" Dan demanded, with his arms spread toward the crowd that had now gathered at the entrance of the hall. "He's not so great."

Josiah staggered, bent in pain. The air wasn't coming, and his vision was going to stars. How had this happened so quickly? He grasped for the hilt of his pistol—but Dan was already lifting his foot for another kick.

That's when Diana shot.

The rifle blast took Dan straight through the chest, sending him stumbling forward. He collapsed onto Josiah. Josiah grunted and heaved the dead weight off him, blood rushing to his face. He was panting as he pulled himself to his feet.

Dan lay sprawled where he fell, his chest bloody. "Damn it, man! It didn't have to end this way." Josiah bit off the words. He reached down, but even before he touched the neck, he knew the man was stone dead. There was no pulse. He jerked his fingers away from that cold, clammy flesh. If he didn't know better, he'd say the man had been dead some time already.

He stood up, giving Diana a nod of thanks, and turned to the crowd. "I'm going to have to ask you all to leave. This is official business now. Have a good night."

Yet no one left.

Instead, they all smiled.

It was the same smile on each face. Turn to 46.

56

Josiah held the door open as Diana pounded inside. Beatriz staggered in a moment later, one arm under her injured brother. Teofilo sagged, breathless, as soon as they came in the door. Josiah slammed the heavy door shut and barred it.

"Will this hold them?" Diana asked, leaning against the inside of the door.

Josiah said, "Solid oak. You'd be amazed how much we had to pay to bring it in. Not much will break it."

"Thank you," Beatriz said, near to tears. "I'm so sorry..." She helped her brother to a chair. He winced as he sat, and Diana saw that there was a trail of blood where he had passed. Josiah went to the boy and pulled aside the bloodstained clothing. The wound on his arm had the shape of teeth marks.

"Josiah..." Diana said. There was a note in her voice that caught his attention. "He was there." She looked up with a haunted look in her eyes.

"I know," the marshal said. He shook his grey head. "There's nothing we can do for him now. But I swear to you, we will get your friend free."

Diana nodded. Tears stung her eyes, blurring her vision. She shook her head, fighting them back. It was all so stupid. Why had she gotten involved in the first place? She never should have fallen for him, never should have let herself...

Beatriz put a hand on Diana's shoulder. "Is he your husband?" she asked sympathetically. Diana flushed. "No," she said, looking away. That was the problem.

Beatriz stepped back, eyes uncertain, then her mouth went wide in an 'O' of understanding.

Josiah put his hand on Diana's shoulder. "Why don't you look around, see what we've got here that we can use."

Diana nodded dully and got to it. The jail wasn't large. A main room with a desk, a single cell in the back. A side room with some beds, and a storage closet. There was also a back door, which she made sure was locked and barred.

She searched the storage closet and brought what she could find out to the front. "We got some ammunition, bandages, and this shotgun. Not as good as the one I left in the wagon, but it'll do." It was a single barrel. She loaded it and laid it on the desk, easy at hand. "How's it look out there?" she asked.

"They've got guns and torches," he said, as she joined him at the window. They were gathering in front of the saloon for now, but it wouldn't be long before they headed this direction.

Diana turned to Beatriz and Teofilo. "What do you know about this?" She demanded, and felt slightly ashamed when the girl paled at her rough tone.

Beatriz said, "Nothing!"

"We've told you everything," Teofilo said, his accent thick with exhaustion and pain.

Diana looked back and forth between them. Beatriz wore the ragged remains of a beautiful dress. Her brother was equally well-dressed and equally tattered, and his fine clothes were stained with blood. She could see the resemblance between them, in the cast of the eyes, the color of the hair.

"Just go over it all again," Josiah said, his deep voice soft. He came over to them and sat down. "Don't leave anything out."

Beatriz met her brother's eyes, and Teofilo spoke, shaking his head. "It had already started before we arrived. Some had vanished."

"We were visiting our uncle. There was going to be a wedding," Beatriz added, and her face twisted up as though she was about to cry.

Teofilo continued, "At first people thought the missing had simply run off or gotten lost out there." He gestured with his chin at the surrounding countryside. "But then more vanished. The town panicked. The wedding, it was called off." He spread his hands in a gesture that he seemed to think explained everything.

"That was not all…" Beatriz said, twisting her hands, "They came back. All the ones who'd gone missing. But they came back changed. Like…" she jerked her head in the direction they had run from.

"Deathwalkers…" a voice came from the darkness.

All eyes turned toward the cell. Walter Korse stood, gripping the bars of his cage. His ice blue eyes gleamed in the shadows.

"If you know something, Korse, speak your mind!" Josiah demanded. Turn to 64. "You will keep your silence, or I will have your tongue before I hang you," Josiah said coldly. Turn to 60.

"Don't listen to him!" Diana said. She didn't like the cool, calculating look in the murderer's eyes. Sometimes she thought she could smell the years of blood on him. She didn't know which was worse, the monsters outside, or the one in here with her.

Josiah shook his head. "She's right. Who's to say you wouldn't turn on us, the second I set you free?"

Diana watched closely as Walter calculated his response. The slight delay spoke to layers of thought within thought. This was a man who shared only what he chose to share. She shook her head. They couldn't trust a word out of his mouth.

Josiah was walking away now. Before he could get far, Korse said, "How are you going to kill Masters?"

Josiah stopped in his tracks.

Still affecting a calm posture, Korse said, "He's going to be back, you know. Guns don't hurt him. Knives don't hurt him. Do you know what to do?"

"Do you?" Josiah shot back.

Walter crooked a smile. "There's one way to find out."

Diana had to look away. He made her skin crawl. But if he could help them defeat Sheriff Buckshot-Face…

Outside, she could hear the vampires gearing up for the next wave. Any moment now, they would swarm the building, and she wasn't sure they could hold this time.

Walter exulted as the marshal said, "Alright, you have one chance." Turn to 70.
"I don't think so. You can rot in there for all I care," Josiah growled. Turn to 59.

A tremendous roar rose from the street. Diana glanced out the front window to see the mob swarm the building—and they were back to fighting for their lives.

Their attackers came in smarter on the second wave. Instead of openly approaching the windows, as if eager to be shot, they looked in and taunted them—making horrible faces, waggling their tongues or calling insults—and then pulled away again before either could get a good shot. Fists and feet banged against the heavy, oaken door, but it seemed to be holding.

One devilish creature lingered at a window as if daring her to take the shot. She levelled the rifle but hesitated. Would it just pull back? But it just stood there with that half-smile on its face.

She fired—and the thing jerked out of sight at the exact same moment. Then it was back, clambering through the window. Swearing, she fumbled with getting a new cartridge into the bolt-action rifle.

"What's the matter? Cat gotcher gun?" It cawed as it climbed in. It was—had been—a teenager. It looked at her with gleeful murder in its eyes, and then Josiah was there. He ripped the monster the rest of the way through the window and threw it to the ground. He put his foot upon its throat and fired a round from one of his twin pistols right into its head.

"Thanks," Diana muttered, as she scared off the next one that showed up at that window.

"Josiah!" a sing-song voice called from the front. "Oh marshal!"

Diana cranked a new shell into position and whirled. Tom O'Day, the trapper, scrambled in the front window. Before she could react, he landed on all fours, crablike.

She and Josiah both fired, but where they had expected him to go down, he went up. In a single, terrible leap, he bounded to the ceiling and held on, scuttling along upside down.

Josiah's eyes bugged out like he'd seen a ghost, but he tracked the paunchy trapper and fired—missing. "Damn you, Tom!" he called.

Diana had to spend her next cartridge keeping a vampire from crawling in the side window. A wild haired woman—she cackled as she dove back, out of the way of Diana's shot. Josiah's gun barked again, but it was another miss.

Tom O'Day licked his lips with glee and dropped right on the marshal from above. His weight bore Josiah to the ground. One of the marshal's pistols went skittering across the floor as Tom O'Day got his arms around Josiah's neck. Turning red-faced, Josiah struggled to pull the arm off his throat with one hand. With the other, he was trying to aim a gun at Tom, but in the mayhem, he couldn't get a clean shot. The vampire hissed and opened his mouth to impossible dimensions. Rows of sharp teeth lined that yawning maw.

"Bite on this," Diana spat, and shoved her freshly-loaded rifle into Tom's mouth. The vampire, startled, looked up at her. She fired.

The back of Tom O'Day's neck blew out, and the paunchy vampire collapsed. Josiah shot over Diana's shoulder. She turned to see another one fall behind her. She gave him a hand and hauled him to his feet.

No more appeared at the windows. The tide had broken, and their attackers pulled back for the moment.

"Need an extra gun?" Walter Korse asked in a drawling voice. Turn to 61.
"I know them, Marshal! I can help you!" Walter Korse hissed, gripping his bars tightly. Turn to 72.

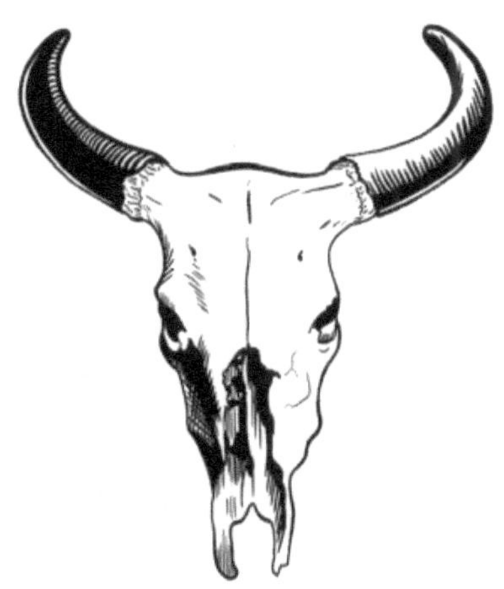

"I don't think so. You can rot in there for all I care," Josiah growled. He turned away, ignoring the seething rage that emanated from the cage. That man had killed his daughter. He would not grant clemency, not even to save his own life.

Diana was looking at him closely, and he felt himself coloring. Then she gave a slight nod.

Outside, the shouting reached a crescendo. "Ready yourself," Josiah said. The two of them unconsciously moved closer to each other, standing back to back as each covered one window, he the front window, she the side window.

The attack came from all directions at once. Turn to 63.

"You will keep your silence, or I will have your tongue before I hang you," Josiah said coldly.

Walter Korse's eyes glittered. He leaned into the bars and whispered with exaggerated motions of his mouth, "Those creatures will tear you apart. They are dead, yet still alive, soulless, yet walking."

"Shut yer mouth!" Josiah snarled.

"Wait," Diana said. "What do you know of them?"

A smile played at the corner of Korse's lips. "Why should I tell you?"

Josiah lifted his gun, a growl rising deep in his throat, but Diana shoved his gun aside. "Walter," she said, "Those things will kill you just as quickly as they will kill us. What are they?"

"Leave him alone. We don't need his help," Josiah growled.

Korse raised his hands, stepping back from the bars with a thin smile. As he turned away, he said, "If you think you can fight vampires without me, be my guest."

"Vampires?" Josiah scoffed. "Don't be ridiculous."

Korse's eyes flicked out the window. "I see four of you, and four dozen Deathwalkers. And they're already dead. Good luck. You're going to need it." He smiled.

Josiah slammed his fist down on the desk. He started to rise, saying, "I warned you."

A rumbling of voices gathered in the street. Turn to 66.

"Need an extra gun?" Walter Korse asked in a drawling voice. The way he figured it, odds were better than even they would all die in this jailhouse anyway. But if he managed to get free, maybe he could have another crack at William Masters. If he just could get his hands on a gun…

But no… a gun couldn't kill William Masters. He had seen that first hand. No normal weapon could.

Josiah crossed to Walter's cell in a few great strides. The attack on the jailhouse seemed to be at a lull, but obviously it would not last. He looked calmly into the marshal's grey eyes, glinting under bristling eyebrows.

"What are you offering, boy?" Josiah asked.

Walter smiled in the shadows. He had him now. "I'm offering you a chance to survive."

"Don't listen to him!" Diana said. Turn to 57.
"I think you should hear him out," Diana said. Turn to 68.

Josiah said, "I don't know what happened to Bill, but that there ain't him." He shoved the corpse with his foot.

Beatriz moved closer and knelt with morbid curiosity. "Is... should it be doing that?"

Both Diana and Josiah leaned in, looking where the girl pointed. The former sheriff's face was a ruined mess. One cheek had been blown completely away, showing teeth and the raw muscle of the jaw. But amidst the blood and shreds of skin, they could see movement. Beetles and worms wriggled in the gore.

Diana recoiled. "Just when I thought this night couldn't get any more disgusting." She turned to Josiah, her face pale. "Marshal, I'm sorry to say that I don't fancy this town. Shall we catch the next train out?"

Josiah quirked his lips in a wry smile. "I'm afraid express service out of Affliction has been cancelled. We'll have to find our own way home."

Diana grimaced and shook her head. "We need to get Garland and get out of here," she said quietly. Beatriz was kneeling closely over the corpse, her face a mask of horrified fascination.

Suddenly the dead sheriff's hand snapped up. It drove into Beatriz, still kneeling beside him, piercing through her and out the other side. The crunch of bone cracked through the small jailhouse. A bloody hand emerged from the girl's back, and a spray of blood landed across the far wall.

Josiah shouted and lifted the shotgun, but he hadn't reloaded the single barrel, and the gun clicked empty.

A terrible, low laugh reverberated through the room as Masters raised his ruined head. "Did you miss me?" He asked, as a bug crawled out of one empty eye socket and skittered across the exposed, bloody cheekbone into his mouth. His tongue darted out to let it in, and he closed his teeth on it with a crunch. He smiled.

"It's not possible," Josiah muttered.

"Anythin's possible with the blessing of a higher power, Joe. Isn't that what you were always goin' on about, back in your preachin' days?" Masters said. He jerked his hand free of the girl's chest. Beatriz fell back, a shocked expression on her face. Furiously, Josiah broke open the shotgun and fumbled for another shell. Some detached part of his mind noted that he was too slow. It was all too slow.

Masters leaped to his feet. His bloody hand locked around Josiah's throat. "You know, Joe, I never did tell you how much you bored me with all that prattle." With terrible strength, Masters lifted him off the ground. Josiah kicked at the open air and grasped at his throat. His head spun and panic tore at the edges of his mind. He couldn't breathe!

Diana fired her rifle directly into Masters' side, but the bullet had no more effect than if it had hit clay. Masters lips—what was left of them—spread in a slow grin. "I could kill you now, but that would be a kindness, Joe. And I have little interest in kindness these days. I'm not done with you, Joe. Not by half." With an effortless motion, he heaved one shoulder and sent Josiah flying across the room.

He hit the stone wall of the jailhouse hard enough to knock the wind out of him. He slid to the floor, gasping, his head ringing. No… he had to do something… a gun… anything!

Masters flung open the door to the jailhouse. "Game's up my friends! Come on in and feast!"

Diana kicked Masters in the small of his back with all her might. Despite his preternatural strength, he had no leverage to stop himself, and he lurched forward, stumbling down the first few steps before catching his balance.

She slammed the door shut. She lowered the bar, turned, and braced her body weight against the heavy door.

"He won't be winning a beauty contest anytime soon," Diana said with a brittle smile. Turn to 71.

"I don't know if we can keep them out," Diana said, her hands shaking. Turn to 73.

<h2 style="text-align:center">63</h2>

The attack came from all directions at once. Vampires rushed up the stairs and started slamming against the main door. Others broke off to surround the building, where they swarmed the windows. Before long, Diana could even hear boots tromping on the roof, sending down light showers of dust with each footstep.

She found herself firing and reloading in a furious blur of activity. Any time a face or body appeared in a window, she shot. Josiah fought by her side, taking the ones she had no time for.

Missing was a luxury she couldn't afford. It took her about as long to reload her rifle as it took for the next monster to start climbing in the window. One shot, one kill. At the front window, Josiah fired at another assailant. Too slow—the monster's quick reflexes saved it. Then the face was up again, leering in triumph. Josiah fired with his other pistol, taking it right in the face with a grim smile.

Stomping above shook dust from the roof. She glanced nervously up. How strong had they build this place? Howling laughter rang out from all sides, only a thin wall away.

Then Diana missed.

It was a lanky man in a fur cap, tumbling in one window. He looked as though he had been none too pretty in life, and now he was rotting and stinking as he pulled himself to his full height. "Keep fighting," He said with a grin, as she scrambled to reload. "Makes it more fun!"

Then Josiah was there, unloading one pistol into the lanky vampire. One shot. Two. Three—his gun clicked empty. The body fell and twitched, and did not rise.

A gunshot cracked out that wasn't either of theirs. Josiah staggered forward, clutching his shoulder in pain. Diana turned to see a vampire gunslinger standing in the front window, grinning as he levelled his gun for a second shot—the shot which would finish the job. Josiah stared, face pale, lips moving soundlessly.

Diana and her rifle roared at the same moment. The gunslinger's head snapped backwards as her shot took him full in the face. Still roaring, she leaped forward and beat him with the butt of her rifle to knock him back. Another was climbing in—too quick! She hadn't had time to reload. She grabbed the shotgun off the desk—where she had set it for just this purpose—and blasted it into the next attacker.

Josiah wasn't moving, just holding his arm and grimacing in pain. Both of Diana's weapons were empty now, and there were fresh assailants at both windows. The prisoner watched with glittering eyes, hands clenched tightly on the bars.

"Don't roll over and die on me, damn you!" she shouted at the marshal. She slammed the next vampire in the mouth with the butt of her shotgun. Josiah jerked into action, firing with his off-hand to scare away one climbing in the side window. It pulled back, and the bullet found no flesh. Josiah started shoving new rounds into the cylinder.

Then a new crash resounded against the front door—so hard it shook the whole jailhouse. The door had held so far, but somehow this was different. Diana threw herself against the door to brace it, but the impact came again, so heavy it knocked the wind out of her and sent her stumbling away. She recovered herself and, cringing, tried again to brace the door with her own body.

This time the slam that came into it was raw pain. She gritted her teeth and forced herself to keep pushing. "Josiah!" She cried.

Josiah was ripping the clothes back away from his arm. A red seam opened in his flesh from one end of the shoulder to the other, where the bullet had passed. It was pumping blood.

"The door won't hold!" Diana shouted. Another impact came, jarring her to the bones.

Instead of responding, he turned his gun and fired four shots in rapid succession, two at each window, driving back the inquisitive faces looking in. They seemed willing to hold back, content that the door would be down soon. Then, with the barrel smoking hot, he held it against the wound in his shoulder. Blood sizzled and flesh burned. Josiah's face became a rictus of pain, but he did not cry out.

When he pulled the gun away, the wound was cauterized. He looked faint and weak, but he was on his feet again.

The next slam against the door seemed like to crack Diana's bones. She fell to the floor in pain. Splinters were appearing in the stout oak. She tried to force herself up, but didn't have the strength. It hurt too much. With a sinking feeling, she realized they would get through that door. There was nothing any of them could do to stop it.

"You're going to die out there," Walter hissed in the cell behind him.

"Everyone dies someday," Josiah said. He closed his eyes and his lips began to move, pulling a rosary from his pocket. Coming up to his knees, he kissed the cross and held it toward the door. "'Many are the afflictions of the righteous, but the Lord delivers him out of them all.' Protect us, Father, in our hour of need."

Fighting through the pain, Diana rallied and came up to her knees, her gun pointed at the door.

And they waited.

The next crash didn't come. Only resounding silence. Her pulse pounded hard in her head. What were they waiting for?

Outside, they heard a howl of frustration. Then voices. "Back off, boys, back off. That door's too strong. We ain't gettin' in this way. But rest assured, they can't stay in there forever. Come on, we got better things to do." It was Sheriff William Masters' voice. And soon, following him, the other voices too began to drift away.

Josiah slumped into a seat and began to laugh. Turn to 84.
Gritting his teeth against the pain, Josiah moved to check the front window. Turn to 79.

64

"If you know something, Korse, speak your mind!" Josiah demanded. He took two great strides toward Walter and grabbed the bars of his cage.

Walter Korse met his eyes without flinching. "I know these beings. They are human no longer. They are Deathwalkers—evil spirits that take the bodies of dead men and women."

A shiver ran down Diana's spine as she heard the words.

"Don't be ridiculous," Josiah scoffed. But his heart was beating quickly, his knuckles white where they gripped the bars.

Korse stared with uneasy intensity. "My mother's tribe told of them as Deathwalkers. Some call them... vampires."

"Vampires?" Diana demanded, "You can't be serious!" She looked to Josiah, as if for confirmation. He shook his head slowly.

Korse went on in the same low drone. "I didn't think the legend was true... but, here they are. They are those who have died but not died. They are blessed with eternal life, but it is not their own. They must steal from the living to feed their own damnation."

"The prisoners," Diana whispered.

Korse nodded, "Their bread and wine."

Diana felt her stomach turn. "They were going to eat those people?"

Beatriz spoke up in a shaking voice, "That's what they said about us! They…" She swallowed. Her brother picked up the train of thought. "They called us food. Said we would go to feed their Goddess."

Korse's eyes narrowed in thought. "The Blood returns..." he muttered.

"What do you mean, man!?" Josiah slammed one of the bars of the cell.

A rumbling of voices gathered in the street. Turn to 66.

65

"Am I… am I going to be okay?" Beatriz asked in a breaking voice. She put one hand to her bloody chest. The hole went so deep into her torso that Diana could see air on the other side.

Josiah's eyes went wide. "I—" he started to speak, but just then a roar rose from the crowd outside the jailhouse. Masters' voice rang out clearly. "Blood for any who can take it! Drink your fill, and let their deaths be a sacrifice to Tezoca!"

Josiah swore and moved to the window, forgetting the girl, and Diana followed one step behind him. A great mass of the people, their eyes flashing red and grinning hideously, rushed up the stairs. Both their guns barked, but they may as well have been shooting into an ocean.

As the swarm hit the door, one wild-eyed man leaped at the window. He grabbed at Diana with a claw-like hand. She had just fired at another target and was forced back, struggling to reload the rifle. Josiah shot the man, and she flashed him a quick grin. "Thanks!"

Others were coming hard after the first, and Josiah was firing, one after another, holding the front window. Then a voice called from the side window, "Beatriz! Come back to me! I was going to take you next!" It was a young man, his head and one shoulder sticking through the narrow window. He looked at the girl with a crazy grin.

Beatriz quailed, sinking in terror against one wall, hands covering her bloody chest. Diana finished reloading, slammed her rifle closed, and fired. The blast knocked the man's head back and sent him reeling out the window. She could hear the crash of his body hitting the ground below.

"We're all going to die!" Beatriz wailed.

Diana gritted her teeth, but she said calmly, "Sweetheart, go sit with your brother. It's going to be all right."

The girl's face was a mask of pain and terror, but she nodded and fled to the nearby room. Their assailants had fallen back to regroup. "Again, boys!" Diana heard Masters shout. "Quickly now! They can't hold us off long!"

"She should already be dead," Josiah muttered, reloading his own guns.

"Maybe it wasn't as bad as it looked," Diana said.

Josiah didn't answer, and she didn't meet his eyes.

A tremendous roar rose from the street. Turn to 58.

A rumbling of voices gathered in the street. Gritting his teeth, Josiah moved to place his back against the stone next to one window. Carefully, he leaned into the window to get a look.

The people—or vampires, or Deathwalkers, or whatever they were—had gathered before the jailhouse. Their faces were drawn in rage, and several of them held torches that gave the street an eerie red glow.

A choking sound came from inside the jailhouse. Josiah turned to see Teofilo tilting from his seat, his chest and throat convulsing. Beatriz let out a low moan and reached to catch him. "Please!" She exclaimed helplessly.

Diana was there in a moment, helping stabilize the shaking man. "Let's get him to a bed. Josiah, don't let anyone in!" She and Beatriz lifted Teofilo and carried him into the next room.

The voices were growing louder outside. "You can't get away with this!" one shouted. "Punish the outsiders!" another cried.

A loud, clear voice rang out across the main street. "What's going on here?" Bill Masters strode into view, and the angry townspeople parted before their sheriff.

One of the townsfolk said, "It's Joe, Sheriff. He opened fire in the dance hall, started shootin' folk left and right."

Josiah sucked in his breath through his teeth. That wasn't how it had happened at all. Yet there had been death tonight, and as marshal, he was responsible.

"Joe, you got somethin' to say about all this?" Masters called, turning to the jailhouse. Some of the townspeople began to holler, but Masters cut them off. "Now, I been friends with Joe a long time. He used to be from 'round these parts. I'm sure he's got a good explanation." He looked around the crowd with a steely eye, subduing them. Then, with a hint of a smile, he turned back to the jailhouse. "Joe, is this true? You kill anyone today?"

Josiah frowned. How could he explain what he'd seen? He couldn't even explain it to himself. He called out the window, "They attacked us, Bill. All we was doin' is defendin' ourselves."

"That's not true!" An outraged cry rose from the crowd. "He and that woman attacked us first! They shot Dan!" More voices joined in a crescendo of anger.

"Now, let the man speak," Sheriff Masters cut them off, and the crowd fell silent again.

What the hell... Josiah rubbed his eyebrows. Nothing he'd seen had made any sense. Finally he called, "Answer me this, Bill. Why you got all those people locked up in the storage room of the saloon? You know about that?"

"Well, that's easy, Joe." The sheriff tucked his thumbs in his belt and rocked back on his feet. "We had a spot of disease here in town. Weren't no big deal, but Doc suggested we set 'em apart a spell. They didn't like it, but weren't gonna do them no harm."

"Not to hear them tell it," Josiah called back. "Disease? What kinda fool do you take me for?"

"Why, haven't you heard? There ain't been no one comin' nor goin' for a spell here, Joe. Why do you think that is? Sure ain't a product of our fine weather." He chuckled at his own joke. "Hell, they looked to be gettin' better.

Probably would have let 'em out in another day or two." The sheriff rubbed his jaw, then said slowly, "Joe, don't tell me you went in there?"

"Yeah, I went in there, 'course I did. Let out whoever I could too. And if you mean what you say, you'll let the rest out."

"Son of a bitch, Josiah, you always were one cussed bastard. That disease is contagious Joe! Don't you realize what you've done?"

Despite himself, Josiah glanced uneasily back toward where Diana had taken the two freed prisoners. Illness was nothing to mess with. Then he scowled and shook his head. "Bill, it weren't like that. Those people were strange."

An angry voice shouted, "Strange? You gonna let him get away with this, Sheriff? That's how come he killed somebody!?"

"Listen, listen," Sheriff Masters said in calming tones. "I'm sure this can all be sorted out. It was just some kinda misunderstanding. Stay calm. Joe, I'm comin' in! Don't shoot! I'm leavin' my weapon behind. I just want to talk."

Josiah lifted his head to look out the window. Masters was handing his pistol, butt-first, to one of the townsfolk. He started up the stairs, slowly, arms held wide, palms open.

Josiah tracked the sheriff with his weapon as he took first one step, then another. And another. He was almost to the door. Bill Masters' lean, familiar face looked older than he remembered, but still just as sturdy and reliable as it had been in youth.

"Aww hell, Bill," Josiah said. He lowered his gun and opened the door, lifting the heavy bar to unlatch it.

William Masters gave him a slight smile and tipped his hat. "Howdy, Joe."

The crowd was hanging back. Josiah eyed them suspiciously, then stepped aside to let the sheriff in, waving his hat to chase out a fly as he did so.

The sheriff took a seat and a deep breath. He gave Josiah a long look, then sighed. "Joe, you and I go back a ways. You know that as well as I do. Hell, you saved my life on Red Bluff."

He paused as if lost in thought, then said, "Remember that damn Injun, with the feathers sticking out behind his ears?" Masters chuckled. "I still remember that whoop he made as he lifted his tomahawk. I dream about it sometimes. Why, if you hadn't been there…" Masters trailed off, then gave Josiah a searching look. "What the hell's going on here, Joe?"

"Something ain't right, Bill. It ain't right at all," Josiah said, pacing and watching the door.

"What ain't right here is you bein' so nervous! Sit down, Joe. No need to stand around like fools. You're the coolest gunman in the West. What the hell'd you see?"

Josiah glanced out the window once more. The townsfolk were waiting, but they didn't look happy. He pulled out a chair and sat down across from the sheriff. As he did so, he noticed Walter Korse, silent in the shadows of his cell, his glittering eyes fixed firmly on the face of William Masters.

Holstering his gun, Josiah took off his hat and ran his hand over his thinning hair. When he closed his eyes, he could still see in his mind's eye the madness that came over the townsfolk. The way that hand had kept moving, right up until the moment it was cut off. The bloody bite marks on that poor Spanish boy's arm. Nothing he'd seen made any sense if he tried to put it in words.

"They had teeth, Bill."

Masters laughed sharply, "We all got teeth, Joe!" He gave Josiah a tolerant look.

Josiah shook his head. "Not like you or I. They bit a boy and… and—" How could he describe it? He took a deep breath and gathered his thoughts. He glanced at Walter Korse out of the corner of his eye. "You ever hear of Deathwalkers, Bill?" he asked.

"Watch out above you, Joe," the sheriff said mildly.

Josiah looked up and didn't see anything. Then he noticed a spider dangling from a thread, just inches from his face. He cried out in alarm and jumped up, knocking his chair over. He swiftly brushed at his cheek. A small mass caught against the back of his hand, and he felt a sharp sting.

Josiah grunted and shook his hand. He saw something go flying away. Tracking it with his eye, he leaped and crushed the balled up spider under his boot.

"You've been away too long, Joe. You've forgotten how to avoid getting bit." Masters was watching him almost with amusement. "You sure it wasn't a spider in that saloon what bit that boy? I ain't never yet heard of the type of man that bites. Unless they got rabies. Here, I'll ask."

Masters got up and leaned out the window while Josiah retook his seat to examine the back of his hand. There were two tiny red dots on his left hand where the spider had bit him. It stung like the devil.

"Hey, any of y'all got rabies? Joe thinks ya bite." Masters shouted out the window. He got a chorus of confused denials and questions. With a wave of his hand, he turned and walked back. "See Joe, ain't nothing wrong with them. I think the question is, what's the matter with you?"

"I agree, what's the matter with you?" Diana said, her rifle trained on Josiah. Turn to 69.

"And you shall know them by the signs that they carry," Walter intoned. Turn to 74.

67

The attack came from all directions at once. Vampires rushed up the stairs and started slamming against the main door. Others broke off to surround the building, where they swarmed the windows. Before long, Walter could even hear footsteps tromping on the roof, sending down light showers of dust with each stomp.

He found himself fighting for his life, beating Deathwalkers back from the windows with no tool but the mop in his hands. He fought in silence, controlling his breath, each motion precise. He had spent too long in a cage; his body wasn't used to this anymore.

One tried to climb in the window, heedless of his mop, and he brought it down hard on the thing's head, then shoved to force the attacker out. Meanwhile, others slammed at the heavy oak door. The bar held, but each impact shook the entire jailhouse, sending dust down from the rafters. Walter glanced upward. How sturdily had they built this place?

"You're going to die, boy," a voice snapped. Walter looked over. A vaguely familiar face—had he known this person in childhood?—glared at him over the black mouth of a revolver.

Walter curiously noted his own lack of fear. There was no time to react, yet the prospect of death caused no emotion in him at all.

The marshal fired an instant before the vampire did, blowing a hole in its head. Walter breathed again. As he brandished the mop to beat back the next attacker—this one with no gun—he wryly called over his shoulder, "You saved my life, Marshal."

"Don't count on it happening again," Josiah growled.

Now a new crash resounded against the front door—so hard Walter could feel it reverberate through the whole jailhouse. Diana ran to the front of the room and threw herself against the door, using her weight to help hold the door while she looked at them with white eyes.

Josiah leaned out the front window to look at whoever—or whatever—had hit the door so hard. But as soon as he showed himself, a stone crashed down on his head from above. He jerked back, reeling in pain. Blood ran down his face.

Walter could hear laughter from above. They were crawling all over the building. He cast about, but what could he do? The only thing saving them was that door. If it gave way…

He ran forward with his mop and braced it against the door, throwing his body weight against the door beside Diana. He was not prepared for the impact which slammed through that oaken frame. It turned his wrists to rubber. He dropped the mop and braced his back against the door, steeling himself for the next blow.

"Josiah!" Diana cried. Her face was white.

The marshal began mumbling something, barely coherent, and Walter realized that Josiah had been knocked senseless. He staggered to a seat and began tearing at his clothes. The door slammed again, causing Diana to cry out in pain. Walter gritted his teeth. They couldn't hold it.

From his shirt, Josiah withdrew a rosary. His voice grew stronger, his mumbles resolving themselves as prayers. The man was praying. Walter stared in disbelief. That was his plan? That was what he had been reduced to?

—SLAM— Walter stumbled forward, his body screaming in pain. Beside him, Diana shook her head to clear it. They looked at each other, and both knew the truth: The door was coming down.

"Many are the afflictions of the righteous, but the Lord delivers him out of them all. Protect us, Father, in our hour of need." Josiah kissed the cross on his rosary and pressed it to the door.

Diana dove away and came up kneeling, her gun pointed at the door. Walter grabbed the mop and readied himself for his final fight.

And they waited.

The next crash didn't come. Only resounding silence met their ears. Against all odds, Walter felt a wild glee rise up in him. It made no sense, but he had missed this. He was free and fighting once more. He didn't even care if he died. Yet in his gut, he knew that, he wouldn't. Not this time.

Outside, they heard a howl of frustration. Then voices. "Back off, boys, back off. That door's too strong. We ain't gettin' in this way. But rest assured, they can't stay in there forever. Come on, we got better things to do." It was Sheriff William Masters' voice. And soon, following him, the other voices too began to drift away.

Walter laughed, leaning against a wall. Turn to 75.

68

"I think you should hear him out," Diana said. She didn't like anything about this man. He was a convicted killer, and the coldness in his eyes made her skin crawl. But she didn't relish dying in this hellhole, and as for finding help… they weren't spoiled for choice.

"Let's say I do let you out, what then?" Josiah asked.

Diana thought she saw Walter smile in the shadows, and her skin crawled.

"You're outnumbered. Outgunned. And there's at least one out there who don't mind gunshot wounds."

"And?" Josiah asked.

Korse leaned closer to his bars. "You know me, Sheriff. You know what I want. I want Masters. Working with you I have a better chance of getting him than if I turn on you." He licked his lips, his blue eyes feverish. "Tell you what, Marshal. Let me out, and once Masters is gone, I'll go with you to the gallows. I'll put the noose around my own neck."

A chill went down Diana's spine. Looking at his burning blue eyes, it seemed he just might do it.

Josiah seemed to be weighing these words. Diana flexed her fingers on her rifle, feeling them sweaty on the grip. Outside, she could hear the vampires rallying for the next wave. She wasn't sure which made her more uncomfortable, the monsters outside, or the one in here with them.

Walter exulted as the marshal said, "Alright, you have one chance." Turn to 70.
"I don't think so. You can rot in there for all I care," Josiah growled. Turn to 59.

"I agree, what's the matter with you?" Diana said, her rifle trained on Josiah. "I thought I told you not to let anyone in." The marshal and his old sheriff buddy were sitting and looking up at her guilty as a pair of schoolboys.

"Easy now," Josiah said, standing and spreading his hands, palm out.

Beatriz was one step behind Diana in returning to the room, and she gasped to see the guns at play.

"What's he doin' inside?" Diana asked, gesturing with the gun at the sheriff. Masters smirked with a glint in his eye that she did not like for one second.

Josiah said calmly, "He's the sheriff of this town. If there's one person we can trust round here, it's him. Besides, he and I, we go way back."

Diana snorted, but before she could reply, Sheriff Masters stood, hat in hand, and bowed to her. "Sorry to startle you, ma'am. I am the sheriff of these parts. It's my duty to clear up any… misunderstandings. I never meant no harm." He still had that smile that just made her want to shoot first and ask questions later.

"Say, Bill, where's your badge?" Josiah asked.

Sheriff Masters looked startled. "Why, s'pose I must have left it this time. You caught me as I was off to bed."

Diana looked closely at the man's face. Was there mockery in that apologetic look? She didn't know what to believe any more.

Josiah grabbed a spare badge from the desk and walked over to Masters. "As long as you're doin' your duty as sheriff, might as well you wear the badge." He stuck the pin into Masters' shirt with force.

"Well, if it'll make the little lady feel better," Masters said with a cheap smile at Diana. He put his hat on and said in what he probably thought was a comforting tone, "I aim to find out what happened here, and make no mistake. Joe." He tipped his hat at Josiah and turned to leave.

"Not so fast, Bill," Josiah said. He lifted the single barrel shotgun from the desk and levelled it at the Sheriff. "You ain't what you say."

Masters' smile grew broad. "Whatever do you mean?"

Josiah fired the shotgun. The tremendous roar of it thundered through the small jail, and the Sheriff's head jerked back, a blast of red splattering the wall behind him. Slowly, his body sank to the floor.

Diana swallowed hard. Beatriz screamed, her hands flying to her mouth.

"No!" Walter cried. His hands gripped the bars of his cell, white-knuckled. "He was mine," he said in a hollow voice. He sank slowly to the floor, empty eyes fixed on the corpse.

Diana could hear shouts of confusion and concern from outside. "I thought he was your friend?" she asked.

Josiah lowered the gun and said, "I must have dug that pin two inches straight into his flesh, and he didn't even flinch. Just like those folks back in the bar."

Josiah said, "I don't know what happened to Bill, but that there ain't him." Turn to 62.

70

Walter exulted as the marshal said, "Alright, you can have one chance." The jangling of keys was like music to his ears, and then Josiah was throwing open the cell door.

Walter gave a mocking little bow and stepped out. The truth was, he had no idea how to kill Masters. Finding out would be his first order of business. But he knew someone who might know…

He moved toward the desk, reaching for the shotgun that still rested there. Diana slid it away from him, keeping her hand on it protectively. Josiah said, "No. No guns."

His voice was firm, and Walter knew it would be useless to argue. Later, he told himself. Trust would come. The stupid ones always wanted to trust. Now that he was out, he had all the time in the world. He gave a thin smile. "Fine, I'll beat them off with my bare hands."

Josiah cast around the small cell.

"They're coming!" Diana hissed urgently. The shouts outside reached a new crescendo, and a new sound erupted—the stamp of many feet.

Josiah mumbled something that sounded like a curse, his eyes burning, and shoved a mop at Walter. "Here, use this!" Walter gave him an even look, but took the mop.

Then the vampires were upon them.

The attack came from all directions at once. Turn to 67.

71

"He won't be winning a beauty contest anytime soon," Diana said with a brittle smile. The thin joke was all that stood between her and panic. "Are you okay?"

"I'm fine," The marshal snapped. He groaned as he got his feet under him, rubbing his neck. He picked up Diana's rifle where she had dropped it when she kicked Masters and handed it to her. Then he brought out his own pistols and made sure each was fully loaded. Finally, he set the single-barrel easy at hand, loaded and ready.

When this was done, he fidgeted, not meeting her eyes. There was something more he wanted to say. "Diana, if we don't make it out of this…"

She moved in front of him and looked him in the eye. "We can, and we will. Together. We will hold them off, because there's nowhere left to run. Are you with me?"

Josiah gave her a grim smile.

"Am I… am I going to be okay?" Beatriz asked in a breaking voice. Turn to 65.

"I know them, Marshal! I can help you!" Walter Korse hissed, gripping his bars tightly. The marshal looked over, his grey eyes glinting under bristling eyebrows. All he needed to do was break through that damned stubborn shell. If he could just make the marshal listen… maybe he could have another chance at William Masters.

But how? If guns didn't work…

"Why should I trust you?" Josiah demanded, crossing to the cell in a few great steps. The attack on the jailhouse seemed to be at a lull, but obviously it would not last.

Walter met Josiah's gaze with cool intensity. "If anyone knows these things, I do. My mother's people had a sworn destiny, to contain this evil. You ended that when you slaughtered them at Red Bluff."

Josiah reeled back as if struck by a blow. Something shadowed his eyes. Confusion? Guilt?

He had him now. He just had to nudge him over the edge. Walter whispered, "I'm the only one left. The least you can do now is let me out to set things right."

"Don't listen to him!" Diana said. Turn to 57.
"I think you should hear him out," Diana said. Turn to 68.

"I don't know if we can keep them out," Diana said, her hands shaking. She closed her eyes. If this was the end… No. This wasn't what she had signed up for. Not here. Not now.

Josiah groaned and got to his feet. "Don't worry. I've been in worse situations than this."

Diana gave him a skeptical look. "Have you?" she asked.

A hint of mischief twinkled in his grey eyes. "No, but I thought if I said it it might make you feel better."

Diana laughed, but it died quickly. Josiah handed her the rifle she had dropped when she kicked Masters, and she automatically reloaded it.

"That was quick thinking, getting him out," he said. "Just hang in there. All we have to do is hold this building. It's good ground. We're safe in here."

Diana nodded. Her hands gripped tightly around the rifle. "Let's do this."

"Am I… am I going to be okay?" Beatriz asked in a breaking voice. Turn to 65.

"And you shall know them by the signs that they carry," Walter intoned. He stood slowly as he spoke. "Their harbingers shall be the insects that crawl upon the earth or fly upon the wind, and their power shall be in the Blood."

Sheriff Masters' mouth twitched in suppressed fury. In a controlled voice, he said, "What nonsense is this prisoner spouting?"

Walter, smiling, said, "They're the old words, William Masters. But you know that already, don't you?"

"Bah! Ridiculous," Masters said. Josiah looked back and forth between the two of them with narrowed eyes, but Walter had no time for the ignorant marshal. William Masters was within his grasp now. Just a few feet away… all he had to do was get him angry enough to come closer. He was probably butchering the words he half-remembered from his mother's stories, all those years ago, but it had gotten Masters' attention, and that was enough. If only he could remember more…

"Nonsense, 'Bill?' Then why do you look so nervous?" Walter said, lacing his voice with mockery and malice.

"Ridiculous. You aren't going to listen to this are you, Joe?" Masters did look nervous, or was that only Walter's imagination?

"Shut up, Korse," Josiah said offhandedly, not even looking in Walter's direction.

"Oh, he's not telling you everything," Walter hissed. "Would you like me to tell him the rest, William Masters? Would you like me to tell him what you really are now?"

"Shut up!" Masters spat, standing up.

Just a little bit more…

Walter quirked a half-smile. "Or should I tell him about the Bled One?" It was a guess, a stab in the dark based on dimly remembered childhood stories. It worked.

Masters stalked across the space to Walter's cell and grabbed the bars. With an effort to control his rage, he hissed, "If you don't quit your babble—"

Now. Walter didn't wait to hear the empty threats. He drew his makeshift knife. In a single quick step, he crossed the distance between them and thrust.

Satisfaction.

The makeshift blade sank deep into Masters' chest, between the ribs. Hot blood spilled across Walter's hands. Beatriz, returning to the main room with Diana, screamed.

That was it. William Masters. "That's for my ma," he whispered into the sheriff's dying ears.

Josiah moved quickly, but it was already too late. When a hand shoved Walter back, he allowed himself to sprawl backwards into the cell, expressionless.

Voices fluttered high and irrelevant. Diana demanding, "What happened!?" Josiah regretting, "I should have warned him about Korse…"

And then—Walter's blood ran cold—William Masters' voice, cool as sin, "Weren't nothin' but a flesh wound. I'll be fine. As for that son of a bitch, you were gonna hang 'im tomorrow anyway, right?"

Walter heard the click of a pistol. He looked up, to see Masters standing tall and the gun pointed right at him.

How?

Time seemed to stand still. He had driven the shaft deep. Memories… He considered rolling aside, but what was the point? He had failed. He closed his eyes. I'm sorry.

A gunshot exploded across the room.

There was no pain.

He opened his eyes to see Josiah holding a smoking shotgun. Where the right side of Masters' face had been, there was nothing but a red mess. The sheriff's body slowly toppled. Walter could hear shouts of confusion and concern from outside.

"He was one of 'em," Josiah said. "Look at that stake. Should have killed a man. The blood goes four inches up the shaft at least. He didn't feel a thing."

Walter's heart pounded in his ears. He slowly pulled himself to his feet, fighting a crazy urge to laugh.

He saw Josiah walk over to the body. The sharpened wooden knife lay nearby for all to see: a bloody testament.

"I thought he was your friend?" Diana asked.

Josiah said, "I don't know what happened to Bill, but that there ain't him." Turn to 62.

75

Walter laughed, leaning against a wall. He turned the mop in his hands. "A fine weapon, all things considered." He turned to his companions. "Aren't you going to thank me?"

"For what?" Josiah growled.

"For doing my part in saving all our lives. But it's nothing. Don't mention it," he added graciously.

"If you don't shut up, I'm going to put you back in that cage," Josiah said.

Walter grinned and didn't say another word.

Diana, meanwhile, was taking a peek out the window. A gunshot sent up shards of wood inches from her face, and she ducked back to cover.

"Bad weather out there," Diana said mildly. "Couldn't see much. Looks as though that sheriff and most of his friends are goin' back to the saloon. Think they mean to dance?"

Walter tuned out the drivel from the others and settled into his own thoughts. There was a chill awareness in his gut that he hadn't wanted to face, but he could hide from it no longer.

It was true.

The things his mother had told him, the legends, the stories… all of it. He'd thought it no more than a tale to help a child fall asleep at night. Even when his grand-uncle, the shaman Dry River, had spoken to him of the destiny of his people… even then, he had not truly listened.

All his life, he'd been motivated by just one goal. From the moment his mother died, nothing else had truly mattered to him. Nothing except vengeance.

Now, here he stood, his hands stained with the blood of those he had hunted down. Only one still remained who had been party to that murder, and he was the same who seemed to have been chosen by whatever dark power moved in this town.

The moon continued to rise, casting a silver square of light into the jailhouse. In the distance, he could hear music and dancing start up again at the saloon. Diana and Josiah were discussing plans, hopeless and clueless, but it wasn't in their nature to give up.

Nor was it in his own.

He had questions, too many questions. But there was one thing that was still clear: he needed to kill William Masters. And to do that, he needed answers. His mother was gone. Dry River was gone. But there was one person who might know the truth…

He found a wall to crouch against, far from his recent cell, and settled in to wait for the night to pass. The actions of the others concerned him little. When the moment was right, he would be ready.

"Sir? There's someone…" Josiah turned as Beatriz appeared in the hall. Turn to 89.

76

"He's dead already. He just doesn't know it," Josiah said. He gripped his gun tightly and turned toward the room.

Diana grabbed his arm. "Are you sure?" she asked.

He nodded, his eyes grim. "I don't see that we have much choice."

Diana lowered her head. Josiah walked into the room. She heard Teofilo's voice briefly, then Josiah's, low and gravelly. A moment of silence. The boy started to protest.

Gunshot.

Then silence. After a moment, Josiah emerged, dragging the body, wrapped in a sheet. "He might get back up. Got to put him outside. Cover me," he said, panting.

Diana stepped with him to the back door and, after listening for a long moment, threw open both the bolts and cracked the door. She couldn't see anyone.

She opened the door fully and helped the marshal roll the corpse down the stairs and out. It tumbled to the dirt, a sad white stain on the otherwise dark street.

Suddenly a voice cried out. "Hey! There they are!" A shot cracked the still night, and Diana threw herself back into the jailhouse. She slammed the door, heart pounding. Josiah reached past her to throw the bolts.

"Did we do the right thing?" she asked, aware of Josiah's stubble near her face.

"I don't know," he said heavily.

The night stretched into silence. Turn to 83.

77

"Why don't you get some rest? I'll keep a lookout," Diana said.

Josiah gave her a grim smile and said, "I don't think I could sleep if I tried."

For a moment, they sat in silence. She felt that she should be thinking, working out a plan, but her mind simply wasn't moving. She was too tired, and it all seemed so unreal.

"What are you going to do when this is all over?" he asked.

She gave a soft laugh. "You mean if?"

"I mean when," he growled, emphasizing the final word.

The outside world seemed so far away. Fairfield, the open trail. When would any of it go back to normal? And would Garland be there by her side when it did?

"Sir? There's someone…" Josiah turned as Beatriz appeared in the hall. Turn to 89.

78

"Korse, what do you think?" Josiah said, gritting his teeth.

Walter turned his dark eyes on him. "So I get a vote now, do I?"

Josiah sighed. "You damn well saved my life, and you know it."

The murderer stared in silence for a long moment, his dark, Indian hair falling around his face. Somewhere, the band holding it back had come off. "I think we should get her Professor friend. Maybe he knows something we don't."

Josiah looked closely at Walter. There was something in his voice, something he couldn't… He mentally shrugged.

"Fine by me," Josiah said. Turn to 92.

79

Gritting his teeth against the pain, Josiah moved to check the front window. He gripped his gun tightly, moving as softly as he could to avoid making noise.

"What are you doing?" Diana hissed. He put a finger to his lips, then leaned in swiftly to look down the street. The townsfolk were gathered around Masters, many of them still holding torches and guns in their hands.

"You lot, keep watch on our pretty little birdies. Make sure they don't fly away," Masters was saying. "The rest of you, come with me. We'll be back."

A shot ricocheted off the window frame about an inch from Josiah's head. For a moment, he clearly saw a man in a window across a street, leveling his gun for a second attempt at murder. Josiah pulled his head back inside to safety, just as the next shot cracked.

"You know if you have a death wish there are faster ways to do it," Diana said.

"Says the woman who came to this town with me," he retorted.

Diana smiled grimly. Still, Josiah pulled himself away from the window, taking a seat near the desk.

"Now hold still," Diana said, coming over to him. "You were hurt."

"I'm fine," he grunted, starting to stand. She pushed him back into his seat.

"Let's have a look at that wound," Diana said. Turn to 88.

80

"We can't risk it," Josiah said, turning away.

"Wait, please!" Beatriz said. "I know her!"

"I'm sorry," he said. "There's no telling what could be out there with her. She could be lying, it could be an ambush… I'm sorry."

The girl's face twisted, and she vanished into the room with her brother. Josiah could hear her sobs. Her weight slid to the floor. He hadn't realized she cared so much. But it didn't change anything.

The old woman's voice still scratched at the door. He turned away.

Back in the main room, Diana raised a quizzical eyebrow. She held her rifle over her lap, preparing to clean it. "What was that all about?" she asked.

Josiah shook his head. "We need to think about what we're doing next. How long can we hole up in here?"

Just then, he heard a long, drawn out hiss, like that of a giant snake. And an even worse sound—that of bolts being thrown open.

He jumped to his feet in time to see a white figure vanish out the back door—a door now swinging open. A cool breeze flowed in to brush his cheek. He leaped for the door and slammed it shut, heart pounding. Had anything gotten in? Where was Beatriz? Had that been her that just left?

He made sure the bolts were securely locked and drew a weapon.

"Beatriz?" Josiah called, looking into the side room. Turn to 87.

81

Josiah leaped to his feet. With a mighty heave, he began to shove the big desk across the room.

"What are you doing?" Diana said in a tense voice.

"When we built this place," Josiah grunted, sliding the desk across the floor, "We put in access to get below the building. Come on!"

He paused, sweating, and reached down to yank up a trapdoor in the floor. Like most buildings, the jail was built off the ground a few feet. This opened into the narrow crawlspace beneath the building, full of spider webs and darkness. "Get moving!" he hissed, gesturing with his other hand.

Diana hit the opening without breaking her stride, hopping and tucking her arms to fall directly into the dark opening. But the explosion caught Josiah before he could get down. A wave of force crashed into him, sending him sprawling as a deafening roar consumed everything. Chunks of stone landed all around him, miraculously failing to crush him as they fell.

Dimly, he recognized that one entire wall of the stone jailhouse had been blown away, including part of the cell at the back of the building. The bars were nothing but broken spars now, twisted by the heat and force of the explosion.

In a moment, strong hands were under his arms, pulling. Walter. He let himself be dragged into the trapdoor and noted with detached relief that the trapdoor was pulled closed over them.

At first he could see nothing. Then lamplight began to play through the cracks in the wooden floor above them, sending thin stripes of warm light playing across the faces of Walter and Diana. They were animated, whispering to each other heatedly, but he could hear nothing except the ringing in his ears.

Dust fell from the floorboards as many boots moved in the room above. He could only hope that the debris of the explosion would make the displaced desk less obvious and obscure the trapdoor they had come down.

With nothing else he could do, Josiah let himself slip into unconsciousness.

He awoke sometime later to urgent prods from his companions. Diana helped him crawl while Walter led the way, scouting. On some signal, they emerged from the dark crawlspace into the open air. His head still spinning, Josiah focused on following Walter's hurrying form.

Soon they had found some other hiding spot, and Walter was bending over Josiah, asking, "How is he?"

Apparently some of his hearing had returned.

"Fine," Josiah groaned. He tried to sit up and failed. His head ached to split.

Walter held Josiah's head and tipped water into his mouth. Who knew where he had gotten it from. Josiah eagerly sipped several swallows, then shook his head. He felt some of his strength returning.

Walter started to move away, but Josiah grabbed his arm tight. Walter turned back, his eyes shining in the darkness. "Why?" he asked.

Walter smiled, but there was no warmth in that smile. "You're going to help me kill Masters." It was a simple statement, nothing more.

Josiah let his head loll back and surrendered to rest once again.

It felt like no time at all had passed when he awoke. Yet the cast of the moonlight had changed. The night seemed still, but he could hear shouts in the distance. Walter sat still as a statue in a shaft of moonlight coming in one window. Diana was huddled in her jacket not far away.

Josiah forced himself to a sitting position. Everything ached, and he had half a dozen stinging cuts where shards of stone had sliced both clothes and flesh during the explosion. "Are we safe here?" he asked.

Walter looked over. "For a time. They already searched this building. We came in right after. They think it's empty, but that won't last forever."

Josiah tried to say something, but all that came out was a groan. He put one hand to his pounding forehead. Soon the ringing had to stop, right?

"We have to find Garland," Diana said, with the air of someone expecting a fight. Walter shrugged.

"Have a plan?" Josiah asked.

"As long as they don't know where we are, we have an advantage," Diana said. "If we can get back to the saloon without being discovered, maybe..."

"Maybe we can get him out," Josiah finished. "It's risky."

"I know," Diana said.

"Fine by me," Josiah said. Turn to 92.

"Korse, what do you think?" Josiah said, gritting his teeth. Turn to 78.

82

"What did you do?" Diana asked.

Josiah gave her a sharp look. "What do you mean?" he asked slowly.

Diana merely held his gaze. A tense moment passed. Josiah sighed and looked away. "I know there's things I ain't proud of."

Diana shook her head. She had a feeling she knew where this path would lead. "It's not just you, though is it? This town... y'all did something wrong."

Josiah picked at the spider bite on his hand, then scratched it vigorously.

"Stop that," Diana said absently. "You'll make it worse."

He grumbled, but moved his hand away. Diana let the silence grow between them, knowing he would speak when he was ready. At last, he did. "This seemed like a fine town at first. Rather, seemed like it would be one someday. But them redskins, the Arahoca tribe, they kept gettin' in our way. We went at it with 'em once and they whooped us.

"They weren't bad folk, not really. Just didn't want us up on their land." Josiah took off his hat and ran his hand over his thinning hair. "They were generous. More'n they needed to be. They let us stay, on one condition. They let us have this valley and all the surrounds, just so long as we stayed out of them mountains." Josiah pointed north. "Said it was sacred."

"And?" Diana prompted, when the marshal paused.

"We agreed. Oh, it worked for a few years. But... well, as time passed, our town grew. Bill and some of the others, they wanted more. Some of the best mining weren't down here, but up in them hills.

"So folks started talkin'. Sayin' we ought to do something. We need to go whoop 'em good. I... well, I guess I got swept up in it. We all remembered what happened last time, so this time we cooked up a plan." He shook his head. Diana felt the pit of her stomach sinking.

"We invited the Arahoca to a feast, all of 'em, and…" he held his hat, turning it in his hands. He looked strangely vulnerable with his bare scalp showing.

"You killed them," she said.

Josiah nodded. He put his hat back on. "The food was bad. We killed 'em while they was sick. Put up a hell of a fight, too. Nearly got us, even with all them conniptions. Me and the boys, we each saved the others' life half a dozen times that night. But after that…" He pursed his lips.

"Were there any survivors?" Diana asked, feeling sick.

Josiah didn't answer. Just looked out the window, where the bluffs could be seen shining in the silver moonlight in the distance. "One," he said finally. "His mother." He pointed at Walter Korse.

Diana glanced over. Korse was still as a stone, not looking at either of them. She shivered, and the hair on the skin of her arms stood on end.

"Sir? There's someone…" Josiah turned as Beatriz appeared in the hall. Turn to 89.

83

The night stretched into silence. No one could sleep, but each passed the time in their own way. Walter simply sat against a wall, eyes glittering in the darkness. Diana cleaned her guns, first the rifle, and then the shotgun they had found in the jailhouse. Then both again. She eyed Josiah's pistols once, but didn't ask for them. He didn't offer.

Josiah sat in the chair behind the sheriff's desk, letting his mind and body relax. But whenever he closed his eyes, he saw Teofilo's face. It was such a young face. He wasn't the first person Josiah had shot, nor even the first innocent person. But there was something different about killing a man in cold blood. The way he had looked up at him, despairing without fighting.

He sighed and shifted in his seat. Why had he even come here? It all seemed so pointless now. Bringing Walter to be hanged where it all started. He was a sentimental old fool after all, and it would get them all killed.

He must have drifted off to sleep, because suddenly Diana was shaking him awake. He grunted, "Hm? What?"

"Shhh," she said. She pointed. He could hear voices in the distance, rapidly drawing closer. His hand went to his gun, but what could he do? They were on the other side of a sturdy stone wall. Hopefully it stayed sturdy. The voices drew right up alongside the jailhouse.

"That's it, boys, just set it right there."

He tensed. It was the voice of Sheriff William Masters.

All three of them looked at the windows, alert. They could hear the sounds of several people moving around just outside the walls of the jailhouse. Something scraped against the west wall, just feet from where they sat.

"That good, sheriff?" one of the voices came.

Masters clapped his hands and in a satisfied voice said, "Sure, son. That'll do. Light it up and let's clear out."

"Dynamite," Walter said, his eyes bright.

Josiah leaped to his feet. Turn to 81.

84

Josiah slumped into a seat and began to laugh. Soon after, Diana joined him, incredulous. "That's it, then?" she asked.

He shook his head. "We're safe for now. That's all I can say." He sighed, testing his joints. His shoulder burned, and his hand was swelling and starting to itch where it had been bitten earlier. He absently scratched at it, gun dangling from his good hand.

"You did good tonight," Diana said, putting her hand on Josiah's shoulder—right on his injury. He winced, and she jerked her hand back, her mouth a little 'O' of shock. "I'm sorry!"

He gave her a wry smile. "I'll be alright. Why don't you take a look outside and see what our situation is. Keep your head down."

Diana nodded and slipped up to a window to peek outside. A gunshot cracked. A spray of splinters erupted from the window frame mere inches from her head. She ducked away and came back over to Josiah.

"Bad weather out there," she commented in a dry voice.

Josiah snorted. "How many?" he asked.

"Hard to say. I saw a lot leaving, but clearly not all."

He nodded. "Could you see where they went?" Josiah asked.

Diana shook her head and said, "Down the street? I don't know, but I don't like it. They'll be back."

Josiah looked around. "Think we should make a break for it?"

Diana gave him a skeptical look. "With two injured? What, should 'Killin' Angel' over there and I carry you all out under gunfire?" Her brow knit. "Or is that three injured?"

A chill went down the back of Josiah's neck. He muttered, "How is the girl, anyway?"

"I'll check on her in a moment, but first…" She reached for his shoulder.

"I'm fine," he grunted, starting to stand. She pushed him back into his seat.

"Let's have a look at that wound," Diana said. Turn to 88.

Josiah threw open the locks and opened the door. He hoped he wouldn't regret this. Outside, a little old lady stood with a shawl wrapped around her shoulders, shivering.

"Hurry!" he hissed, waving the woman inside. He looked either way, but could not see any other figures lurking in ambush. She gratefully tottered through the door, and he locked it again behind her.

Beatriz screamed—too late. As Josiah was locking the door, his back was to the old woman. Her hands clasped, claw-like, around his throat. With preternatural strength she yanked him off balance and forced him to his knees.

Diana shouted in alarm while Josiah thrashed monstrously, trying to get his leverage to fight back. He managed to get his feet under him and heaved with all his might, lifting the old woman off the floor as he stood to his full height. Her weight pulled him staggering backward, into the main room.

Suddenly his gun was wrenched from his fingers. The old woman threw it with terrific force—a well-aimed blow that struck Diana on the forehead. She tumbled back, senseless, her own weapon falling from her hands.

Josiah grabbed at the weakened hold on his neck, but the old woman's fingers returned to his throat almost immediately. They tightened with inexorable force, choking the breath out of him. She cackled in infernal glee.

Out of the corner of his eye, he could see the old woman lifting her own full body weight to bring her mouth to his neck. Her lips were spread impossibly wide to show a row of long, filthy fangs. She spread her teeth, leaning in to rip a chunk from his neck.

That's when he fired.

It was a glancing blow with his off-hand pistol, but she shrieked in fury and her grip released from his neck. He gasped in the pleasure of breathing. He stumbled, finding his balance. Still seeing red, he whirled, searching for his assailant—but she was nowhere to be seen.

Walter laughed, a low, eerie sound. Josiah spun again, but the old woman wasn't there. Josiah whirled on Walter, but came up short when he saw the direction Walter's blue eyes were looking—up.

Josiah followed his gaze to the ceiling. Grandma Sews was clinging to the roof beams like a bat. She hissed, showing her fangs, and dropped down upon him.

Josiah threw his arms up, deflecting her teeth, but the shocking strength in her limbs bore him to the ground. He rolled, his gun skittering away, fighting to keep her limbs and teeth off of him.

In an agony of effort, Josiah came to a painful realization. She was stronger than him. Despite her tiny frame, her fragile-looking bones, and her dead, limp skin, she slowly overbore him. He couldn't even reach for a pistol—he had lost both in the struggle now.

He wrenched with all his effort, but it was like fighting a mountain. His neck muscles strained to the point of breaking, yet still she bore him down. He could feel her fetid breath on his neck, her teeth grazing at his skin.

A gunshot rang out, and the old woman went limp in his arms. He threw her off, spotting a red bullet hole in her temple.

He looked over. Walter was holding the gun Josiah had dropped.

For a long moment, the two men stared at each other. Then Walter spat and tossed the gun to the floor, sliding it toward Josiah. He turned away without saying a word.

The old woman's body hissed as it seemed to deflate, but Josiah had no attention to spare for her death throes. Diana was recovering on the ground, her hand going to her bleeding forehead. He reached out to help her up. That's when he felt the cool brush of a breeze against his cheek.

He grabbed his gun and moved toward the back of the building. As soon as he rounded the corner, he saw the back door was swinging open in the night breeze. A chill wind rustled in through the opening, caressing his cheek and tousling his hair.

Josiah leaped forward and slammed the door closed, locking each of its bolts. He glanced around. Had anything gotten in?

"Beatriz?" Josiah called, looking into the side room. Turn to 87.

<h1 style="text-align:center">86</h1>

The night stretched into silence. No one could sleep, but each passed the time in their own way. Walter simply sat against a wall, eyes glittering in the darkness. Josiah sat in the chair behind the sheriff's desk, his eyes and moustache drooping as the long, slow minutes passed.

Diana cleaned the guns. First her rifle, then the shotgun that had been left in the jailhouse. Then she did both again. It gave her hands something to do, her body something to do. Her mind something to do.

How long could they wait like this? And what would come next? The vampires wouldn't just turn and leave. Would the sun rise on a brand new day, or would the night end in some new disaster to make them fight and run once more?

Her thoughts returned, always, to Garland. Where was he right now? Was he in pain? Hungry? Her heart hurt to think of him suffering.

She shook her head, her thoughts travelling familiar paths of self-recrimination. Why had she chosen a man so… unpredictable? A man so much like her father.

Had she even chosen him? She had never meant to be so bound to him. She had thought… no, she hadn't thought. That was the problem. If she had, she wouldn't be in this mess, now. She shouldn't have let him get so close.

But it was too late for all that now. Here he was, and here she was. If she could just find a way to get them both out alive…

"Ma'am?" a voice came from the hall.

She looked up sharply. Teofilo stood shadowed in the darkness, his thin frame standing erect.

"What is it?" She asked. She let her fingers fall casually on the shotgun.

"I was just thinking," he started. He licked his lips. "I was thinking, I'm a mite hungry."

Josiah raised his head and looked, bleary eyed, at the young man. "We got some rations. Here," he started to reach for a bag.

"That's not… I don't…" Teofilo said. He took a few steps toward Diana.

"Stop right there," Diana said, lifting the shotgun.

"I just…" he took another step forward and reached out his hand as if to touch her. A look of pain and confusion crossed his face. He shuddered and said, "I'm so thirsty." His eyes fixed on her neck. Diana was aware of a coldness radiating from him. The young man had no body heat at all.

Then he opened his mouth, and kept opening it, wider and wider, past impossibility, revealing rows of small, sharp teeth.

Diana pulled the trigger. The shotgun leaped in her hands like a living thing. Teofilo stumbled backward, his chest a ruined, gaping mess. His mouth closed again, returning to human dimensions. Human lips, curled in pain and hurt. Then stillness. He slumped to the floor, unmoving.

Josiah was standing by her side.

"Damn you!" she said, shoving the gun into his hands. "Why didn't you do it? Why didn't you do it earlier?"

He said nothing.

She took a deep, shuddering breath. "We can't stay here. We have to—"

"Do what? Even if we could get out. Go where?" Josiah demanded.

She didn't have an answer.

Just then they heard voices. She held very still as the voices drew closer, coming up right alongside the jailhouse.

"That's it, boys, just set it right there."

She tensed. It was the voice of Sheriff William Masters.

They all looked up. They could hear the sounds of several people moving around just outside the walls of the jailhouse. Something scraped against the west wall, just feet from where they stood.

"That good, sheriff?" one of the voices came.

Masters clapped his hands and in a satisfied voice said, "Sure, son. That'll do. Light it up and let's clear out."

"Dynamite," Walter said, his eyes bright.

Josiah leaped to his feet. Turn to 81.

87

"Beatriz?" Josiah called, looking into the side room. He held one pistol raised cautiously as he edged around the corner, not making himself a target.

Teofilo was sitting up in one of the beds. "What's going on?" he asked blearily. "I heard something." The young man's skin was white and clammy. Josiah didn't have time for him right now. Where was the girl?

There! He spotted a corner of her dress. She was laying on the floor in a corner of the room. He moved closer… but something didn't seem right.

As he drew up next to the body, he realized it was not Beatriz. The thing inside her dress was only her flat, discarded skin. The loose sheath of skin was dry and translucent, like a snakeskin left behind when the snake was done with it. He recoiled.

Diana appeared in the door. "What's going on? Is everything alright?"

Josiah pointed at the skin on the floor, inhabiting the girl's dress. "We've lost Beatriz," he said.

Diana looked at it and her face reflected the disgust Josiah felt.

"What is it? What's going on? Is my sister... is she alright?" Teofilo asked. He was trying to struggle free of the sheets that still entangled him, but he was weak, too weak. The bite on his arm shone clearly, an angry red against the pure white of his skin.

Josiah pulled Diana out of the room. "What about him?" he asked, jerking a thumb back toward where they had come from.

Diana swore. "If Beatriz turned, there's no reason he won't either."

Josiah looked over his shoulder. He could hear the young man coughing. "But if he's not..."

"...we would be killing an innocent man," Diana finished the sentence. "I don't like it any better than you do."

Josiah scowled.

"He's dead already. He just doesn't know it," Josiah said. Turn to 76.
"He's still innocent. I won't let him come to harm," Josiah said. Turn to 90.

88

"Let's have a look at that wound," Diana said. She lifted his arm and pulled the shirt back gingerly. The bullet wound was a long, red welt across the shoulder. She raised an eyebrow and said, "Cauterized it already?" She whistled, then said, "You're lucky. It could be a lot worse. You should be fine, just try not to use it for a few days."

"Right," Josiah said with a grimace.

Diana rifled through the meager supplies in the jailhouse and came back with a bandage. In the distance, they could hear music and dancing picking up once more at the saloon. How could those... things just go back to dancing and singing?

She cleaned the wound as well as she could with what she had. While she worked, her mind turned over all that had happened. The town, the vampires, the regular people. And where was Garland now? Would he survive to give her a chance to rescue him? Would she survive to have a chance at it?

At last she sighed and asked, "What bet with the devil did this town lose?"

Josiah was very still. "Life here was never easy, but..." He closed his eyes, his moustache drooping, and for a moment he looked old and tired. He said, "Something has been rotten here for a long time. We thought we were heroes..." He shook his head.

She looked closely at him. In this man was sorrow, loss, and a drive for revenge, but under all of it... were those lines of guilt around his eyes?

She finished the bandage with a neat knot and sat next to Josiah.

"What did you do?" Diana asked. Turn to 82.
"What did Korse do to you?" Diana asked. Turn to 91.
"Why don't you get some rest? I'll keep a lookout," Diana said. Turn to 77.

89

"Sir? There's someone…" Josiah turned as Beatriz appeared in the hall. The girl was pale as a ghost and wringing her hands.

"What is it?" he demanded.

She pointed. "At the back door," she said. "The bolted one. It's Granny Sews."

Josiah gave Diana a look and stood up. "Watch these windows." He followed Beatriz into the little hall that connected to the bunk room, the storage closet, and the back door. It was double bolted, as it had been all night.

He drew one gun and held it lightly as he called, "Who is it?"

"Beatriz, is that you honey? Are you in there?" It was the voice of a little old lady, cracked and faint.

"Who?" He whispered to Beatriz.

The girl said, "She's a little old lady around town. She makes dresses; that's why they call her Grandma Sews." Louder, she said, "Yes, it's me Grandma! I don't know if we can let you in!"

"Please help me!" Grandma Sews called in a thin, panicked voice. "There are so many of them!"

There were no windows for Josiah to look out on this side of the building. He hissed to Beatriz, "Where'd you see her? She with the prisoners?"

She furrowed her brow. "Yes, I think so. It was dark, but I believe she was there."

"Please hurry!" the little voice croaked.

Josiah threw open the locks and opened the door. Turn to 85.
"We can't risk it," Josiah said, turning away. Turn to 80.

90

"He's still innocent. I won't let him come to harm," Josiah said.

Diana gave him a steady look. "Are you sure?" she asked.

He gave her a tight smile. "No."

She lightened a little, a smile growing on her face. "Well that makes two of us." She went to the door of the side room and looked in. Teofilo was still sitting on the bed, wrapped in nothing but a sheet. He held his head in his hands.

"Where is Beatriz?" he asked.

Diana swallowed hard. "She's gone. I'm sorry."

He looked at his hands. They were shaking. He nodded. "Will I be safe here?" he asked.

"Try to get some rest. We'll do the best we can," she said.

He pulled up the sheet and lay down.

"Will he be okay?" Josiah asked as she returned to the main room.

"Will any of us?" she asked.

The night stretched into silence. Turn to 86.

"What did Korse do to you?" Diana asked.

Josiah looked down, his hands clenching each other tightly. For a moment, she thought he would lash out. Or refuse to answer. But he spoke.

"It was Cora. My little girl," he began. "It was on her wedding day. The boy she married was on Korse's list, and he didn't have no mercy to spare that day."

Diana caught her breath, and her hand went to her belly. She couldn't imagine. "I'm so sorry," she said. The words seemed inadequate.

His eyes looked faraway, and she knew he was no longer seeing the interior of the small jailhouse. "We were in an army camp, toward the end of the war. Must have been… '64, autumn of '64. The cannons were booming when I first clapped eyes on Korse.

"Well, the cannons were always booming. You could go whole days without that sound ever stopping…

"I didn't recognize him right away, but I knew there was somethin' funny 'bout him first time I saw him. Thought he showed promise at first, truth be told. Then he took an interest in Cora."

Diana watched Josiah's face in silence. It was a strong face, lined with years and pride, with a drooping grey moustache that quivered as he spoke. In the distance she could hear the music from the saloon.

Josiah shook his head. "But Cora and Toby, well, they'd taken a shine to one another. Cora, she had a choice to make. Toby was an army captain, a good man. Reliable. He'd been like a son to me, ever since Red Bluff. It was a good match.

"Korse, he was a nobody. She turned him down." He sighed and looked at his hands. "I guess that was too much for him. After her and Toby married, once it was final… He killed 'em both. They hadn't been married but an hour."

Diana's eyes drifted to the cell, where Walter Korse sat, his face sunk in shadows. He could hear every word. What was going on behind those cold blue eyes? What had he thought that day? Why had he done it?

What was he thinking right now?

"Sir? There's someone…" Josiah turned as Beatriz appeared in the hall. Turn to 89.

"Fine by me," Josiah said.

Walter raised a hand sharply, and all three of them fell silent.

"We'll find them. They can't hide forever," a voice was saying. The voice, along with the sound of boots, was coming up along one side of the building they hid in.

"When we do, I want the woman," another voice said, and this brought nasty chuckles all around.

Josiah looked to Diana, who silently checked that her rifle was loaded. Her face was stony.

The voices faded as their owners moved on, and Walter mouthed, "Let's move." He led the way out of the building into the cool night air.

Josiah followed as Walter led them between buildings and around corners, often pausing to listen, look, and hide as one group or another passed them by. It seemed that many of the vampires had gotten bored of the hunt, and were simply waiting for their prey to show themselves once more.

"This is the hard part," Walter whispered. "We need to cross the street. Any ideas?"

Diana said nothing, but looked with strained eyes at the saloon visible between the buildings. A bit of light gleamed in the windows, and even from here they could hear the piano music.

"There's only one way to do it, and that's to do it," Josiah said. He moved forward until he hunkered at the forward edge of the nearest building and peered out into the street. He saw a bit of movement at the far end of town, but that was all. Where had the vampires gone? Had they really all returned to partying and dancing in the saloon?

There was no time like now. He gestured sharply, and all three ran hunched and quiet across the street. They came to a rest, hearts pounding. No alarm rose from the street behind them. Josiah dared a tight grin. "So far so good."

They knelt now in the alley beside the saloon; from here the piano music jangled loudly. Numerous voices talked and laughed in the main room. If they were the least bit disturbed by the casualties they had suffered earlier in the evening, their voices didn't show it.

Josiah grimaced and led them down the alley to the hole which he knew would open into the back room where the prisoners were held. He would get those innocent men and women out if it was the last thing he did. He hoisted himself up to look in.

Nothing.

The room was completely bare. All the prisoners gone.

He swore under his breath and Diana asked, "What is it?" Without waiting for an answer, she stood to look in as well.

Josiah met Walter's eye and said, "They're gone." The murderer nodded.

Diana put her back to the wall and slid down to a kneeling position. Josiah caught the look of anguish that flashed across her face. He put a hand on her shoulder. "We'll find him. Somehow."

Diana nodded and put her hand on his, but said nothing.

"We can't stay here," Walter said.

Josiah's eye fell on the steeple of the church at the end of town. They had come closer to it in their mad flight through the darkness.

"The church," Josiah said. "We can hide there until daybreak."

The sound of a door opening came from around the corner, and a handful of voices, raised in laughter, spilled out into the street. Boots tromped on the porch in front of the saloon.

Walter pointed swiftly toward the back of the alley. Nodding, Josiah hurried after him. No sooner had they gotten out of sight than they could hear the crowd pass by the alley, mere feet from where they had been hiding just moments ago.

Josiah let his breath out slowly, heart pounding.

"It's not going to be easy to get there," Walter whispered, so softly Josiah could barely hear him. Josiah looked to Diana. She was still lost in her own private misery.

"Do you have a better idea?" Josiah shot back.

Walter shook his head. He looked toward the church, eyes going far away as he contemplated their next move. "We can either try to stay out of sight between the buildings, or swing wide around town and approach the church through the graveyard."

Josiah sighed.

"Let's swing wide and go through the graveyard," Josiah said. Turn to 99.
"Let's stay close to the buildings," Josiah said. Turn to 96.

93

Josiah reached for his rosary, forming the words of a prayer on his lips. "Jesus, Mary and Joseph," he said, holding the rosary high so the cross hung above Diana. "Lord protect this woman in her time of need, for she knows not what she does. 'For I say, walk in the spirit, and you shall not fulfill the lust of the flesh.' Bless her and keep her, protect her from harm and free her from pain."

Diana cried out in pain, hands going to her head. She looked up and her eyes flared. "Stop that!" She growled, but her knees buckled and she sank to the floor.

Laughter echoed around the room. Turn to 98.

Josiah put the revolver to his own head. Staring at the hideous skull mask that had once been his friend, he slowly, deliberately, cocked the hammer one last time. "I won't end like you, Bill."

"Oh come now, you don't want to take that way out." Masters' face couldn't make expressions, but Josiah couldn't help but feel that he was grinning as he said, "Besides, don't think that'll stop us from recruiting you."

"The Lord will save my soul. I will never be one of you."

Masters scowled. "Don't do it Joe. We could use a man like you!"

The metal barrel quivered against Josiah's temple, still hot from shooting, so hot it burned his skin. He swallowed hard. He closed his eyes and whispered, "Lord forgive me for what I'm about to do."

He saw the light.

The End.

"KNEEL!" The reverend's thundering voice swept across the room.

Walter's eyes widened slightly, but he did not immediately move. Then his body began to tremble as the reverend's terrible will forced him to his knees. Josiah's stomach sank as he watched Walter bow his head before the maniacal priest.

Reverend Zeke laughed, a long, full, belly laugh that spread across the room. He turned, surveying his conquests. "What shall I do with each of you now? Oh… the possibilities. I'm sure the Bled One doesn't need ALL of you alive…"

Josiah tried to move, but the pain in his limbs was too great. He steadied his mind and forced aside the pain, bending all his will to bear on one arm. The arm twitched. It moved. He was reaching for his gun!

And then the reverend's will clamped down on him again, and Josiah screamed. His arm curled in against his body, every muscle clenching so tightly that the whole limb burned.

Out of the corner of his eye, Josiah saw movement. He tried to breath, turning his head to see.

Incredibly, Walter was standing. He pushed upward as though fighting a tremendous waterfall that crashed upon him, each gallon of water pressing him down. Yet he stood.

The pressure on Josiah eased as the reverend whirled on Walter. Eyes wide with rage, he held out a hand and cried, "Prostrate yourself before me, worm!"

Walter's body seized and shook. Every line of his body quivered with what Josiah knew must be excruciating pain. For a moment, he began to sink again… then, slowly—ever so slowly—he lifted his head and looked right at the reverend, eyes blazing like twin fires.

"No…" Reverend Zeke murmured, driven back a step by the hate in those eyes.

The pressure seemed to drop off Walter, and he drew himself to his full height with a slow sigh. He squared his shoulders, and something in the tension of the motion told Josiah he was still fighting for every inch.

"Kneel before me!" The reverend screamed.

Walter's neck bulged with tendons. His eyes popped in their sockets—but he never took his burning gaze off the reverend's face. He lifted his gun, slowly but surely.

The reverend let out an animal howl.

Suddenly Josiah could move his limbs. Breath came into his lungs in ragged gasps.

Walter fired and the gunshot sang out, but he was too late. The reverend—moving with blinding speed—leapt toward the criminal. He grabbed Walter's gun arm and forced it up, sending the next shot wide. A sickening crack followed, and Walter's wrist bent unnaturally backward, the gun falling from his hand.

Walter's face blanched, but he made no sound of pain. He used his other hand to swing, striking the reverend across the face. His fist slammed into the reverend's jaw, but the vampire seemed not to even notice the impact.

The reverend swelled with power and the pleasure of his victory. He seized Walter by the neck and lifted him with one hand. A darkness gathered around them, shrouding out the lights of the candles and obscuring Walter's struggling form.

"You think you can defeat me, one of the Chosen of the Bled One?" The reverend's eyes took on a reflective, reddish gleam. He opened his mouth... and kept opening it, revealing long, hideous white fangs going in rows deep into his mouth.

Josiah He rolled over, coughing in pain, and tried to gain his feet, but every muscle flared with pain after his ill-treatment. He grasped for his gun, but his hand kept missing.

Reverend Zeke laughed, an awful laugh that reverberated through the church. He lifted his free hand. Blood from Walter's desperate shot trailed down his wrist, and the reverend stared at it as though fascinated. He extended an unnaturally long tongue and licked the blood with obvious relish.

Then a rifle shot cracked, the powerful sound echoing throughout the church. Reverend Zeke's head snapped forward. His body collapsed, revealing a spray of blood on the far wall behind him. He slid to the ground, his head a ruined mess. His corpse twitched once, and then did not move. Walter, released, staggered to lean against one wall.

"Take that you son of a bitch," said Diana. She stood by the altar, rifle held steady in both hands.

"Diana..." Josiah forced himself to his feet. Every muscle screamed in pain. It took all his effort, and a hand leaning on the nearby pew, to simply stand on two feet. He felt every minor injury, even the little spots where debris from the explosion had torn through his clothes. His left hand ached with the spider bite, and his head throbbed from the tension of fighting the reverend's will.

Josiah recovered his gun and went to the fallen reverend. Turn to 103.
Josiah went to Diana's side. "Alright?" he asked. Turn to 107.

"Let's stay close to the buildings," Josiah said. "I'll feel safer if we're not out in the open." He didn't consider himself a superstitious man, but it was also true that he didn't relish the idea of stealing through the graveyard on this night, of all nights. He didn't say that part out loud.

Walter looked like he was about to say something, but whatever it was, he held his tongue. He gestured and began leading the way between buildings as he could, working them ever closer to the church at the end of town.

They were almost there, when voices inside one of the buildings stopped them all in their tracks. It was the building right beside them, dark, one they had presumed empty.

"I'm tellin' you, they ain't here!" one was saying.

"We got to keep looking! That's what the sheriff says. You want to tell him why we didn't?"

"Hell, how will he ever know? They probably long gone by now, riding out across the Devil's Anvil, never to be seen again."

A door opened, and one of the vampires stepped down into the alleyway right between Walter and Diana.

Flashing into motion, Walter struck the man's neck with the blade of one hand, crushing his windpipe. The vampire staggered, making gurgling noises, and Diana brought down the butt of her rifle hard on his head.

"What the…?" The other vampire started backward. His eyes widened and he opened his mouth for a holler, when Walter's knife sprouted in the man's throat. Where had Walter gotten a knife? It was too late to ask now.

Josiah gripped his pistol, heart pounding. There had been nothing he could do. If he'd fired the pistol, the whole town would have heard him.

Walter eased the second body down and laid him next to the first in the alley. Then he rearranged some of the boxes nearby to conceal them.

Josiah watched thoughtfully as Walter finished hiding the bodies. The man had proven himself resourceful. He had, in fact, saved Josiah's life on at least two occasions now, just in the last hour. As Walter finished his work, Josiah put a hand on the man's shoulder. Walter turned. Josiah drew one of his pistols and held it butt first out to Walter. "Here, you'll need this."

Walter met Josiah's eyes for a moment, then nodded and took the gun. "I thought you wanted me dead, Marshal?" he said, spinning the cylinder to check that it was loaded.

Josiah frowned. "You're not a free man yet, Korse. You've killed too many to go free, including someone I loved very much." His face darkened, but he continued, "But right now, we need you. If you can help us free some of the lost souls trapped in this town, it could go a long ways toward balancing the scales when you get to the other side."

Walter's eyes glinted as he drawled, "So glad I have your approval."

Josiah scowled. "Come on, we're almost there."

"Are you sure we'll find sanctuary in the church?" Diana asked. Turn to 102.

"Walter! Come back here you son of a bitch!" Josiah hissed. He leaped out and threw open the door to the outbuilding. It was unlit, but even in the darkness he could see the gleam of many pairs of eyes, all looking up at him. The prisoners! Here they were! Josiah hated to see them thin and broken like this.

He raced his eyes over the crowd, and noticed two things… Walter Korse wasn't here, and neither was Garland Enfield.

His mind spun. No… he couldn't let this happen. "Did a man just come through here!" he demanded, stepping into the room. "Where's Professor Enfield?"

From somewhere back the way he had come, he heard a scream... Diana.

Most of the prisoners just stared, but a few nodded their heads and pointed back out the way he had come. He turned and scanned the dark streets. There— figures moving. He hadn't gotten away yet.

The killer was crossing the street in the dim light of false dawn, shepherding Diana's friend before him at gunpoint. He held the gun in his left hand; the right dangled at a terrible angle. Korse paused and looked back, as if sensing Josiah's pursuit. For a moment, the two men made eye contact across the dark street.

"Josiah!" Diana screamed, a terrible urgency in her voice.

Walter began to run, dragging the professor along with him.

"You filthy bastard," Josiah said. He lifted his gun, but it was hard to get a bead on the moving target, and his muscles were still trembling from his ordeal in the church.

Diana screamed again, an inchoate cry of fear and rage. Josiah clenched his jaw. He could still make the shot…

Josiah couldn't let Walter escape, not now. Turn to 101.
Josiah couldn't let Diana down, not now. Turn to 108.

Laughter echoed around the room. Josiah looked toward the sound, to see a priest step forth out of the vestry. He was tall and young, with the kind of clean good looks that get a man into politics. "How good of you to join us!" he said in a silky voice, clapping his hands.

With a shock, Josiah realized he recognized the man. "Ezekiel Smith… all grown up," he said slowly. He recognized the features of the Smith family, but Ezekiel was even taller than his father had been.

"Josiah! What a pleasure to have you return to us. Don't be cold, everyone from Affliction just calls me Zeke now." The priest gave him a smile that was just a little too broad. "Reverend Zeke, that is."

Diana was still kneeling near the altar, shirt half-open, eyes unfocused. Her breath came in short, rapid heaves. Josiah growled slowly, "Whatever you're doin' to the lady, I suggest you stop it now." He swept back his coat to show one gun.

The reverend gasped when he laid eyes upon her. "Such sin, and in the house of God!" He started to move toward Diana, but Josiah stepped in his path, blocking his way. Zeke hissed at Diana, "You should be ashamed of yourself, you sinful creature… but then… I like it that way." He finished with a leer.

Diana shuddered. "Step back," Josiah said, drawing his revolver.

The reverend looked at him, eyes blazing. With a sudden flare, the muscles in Josiah's arm cramped so badly that he dropped his gun.

Reverend Zeke made an affronted expression. He stepped past Josiah and held up his hands to Diana as though illustrating a beautiful piece of artwork, saying, "Are your senses so dulled to life, to pleasure, that you cannot appreciate a beautiful creature such as this?"

Diana's face was tilted back, lips parted. Her prettiness was never more apparent, but the wrongness of what was being done to her offended Josiah to his core. His heart pounded in his chest in both rage and fear. Every instinct screamed at him to run from this church immediately, or destroy it. "This is no house of the Lord," he said softly.

Reverend Zeke laughed. "Oh, this is something much better! This is the beginning of the end, the seat of the blood of transformation that will remake this world. And I will be its vanguard, carrier of the holy message, first to whom all must bow… or die!"

"Let her go," Josiah demanded. He flexed one hand, found he could move it.

"Oh?" Zeke said. "Would you take her place? I was going to have her dance for us, but perhaps you would prefer to do the dancing?"

"I will see you in Hell for this…" Josiah growled. He pushed his body—he could move! Quickly, he dove to the floor to grab the gun he had dropped. Rolling, he came up with the gun pointed at the reverend—and found that his finger would not move to pull the trigger. "Damn you!" he shouted, before his tongue froze in his mouth. Panic welled up as he realized his helplessness.

Reverend Zeke took a few steps closer, his eyes fixed on Josiah. "I always thought you looked a little like a monkey…"

Josiah fought to move, but as he tried each limb, the muscles in it seized, until he could not even twitch his littlest finger. The unrelenting tension began to turn from ache into pain.

The reverend laughed again. "Dance for me, monkey!" He cried. He jerked his hand up in a sharp motion, fingers clawed like a puppeteer—and Josiah danced. His body leaped and cavorted. He found himself flinging his limbs this way and that. He jumped up onto a table and did a jig, then crouched and hooted like a monkey.

"Stop it! Leave him alone!" Diana cried, one hand holding her shirt closed.

Josiah fought, but each attempt to control his own muscles only brought him blinding pain. With terrible consciousness, he was forced to watch as his body dropped to all fours, then scratched itself under the armpits. Hideous howls and honking noises emerged from his own throat.

Diana was moving, reaching for a gun. Then the reverend's other hand lashed out, and Diana's body seized up as each muscle tightened to its fullest capacity. Josiah struggled to move and could not.

"Would you like to dance, too?" the reverend asked darkly. Diana's eyes darted from side to side in panic. Josiah howled inside his own mind in impotent rage, even as his body still crouched like a monkey.

"Let them go." Walter's voice, deadly quiet, cut across the room. Turn to 104.
A gunshot interrupted the reverend's maniacal laughter. Turn to 100.

99

"Let's swing wide and go through the graveyard," Josiah said.

Walter nodded. He led them on a long, low course away from the town, taking shelter behind storage buildings and haystacks as they were available, or huddling low in the moonlight as they crossed bare ground. No one hollered.

Soon enough they found themselves at the edge of town. The only thing still between them and the church was the town graveyard. It was a wide, irregularly fenced area of earth set aside for burials. Here and there a stone monument marked the site of some notable's final resting place, but most of the mounds were marked with nothing but a wooden stake.

Diana shivered, moving unconsciously closer to Josiah. Her warmth near him was not unpleasant.

"Come on, the dead don't bite. Usually," Walter said with a twist to his lips.

Josiah didn't consider himself a superstitious man, but entering the graveyard on that night, of all nights, was one of the hardest things he had ever done. Nevertheless, once his skin stopped crawling, he started to feel a certain peace steal over him.

"It's not too bad, is it?" Diana asked. Her voice had a melancholy tone as she looked out over the wooden stakes.

Josiah nodded. "They're resting. As they should be. It's those others who aren't right."

Diana was trembling with the cold, and Josiah nearly put his arm around to warm her. Then she was moving again, leading the way between the mounds of cold earth.

Someday, they would all wind up in a place like this. But Diana was right. This death didn't sound so bad. The Lord would be ready for him, when his time came. It was turning into one of those monsters back in the town that scared him.

Before he knew it, they were standing at the fence marking the far side of the graveyard. Only a small space of open ground separated them from the church now.

Josiah turned to Walter, regarding him with a steady gaze. The man had proven himself multiple times tonight. Every instinct screamed at him not to trust the murderer, and yet… they wouldn't have made it through the night without his help. He said, "Whatever happens in there, you'll need this." He drew one pistol and held it out to Walter, handle first.

The criminal raised an eyebrow. Josiah scowled. "Just remember, you're still hangin' once it's all through. Till then, we need all hands on deck."

Walter twisted his lips in a mocking smile, but he took the gun.

"Are you sure we'll find sanctuary in the church?" Diana asked. Turn to 102.

100

A gunshot interrupted the reverend's maniacal laughter. Blood sprayed from an opening that appeared in the tall priest's chest. Behind the reverend, Walter stood, holding a smoking gun. He stepped out from the shadows, lowering his gun.

But the reverend did not fall. Instead, he looked down and touched his chest. His fingers came away bloody. He grunted in surprise, and the wound began to close. He turned to face Walter, a grin growing. "The would-be hero…" he purred.

Walter's eyes went wide and fierce. He jerked the gun up once more, drawing a bead on the reverend's head.

"KNEEL!" The reverend's thundering voice swept across the room. Turn to 95.

101

Josiah couldn't let Walter escape, not now. The running figure would be hard to hit… harder still to make sure not to hit the hostage. He tracked their movement, using both hands…

He took the shot. A single report broke the pre-dawn silence.

Walter fell forward, staggered another few steps, and then collapsed in the dust. He lay there unmoving, and Josiah felt a grim satisfaction.

The young man, Diana's friend, looked this way and that in abject terror, then turned to run. Josiah called after him, but he did not stop. Diana screamed again.

This time, it was not a scream of fear, but one of raw pain.

Heart pounding in his throat, Josiah turned and ran back into the church. Where the reverend had fallen, there was nothing but a stain of blood on the ground, already black and crusting.

Laughter.

Josiah looked up toward the altar. Diana's body was draped over the knees of Reverend Zeke. Her head tilted back horribly, showing two bloody gashes across her neck. "Diana!" Josiah shouted. She did not move.

"You're too late, my dear, old Uncle Joe," Reverend Zeke said in piteous tones. His mouth was stained with blood. It ran down his chin, dripping onto his robes.

"Diana…" Josiah whispered.

"I want you to savor the feeling of failure," Zeke said, standing. He held out Diana's body with one hand, and let it drop limply to the floor, where it rolled down the stairs to lay at the front of the nave, eyes staring glassily at the ceiling.

The reverend's laughter resounded through the room, filling the nave. Josiah felt it shake in his bones.

Josiah fired, not giving the priest a chance to use his power. The shot took Reverend Zeke in the chest. He staggered back, touched the red wound, then looked up at Josiah and laughed.

Josiah fired again. Then again. The priest just kept laughing and laughing, without pause, like a man might laugh at a kitten. Josiah kept firing, advancing on the priest until his gun was empty. After three successive shots to the head, the priest finally went down, his body twitching on the floor.

"It's no good," a drawling voice said from one side.

Josiah whirled to see Sheriff William Masters standing in the doorway to the church. Josiah looked away, his jaw clenched. "What the hell do you know?"

"More than you'd think, old man." Masters walked into the room, his thumbs hooked into his belt loops, spurs clinking with every step. He looked at Diana's lifeless body, and the bullet-riddled carcass of the priest.

"Not bad, though," Masters clicked his tongue. "Should take him a minute or two to get up from that one."

In the light now, Josiah could see Masters' face for the first time since the jailhouse. His face had been wrecked by the shotgun blast. The skull was showing in most places, occasionally with deep pit-marks where individual shot pellets had scored it. His mouth was nothing but a death's head grin. But the eyes, the eyes were burning orbs of red light, deep within the skull.

"Why you fightin' us, Joe?" the hideous sheriff said. He spread his arms. "This is the future. You can't stop it. Nobody can."

Josiah lifted his gun toward Masters, but the former sheriff simply laughed. "What good is that goin' to do, old friend? By my count you've got, what, one bullet left in that piece? Think that'll do the trick, where a shotgun didn't? I'm one of the Chosen, get it? Not like those scum you been shootin' up left and right. We ain't thralls. We don't die so easy." He stepped closer to Josiah, a grotesque smile on his death's head face.

"See, the thing is, we're already dead. Cheated death, right? He don't come back a second time."

Josiah trembled, his gun hand shaking.

"Didn't you ever want to live forever, Joe? If so… well, I got someone you should meet. She'll do right by you. What do you say?"

Marshal Josiah da Silva knew, in his bones, that his time had come. His body was on fire from a dozen aches and injuries. He was out of ammo, exhausted, and had no friends. There was only one thing left to do.

"Alright," Josiah said. "Sign me up." Turn to 105.
Josiah put the revolver to his own head. Turn to 94.

"Are you sure we'll find sanctuary in the church?" Diana asked.

"What choice do we have?" Josiah growled.

He regarded the small church that served the town of Affliction. He had helped build that church, years ago. He could still remember putting the roof on, raising the cross. The way the town had cheered once the cross on top was finally set in place. It was the finishing touch, and they had felt, briefly, that the town might be blessed.

Then Red Bluff happened…

Somehow, that cross reaching to the sky no longer gave him the same reassurance it once did. But it was the house of the Lord, his Father, and surely some solace could still be found there.

"It's as good a place as any, and better than most," he said. He glanced briefly in both directions. It didn't seem that any of their pursuers were currently watching. "Now, go!" he called, and started to run across the street. But at that exact moment, he noticed movement just a few buildings over.

"Stop!" he hissed. He flattened himself against the wall, aborting his dash across the street—but Diana was already going. His heart pounded in his chest as he watched her, crouching low, hurry to the nearest shadows. Glancing down the street once more, he saw that no one seemed to have noticed her.

Diana looked back at him and Walter and gave them a nod and a smile, then began working her way along the side of the church. There was a side door which she vanished into.

Once the vampires down the street had passed out of sight once more, Josiah said to Walter, "Come on." Moving swiftly and quietly, the two of them followed Diana across the street and in through the small door.

The interior of the church was dimly lit and smoky. The wooden walls seemed dark and heavy, oppressive. The aisles were lined with arrays of votive candles, dozens of them, their tiny flames giving the room what little light and warmth it had.

"Hello boys," a feminine voice came from near the altar. They both looked at once.

Diana stood there, her jacket off and draped across the altar. Her eyes were unfocused, and her voice sounded dreamy. As they watched, she took off her hat, set it on the altar, and shook out her hair.

Walter and Josiah looked at one another.

"Diana…" Josiah started to say.

She put her finger to her lips. Eyes half-lidded, she stepped toward them, letting her hips sway with the rhythm of her steps. She put her fingers to her shirt and started fiddling with the buttons. She shuddered—a look something like pain crossed her face. Then the spasm passed and she looked up at them with an empty smile, her eyes glazed. She undid the top button of her shirt, showing a bit of her undershirt.

Walter drew his gun and made a silent gesture with his head toward Diana, as if to say, 'you deal with her.' Then he prowled into one of the darkened aisles, eyes keenly searching out the corners of the building.

"Diana, stop," Josiah growled. "We have business to take care of."

She giggled, "I want to take care of business..." Her voice had a strange, throaty quality to it. She rolled back her head and began to sway, dancing to music only she could hear. She brought her hands up to touch her belly as she moved. It was the kind of dance that could kill a man.

Josiah blanched and averted his gaze, suddenly uncomfortably aware of how long it had been... "Woman, get ahold of yourself!" he demanded.

In that same, strange voice, she said, "Josiah, don't you want..." A spasm of pain crossed her face. Her body tensed and she stumbled to one knee. "What's... happening...?" she gasped.

"Diana!" Josiah cried. He hurried to her side and grasped her shoulder tightly. "Pull yourself together! We are here to save people. We need you. I need you!"

She looked up at him, and her eyes were completely unfocused. "Do you, now?" she asked with a low laugh. "Tell me how much you need me..." She tossed her head, and her loose hair fell around one shoulder.

"Diana, snap out of it!" Josiah slapped her across the face. Turn to 106.
Josiah reached for his rosary, forming the words of a prayer on his lips. Turn to 93.

103

Josiah recovered his gun and went to the fallen reverend. The priest's long body lay stretched out, face down, in the south transept. He did not stir as Josiah nudged the body with his toe. Nearby, a door swung loosely, revealing the cold air of night.

"You did good," he said to Diana.

"Thanks. So did you," she replied in a tired voice.

But Josiah knew that he had not. He had been trapped, unable to act, and the memory sent chills down his spine. "Let's leave this part out when we tell the story," he said, thinking of the monkey dance.

"Agreed!" Diana said fervently.

Suddenly Josiah looked up, eyes narrowing, and scanned the small church. "Where's Walter?" he asked.

She shook her head. "I didn't see."

He cursed under his breath. He moved to the door—outside was a covered path between the church and a small outbuilding, probably used as storage for the church. Another door swung gently into that building.

"Walter! Come back here you son of a bitch!" Josiah hissed. Turn to 97.

"Let them go." Walter's voice, deadly quiet, cut across the room.

The reverend turned. Walter stepped out of the shadows behind him, gun aimed firmly at the reverend's head. A twisted smile spread across Reverend Zeke's face. "If I must," he said, and let his outstretched hand open.

Josiah felt the pressure fall from his body, but the pain of overexertion caused him to double over. His muscles screamed. Even his jaw quivered. Every limb had been clenched so hard by the awful dancing, he could barely move except to tremble.

Walter smiled, his finger moving on the trigger.

"KNEEL!" The reverend's thundering voice swept across the room. Turn to 95.

"Alright," Josiah said. "Sign me up." He lowered his revolver, putting both guns back in their holsters. He squared his shoulders and looked at Masters, waiting.

Masters spoke, and satisfaction oozed from his voice. "That's right, that's good Joe. We could use a man like you. You just hold still right there for a moment."

Josiah felt a presence behind him, a shadow growing... swallowing him. Some part of him screamed, but it was all he could do hold himself still. All the light in the world was fading as the shadows slowly engulfed him, until even the candles were little more than glowing motes, far away.

From behind, he heard the reverend laugh, a low, bone-chilling chuckle. Two impossibly strong hands gripped his shoulders. Then searing pain pierced his neck.

The light fled.

The End.

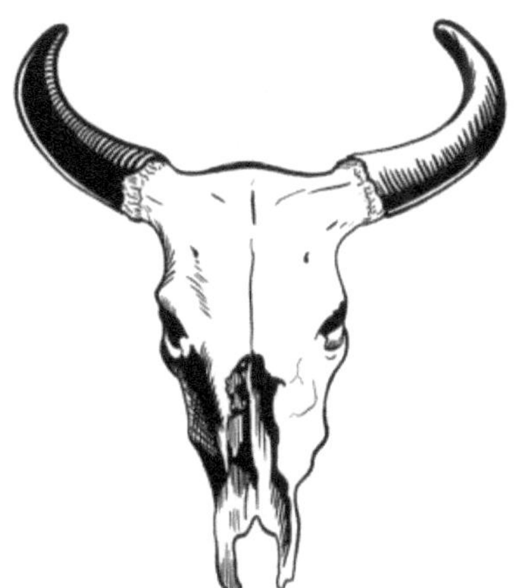

106

"Diana, snap out of it!" Josiah slapped her across the face.

The woman's eyes glowed as she looked up at him. One hand drifted to her cheek, as a kind of smile played around her mouth. "Marshal," she said, "So forceful… do it again."

Josiah tried to take a step back, but Diana, her eyes completely foreign to him, held him tight and pressed her body against his, making soft noises that would have been tempting at another time. He tried to push her away without hurting her.

"Damn you, what is wrong with you?" he demanded.

Laughter echoed around the room. Turn to 98.

107

Josiah went to Diana's side. "Alright?" he asked.

Diana shrugged. "I've been better. Just give me a minute." She finished buttoning her shirt, then threw on her jacket and sat down. Looking at her, he realized her hands were shaking.

He nodded and looked away, giving her the meager dignity of privacy. "You did good," he said to her.

"Thanks. So did you," she replied in a tired voice.

But Josiah knew that he had not. He had been trapped, unable to act, and the memory sent chills down his spine. "Let's leave this part out when we tell the story," he said, thinking of the monkey dance.

That got a weak laugh out of her. "Agreed!" she said.

Suddenly he looked up, eyes narrowing, and scanned the small church. "Where's Walter?" he asked.

She said, "I don't see him."

He cursed under his breath. He moved toward the shadows behind where the reverend had fallen, where he had last seen Walter. Deep in those shadows, a door swung loosely on its hinges. He leaped to that door and shoved it open. Outside was a covered path between the church and a small outbuilding, probably used as storage for the church. Another door swung gently into that building.

"Walter! Come back here you son of a bitch!" Josiah roared. Turn to 97.

Josiah couldn't let Diana down, not now. He turned and dashed back into the church, ignoring the exhaustion that tugged at his body. Where the reverend's body had lain, there was nothing but a stain of blood on the ground.

"Help…" he heard a strange voice croak. Diana.

He looked up—she was kneeling in front of the reverend, who stood above her with his arms raised as if to greet the heavens. Diana's body shook with the effort of resisting his control, but she couldn't, not completely. She stood, slowly… and the reverend's hands came down to embrace her neck with a gentle, almost loving touch. The reverend opened his mouth, showing rows of long, white fangs.

Josiah fired. He didn't have time for perfect aim, and he needed to make sure he wouldn't hit Diana—the shot took the reverend in the shoulder.

The tall priest whipped around, eyes blazing.

"Let her go, you son of a bitch." Josiah fired again, sinking another bullet into that robed body.

The reverend raised one arm, fingers open in a claw. His eyes blazed, and again Josiah's muscles clenched uncontrollably, sending shivers of agony through his body. He was frozen, his own form slave to another's will.

Then his arm began to move—lifting his revolver toward his own head. He resisted, but it did no good. He cried out with the pain of fighting it, but the gun kept rising. It was almost to his face now. His fingers trembled. He could see the black mouth of the barrel turning toward him.

Then another shot rang out, this one from Diana. The revered fell backward, a bloody hole in his face—but he simply laughed, a strange, gurgling sound coming through broken teeth. "There is nothing you can do!" Reverend Zeke gasped through his laughter. "Don't you get it? You're totally helpless!"

Josiah, in control of his own body once again, stepped forward, and both of them fired on the reverend. The tall priest spun from the force of the blows and fell to his knees.

He just kept laughing as he fell. "Go on, hit me with your best shot. You can't stop me! You can't stop any of us. Not her Chosen." Zeke ranted, his voice broken and strange through his ruined mouth.

The force of their bullets drove him to the ground, but as soon as their firing paused, he started pulling himself back up. "I can do whatever I want to you, and you can't stop me," he burbled.

Josiah closed his eyes. His gun was empty, and why reload? The monster that Zeke had become was right: they couldn't stop him. If bullets did no good, what power on earth could hurt him? He tilted his head back, feeling a bone-deep weariness. The high arches of the church rose overhead. At least, if he had to die, it would be here, in the house of God.

A strange pity came over Josiah, not for himself, but for Zeke. He had known this man as a boy. He had been a quick, bright boy, all smiles. Josiah may die, but he had lived as well as he could, and a place waited for him in the house of the Lord. Little Ezekiel was the one who would kill him… and that bright little boy would never have wanted that. Would never have wanted to become what he had become.

Josiah looked down at the monstrosity rising before him. It's teeth were healing, shards gathering together to form whole fangs. He could see a shadow of the boy's smile in the monster's smile, and his heart ached.

He reached out and touched Ezekiel's face. "I forgive you," he said quietly.

"What?" the reverend stopped.

"You didn't want this." Josiah gestured at all that surrounded them. He closed his eyes and held his rosary tightly. "Forgive him Father. He knows not what he does."

Tears of blood appeared on Zeke's face. His features contorted in expressions of rage, grief and fear. "No, no…" he whispered. He clawed at Josiah's clothing. "Take it back!" he wailed.

Josiah felt a power move through him, and he thought of the Holy Ghost. Not knowing what he did, he placed his hand on Ezekiel's forehead and closed his eyes. Holding the rosary in his other hand, he intoned, "For he has delivered us from the dominion of darkness and brought us into the kingdom of the Son he loves, in whom we have redemption through his blood, even for the forgiveness of sins."

The reverend screamed and clutched at Josiah's hand, but seemed not to be able to touch his skin. "I didn't mean to!" he wailed, and it wasn't the voice of a grown man, but a little boy, broken and ashamed.

"The Lord will forgive you. Be at peace," Josiah said, and something happened. A great, rushing power seemed to leave Ezekiel's body. His mouth yawned wide, showing those rows of teeth—but something boiled in those depths. He collapsed back to the ground, his body lifeless.

A centipede crawled out of the mouth, then another, and then insects came boiling out of his wide open mouth, out of his eyes, his ears. They tore their way out of his skin.

Diana jumped back, leaping up onto a chair to avoid them. There were hundreds of them, thousands of them. They fled the room in a black tide so thick she couldn't distinguish one from another. Josiah simply stood, his face serene, and the insects did not approach him, but left an open circle around his feet as they swarmed past.

Diana watched with a sort of horrified fascination as the living tide of insects slowed and vanished into the shadowy corners, escaping the building by whatever means they could. At last, the room was silent.

Josiah slumped, letting his head rest against his chest, and the room seemed darker somehow.

A new sound punctuated the silence. Then another. Diana realized it was clapping. The slow claps echoed through the room, bouncing from one end of it to another. With effort, Josiah raised his head and looked around.

Sheriff William Masters was standing in the shadows against the far wall, near the door. He stepped forward into the light, and they could see his face clearly for the first time since the jailhouse.

It was a ruined mess, all the flesh of his cheeks and lips torn off by the shotgun blast. His skull shone through, bloody and marred by patches of torn skin. Here and there it was pitted, where individual shot pellets had torn into the bone. His mouth, what was left of it, was frozen in a bloody death's head grin.

But his eyes were two orbs of red light, burning deep in the shadows of the eyesocket pits.

"Well done," Masters said, in a surprisingly clear voice that came out of that skull mouth. "Very resourceful." Masters looked down at a scorpion scuttling by beneath him and casually stepped on it, grinding it beneath one boot-heel.

"What do you want?" Josiah said, his voice tired.

Masters approached them, his boot squishing with every step. "Hell, Joe, I'm here to offer you a job! You proved yourself here. We could use a man like you."

"Like hell," Josiah said.

Masters raised his arms to encompass the entire town of Affliction. "This is the future, old friend, like it or not. We will be kings, as we were always meant to be. You could have a temple of your own—a palace—servants by the dozen." He looked at Diana, "Hell, you could even have this pretty thing for your very own."

"Don't you dare," Diana said, her voice a whiplash.

Josiah stepped out into the nave and slowly walked up to Masters. He hooked his hand on the butt of his revolver and said, "I don't like you. I don't like what you do. I've never liked what you do, truth be told. All the way back to Red Bluff. You ain't a good Christian, and you ain't never been."

Masters started forward, but Josiah drew the gun with lightning swiftness and held it pointed at Masters' face.

The former sheriff laughed and raised his hands. "I counted, Joe. That gun is empty, Joe. By the time you move, I could tear your head off."

Josiah's aim didn't waver. "Might be you're wrong. By my count, I got one bullet left."

Masters sighed. "I'd love to dance, Joe, but I've got places to be. Time for this ball to end. Maybe tomorrow night." With that, he tipped his hat, turned on his heel, and left. He slapped the wall of the church twice on his way out, a kind of farewell.

Josiah lowered the gun and checked inside. It was, in fact, completely empty. He re-loaded it, and Diana followed suit with her own weapon. "What did he mean?" she asked.

Josiah didn't answer. Moments later, the light of the rising sun pierced through the stained glass window, illuminating the church in brilliant colors. Josiah looked up and closed his eyes, letting the light fall on his face.

Day Two. Turn to 109.

A little girl, not more than nine years of age, sat on the end of the counter. She was kicking her feet in the air, watching the dancers with no expression.

Day Two

Walter levelled the long-stemmed looking glass, trying to keep the sight of the church from jumping as he held it with his one good hand. He shifted position, letting one of the rocks dig into his hip for the sake of getting a sturdy place to rest the glass.

Through it, he could see the marshal and his woman. They stood talking outside the doors of the church, the rising sun clearly illuminating their faces.

Around them was a bustle of activity. He swept the looking glass left and right, then pulled it away from his eye to make sure he wasn't missing anything. It seemed the prisoners they had freed were scouring the town for anything with wheels. They had even managed to find a few surviving animals to pull the assorted wagons they gathered. Must have raided the nearby ranches.

Soon, he presumed, the surviving townsfolk who hadn't been corrupted would be sent out across the Devil's Anvil, toward safety. With good fortune, the marshal and the woman would go with them. But he knew well enough not to count on good fortune.

He shifted down to make sure his head wouldn't be visible among the rocks and glanced back to his own prisoner. Professor Garland Enfield lay tied up in the back of the woman's wagon. Those freed prisoners wouldn't have had to scrounge so hard if he'd left the wagon. He allowed himself a twist of a smile. What fools they were.

He'd found good supplies in that wagon. The mining equipment wasn't much use to him, except perhaps the dynamite, but there was water, food, a shotgun, ammunition and more. In addition, he had the pistol the marshal had given him. All of it would be useful, but right now, he was most interested in the bandages.

His right hand throbbed painfully, and he forced himself to unwrap it. The makeshift bandage was bloody, which was a bad sign. The bone must have cut free of the skin when that bastard reverend broke it.

He sucked in through his teeth when the bandage came off completely. The wrist was bent at a hideous angle, a jagged spur of bone sticking out, bloody and exposed to the open air. The entire area was discolored and sticky with blood. He tried to move it.

—pain—

Blinking, he gathered his breath and considered his options.

He looked around: the little mining camp they were hunkered down in seemed all-but abandoned. It was unlikely further supplies could be found here. He would use what he had.

Holding the wrist very steady with his other hand, he stood and went to the wagon. Professor Enfield's eyes tracked him, but he could neither speak nor move, thanks to the ropes binding him and the gag over his mouth.

Using his left hand, Walter rooted through the various supplies until he found whiskey. Popping the cork out with his teeth, he poured the juice liberally over his right hand and wrist. It stung, but almost in a good way.

He didn't want to think about what came next, but there was no avoiding it.

Walter eyed the Professor, wondering if the man could be trusted to help. Turn to 117.

Walter eyed the wrist, weighing whether he could do it on his own. Turn to 124.

110

"What's the story with you and Sheriff Masters?" Diana asked.

Josiah sighed. "Bill and I go way back. Way, way back. Hell, we met on a cattle drive 'fore either of us came out this far West. I thought he was a good man, once."

"Something changed?"

Josiah snorted. "Took a while, mind. We were thick as thieves for a long spell." He took off his hat and turned it in his hands, straightening the brim here and there. Diana noticed that his hair was thinning toward the top. He gestured broadly with the hat, saying, "Him and me, we built this town. Us and a few others. None of this would have been here if not for us."

"That's something to be proud of, right?" she said.

He nodded once or twice, not meeting her eye. "Maybe, maybe… It was that massacre at Red Bluff what did me in for him. I just didn't feel right about things afterward. Oh I spoke up, but he didn't see it my way. I guess that's when we started to part ways. That and…"

"What?" Diana prompted.

"Abe Korse takin' that Injun girl. That didn't sit right with me neither. But Bill stood up for him, and that was that. Was around then my wife died, givin' birth to Cora, and I didn't see much reason to stick around after that. Especially not with a little one." He coughed. "She deserved a better life than… this." He gestured vaguely with the hat once more.

"But I heard things, you know. Things about old Abe Korse and that girl, and the kid she bore him, and the way he treated them both. I s'pose I should have said something then. Done something. But Bill and the others, they didn't see no wrong. So I just left.

"Now… well, it is what it is." He put the hat back on his head. A breath of wind gusted down the street, sending a dust devil spinning from nowhere to nowhere.

"What happened with the Reverend?" Diana asked. Turn to 123.
"What's riding Walter Korse?" Diana asked. Turn to 127.
"Better get some rest," Diana said, standing up and stretching. Turn to 119.

111

Walter stared at the canyon, searching his memories. Yes… he'd been standing in this very spot with his mother. It must have been one of the last times he'd seen her alive.

He could remember the wind tugging at her hair, her clothes, her very soul, as if it would pull her away from him. Sorrow had seeped from her; that he could remember. It was like the life blood pulsing from a dying animal. That sorrow had always been a part of her… somehow he had known that, even at such a young age. But here, standing in this place, it had been open and raw.

She had told him then of their people, the Arahoca, of how once all this land had been their home, not the home of their killers. She told him the stories… stories he now felt stirring in the misty depths of his memory, but could not distinctly remember.

They had looked into this canyon, and talked, and hurt, and even as they hurt, they loved. She loved the past, the family they had lost, and him. He loved her so hard it hurt, so hard he swore he would dry her tears and make her happy, as soon as he was big enough to do so.

Walter turned away, saying, "Ghosts live in that canyon. Leave it be." Turn to 121.

112

Walter drew his knife. The professor's eyes went wide. Walter put one foot on a rock and leaned in above Enfield, idly toying with the knife. He said, "Now, this didn't go so well last time, so we're going to try again."

Professor Enfield made a frightened, groaning sound.

"Now, don't be like that!" Walter said. He tossed his knife, catching it by the handle. "I just need to know one thing."

"Wh… what?" Enfield mumbled.

Walter considered his words, then said very slowly, "How do I kill William Masters?"

Professor Enfield closed his eyes, trying to roll away. "I don't know! I don't know anything!"

"That just won't do, Slick. Don't mind if I call you Slick, do you?" He twirled the knife.

The professor jerked his head in a reflexive gesture, still not looking at Walter.

"Look at me when I'm talking to you!" Walter barked.

Enfield's eyes flew open. "Please," he begged, "Leave me alone! You have no idea what's going on here!"

"I know more than you think," Walter said. Turn to 125.

113

Walter Korse pulled himself out of a brief, pain-filled sleep. He rolled over to see the heavy afternoon sun glowering in through the window of the little shack he had hunkered down in. He sat up quickly, shaking off the grogginess of sleep. Looking at the level of the sun, he could see he'd been out longer than he meant to be. It made sense; his body would need time to recuperate from an injury as bad as his wrist.

He looked down at the arm. It was unchanged, still in the splinted bandage. Some blood had soaked through, but by now it was a dry rust-brown. No fresh blood. That was good. He considered changing the bandage, but the sun was already getting low. He was running out of time.

The desert air struck him, dry and windy, as he came out of his refuge. A semi-circle of crude shacks deteriorated here in the sun. Once they had provided storage to support a mining operation here, but it was obvious that the tiny mine hadn't been active in years, at least. Walter could remember playing up here once in a while when he was little. While the miners worked, he and the other boys could play among the stones, long as they stayed out from underfoot.

He walked to the edge of the rocky ridge at the south end of the camp. From here he had a hell of a view; he could see all of Affliction and surrounds, but a quick scan of the town showed no activity. It would still be a time yet before sun set and the vampires arose, but the marshal might give him trouble before then. Or the woman could come looking for this professor.

He needed a plan. And he needed answers. The professor had fainted as soon as he drew the bowie knife last time; maybe a few hours rest would make him more talkative. On the other hand, it might be best to explore the area while he still had some light.

Walter decided to look around the mining camp. Turn to 122.
Walter returned to the wagon to try again with interrogating the professor. Turn to 116.

Diana looked out at the rising sun, white and hot. A cool breeze still blew over the town, but she could already feel the promise of desert heat in the sun's touch on her cheek. To the east, the air was shimmering above the Devil's Anvil.

"Think they'll make it?" she asked, turning to Josiah.

Josiah nodded slowly, looking at the haphazard caravan setting out before them. "They should be fine. Long as they stick to the road and don't stop till they're in free country." Josiah turned his face to eye her.

"What?" she asked.

"'Course, this means we only got the one horse between us. We can't leave so easy, not by day anyhow."

Diana put a hand through her hair and took a seat on the porch of the saloon. "Where do you suppose all the vampires go in the daytime?" she asked.

Josiah shrugged, moving to sit near her. He absently rubbed his swollen left hand as he sat. That spider bite was worse than he'd thought at first. It ached whenever he used the hand. And it itched like hell. He pulled his hand away and tried to think of anything except scratching it.

Diana pulled out a bit of chew and stuck it in her mouth. "I wish that bastard of yours hadn't taken my wagon," she said.

"What all'd you have in there, again?" Josiah asked.

Diana shrugged. "Goods for the road, plus some things I thought I could sell here. Food, water, liquor." She made a face. "My shotgun. Dynamite."

"Dynamite?" Josiah shot her a glance.

"I told you. It's a mining town. Thought they could use it."

Josiah swore, then asked, "How much?"

"Plenty," Diana said sourly. "But don't worry. He missed this bag." She gave him a wicked grin and held up a burlap sack with several tube-like shapes inside.

"Hell and damnation, woman!" Josiah's eyes widened. "You carry that with you?"

Diana gave a dark smile. "It never hurts to be prepared. You ever been a lady, traveling alone?" She looked at him.

Josiah grunted.

Diana shrugged and sat forward, leaning her elbows on her knees. "Bandits like to go for wagons like mine, but nothin' spooks horses like a stick of dynamite in the middle of 'em." She laughed, then added. "Besides, if worst comes to worst... I'd rather take a few of 'em with me."

Josiah gave her a long look, then said, "Yer a tough woman."

"Don't look so glum, Marshal," she said. "Ain't happened yet, probably never will. You want some chew?"

He shook his head. "Why didn't you use that last night?" He asked.

She shrugged. "It wasn't in the jailhouse with us. I didn't think to grab it till later."

As she chewed, he readied his own pipe and tobacco. Within a few moments, he was puffing away. The rising sun gave him a wakeful feeling, but the aches in his body refused to go away, reminding him he would need sleep.

Diana regarded the marshal.

"What happened with the Reverend?" Diana asked. Turn to 123.

"What's the story with you and Sheriff Masters?" Diana asked. Turn to 110.

"What's riding Walter Korse?" Diana asked. Turn to 127.

"Better get some rest," Diana said, standing up and stretching. Turn to 119.

115

"What happened, Professor?" Walter asked.

The professor shook his head. He let out another, haunted moan. "I found her. Deep in the mountain. I found her in the temple, just where the old writings said she would be." He looked up at Walter, and something in his eyes made Walter's skin crawl.

"Who?" Walter asked.

The Professor licked his lips and whispered, "Tezoca, the Bled One."

Walter felt a shiver run down his spine. He knew that name... somewhere, from his earliest memories, he knew he had heard it before. He seemed to remember a campfire, stars... his mother nearby. Or was that simply his imagination? Wishful thinking? He shook his head and asked, "Alright, then what?"

Enfield looked away. "She began to take the town. Just a few at a time, at first. Then more. Then... all..."

"How come some of them die like normal folks, and others don't die at all?" Walter asked. Turn to 120.

"How can I kill William Masters?" Walter asked. Turn to 126.

116

Walter returned to the wagon to try again with interrogating the professor. He went to the wagon and shook it—but something was wrong. The blankets looked stacked oddly. Walter threw back the blankets—nothing was there.

Walter swore. He looked sharply in each direction. How far could the professor have made it? Skin and a little blood on the ropes tied to the wagon showed how the Professor had gotten away, but Walter could see no sign of the ropes that had bound the professor's hands and feet—he must still be partially tied up.

Walter's eye fell on a small path leading up from the mining camp, up to... No!

Taking the path in great, loping strides, Walter ascended the steep, rocky slope. Turn to 118.

117

Walter eyed the professor, wondering if the man could be trusted to help. With one hand, he reached out and ripped off the gag he had stuffed into the man's mouth.

Enfield flinched as Walter stood over him. That suited Walter just fine.

"Don't hurt me!" Enfield whimpered.

Walter shook his head in disgust. No… the way the professor was cringing and cowering, there was no way he would have the guts to do what needed doing.

Besides, trusting was the quickest way to get killed.

Walter eyed the wrist, weighing whether he could do it on his own. Turn to 124.

118

Taking the path in great, loping strides, Walter ascended the steep, rocky slope. The view opened up beneath him, showing the entire expanse of the valley the town of Affliction lay in, and even farther south, the high, black mesas and wide, salt desert in the distance.

As he rounded a bend, he caught up with the professor, wriggling and still partially bound, laying dusty and exhausted on the path. Walter came to a stop, the wind whipping his long hair as he looked down at the gasping professor.

"Going somewhere?" Walter asked.

"You can't keep me like this!" Enfield said, tears standing in his eyes.

Walter looked up the path, then back down at the whimpering professor. "Where'd you think you were going, anyway?"

The professor looked up the path, to where it ended in a narrow slot canyon opening up in the side of the mountain.

As Walter followed his gaze up to the entrance to that narrow canyon, a cold chill ran through his bones. He knew this place. "You don't want to go that way," he said.

Enfield looked up at the canyon and thrust his jaw out belligerently. "Why not?"

Walter couldn't explain the dark feeling that came over him whenever he looked at the opening. It lay between two massive slabs of rock, a canyon so narrow that you could touch both walls as you stepped into it. Once, so he had been told, his people had lived down that canyon.

Walter stared at the canyon, searching his memories. Turn to 111.
Walter turned away, saying, "Ghosts live in that canyon. Leave it be." Turn to 121.

"Better get some rest," Diana said, standing up and stretching. The sun was starting to get higher in the sky now, and Diana could feel her eyes drooping after the sleepless night.

Josiah sat for a long moment, still as a picture. Then he shook off the weight of his thoughts and stood. "Yup." He touched his hat. "There's some good beds still in the saloon. You can have the first pick. You sure you want to stay? We could ride double far enough to catch up with those folk." He nodded out at the desert, where the last of Affliction's survivors could just be seen cresting the hill.

Diana's jaw tightened. "I can't leave Garland here, all on his own."

She was aware of the marshal giving her a long look, but he said nothing. Finally Josiah said, "I'll find Korse if it's the last thing I do. Stick with me and we'll find your man as well."

Diana asked, "There wasn't any sign of 'em?"

Josiah shook his head and tucked his thumbs in his belt. "Korse knows how to cover his tracks, I'll give him that. He's a damn devil in the wild. Did I mention it took me five years to catch him?"

"It better not take another five…" Diana said.

Josiah snorted. "Korse wants Bill, and Bill… well, he'll be back come night. We just need to wait and flush 'em out. Now go get some rest."

Diana nodded. She still needed to take care of herself as best she could, in her condition. She tipped her hat to the marshal and went in search of the bed with the cleanest sheets.

Walter Korse pulled himself out of a brief, pain-filled sleep. Turn to 113.

"How come some of them die like normal folks, and others don't die at all?" Walter asked.

The professor chewed on the inside of his lip, not looking at his tormentor. For a long time, it seemed he might not answer. At last, he replied, his voice almost too quiet to hear, "Not all are made the same… some are turned the quick way, while others are truly claimed by her. And others… she does not turn at all, but merely uses her will to control them."

"Some of them don't seem to care if they get shot," Walter said.

Enfield looked up, his eyes dark and wild. "Her true children. Her Chosen. These are the ones she bites personally. Not personally, but with one of the insects from her own body."

Walter narrowed his eyes, listening.

The professor, breathing shallowly, continued, "They inherit a measure of her power. They can control the minds of the weak. They can spread the bite, but their children become lesser ones, with little power. These Chosen Ones... they can't be killed."

Walter looked out over the town below, his gaze on the setting sun. "Anything can be killed..." he said.

Enfield shook his head. "Not these."

Walter grabbed Enfield's collar. "Don't lie to me. I'll ask you one more time." Walter took a deep breath.

"How can I kill William Masters?" Walter asked. Turn to 126.

121

Walter turned away, saying, "Ghosts live in that canyon. Leave it be." He knelt and hefted Enfield to his feet with one arm scooped under his shoulder. The man could barely walk with his ankles tied, so Walter half-carried him down a few steps.

As they descended the path, an idea came to Walter. He looked for the little nook where he had once played, where he could call into a crack in the rock and tease the miners below with the sound coming apparently from nowhere. He smiled when he saw it.

He laid Enfield down in that nook, saying, "Why don't you just rest here until I'm ready for you."

The professor looked exhausted and scared, but nodded as he nestled down into the nook, away from the wind. "Just don't let them get me again! Please..."

"They won't find you here," Walter said. He looked out over the town below. The sun was lowering, but he still had time. "Now, I just need to ask you some questions. You weren't very helpful this morning, and I don't like that."

Enfield looked up, shivering. His slightly-too-long hair fell in his face, disheveled and curly, and his spectacles were askew. He didn't have the hands free to fix them.

Walter decided to take a gentle approach. Turn to 128.
Walter drew his knife. Turn to 112.

122

Walter decided to look around the mining camp. There were no more than a dozen buildings, mostly collapsing shacks. Down the ridge a ways, he could see an empty mill building which might be useful. It seemed to be in better shape than most here at the camp.

The mill was about halfway down the slope toward the town. If he needed to make a break for it, that could be a good hiding place.

He took the time to go from building to building in the old mining camp, looking in each for anything of use. He found precious little: a few shovels and picks, some rusted and splintering wheelbarrows.

Last but not least, he turned his attention to the mine shaft. Old rails emerged from it, a relic of a more productive day. As he approached the black, gaping opening, he felt a chill. He never had liked the underground. As a child he had been afraid of this place.

Nevertheless, he took a few steps inside, letting his eyes adjust. The walls were rough-hewn, and the tunnel went deeper than he could see.

Suddenly he heard a strange scraping and grunting sound. He started—Enfield? It sounded like the professor, but how could that—

Walter realized what it was. As a kid, playing among these rocks, he had discovered there was a spot on the path above where he could speak through a crevasse in the rocks and be heard by the miners here in the mineshaft.

That meant Enfield was on the path above.

His stomach sank. That path led to the place one must not go.

Jaw tight, he ran out of the mineshaft and up to the path. On the way, he glanced in the wagon. Sure enough, the professor had slipped his bonds, leaving a bit of blood and skin behind. Walter swore.

Taking the path in great, loping strides, Walter ascended the steep, rocky slope. Turn to 118.

<h3 style="text-align:center">123</h3>

"What happened with the Reverend?" Diana asked.

Josiah stared out at the rising sun, his hand going to his throat. He idly ran his fingers over the cross pinned to his cravat. "I don't know," he said truthfully.

"Those words you said… how did you…?" Diana couldn't find the right question.

"It just came to me, I guess."

"Are you a man of faith?" Diana asked.

Josiah laughed bitterly. "I used to be a preacher, longer ago'n I care to remember. It was after I left Affliction, but before…" he trailed off. Now his fingers drifted to his marshal's star. He unpinned it and held it up to the light. "I left preachin' when I went back to marshalin'. About five years ago."

The sunlight caught on the gold star and reflected back, striking Diana in the eyes.

"What's the story with you and Sheriff Masters?" Diana asked. Turn to 110.

"What's riding Walter Korse?" Diana asked. Turn to 127.

"Better get some rest," Diana said, standing up and stretching. Turn to 119.

<h3 style="text-align:center">124</h3>

Walter eyed the wrist, weighing whether he could do it on his own. Slowly, he nodded. Wouldn't be easy, but easy had never been his way.

He looked at Enfield, grimaced, and laid his injured hand on the wood platform of the wagon, where the professor could watch. He grabbed the whiskey and took a long swallow for himself. Then he poured a little more over the open wound. That would be all the anesthetic he got.

It wasn't getting any earlier.

He grabbed his right hand in his left and pulled.

Pain—blinding, white hot pain—shot up his arm and threatened to blank out his mind.

—No, Pa, stop! He was a child, crying as the whip lifted above his back—

He clenched his jaw and focused. He pulled, stretching the muscle and skin, until the broken bone popped back inside his flesh.

—The whip cracked down. He could smell the leather of it. He could see the spots of blood that splashed up onto the far wall—

Vaguely, Walter was aware of his flesh tearing, the jagged bone cutting its way through muscle and skin. Blood spurted from the wound. He pulled.

—He lay on the floor of the basement, his small body doubled over in pain. Bruises bloomed bright and blue all over his body. When he threw up, there was blood mixed in—

Walter could feel the lines of his bones; he aligned them. The walls of his mind held under the pressure of the pain, a tidal wave of pain.

But there was a limit, and he was reaching it.

—he cried, holding himself, whispering, "mother," and as the tears fell, he hated them. Hated himself. And hated the man who had taken her from him—

The bones lined up and Walter released the hand, letting the jagged pieces of bone merge like puzzle pieces. The grinding noise they made as they came back together almost threatened to bring the walls crumbling down. But he was done now.

Done.

And his eyes were still dry.

Why had he thought of those things? Strange. It had been that moment, years ago… that moment he had made up his mind. He was done with tears. They would pay. They would all pay.

Walter grabbed the whiskey and took another quick swallow. Then he started to tie on the splints he had prepared. It hurt, but it was nothing compared to moments before.

Enfield was staring at him, eyes wide with disbelief and fear.

Walter finished wrapping the splints and regarded his work. The hand was straight. Bloody, but clean. And protected, more or less. He knew he had damaged the flesh more in setting the bone, but what choice did he have?

The hand might never be the same, but he wouldn't need it much longer anyway. The last one was close. Either way, it would be over soon.

With his good hand, he drew a knife: the long kind of Bowie knife good for everything on the plains. Not least, good for scaring city folk with.

He stepped in until he loomed above Enfield and put the knife alongside the professor's soft neck. In a silky voice, he asked, "Now, why don't you tell me all about William Masters?"

Diana looked out at the rising sun, white and hot. Turn to 114.

"I know more than you think," Walter said. "Does Tennessee ring a bell?"

Enfield stared at him with blank eyes.

"A little saloon called the Wagon Wheel? November, two years ago? Sound familiar?"

The professor straightened a little, his eyes narrowing with comprehension. He licked his lips. "That was you…"

Walter turned his face into the wind and gave Enfield a smile. "Yeah, that was me. Now you're getting in the right mood. And do you remember what we talked about then?"

Enfield looked around, his eyes darting this way and that like a trapped rabbit. He licked his lips, his breath coming in short, shallow gasps.

"Don't be like that Mr. Professor. You had some questions for me, remember? What were they?"

Enfield's words came in quick bursts. "I asked you… about… Affliction. And about… the Arahoca."

"That's right. My tribe. My people." Walter's face twitched. "You also talked quite a lot. Quite a lot, Mr. Professor. Do you remember what you talked about?"

Enfield shook his head, shifting in his bonds.

"You talked about the Deathwalkers, Mr. Professor. You didn't need me to tell you the legend. You knew it already; better than I do. You talked about a myth. Of a buried temple, that my people were supposed to protect. Guardians or some such. And you talked about comin' here and diggin' it all up."

Enfield stared at him with wide eyes, like a rabbit who sees its predator too late, and knows there's nowhere to run.

Walter eyed the professor with a hard gaze. "So there's no point in lyin' anymore, Slick. See, I already know you're the rat bastard responsible for all this." He gestured vaguely in the direction of the town. "So why don't you tell me what happened?"

A low moan escaped from Enfield. He buried his head in the rocks, as though hiding from the wind and sky. When he looked up, he said, "It wasn't supposed to go like this! It wasn't!"

"What happened, Professor?" Walter asked. Turn to 115.
"How can I kill William Masters?" Walter asked. Turn to 126.

126

"How can I kill William Masters?" Walter asked.

Enfield shook. "I don't know! I don't know! He's one of the Chosen Ones. He can't be killed!"

Walter turned away in disgust.

The professor writhed in his bonds among the rocks, moaning, "The world is doomed. They will spread across it like a plague of locusts, devouring… eating… destroying… Nothing can stop them now…"

"Sunlight?" Walter asked.

Enfield moaned, "It hurts them, but they can always just come out at night."

Walter leaned in, "What about stakes? In some of the stories that works."

The Professor spat, "Why don't you ask Masters very nicely to sit still while you drive a stake through his heart, and tell me how it works?"

Walter knelt and grabbed Enfield's collar, shaking him. "Something has to kill them! Cutting their heads off?"

Enfield winced and cried, "I don't know!"

Walter looked out at the sun, getting low to the horizon. He stood up. "Dynamite. Blowin' them to smithereens ought to do the trick, if anything does."

The Professor turned his head back and forth, smoothing out where his collar had dug into his neck, watching the taller man.

Walter stepped out to the edge of the rocks, looking down not only at the town, but at the little mining camp below. The stolen wagon was still there, and in it, with the other mining supplies, enough dynamite to blow the whole town to kingdom come.

Walter turned to leave, but Enfield's voice arrested him, "Korse. Walter."

Walter turned around, looking at the small man bent among the rocks, in the lee of the wind. The Professor looked back with dark, calculating eyes. He shoved himself up into a sitting position, and he said in a soft voice, "I have a proposition for you…"

Josiah stretched his aching bones. Turn to 129.

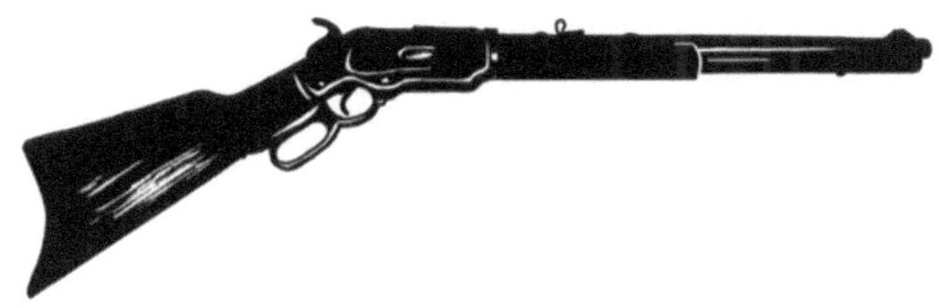

127

"What's riding Walter Korse?" Diana asked.

Josiah sighed. "There's been no shortage of evil happenings in this town. Wish I could say it wasn't so, but it is."

Diana waited, hoping he would go on. But Josiah's dry voice was as silent as the empty town around them.

After a spell Diana shifted, and the sound seemed to shake the marshal awake. He took a deep breath and began to speak, "I don't right know what happened to Korse. All I know is, after it was done, his ma was dead, he'd killed his own pa, and he was out to kill the rest of the Band of Brothers."

"The Band of Brothers?" Diana asked.

"The old gang. At Red Bluff it was me, Bill Masters, Abe Korse—that's Walter's daddy—and a few others. Toby McCann, too, if you count him, but he was pretty young at the time. Anyway, all I heard was Abe was dead at Walter's own hand, and little Walter—not so little anymore—was out for all of 'em."

"Even you?"

Josiah shook his head. "Not me, no. I had left town by then, so I wasn't part of whatever it was."

The two of them sat in silence, each lost in their own thoughts. Dream-figures moved through Diana's mind as her exhaustion caught up with her. She saw ancient Indians and horsemen riding across the plains. A single man, a young half-breed, driven by a spirit of hatred so strong that he had no face, pursuing his vendetta through the years, riding down his enemies one by one.

Diana shuddered. If William Masters really was the last one on Korse's list, she wouldn't want to be him, not even with whatever vile powers he had now.

Josiah let out a heavy breath. "Well," he said.

"What happened with the Reverend?" Diana asked. Turn to 123.
"What's the story with you and Sheriff Masters?" Diana asked. Turn to 110.
"Better get some rest," Diana said, standing up and stretching. Turn to 119.

128

Walter decided to take a gentle approach. He used his good arm to lower himself to a sitting position near the bound professor. There, he painstakingly pulled out his tobacco pouch and rolled a cigarette with one hand, leaning down into the lee of the rocks to light his match out of the wind.

Professor Enfield watched this process with wide eyes.

"Listen, Slick," Walter said. "You don't mind if I call you Slick, do you?" He took another drag on the cigarette, enjoying the feeling of the tobacco spreading through his body. It numbed the pain.

The professor licked his lips. "What do you want?" he asked in a cracking voice.

"I just need to know one thing…" Walter considered his words. In a very deliberate voice, he said, "How do I kill William Masters?"

Enfield jerked his head in a quick shake. "I… I don't know! I don't know anything!"

"Now, see, that's the problem. Because I think you do know." Walter leaned in close. "And I think you're going to tell me."

"No… please… leave me alone! You have no idea what's going on here!" The professor cried.

"I know more than you think," Walter said. Turn to 125.

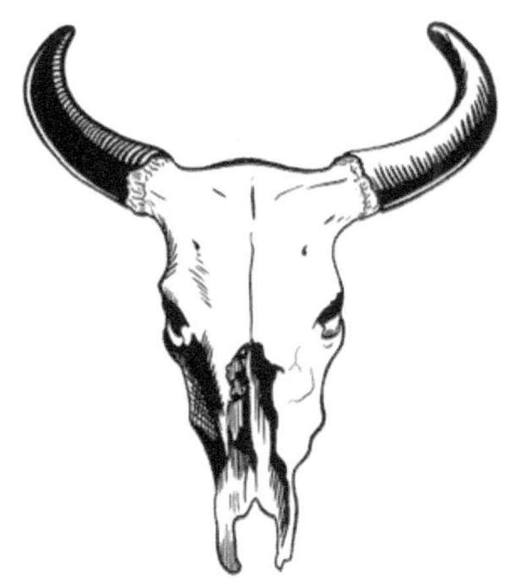

129

Josiah stretched his aching bones. Fighting off grogginess, he pushed himself up off the bed he had collapsed in. It took him a moment to convince his legs to stand. So much hurt from the events of the night before, he wasn't sure where he ended and the pain began.

He stood, feeling the pops and creaks as he stumbled, finding his balance. He put one hand on his back, letting out a low groan. It was a good thing no one else was in here to witness his indignity.

Slowly, he made his way downstairs. The saloon was a wreck. It didn't look like anybody had bothered to clean in weeks. It hadn't been as obvious when the place was in use at night, but in the daylight…

"Mornin'" Diana said, offering him a steaming bowl of porridge. She glanced out the window, at the setting sun. "Or somethin' like that."

"Thanks," Josiah said, taking the bowl. He found an intact stool to sit on at the bar and began to eat.

"What's the plan?" Diana asked.

Josiah grunted. "We wait."

"Here?" Diana asked, one eyebrow going up.

"Not here." He gestured with his spoon. "Somewhere out there. Somewhere hidden. Somewhere with a good view." He took another bite of the porridge. "Good grub. Thanks."

"No problem," Diana said in a wry voice. She sighed. "So that's it. We wait."

Josiah said, "Masters will show himself, and wherever he is, Korse will be. It's our best chance at finding your man."

"I know," Diana said, sighing. "It's just…"

Josiah gave her another studying look, noting the way her hand drifted to her belly when she thought he wasn't looking. "We'll find him," he said.

"Thank you," Diana said. She came around the bar to give him a kiss on the cheek. Turn to 136.

"Thank you," Diana said, turning away. Turn to 142.

130

"Wait! Korse, where is Professor Enfield?" Diana demanded.

After a long, stubborn moment, Korse turned his eyes to her. Something in them made Diana shiver.

The killer gave her a crooked smile and said, "Your man is waiting for you. Up in the mining camp. Follow the road north from town… but don't go too far." He turned his attention back to the horizon, as if he could see his next life waiting for him there.

Josiah bent his head in prayer, rosary in one hand, the other on the lever that would drop Korse to his death.

Diana lifted her rifle. "Josiah, don't do this," she said in a cool voice. Turn to 144.
Diana turned away. Turn to 131.

131

Diana turned away. She caught her breath as her eye fell on a swarm of dark shapes moving quickly up the hillside toward them. "Josiah!" She called.

The marshal looked down and swore.

Diana fumbled with her rifle, trying to find a clear figure to take aim on, but in the shadows, it was too hard to pick out a sure target.

Josiah stepped to the edge of the platform as the vampires approached.

"An execution and you didn't invite me?" Sheriff Masters said, coming up the hill. Turn to 145.

132

"Let's check this level," Josiah said and went into the den. He didn't recognize the house from his days in Affliction, but it had been a long time since then. The house looked like it had been abandoned for months, if not years. A mirror was cracked over a fireplace, and the upholstery on the furniture was dusty and torn.

Diana watched the door while Josiah moved to the kitchen. His spurs clinked with each slow step. Red light from the setting sun illuminated the kitchen, falling in brilliant profile on a painted portrait of a young lady. Silverware gleamed as the shifting sunlight travelled across it.

Josiah pushed open a door next to the wood burning stove. It was dark, a pantry. During the moment it took his eyes to adjust, he heard something—a faint, shifting noise.

He held his breath. There was no other breathing in the room to be heard, and he started to relax. But as his eyes adjusted, the shapes of several bodies curled on the floor became clear.

At first he thought they were dead. Then one of them moved.

Josiah stepped back out of the pantry, letting the door fall silently closed, heart pounding. "Diana," he hissed, crossing the kitchen back over to her.

"What?" she asked, following his lead and whispering.

"The dead…" Josiah said. "They are in that room. The vampires!"

Diana's eyes went wide. "How many of them?" she asked.

Josiah thought. "Three. Maybe four."

"Well," she said, rocking on her heels. She looked at him and raised one eyebrow, an unspoken question.

Josiah jerked his head toward the sleeping vampires and put his hand on his gun. Turn to 147.

"We don't have much time," Josiah said and went up the stairs. Turn to 151.

133

Walter's flinty eyes did not acknowledge the marshal. He looked at the sky, his face as distant and unreadable as the stars he stared at.

Josiah grunted and heaved the criminal up to a standing position. Korse did not cooperate, so Josiah was forced to hold him up while looping the noose around his neck. Korse only took the weight on his own legs once the noose was tied securely. He held his chin high and proud, the sharp cheekbones of his Indian ancestry carving deep pools in the shadows of his cheeks.

"Wait! Korse, where is Professor Enfield?" Diana demanded. Turn to 130.

Diana lifted her rifle. "Josiah, don't do this," she said in a cool voice. Turn to 144.

134

Josiah nodded. "You just stay right there a spell," he said. "This won't take but a minute."

Masters touched the brim of his hat in a mockery of polite patience, and Josiah took several cautious steps backwards, unwilling to turn his back on the vampire. Masters met his eye and grinned.

Carefully, Josiah backed up until he could place one hand on the lever that would drop the gallows, hanging Walter Korse. He looked over—Korse was gone.

The rope swung in the wind, a clean cut through the noose.

"Damn," Diana hissed nearby.

Josiah cast about frantically. His attention had only been away for a moment. Korse couldn't have gotten far.

A raucous, grating laughter raked at Josiah's ears. It was Bill Masters, bent nearly double, slapping his knee. He made a show of wiping a tear away from one eye. "I saw him goin'," Masters admitted. "Just couldn't help myself. The look on your face, Joe… well hell, almost makes me wish I didn't have to kill you, so's we could laugh about it together."

"Which way did he go!?" Josiah demanded, stepping forward.

"Sorry, old boy," Masters said, still recovering from his fit of laughter. "Come on, lads, kill 'em both! We'll catch the half-breed next!"

Vampires swarmed toward the platform. Josiah swore and fired. His shots hit the first vampire lunging toward them, blowing it backward before it came anywhere near. But more were coming, their long teeth and sharp, distended fingernails looming in his vision. He fired again and again, hearing Diana's rifle boom nearby.

Now they were climbing up onto the platform. He turned this way and that, firing, but they were climbing faster than he could kill them. He was surrounded.

"Masters!" A voice rang out. It was Walter Korse. Turn to 155.

135

"Stay put," Josiah said. "Don't get found." They couldn't run. If they ran, they would be caught and killed. But how long could they hide here?

He looked across at Diana, whose tension showed her fear. He had to protect her, but how?

The ruckus and clatter of the search began to rise from the streets below, vampires howling with laughter as they tore apart the first few houses. Down below, Josiah heard a door slam open.

"Hellooo!" A singsong voice called out from below. "Come out, come out wherever you are!" The words floated up to them, twisted in sadistic pleasure.

Diana gripped Josiah's arm. He put his finger to his lips.

A crash came from downstairs. The searchers had knocked something over. Then another. Voices. Laughter. The vampires were having fun…

"As soon as they come upstairs…" Diana hissed.

Josiah nodded. There was scant cover, nowhere for them to properly hide. He got out his one remaining pistol. He didn't like that Korse had taken the other. If anything happened to this gun, he had no backup. He would just have to make sure he didn't drop it.

Diana shook her head with a dark look and readied her rifle. She scanned the room and took refuge behind the pitiful shelter of an armchair, gun aimed at the door.

Footsteps on the stairs. They could hear the creaking of floorboards. The voice sang again, "If you're up here, I'll find you…"

Josiah clenched his jaw. Once shots were fired, the whole town would know where they were…

Bang! Bang! Two shots.

"What was that?" One of the vampires called from the stairs.

It took Josiah a moment to realize the shots had come from outside the window. He spun up onto his knee to look out, pushing aside the lace curtain with the tip of his six-shooter.

Walter Korse stood on a nearby hilltop, coat blowing in the wind, gun smoking in his hand. "Masters!" Korse bellowed his challenge.

Sheriff Masters stepped forward, grinning and gesturing for the other vampires to stand down. He tipped his hat to Korse, and in a laconic voice said, "Howdy, boy. Come on down here and let's talk."

Korse's gun leapt, sending up a puff of black smoke, and the sheriff's hat flew off his head.

Now Masters scowled. He walked over to the hat and knelt—but as he reached for it Korse's gun popped again, and the hat leaped away. One more time, Masters reached for the hat, and one more time Korse shot it out of his grasp.

Finally Masters turned back to the criminal, his ruined face dark with rage. His balding head shone in the evening light. He pointed to Korse and called, "Kill the mongrel half-breed!"

A howl went up from the vampires, and they coursed toward the hill where Walter stood. Walter flashed a fierce smile—and ran.

Masters himself howled as he saw his prey fleeing. He broke into a long, loping gait, bent over like an animal, and tore off chasing Walter up the hill.

A curse came from the stairwell, not far away. The door at the top of the stairs opened, and a leathery face looked in. The vampire scanned the room once, then scowled, slammed the door and left.

Josiah stood up from where he had crouched behind the bed and made eye contact with Diana, who stood up from behind her chair. Both spontaneously broke into a grin. It was nearly unbelievable that the vampire hadn't noticed him, but Walter's timely interruption had created just enough of a distraction.

But the smiles faded quickly. They were still surrounded by enemies and no closer to success.

Diana moved to the window to watch the wild chase into the hills. "What do you think his game is?" she asked.

Josiah moved to the door, where he listened until he heard the vampires downstairs leaving the building. He shook his head. "Whatever it is, it'll end with Bill's head on a stick. But I'd lay odds if we catch up with Korse, we find your friend."

Walter ran. Turn to 161.

136

"Thank you," Diana said. She came around the bar to give him a kiss on the cheek.

Josiah snorted, but he hid a smile beneath his moustache. Pushing away his bowl, he pulled out his ammunition pouch and dumped the remaining rounds out on the counter. He gave a contemplative sigh.

"What are you doing?" Diana asked.

Josiah didn't answer right away. He spread out the ammunition, standing each piece up side by side. Then he rummaged in his pocket and pulled out his rosary. Lowering his head, he held the rosary above the bullets and waved the cross above each one.

He intoned, "Lord in heaven, blessed be thy name. Thy will be done. Thy kingdom come. On earth as it is in heaven. Watch over me today, Father, for I walk in the valley of evil. Hold my hand as I aim thy weapon, and guide my steps as I walk for you."

Josiah hesitated, then said, "Amen." He tucked the rosary back into his pocket.

Diana looked around. She held one hand out as though expecting rain. "Don't feel like nothin'."

Without looking up, Josiah said, "The Lord works in mysterious ways. The way I figure it, we can use all the help we can get." He lifted a bullet, pulled out his knife, and carved a shallow cross in the tip of the soft lead. "Help me carve crosses in these."

Shrugging, Diana moved to join him.

When they were done, Josiah poured the ammunition back into his belt pouch and stood.

"Think that'll help?" Diana asked.

Josiah said, "Asking the Lord for help never hurts. Let's move." He went to the window and pulled aside the shutters, looking both ways down the street.

The street was as deserted now as it had been the moment they arrived in Affliction. Turn to 152.

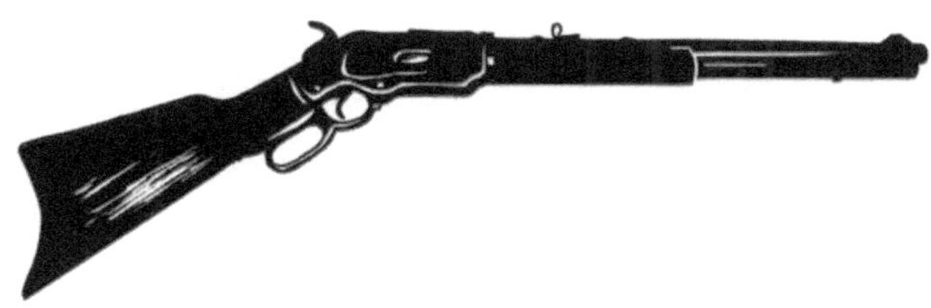

137

Josiah struck first. He threw a jab with his left, disregarding the ache of the spider bite, then followed it with a cross from his right. Korse dodged back, quick as a devil, and threw a punch of his own. Josiah took it with a grunt, then grabbed the murderer and pushed him to the ground.

They hit the floor heavily, Josiah's greater weight crushing Korse. Something caught Josiah alongside the head, making the world spin for a moment. Josiah bore down, striking and feeling the blows hit flesh, but Korse writhed underneath him like a man possessed. In a moment, the killer wriggled free and leaped back, nearly vanishing in the darkness.

Josiah got to his feet more slowly, keeping a wary eye on his opponent. Korse didn't give him a chance to recover—the killer came in with a hook that Josiah barely caught on his forearm. He stepped in, pushing up as he threw an uppercut. Korse dodged back, and the power blow caught only air.

A couple light hits caught Josiah on the face, but there was no weight behind them. Josiah tasted blood on his lips. It didn't slow him. He lashed out with a jab when he saw the opening, and felt the satisfaction of impact.

Korse staggered back, breathing hard. "Don't think this is over, da Silva," the murderer said.

Josiah smiled and wiped blood off his cheek. "I'll see you hang if it's the last thing I do."

Korse shot forward with two quick lefts. Josiah blocked them easily—and then a kick was coming, already almost on him.

The kick hit Josiah hard, knocking the breath out of him. Turn to 148.
Josiah caught Walter's leg and threw him. Turn to 143.

138

"I'll see to it," Josiah said. With a sigh, he grabbed Korse under the armpits and heaved him up to his feet, then pulled him over to the noose.

Walter closed his eyes while the marshal looped the noose around his neck. His eyes were dry, which he wondered at. Perhaps this life was not such a bad thing to lose. He let his memories drift, seeing the ranch house where he had been raised, hearing his mother's song…

The marshal stepped away, leaving the rope chafing around Walter's neck.

"Wait! Korse, where is Professor Enfield?" Diana demanded. Turn to 130.
Diana lifted her rifle. "Josiah, don't do this," she said in a cool voice. Turn to 144.

Josiah shook his head. "So you can shoot me in the back? I don't think so." He rested his hands on the butt of his pistol and grinned, showing teeth. "Now you lot back away real slow, and we can talk this over later." Cursing inside, Josiah realized he had never gotten his second gun back from Walter. Well, there would be time once the killer was hung. Had to get there first.

Masters laughed, looking around at his fellows. The other vampires, bent and misshapen, looked on, their long teeth nearly dripping with saliva in anticipation. "Joe thinks he's a big man. Say, Joe, think you can take on all of us?"

Josiah inclined his head slightly. "One way to find out." He shifted his grip on his pistols ever so slightly.

"Josiah," Diana growled, and something in her tone made him glance back to the gallows.

The rope was swinging loose in the wind, a clean cut through the noose.

"Well damn it all, ain't that a bitch," Masters said in mock solicitude. "Guess we'll have to finish this the old fashioned way." He grinned, reaching for his guns.

Josiah cast about, mind spinning. The only direction Korse could have escaped would have been if he'd slipped off the back of the platform and gone down the other side of the hill. He couldn't be far yet.

Sheriff Masters shot into the air and let out a whoop. "Git 'im boys!" he cried. "We'll catch the half-breed next!"

Vampires swarmed the platform. Josiah swore and drew, firing quickly. The two shots blew away the first two vampires to touch the platform. Diana fired a shot at Masters and hit, but the sheriff just laughed. She cursed and worked the bolt action, struggling to reload.

Now they were climbing up onto the platform. He turned this way and that, firing, but they were climbing faster than he could kill them. He was surrounded.

"Masters!" A voice rang out. It was Walter Korse. Turn to 155.

"Make it quick, Marshal," Diana said. She took out her rifle and moved to the far corner of the gallows platform, resting her rifle on it as a stable shooting surface. She checked the sights and kept one eye on the town while Josiah worked.

The marshal was checking the knots of the hangman's noose, making sure each coil was secure and the measurements correct. He tugged the last of it and nodded, satisfied. Kneeling next to Walter Korse, he said, "Any last words, murderer?"

Walter's flinty eyes did not acknowledge the marshal. Turn to 133.
"Go to hell, da Silva," Walter said. Turn to 149.
"Kill Masters for me…" Walter said. Turn to 154.

"We need to move," Josiah said. "Follow me." He crouched low and moved quickly but quietly back to the stairs. Diana followed him, cringing with every squeak of the floorboards.

"If they're tearing this town apart, we won't be safe here," Josiah hissed.

"Where will we go?" Diana asked.

Josiah shook his head. "Out of town, perhaps. We'll figure it out." He eased open the door to the stairwell. Listening for a moment, they could hear no disturbance below. "Quietly!"

The two of them slipped down the stairs, stepping close to the wall to avoid creaking as much as possible. The lace curtains on the windows provided a slight barrier to anyone looking in; Diana hoped it would be enough.

"I saw a door at the back," Josiah whispered. Sounds of celebration and the hunt could be heard echoing throughout the town. Howls of hunger and excitement, wicked laughter. Now, as the twilight faded, the red glow of torches were beginning to appear. These caused dancing shadows on the wall of the building across from them.

"Where the hell is Korse?" Josiah muttered, pausing at the back door to listen. Hearing nothing, he gestured and began running in a low crouch. Diana followed him, keeping her rifle at the ready.

As they moved between buildings, Diana caught a glimpse in one window and out another, completely through the building on their left. Vampires. Close.

With no time to speak, Diana lashed out and grabbed Josiah, pulling him into the alcove of a side doorway. Just in time. The vampires passed so close Diana could smell the blood on them.

"In here," Diana said. She pushed open the door at the back of their alcove. It opened into complete darkness. "I think it's safe," she hissed, as Josiah started to duck in after her.

A flash of movement in the darkness—a crack of impact on bone—and Diana collapsed. Walter Korse stood above her, his face gleaming in the darkness. One hand held a gun by the barrel—it's grip wet with a slick of blood. Diana...

Josiah went pale with fear for his friend—she lay unmoving—then a dark rage burned inside of him. He whipped out his gun—but the laughter of vampires nearby stopped him from firing.

"Marshal..." Walter said, with a hint of a smile.

"Korse." Josiah spat the name like a foul word.

Walter struck first. Turn to 153.
Josiah struck first. Turn to 137.

"Thank you," Diana said, turning away. Leaving her food abandoned, she drifted to the window to look out, not at any one thing, so much as at her own thoughts.

Josiah sighed. Masters had a lot to answer for after all this. And Korse no less. He shoveled the last of his food into his mouth. Pushing away his bowl, he pulled out his ammunition pouch and dumped the remaining rounds out on the counter.

Diana looked back at the sound of the rounds clattering across the counter. She watched as he spread out the ammunition, standing each piece up side by side. Then he rummaged in his pocket and pulled out his rosary.

Lowering his head, he held the rosary above the bullets and waved the cross above each one. He intoned, "Lord in heaven, blessed be thy name. Thy will be done. Thy kingdom come. On earth as it is in heaven. Watch over me today, Father, for I walk in the valley of evil. Hold my hand as I aim thy weapon, and guide my steps as I walk for you."

Josiah hesitated, then said, "Amen." He tucked the rosary back into his pocket.

Diana nodded toward him. "That work?"

Without looking up, Josiah said, "The Lord works in mysterious ways. The way I figure it, we can use all the help we can get. I need another moment." He lifted a bullet, pulled out his knife, and carved a shallow cross in the tip of the soft lead.

Shrugging, Diana turned to gather her things. By the time Josiah had finished preparing his ammunition, Diana was ready to go.

"You always do that?" Diana asked.

Josiah said, "No. I figure asking the Lord for a little extra help today can't hurt. Let's move." He went to the window and pulled aside the shutters, looking both ways down the street.

The street was as deserted now as it had been the moment they arrived in Affliction. Turn to 152.

Josiah caught Walter's leg and threw him. The killer hit the ground face first and did not get up.

Josiah stood panting for a moment, leaning over to rest his hands on his knees. After a few quick breaths, he wiped blood and sweat from his face and knelt to bind the fallen criminal.

A stirring near him caught his attention, and he looked over to see Diana sitting up. She put her hand to her forehead, eyes still unfocused. "What happened?" she asked.

"Korse," Josiah grunted, securing the bonds on the killer.

A muffled crash sounded through the walls, and they both looked up. Josiah said, "They're breaking into the next building over. Can you walk?"

Diana pushed herself to her feet, swaying only slightly. "I think so. Let's go."

Josiah wrapped his arms around Korse and heaved, throwing the bound killer over his shoulder. He grunted with the effort and let Diana lead the way out of the building. She pushed open the back door, checked to make sure the way was clear, and nodded. The two of them ran for the cover of the next building up.

This was a little home set back from the main road. They circled around behind it and knelt against the back wall to rest. A cool evening breeze drifted to them from out across the open land, drying the sweat on their brows.

Josiah pointed to the hill they had passed on their way into town. The gallows stood stark and black, silhouetted against the starry night sky. "There," he said.

Diana followed his gaze. "Now?" she asked.

"It's what I came here for," Josiah said. He heaved Walter Korse's still-unconscious body over his shoulder and set off.

Diana followed, scowling. Sheriff Masters and his vampires seemed to be methodically taking the town apart, one building at a time. They had gotten away ahead of the search, but how long would it take them to search the town? And how long to find the tracks leading up to this lonely hill?

Josiah threw Korse down on the platform of the gallows, panting like a bellows. Sweat beaded on his cheeks and forehead, gleaming in the starlight.

Korse stirred and groaned as he shifted—and found his arms tied. He lifted his head and looked around. He showed no reaction as his eyes fell on the gallows looming above him.

"Take a good look, Korse," Josiah said. "It'll be your last." He climbed up onto the gallows platform and checked the rope.

Diana glanced back toward the town. They would be perfectly visible here if anyone bothered to look up, with only the meager cover of darkness to conceal them.

"Are you sure you want to do this, Josiah?" Diana asked. Turn to 146.
"Make it quick, Marshal," Diana said. Turn to 140.

144

Diana lifted her rifle. "Josiah, don't do this," she said in a cool voice.

"Diana…" Josiah said slowly.

"I mean it," Diana said. "Step away from the lever."

Josiah looked down the barrel of her rifle, jaw tight and fists clenching and unclenching. Finally, he stepped away. "Diana, you don't understand what this man has done."

Diana shook her head. "No, you don't understand—"

Suddenly a voice interrupted them.

"An execution and you didn't invite me?" Sheriff Masters said, coming up the hill. Turn to 145.

145

"An execution and you didn't invite me?" Sheriff Masters said, coming up the hill. He looked from one of them to the other. His ruined face might have been grinning. "Well, isn't this a festive scene? I'm hurt, Joe! I thought we were friends!"

Josiah pushed back his coat to show his gun. "What do you want, Bill?" he asked.

"Joe, Joe, Joe… why you always got to be like this? So stiff all the time. Relax, cut a jig. Have a little fun!"

Josiah stiffened. "I got a job to do, Bill, so unless you aim to interfere…"

Masters heaved an affected sigh. "Well, Joe… about that. See, I can't let any of y'all live. That's the thing. Hard on me, it is, us goin' back so far and all, but my hands are tied! So, well, tell you what—sure! Why don't you go on and kill him for us and get it over with. Then we'll finish up, you and me. What do you say?"

Josiah nodded. "You just stay right there a spell." Turn to 134.
Josiah shook his head. "So you can shoot me in the back? I don't think so." Turn to 139.

146

"Are you sure you want to do this, Josiah?" Diana asked.

The marshal did not respond right away, but she could sense his displeasure in his silence. She glanced up at him; with his back to the sky, his face was shadowed even from the starlight. He was checking the knots of the hangman's noose, securing each coil.

Diana moved closer to him and looked up. She said, "With so many dead, can we afford to lose one of the living?"

"He's not the kind of man you want alive," Josiah said, his voice low and hollow. He jerked the last part of the knot savagely.

Korse's eyes flickered in the darkness, watching this.

Josiah knelt next to the bound killer. "Any last words, Korse?"

Walter's flinty eyes did not acknowledge the marshal. Turn to 133.
"Go to hell, da Silva," Walter said. Turn to 149.
"Kill Masters for me…" Walter said. Turn to 154.

147

Josiah jerked his head toward the sleeping vampires and put his hand on his gun. Diana nodded, readying her rifle. They took up positions on either side of the door before Josiah reached out to open it. The figures inside did not stir.

Josiah frowned. The light of the sun did not quite fall at the right angle to go straight into the pantry, but it was close. "Cover me," he said. He sheathed his pistol and stepped into the room. He reached down and took one of the figures by the feet and pulled.

Diana kept her rifle trained on the comatose figure as Josiah pulled a man into the sunlight. As soon as his face hit the light, his eyes flew open. He let out a shrill, keening scream, and smoke began to rise from his flesh.

Diana fired.

The man's head flew back—dead—but now the others were up. They shifted groggily, hissing and staring. Josiah grabbed another with main strength and threw it out into the light. It was a woman. She looked at the sun and howled before her skin caught fire.

Diana, not wanting to waste the bullet, grabbed a chair and slammed it down onto the woman's neck. She collapsed, flames licking up and down her body from the sunlight.

Two more gunshots erupted from inside the pantry, then Josiah came out, splattered with blood.

They met each other's eyes, and neither said a word.

The sunlight shifted lower.

"We don't have much time," Josiah said and went up the stairs. Turn to 151.

148

The kick hit Josiah hard, knocking the breath out of him. Walter followed up with a crack to the head that sent the older man reeling. The next one dropped him like a poleaxed bull.

As the marshal's body fell heavily to the floor, the woman started stirring. Walter wiped blood from his eye and drew his pistol with his one good hand. He held it trained on her as she awoke.

"Wha—" she murmured, but fell silent as she saw him.

Walter put one finger to his lips, positioning himself where a shaft of light coming in through the shutters would fall on his face. The woman's eyes widened. Walter jerked a thumb toward the window. The vampires were ransacking the next building over. They would be here any moment.

The woman groaned softly, pulling herself to her feet. Then she saw the marshal, stretched out cold on the ground. "What have you done?" she hissed.

"He's still breathing," Walter whispered back. "What happens next is none of your business."

"What are you going to do to him?" Diana demanded.

Walter lifted his pistol into the light, to make sure she saw it. She drew in her breath. He said, "Better than he would have done to me. Professor Enfield is up the hill, by the old mill building. He's waiting for you. Get out of here."

The woman's eyes narrowed in anger, but she backed away. "If you hurt him…" she said.

"If he comes to harm, it won't be at my hands. Go." Walter held the pistol trained on her.

Diana narrowed her eyes, but looked at the gun Walter held on her and backed away.

"Go!" Walter said, tracking her with his weapon. The woman stepped out into the moonlight, then let the door fall closed behind her as she turned up the hill.

Walter looked down at the fallen marshal. He knelt… yes, the big man was still breathing. Walter smiled. "Now here's a stroke of good luck, you turnin' up like this… after what the professor told me. How strong is your faith, Mr. da Silva?"

Walter took the marshal's gun and hefted it.

Diana struggled up the slope, panting and swearing. Turn to 185.

149

"Go to hell, da Silva," Walter said. He met the marshal's eyes—and spat in his face.

Josiah wiped it away. "Serves me for asking… filth like you," he muttered.

Josiah grunted and heaved the killer up to a standing position. Korse stood proudly while Josiah looped the noose around his neck. He held his chin steady and high, the sharp cheekbones of his Indian ancestry carving deep pools of shadow on his cheeks.

"Wait! Korse, where is Professor Enfield?" Diana demanded. Turn to 130.
Diana lifted her rifle. "Josiah, don't do this," she said in a cool voice. Turn to 144.

150

"Go to hell," Josiah said. Korse stiffened, his face twisting slightly in a snarl.

Josiah grabbed the killer under the armpits and heaved him up to his feet, then pulled him over to the noose.

Walter clenched his jaw while the marshal looped the noose around his neck, holding his head proudly. The sharp cheekbones of his Indian ancestry carved deep pools of shadow on his cheeks. His eyes stared into an unknown distance.

"Wait! Korse, where is Professor Enfield?" Diana demanded. Turn to 130.
Diana lifted her rifle. "Josiah, don't do this," she said in a cool voice. Turn to 144.

"We don't have much time," Josiah said and went up the stairs. The upper floor opened out onto a small hallway, with rooms in each direction. Josiah checked them each, pistol in hand, and when he came back into the hall, he gave Diana a small nod.

"In here," he said, gesturing toward the master bedroom. It was conveniently positioned with windows opening out in two directions, giving them a broad view of much of the town—including the sunset.

Diana took up position at one of the north-facing windows, using the tip of her gun to part the lace curtains so she could get a look at the town. Josiah moved to a west-facing window. He rested some of his weight on the edge of a ladies' jewelry table, using one hand to hold the curtains open while he held his pistol in the other.

The last light of the setting sun illuminated the town and sky in brilliant purples and reds. For a moment, the town looked as though it were a hundred years old, decayed beyond recognition. A lone tumbleweed bounced gently through the empty streets.

The sun glowed brilliantly as it sank behind the mountains; then, with a final flash, it was gone, leaving purple twilight in its wake.

The reaction was almost instantaneous. An inchoate howl rose from the town, coming from multiple directions, all around them. From secret places, dark places throughout the town, vampires boiled forth, gathering in the streets.

"Just in time," Josiah muttered, catching Diana's eye.

Diana nodded. She caught her breath and pointed. Josiah followed her finger, looking back through the window at the church that loomed at one end of the town.

The church doors flew open, and Sheriff William Masters stepped out. His face was still ruined from the shotgun blast in the jailhouse. He didn't even look human anymore, more like an abomination risen from hell.

Masters raised his hands. Standing on the patio of the church, he had a commanding view of the main street. Vampires flocked to him like flies to rotting meat.

"Friends! Brothers!" he called. The still-gathering crowd of vampires fell silent and his words came clearly to the ears of the living listeners. Masters looked over the crowd. He announced, "Our beloved town has come under attack. Attack by villains—outsiders—who do not understand us, do not respect us, and seek to destroy us."

The hairs on Josiah's arms stood up. Whatever was coming, he wouldn't like it.

Masters spoke with the force of a preacher before his flock. "Some of these outsiders may once have walked among us. But they are of us no longer! I say to you, that Joe—yes, our own Josiah da Silva, once my brother, as he was yours—has turned against us. He walks now with Indians and women. He is no longer a man!" A chorus of boos and shouts of hate and derision followed this announcement.

"He chooses these godless ones over his own folk! He knows not the Bled One! And yes, he would destroy our Goddess if he could." Sheriff Masters' voice fell low, as if with sorrow.

Screams of rage and fury rose from the vampires. Cries of "Kill them! Feast upon them!" chorused back and forth through the street.

Masters raised one hand to quell them. Above him, a vulture descended from the sky to perch on the cross at the tip of the church.

The sheriff said, "Their blood shall grace our lips. Do not fear. Our Goddess has made a promise to us. We must deliver the traitors unto her, and she will deliver all the world unto us. For we are the meek, and we shall inherit the Kingdom of the Earth." He raised his arms, and the vampires howled.

"We, my brothers and sisters, will be as kings among men! We shall rise like a tide and sweep over the living. We shall judge them! Those who are trustworthy will join our ranks. The rest… they will be as the blood and the flesh of Jesus Christ, for us to feast upon!" His eyes gleamed with unholy light.

Quietly, but in a voice designed to carry, he said, "It is our destiny to rule this world." He fell silent, and the crowd roared with approval. He watched them, nodding. Then he made a small gesture with one hand. Several of his henchmen dragged forward a handful of innocent men and women, who struggled against their bonds.

Josiah swore. He met Diana's eyes briefly. Her face was drained of color.

Masters placed a hand almost affectionately upon the cheek of one prisoner. Then he turned to the crowd. "Our Goddess has had her fill, for now. There is only one whose blood she yet desires. These," he swept a hand among the prisoners, "are her gift to us!"

This time, the howl of the vampires was one of pleasure, hunger, anticipation. Masters spoke, his words creating a silence that they dropped into like rain, "Drink, and when you are done… find them. The Goddess has told me they still lurk among us. Find them, and bring them to me."

Masters grabbed the hair of the man beneath his hand, and wrenched, lifting the hapless prisoner by sheer strength. Almost lover-like, he pulled the man close and sank his fangs into the fellow's neck.

The vampires screamed and clamored as the prisoners were distributed among them. Josiah lowered the curtain, averting his eyes as the blood began to run.

Diana was looking at the floor, her eyes sick.

"There's nothing we can do for them," Josiah said, crouching and holding his gun in both hands.

Diana nodded miserably. "What now?"

"We need to move," Josiah said. Turn to 141.
"Stay put," Josiah said. "Don't get found." Turn to 135.

The street was as deserted now as it had been the moment they arrived in Affliction. The sun was a red disk glowing in the western sky, rapidly sinking toward the horizon.

"Nothing," Diana grunted, joining him at the window.

Josiah said, "There's the church, but they'll look there. Or we could hide in that manor house." He pointed across the street. "We'd get a good view from the second floor, and it'd be safe—unless we do something to give ourselves away. There's also that old mill building, up the hill a ways." He pointed, and Diana could see the large, decrepit mill on the outskirts of town.

"What do you think?" Josiah asked, squinting at the town.

Diana nodded toward the manor house. "I think the big house is our best bet. We'll have cover and a good view. And it's right in town, so there'll be places to hide if we need to get out quick."

Josiah nodded. He opened the door, and the two of them moved out into the street, guns at the ready. He held his one remaining pistol, while she had her rifle.

The street was painted red by the setting sun. He had to avoid looking directly west for fear of being blinded, and he didn't like that he couldn't see that direction. He hurried across the street and into the manor house on the far side of the road.

The building had once been home to one of Affliction's wealthier families. He found himself in a small entrance foyer. A den opened off to one direction, a kitchen to the other, and stairs straight ahead.

She came in a moment later and carefully shut the door behind her. "Which way?" she asked, holding her rifle loosely.

"Let's check this level," Josiah said and went into the den. Turn to 132.
"We don't have much time," Josiah said and went up the stairs. Turn to 151.

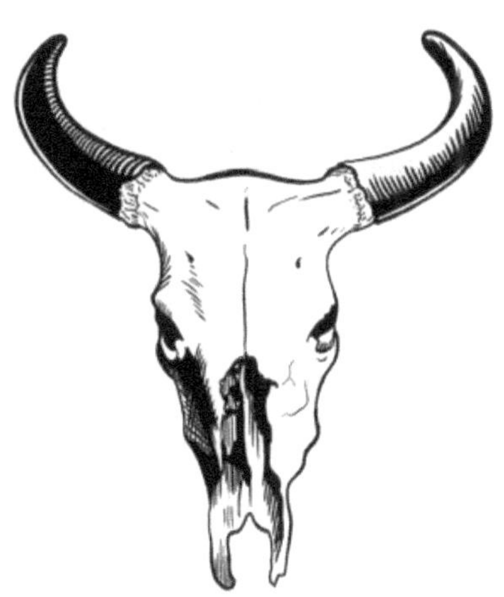

153

Walter struck first. His fist lashed out like a striking snake, catching the older man alongside the head. Josiah growled and stepped forward, putting his weight behind his counter punch.

Walter danced back, barely avoiding the heavy blow. He hadn't expected the older man to be so resilient, or so quick. His eyes narrowed.

Now it was the marshal's turn to smile. A dark, heavy smile that promised pain. Walter threw another jab, backing up to give himself some space. He cursed his injured right hand. He was playing with a stacked deck. But he could still win.

Marshal da Silva came hard and fast, forcing Walter to dance. But in the movement, he saw his opportunity—as the marshal came rushing forward, Walter dropped to one knee—bracing with his left hand only—and swept out a leg. Da Silva grunted heavily and came crashing down.

Walter was up in a heartbeat, knife gleaming in his hand. With a swift movement, the knife flashed downward.

Josiah rolled out of the way barely in time. He retaliated with a quick strike at Walter's arm. Pain shot up the arm, and the knife clattered from his grip.

Walter jumped back, shaking his hand to free it from the painful tingling of a nerve strike. This gave the marshal time to get to his feet, nose bloodied, but ready for a fight.

Walter didn't give him time to recover. He shot forward, faking with his left before coming in with a kick. Most men didn't expect kicks; when one came it caught most fighters cold, but it was a risky choice against an experienced brawler.

The kick hit Josiah hard, knocking the breath out of him. Turn to 148.
Josiah caught Walter's leg and threw him. Turn to 143.

154

"Kill Masters for me…" Walter said. His eyes looked down, into shadows and darkness.

Josiah rubbed the stubble on his chin. After all the years of hunting, it was strange to find the moment had finally come. At last, he could send the spirit of his little girl on in peace. But now that he was here, it was a hell of a thing to look upon a man and know that soon he would be dead at your own hand.

The universe hadn't done this half-breed any favors. It had turned him into the man he was. And yet… no one else had pulled that trigger.

"Go to hell," Josiah said. Turn to 150.
"I'll see to it," Josiah said. Turn to 138.

155

"Masters!" A voice rang out. It was Walter Korse. He stood at the crest of the next hill, silhouetted against the night sky. Sheriff Masters turned to look that direction, and the other vampires paused, following their master's lead.

Korse let out a wild laugh, throwing his head back. "Tonight is your last night, William Masters! Come and get me… if you can!" The words rang with prophetic resonance, echoing across the valley. But Sheriff Masters merely snarled and turned away. "Finish him," he growled, pointing to Josiah. "We'll get the half-breed later."

The outlaw fired, but from so far away, his bullets merely puffed in the dust at random. Josiah thought he saw one hit the vampire sheriff, but if it did, Masters didn't even flinch.

The vampires moved toward the gallows again, this time more careful in their approach, staying low and out of sight. With Josiah's guns primed and ready, each was reluctant to be the first over the lip onto the platform.

Josiah took advantage of the moment to level a shot at Sheriff Masters himself. "Lord, thy rod and thy staff, they comfort me," he whispered as he squeezed the trigger. He felt something move in him, a certainty, a faith, that this shot would fly true.

Time seemed to slow. Masters' eyes widened, as if the same realization came over him. The shot was good; Josiah could feel it in his bones the moment he pulled the trigger. He almost seemed to watch as the bullet speared across the gap toward its target.

Masters flinched back, nearly falling over with his haste. The bullet grazed the edge of his scalp, and where it touched, a thin line of burnt, black skin was left in its wake. Despite the darkness, Josiah thought he could see a small trace of white smoke rising from the shallow wound.

Sheriff Masters backed away into the darkness, hand holding the place where Josiah's bullet had nicked him. "You lot, finish them!" He howled. "I'll get the mongrel!"

The sheriff turned and ran in the direction of Walter Korse, trailed by a number of uncertain followers, but to Josiah it looked more like he was running away. Josiah's mouth twisted in a wry smile.

Yet as the remaining vampires returned their attention to himself and Diana, his smile vanished. The vampires, over a dozen of them, regarded them with tongues slavering in the anticipated delight of their forthcoming feast.

"Ready?" Josiah asked, clicking six new bullets into his revolver—each with a cross carved into its head.

"Ready," Diana echoed, lifting her freshly loaded rifle.

The vampires swarmed forward.

Walter ran. Turn to 161.

156

Walter vanished into the shack that held his detonator. He grinned to see it waiting for him, gleaming lightly in the darkness. A coil of fuse reached from it out the door, into the clearing, where it was buried under a thin layer of dust. From there, it led across to the opening of the old mine shaft. All he had to do was make sure Masters was in the mine…

He crouched in the darkness. He had chosen this shack because it had a clear view of the mine entrance. The vampires were clustered around it, listening, presumably, to Enfield's rantings from 'within' the mine. He smiled.

Now the vampires moved in. Now Masters moved.

Now.

Walter reached for the detonator, but just then he felt something drop onto his hand—a centipede. It was massive, as big as one of his fingers, crawling across his skin. He jerked reflexively, stifling a shout. The insect flew off his hand and slammed into the wall. But more were boiling up from the sand now.

Walter jumped, staying on his toes to avoid them. He crushed one, then another with his boots.

There was no time. A quick glance out told him Masters had entered the cavern.

Walter brushed a bug off the detonator and slammed it closed. Was he already too late? A sparkle of fire started burning toward the mine entrance.

It would be fast enough. It had to be. He watched the sparkle blaze its way across the clearing. Too slow. Too slow! Masters was still inside, but for how much longer?

Walter stepped out. What he needed was a distraction. Just as one vampire's eye fell on the sparkle, Walter fired. The bullet hit. It was a clean kill shot, dropping the alert vampire before he could shout warning to the others.

Yet the others heard the gunshot and turned to face him. "Get ready to meet your maker," Walter said with a smile, levelling his gun.

All of them scrambled for their weapons, ignoring the tiny spark that burned toward the mineshaft.

Walter started firing, moving and firing. He just needed to hold their attention; he didn't need to land shots.

Then Masters emerged from the mineshaft. Walter's breath froze in his chest. Time seemed to move slowly as Masters' eye fell on the sparkling light of the fuse, then looked up toward Walter.

Only a second longer... Walter levelled his weapon, but everything was moving too slowly.

Masters coiled his legs beneath him. He leaped, his powerful, bunched legs sending him sailing through the air.

The mine exploded behind him. The force of the explosion sent vampires hurling like dolls in all directions, crushed by either the explosion or the falling rocks that sailed out with it.

The blast hit Masters mid-air, propelling him even faster than he was already leaping. Flames licked at Masters, setting his coat on fire, but the man snarled in pure fury, curled forward into a controlled flip, and landed catlike on his feet. His eyes burned as they fixed on Walter.

Walter felt the pit of his stomach drop out inside him. He had pinned everything on this moment, and it had failed. It wasn't his last trick, though...

Walter stumbled back, his panicked mind casting about for escape. Turn to 173.
Josiah swore and rubbed his jaw, looking at the bodies that surrounded him. Turn to 162.

157

Finally, Walter dashed into the mining camp. His broken wrist throbbed. His rage was cold, tempered by years of patience, but the moment was upon him, and he burned with his need to complete the thing.

Enfield, if he held his part of the bargain, would be in the nook above that would carry his voice down to the mines. Now was the moment of truth. He ran to the mine entrance and shouted, "Now!"

After a moment, he heard rustling, and then Enfield's thin voice coming through the crack in the stone. "I'm ready!"

The illusion was complete. It really did sound like the professor was deeper in the mineshaft. He didn't have time to wait—the vampires would be hot on his heels.

He ran for the little shack where he had hidden the detonator. But before he could make it, the first vampires crested the hill.

Walter threw himself behind a dusty wheelbarrow, crouching to avoid being spotted. This flimsy cover would only last moments, though... he had to get somewhere safer. Ahead a crumbling shack could provide cover, or to the right a drainage ditch encircled the encampment, running along the foot of the hillside.

Walter dove into the drainage ditch. Turn to 165.
Walter ducked into the nearest shack. Turn to 171.

"What's the plan?" Josiah asked, checking his pistols.

"You could start with an apology," Walter said, eying Josiah.

Josiah stared after him. "The hell?"

Walter just shook his head. "Let's just stick to business." He moved toward the front of the building and knelt next to a window. With his good hand, he parted the blinds slightly, looking out on the dirt road before them. "I figure it won't be long before they figure out we're not in the camp above, nor the town below. At that point, there will only be one place left to look."

Josiah clenched his jaw. "We're outnumbered, and one of them can't die. What exactly is your plan?"

Walter looked up. "What about the power of faith? Think you got that under control?"

Josiah looked sour, but said nothing.

The vampires were coming up the street now, in two groups, one from below, and one from above, just as Walter had said.

Josiah looked out and said, "So we just charge out there and start firing? That sounds like a fast way to get killed."

"Well they can't come in after us," Walter said.

"Why not?" Josiah asked.

"Look around."

In the dim light, Josiah could still see the dynamite that lined the walls.

Walter cracked a half-smile. "They come in, we light it up." He made a silent explosion motion with his hands.

Josiah stared at him, his moustache twitching.

Walter grinned without humor. He stood up, stretching his knees, and gestured at the window and blinds. "What do you see?" he asked.

Josiah knelt down next to the window and parted the blinds to look out. "They're gathering, and they're angry. It won't be long now."

"Well," Walter said. He stood, drew his pistol, and hefted it in one hand. He eyed the back of the marshal's neck, right where the hairline ended at the base of the skull. With a single quick motion, he slammed the butt of the gun down.

Josiah let out a soft grunt and slid down the wall, instantly unconscious.

"Admit it, you had that coming," Walter said, kneeling next to him.

Diana followed Garland into the darkness. Turn to 193.

"You two love each other," Josiah said.

Diana smiled. "That's why I came out here." She took Garland's hand in her own, and the professor turned to regard her with his owlish eyes.

"He has eyes only for you," Josiah said, putting a hand on each of their shoulders. "Now git out of here. Go live on a farm somewhere. Live the life I wish I had."

Diana's face turned serious. "What are you going to do?"

The marshal rubbed his jaw. "I reckon I'll do what I can to stop this madness."

Diana turned to look at Garland. The professor met her gaze, then stammered, "It does seem… we should help…"

Josiah shook his head. "No. You've got a whole life ahead of you."

Diana took a deep breath, her hand drifting to her belly. She carried a new life there, already growing. She wasn't just risking her own life anymore… but what kind of world would she be raising her child into?

"We'll stay and help," Diana said. Turn to 188.
"Maybe we should go… thank you," Diana said. Turn to 184.

"Put your hands up," Marshal da Silva said, and Walter heard the click of a pistol.

Walter stiffened. He raised his hands, turning slowly. It was that damned marshal. Rage flooded Walter, and then it changed within.

He began to laugh.

The marshal's eyebrows knitted. "The hell's wrong with you?"

Walter bent, gasping for breath as laughter took over. It was just too much, after everything, to find the marshal here waiting for him.

"I was so close," Walter said, aware his voice was close to breaking, but unable to stop it. "You won. You got me." He turned to face the marshal, hands raised, with a small, strange smile on his face.

The marshal's eyes narrowed. His finger twitched ever so slightly, preparing to pull the trigger.

The sound of a distant explosion came to the room.

"Diana," the marshal breathed. His eyes flicked left—momentarily averting his gaze from Walter.

Walter acted without thought. He spun, raising his foot in a swift kick. His foot slammed into Josiah's hand, knocking the gun free and sending it spinning across the floor.

"That should keep 'em busy." Diana's voice came up the stairs from the back door.

Walter ignored her. He flew at the marshal, too furious to even draw his gun. Another kick sent the older man reeling, even as he reached for the fallen pistol. And then Walter was upon him, pounding—but instinct betrayed him. Walter tried to hit the marshal with his broken hand, and the bandaged wrist gave out in a brilliant haze of pain.

Iron fingers wrapped around Walter's broken wrist. Blinding pain, crippling pain shot through Walter; his knees buckled. Josiah rose, twisting the murderer's wrist, feeling the man crumple under his strength.

"What—? Stop this!" Diana called.

Josiah turned, and in that moment of distraction Walter twisted away. Josiah could feel bones grinding under his fingers as the murderer ripped his arm free, but Walter didn't let out even so much as a grunt. He simply pulled his wrist away and vanished into the darkness between rows of shelves.

Josiah swore and grabbed his gun, turning toward the darkness. Diana put a hand on his shoulder, stepping into his path. "Cut it out, now," she said. "We need to work together against those things."

"The hell are you talking about?" Josiah demanded. "I came here to kill him! Him! Not get sucked into some nightmare!"

Diana's eyes flared. "What's happening here is bigger than this," she spat. "I don't care what he did to you—he's alive. And we need all the living we can get." Slowly, she said, "You have to stop now."

Josiah took a deep breath. His hands trembled.

"Fine," Josiah said, holstering his gun. Turn to 164.
"Like hell," Josiah growled. He shoved Diana out of the way. Turn to 170.

<h1 style="text-align:center">161</h1>

Walter ran. The bright moon burned above him, and his vampires gave chase. His feet pounded bare earth, all his energies, all his life and self bent toward this moment. As he ran, a wild glee filled him. One way or another, this would all be over tonight. The last man on his list was within his grasp.

Gunshots rang out from behind. He could barely hear them over the pounding pulse of his own breath, but he could see the puffs of dust that rose up from the hillside around him as the bullets struck dirt.

His goal was the narrow trail which led up the mining camp, to the trap he had laid. But the trail was still too far away, and he would be an easy target. On the left side of the trail lay the old mill building, but this was no time for holing up. Instead, he veered into the broken terrain off to the right side of the trail.

Rocks suddenly loomed all around him, towers of broken stone. This maze would provide ideal cover while he picked his way toward the mining camp above.

A bullet chirped off of a flat face of stone near him, and Walter ducked behind the rock formation, putting its bulk between himself and his assailants. As he drew his gun, he realized an insane grin split his face.

"Masters!" Walter shouted, unable to contain himself.

"Walter Korse," the sheriff growled somewhere not too far away. "Come on out and make this easy for yourself."

"You remember what you did, Masters? You remember." Walter leaned out and picked out his targets. Two vampires prowling through the stones. While he drew his aim, one of them noticed him, gestured to the other, and Walter fired.

Two shots. Quick and clean. Both vampires went down. Walter felt like laughing. Instead, he flattened almost to the earth and moved quietly to a new position, higher on the hillside.

"I don't know what you're talking about, Walter. Listen, yer pa was a good man. Come on out and we can work this all out."

Walter clenched his jaw, his glee evaporating into rage that gnawed at his insides. "You remember, you bastard! Don't say you forget!" He peeked out from his new hiding place. Masters was standing on a broad rock, making himself an easy target, but Walter didn't take the bait. He knew it would take more than mere bullets to bring the man down.

Masters chuckled. "Look, things may have gotten a little out of hand. It was just boys being boys. You'd have done the same."

Walter closed his eyes to avert the vertigo of emotion that swept over him. His mother's screams still sounded harsh in his ears. He could still hear them, as if it had been only moments ago instead of years ago.

Swallowing his hatred, Walter swarmed up the mountain. He had to lure Masters to the mineshaft...

Behind him, he heard Masters giving orders to his men. Walter swallowed. Moving around the field of rocks, they might be able to move faster and cut him off from above.

Walter reloaded. He would have to fight. Turn to 167.
Walter broke into a bent run. Speed was of the essence. Turn to 169.

162

Josiah swore and rubbed his jaw, looking at the bodies which surrounded him. The vampires hadn't fought well, but there'd been a lot of them. With he and Diana fighting back to back, they'd left the place looking like a graveyard without any undertaker.

"Did you see where he went?" Diana asked, coming up next to him. She held her still-smoking rifle in both hands.

"North, into the hills," Josiah answered.

"Think Garland is still with him?" Diana asked, staring up at the mountains that loomed black against the sky to the north.

"Best lead we've got."

"Then we'd best be moving," she said, reloading her gun.

Josiah nodded, and the two of them set off at an easy jog, following the trail left by the mob of vampires that had chased Walter. As they left the town, the moon rose, making the night seem less dark. The sloping ground stretched wide and barren all around them, and the mesas glowing in the moonlight ahead looked almost beautiful.

A distant explosion boomed, and a gout of flame erupted from the mining camp above them. Illuminated against the light of the explosion, they could see several figures scurrying and scattering before the blast.

"Son of a bitch..." Josiah breathed.

"What was that?" Diana asked.

"Walter," Josiah said, and set his jaw. More motion was coming from up ahead, figures running this way and that. "We need cover. In here," Josiah said, and he gestured toward an abandoned mill building up ahead, between the trail and a grove of juniper trees.

The two of them hurried up the hill to the old building and let themselves in. The dry wood creaked as they opened the door.

Diana stopped dead in her tracks. "Josiah…" she breathed, "the dynamite."

It lined the walls, hundreds of sticks of the stuff. Josiah swore.

"We've got to get out of here," Diana said.

"Too late." Josiah pointed. A mob of vampires was swarming down the trail outside, tearing up the underbrush as though searching for something—or someone.

Diana looked out the window and swore. "Stay here," she said. "I'll draw them off." She grabbed a couple sticks of dynamite. Before Josiah could say another word, she was out the back door.

"Damn that woman," Josiah muttered. He followed her to the door and looked out. She was running through the juniper grove. That would give him a few minutes, at least. Best use them.

He turned to look up the hill, wondering where Korse and Enfield would be found—and was surprised to see another shadowy figure moving through the trees, coming toward him from the opposite direction as the way Diana had gone. Josiah's eyes went wide. It was the killer, Korse.

He stepped back, taking position behind the door, and drew his pistol. He could hear the man's progress as he approached. A pause, and then several quick footsteps brought him to the building.

A moment later, the dark figure slipped in the door.

"Put your hands up," Marshal da Silva said, and Walter heard the click of a pistol. Turn to 160.

163

Diana watched as vampires descended on the mill. They came from both above and below, hot in their anger. Their voices rose in confusion and rage as each group discovered that neither had found their quarry—and then all turned toward the mill.

Diana swore, abruptly and fiercely. She kicked a tree, shaking its leaves.

Josiah moved closer to her.

"He could be anywhere," Diana said in a small voice. She hugged herself.

A rustling in the trees arrested both their attention. With one motion, they each drew steel and pointed at the sound.

"Diana?" a tremulous voice called from the darkness.

Diana hesitated, lowering her weapon. "Garland?" She called back.

A dark shape emerged from the depths of the juniper grove. "Garland!" Diana called, and threw herself on him in a massive embrace.

Garland Enfield blinked owlishly and slowly put his arms around her in return.

"What are you doing here?" Diana asked, pushing away to look him in the face.

"Walter told me to wait…" Garland looked around. "Where is he, anyway?"

Diana's jaw clenched. "He's gone."

Garland's eyes grew wide. "What? No—he can't be—where is he?" The professor jerked under Diana's hands, and he almost started toward the mill building.

"Easy," Diana said, holding him tightly. "You can't go in there. Even if he's still alive, the vampires are taking the building."

It was true. Even as they watched, the vampire mobs were converging on the old mill building, swarming in from all directions.

Garland relaxed. "Oh, alright then." He blinked under his glasses, watching the vampires ransack the building. He turned his attention to Josiah. "And you are?"

"Marshal Josiah da Silva," Josiah responded, putting out his hand. The young professor took it and shook vigorously, saying, "Ah, yes, we met at the saloon. Forgive me, my thoughts are so scattered these days."

Diana stepped forward and took Garland's arm. "Let me get a look at you," she said, turning his face to hers. "I thought I'd never see you again."

Josiah regarded the two in the near-darkness. He hadn't seen Diana as the kind of woman to fall in love, but then, he'd never met a woman like her before. To see her with the professor was to see a completely different side of her.

He stepped forward to get their attention. "You two need to get out of here."

"We all need to get out of here!" Diana replied.

Josiah shook his head. "We don't have the cart. We'll never outrun them on foot. There's only one horse left. You two should take it and go."

Diana hesitated. She looked at Garland and their hands met and clasped. Yet when she looked back at Josiah, there was steel in her eyes. "If you can't come with us… we'll stay. We need to finish this together."

Josiah sighed. "You have to go."

Diana's jaw stiffened and she took a step closer to him. "Why's that?"

"You have a child on the way," Josiah said. Turn to 174.
"You two love each other," Josiah said. Turn to 159.
"You have people waiting for you back home," Josiah said. Turn to 172.

"Fine," Josiah said, holstering his gun.

Diana blinked. "You'll let it go?"

"For now," Josiah growled. He rubbed his stubbled jaw, thinking of the horrors he had seen since coming to this town. "Maybe it's best the living stick together."

Diana saw a shadow behind his eyes. He looked like he wasn't saying everything, but she didn't push it. She called into the dark interior of the mill, "You hear that, Walter? You can come out."

After a moment, Walter's form appeared, long and lean and cloaked in shadows. "That's what I've been trying to say all along," he said, touching the brim of his hat. If he was white with the pain he had just felt, it didn't show in the darkness. But he was favoring the right arm.

Josiah gave Walter a long, hard stare. Then, in cold, slow tones, he said, "You killed my daughter, you son of a bitch. You will still pay."

"Fine," Walter said, meeting the marshal's eyes without expression.

"I can't believe I nearly let her marry you…" Josiah muttered, turning away.

Walter let out a short bark of a laugh. "You think I was the monster? You don't know the man you married her to."

"Toby McCann?" Josiah asked, puzzled. "He was a good kid. Fought with us at Red Bluff."

Walter stared, unblinking. Josiah was the one who looked away. He said gruffly, "Come on, anyway. We need a plan."

Diana let out her breath. She hadn't even realized she'd been holding it. She said, "They could come back at any time. Walter, where the hell is Garland?" She rounded on the one-time prisoner.

Walter turned his gaze to her for the first time. His eyes were black and empty. "He's waiting for you." A few long strides brought Walter to the back door of the mill. He looked out at the juniper grove and called, "Come on in, Mr. Enfield."

A rustling could be heard in the bushes, and then a figure emerged from the cover of the trees. It was Garland Enfield, looking slight and fearful. Walter gestured with his good hand, beckoning him forward, and the professor broke into a shaky run to cross the distance.

Below, toward the town, the voices of the vampires were increasing in agitation and anger. A red glow came from where Diana's dynamite had started a fire.

As Professor Enfield topped the steps, Diana caught him in a rough embrace. "I can't believe it's really you," she said.

Walter grabbed the slight man's arm. "We had a deal. You owe me something."

Diana released him from the embrace and Garland adjusted his glasses, glancing nervously from Walter to Josiah. "My best guess is… well, I don't know for certain, but I think I can make an educated guess that—"

"Get to the point," Walter growled.

"I think… faith can kill them," Garland said. "Only one whose blows carry the power of the Almighty can hurt those who are Chosen by the Bled One."

Walter stared, a muscle in his jaw twitching. Garland nodded toward Josiah. "There's your man, Mr. Korse. Stick by his side if you want to kill Sheriff Masters."

"You're sure?" Walter asked.

"No, but if anyone could do it, it's him. He used to be a preacher."

Walter looked over at Josiah, who met his gaze. Walter made a faintly disgusted sound.

"Are you okay?" Diana asked the young professor. He nodded absently. "Yourself?" he asked. She smiled, then her face turned serious. "Damn you for disappearing on me! I thought you—I thought…"

Garland opened his arms, and awkwardly took Diana into an embrace.

"Get somewhere safe," Josiah said, touching Diana on the shoulder. "We'll take it from here."

Diana pushed Garland away, dashing away her tears. She looked up at Josiah. "Are you sure?" She looked like she wanted to stay, but instead of drifting to her guns, her hands drifted to her abdomen, as if holding her own belly in a gentle embrace.

"Go," Walter said. "Before they get here."

The sounds of the vampires could be heard getting louder now. Whatever distraction Diana had engineered had lost its hold on them.

"There's a horse tied up behind the church. Be safe!" Josiah said, and ushered the two out the door.

Diana flashed a quick smile back at the men, and she and Garland hurried across the short distance to the grove, where they were swallowed by the shadows under the trees.

"I still don't trust you," Josiah said, reloading his pistols. Turn to 166.

"What's the plan?" Josiah asked, checking his pistols. Turn to 158.

165

Walter dove into the drainage ditch. He hit the ground and rolled, bringing himself to a rest prone at the bottom of the shallow indentation.

He could hear the vampires' voices, raised in rage and frustration as they searched the camp. Masters wasn't far behind, his voice like a bellows as he called orders, demanding Walter's head at any cost.

Carefully, Walter shimmied along the ditch. It would take him close to the shack where he had hidden the detonator, but not all the way there. It would have to do.

Just as he was wondering what distraction could pull their attention so that he could cover the last bit of open ground, a shout came up from one of the vampires. "Hey! Hey boss, over here! It's Professor Enfield. He's in the mine!"

All eyes would be on the mine. Without hesitation, Walter raised himself up. A quick glance showed he was right—he darted forward, moving silently.

Walter vanished into the shack that held his detonator. Turn to 156.

"I still don't trust you," Josiah said, reloading his pistols.

Walter watched Diana and Enfield leave out the back door. He took out a slightly crumpled cigarette and, with some difficulty, managed to light it despite his broken hand. "You shouldn't," he said.

Josiah watched the match flame warily as Walter shook it out, his eyes flicking to the dynamite lining the walls. "What's the point of all this?" he asked, gesturing toward the hundreds of sticks that surrounded them.

"A promise." Walter grinned without humor. "They come in here after us, I promise they have hell to pay."

Josiah grunted, shaking his head. The man was mad.

A sound from the road caught both their attention. "Looks like I may have to keep that promise," Walter said. Both men moved to the front of the building, positioning themselves at windows to look out.

The vampires were gathering in front of the mill, confusion and anger in their voices as the group from above and the group from below met and each discovered neither had found their prey. One by one, the group's eyes turned toward the mill building.

"How do you want to play this?" Josiah asked, peering between two blinds to look out at the street.

"Well," Walter said. He stood, drew his pistol, and hefted it in one hand. Just as the marshal began to turn, he slammed the butt of the gun down on the back of Josiah's neck.

The marshal collapsed with a soft grunt.

Walter sucked on his cigarette, making a red glow in the darkness. "I said you shouldn't trust me."

Diana followed Garland into the darkness. Turn to 193.

Walter reloaded. He would have to fight. Staying silent, he slipped from the cover of one rock formation to the next. The land was broken and uneven, but he nimbly hopped from stone to stone, timing his movements to avoid being spotted by the vampires who were slowly surrounding him.

He picked his targets, deciding to gun for the two on the right first. They were closer, and by moving that direction, he could take them before they got support from the others.

The look on their face when he stepped out from behind a bulbous tower of stone was priceless, yet short-lived. They had their guns out, but he was faster, and they both dropped.

His gunshots echoed across the hillside and were answered in seconds by more coughing shots from all directions. Bullets whizzed past, cracking against stone and sending up chips of sharp rock from each place they hit. Walter ran, disappearing into the tumble of stones before they could get a bead on his exact location.

"Damn you, boy!" Masters shouted. "Your pa wouldn't have wanted you to end this way! Hunted like a dog on the mountain!"

Walter smiled. What his pa would have wanted didn't matter. He had seen to that when he planted a bullet in the man's gut nine years ago. He'd been twelve years old. It was old enough to run away, old enough to lie about his age and join the war. Old enough to kill a man.

He didn't talk now; that would give away his location. He hid, and when the vampires drew close, he stepped out and assassinated them. One after another.

He had always been good at killing. He'd started young. Yet he also knew there was only one way to bring down Masters. With the fall of one more vampire, the path up the hill was clear. Walter took it.

Finally, Walter dashed into the mining camp. Turn to 157.

168

Walter rolled over, seeing white and feeling nothing but pain. He knew in his gut that the bullet that had torn through him had severed something that must not be severed. He would not recover from this wound. It was only a matter of time.

"Damn you." He cursed Josiah in his mind. "Kill the bastard for me."

His mother rose in his mind, so quick and fierce that tears stung his cheeks. "I'm sorry…" he whispered. "I'm sorry."

A banging rose him from his stupor—he looked up to see multiple vampires entering the room. At their head: William Masters. The sheriff looked down at him with a twisted grin.

"Go… to… hell…" Walter croaked. He slipped his gun from his holster. Without breaking eye contact with Masters, he leveled the gun at the nearest stick of dynamite. The gun shook in his hand. Masters' eyes narrowed, then widened, as he saw what Walter aimed at. He glanced around, taking in the dynamite that surrounded them both.

Walter squeezed the trigger—and a vampire foot kicked the gun out of his hand. The report sounded wrong. Too fast, too hollow. The bullet missed.

A choked sob tore from Walter's throat. He rolled away from the hands that grabbed at him. As he turned his body, blood poured out of the wound in his chest. He watched it spill between the broken floorboards to sink into the thirsty earth.

"The Blood returns," he whispered with parched lips. Strong hands grabbed him, and he knew no more. The Blood returns. It always returned.

Diana watched as vampires descended on the mill. Turn to 163.

Walter broke into a bent run. Speed was of the essence. The vampires were moving in pairs all around him, some skirting the field of stones, looking in to catch glimpses of him and take potshots as he ran, while others pursued him through the broken terrain.

Bullets periodically whizzed by, sending up shards of shattered stone when they hit one of the rock formations. Walter ignored them. Either one would hit, or it wouldn't… and he was running quickly enough and staying low enough that he knew he would be a difficult target.

The vampires ahead would be a problem… they were getting too close, too fast. At least one pair would be in his way.

He veered in that direction. If he couldn't go around the problem, he would go through it.

A bullet zipped by his ear, so close he could feel the heat of it searing his skin.

"Walter!" Masters roared somewhere nearby. "What do you think you're doing? You can't get away. You're just makin' me draw it out. I don't want to do that, boy. I liked your pa; least I can do is put his son down with the Lord's mercy."

Walter's rage was cold as he stepped out with a smile. The two vampires blocking his path had just turned away, and he planted a bullet in each. He shouted, "Go to hell, Masters! Curtis, Bo, Toby… they're all waiting for you there. I got 'em all, Masters. Even my pa. He's waiting there for you too."

Masters snarled. Walter moved past another pillar of stone into plain view of Masters, and the vampire fired rapidly. Walter didn't linger—as soon as he made himself visible, he ducked back into cover again. He listened with a smile until Masters' gun clicked empty, then ran up the hill.

Masters, reloading, wasn't able to take the shot. Some of the other vampires, the quicker and smarter ones, took shots, but none had Masters' aim.

Finally, Walter dashed into the mining camp. Turn to 157.

"Like hell," Josiah growled. He shoved Diana out of the way. He leaped forward, looking behind the row of shelves where Walter had disappeared. Nothing.

"What's the matter, Marshal?" the murderer's taunting voice came from somewhere inside the old building. "Too angry to think straight?"

"You killed my daughter," Josiah growled.

A gunshot rang out, and Josiah ducked down reflexively. Chips of wood erupted just above his left shoulder. He glanced around, trying to locate where the shot had come from.

The interior of the mill was dark; with only the faint moonlight coming in the windows, it was almost impossible to spot a thing. Josiah held himself as low as possible, trying to stay hidden while he listened for sounds of where the murderer was.

Then he heard it—footsteps along what sounded like the upper level of the stamp battery. Josiah leaped up and fired, emptying his revolver in the direction of the noise. He heard bullets ringing off of the metal stamps and their frames, but no cry of pain.

"Damn it, Josiah! You'll draw them all to us!" Diana's silhouette appeared against a window, looking out, her own gun drawn.

"Keep shooting, Marshal," Walter's mocking voice came. "Maybe you'll hit the dynamite I've laid in and put us all out of our misery."

Josiah hunkered down, reloading his gun. He was confident the killer didn't know where he was either, or he would have fired already. If he kept the man talking… maybe he would reveal his position. Josiah ground his teeth and called out, "Why did you propose to her?"

No answer.

Josiah finished clicking the new set of bullets in and rolled the revolving chamber back into position. He looked out between the shelves. Where the hell was Korse?

Josiah called, "What I mean is, if you didn't love her, why ask her to marry you? And if you did, well then why the hell did you do it?"

Josiah's only answer was a salvo of bullets. He ducked behind cover and closed his eyes, and in that moment, he no longer saw the dark interior of the Affliction mill; he saw instead his daughter's face, her white dress fairly glowing under a full Virginia moon.

And for a moment he saw, too, a much younger Walter Korse. Unscarred, though a smile had seemed strange on his face even then.

Josiah jerked himself back to the present, not wanting the memories. His eyes found a still-hot bullet hole not inches from a stick of dynamite. He breathed out. Too close.

"Damn it, both of you! They're coming back!" Diana hissed.

"You know what really kills me, Walter?" Josiah called out. "I almost said yes, too. Before I knew what you were."

A low chuckle echoed around the room. Walter's voice came low and steady, "You think you almost married her to a monster… you don't know the man you did marry her to. You don't know what he did."

"Toby McCann?" Josiah's tone was puzzled. Toby had been a good kid. Quick, kind, with an easy smile and good nature. He'd been part of the Band of Brothers, back in the day, one of the founding members of Affliction. The youngest of them, barely more than a boy at that time. But after all they'd been through together, Josiah had trusted him. That's why he'd given his blessing for Cora da Silva to become Cora McCann.

"He was there, Marshal. He participated. He didn't like it, no, not like the others did. But he didn't stop them."

"What do you mean?" Josiah growled.

Walter laughed, a low, ugly sound. "Didn't you ever wonder why? Toby was there." He spit the words.

Josiah's throat clenched, so that it was almost hard to speak. "Whatever he did, it had nothing to do with Cora!"

"She got in the way!" Walter spat. "I didn't make her do that; she did it! Damn the girl. She jumped in front of him… I never…"

Josiah cried out in rage, stood, and fired blindly at the spot the voice came from. In the flash of light from the explosion in the chamber, he saw Walter's dark form, at one end of the stamp battery, on the upper level. He fired again. And again.

Walter was moving, quickly. In each flash, his body was in a different place, and Josiah knew the frustration of shooting and missing. Then, in the last flash, he saw Walter leveling his gun to return the shot.

Josiah swore and dropped, but not before a bullet stung the skin on top of his shoulder. He touched it, and his fingers came away bloody. There was no time to rest. Staying low, he moved slow and quiet along the length of the aisle, looking for a different vantage point.

He could hear Walter's breathing, heavy and raspy. Maybe he had been hit, after all. When his voice came, it was strangely devoid of all emotion. "I didn't want to kill her. She made her choice when she married McCann. She made her choice."

"Damn you both," Diana swore. Standing near the door, she lit the fuse on a stick of dynamite, and the sudden glow caused both men to look at her. She held the rifle loosely in her other hand, ready for action.

"If you boys are done playing, we have an actual problem. The vampires are coming back. In about twenty more seconds, they're going to overrun this building."

It was true; all three of them could hear the mob getting closer.

Josiah growled, "Help me, Diana. He killed my daughter."

Walter's eyes flashed. "I know where your man Enfield is. Help me and I'll take you to him."

The fuse slowly burned down.

Diana shook her head. "I can't believe you two." She turned and hurled the dynamite into the night.

In the lingering glow, both men turned their eyes from her, to each other. With one motion, they each rose, levelling their weapons at each other. It would be mutual suicide.

But she was fresh—she was faster. She could save one of them.

Diana levelled her rifle and shot Walter. Turn to 175.
Diana levelled her rifle and shot Josiah. Turn to 180.

171

Walter ducked into the nearest shack. It had clearly been abandoned far longer than the few months of the town's recent troubles; the door nearly fell off its hinges as he swung it open. He waited inside, heart pounding as the vampires searched the camp. Their voices rose in rage and confusion. They must not have spotted him.

But they would be here in moments. He moved to the back of the shack and kicked out a loose board, trusting that the noise the vampires were making would more than cover the sound of the splintering wood.

Behind, he heard Masters' voice, calling out commands and threats. Walter slipped out through the gap in the boards, twisting his scarecrow-thin body through the narrow opening. He froze. A vampire was mere feet away, its back to him.

The thing was examining another abandoned shack, but in a moment it would turn to him. If he fired his gun, he could easily bring it down, but he would give away his position, and the entire horde of them would be upon him in moments.

Barely daring to breathe, Walter held still. The vampire was close enough that Walter could have hit him with a shovel, had he one to hand.

"Hey! Hey boss, over here! It's Professor Enfield. He's in the mine!" One of the vampires shouted.

"What?" Masters snarled. "Out of my way."

Yes. Now would be the moment. He had to get to the detonator!

The vampire looked up, his attention riveted on the mine. As the vampire began to move, Walter moved also, timing his steps so that each footfall landed with one of the vampire's own.

In moments, he was able to get out of sight behind a tumbled down wall. The shack he needed was feet away. He had made it. But was he in time?

Walter vanished into the shack that held his detonator. Turn to 156.

172

"You have people waiting for you back home," Josiah said.

Diana gave a confused laugh. "The only person I'm waiting for is right here," she said, taking Garland's arm.

Josiah's brow furrowed.

Diana turned and said, "We can't leave you to face these things on your own. Right, Garland?"

Garland missed a beat, then laughed nervously and said, "No, of course not! We'll help you, of course." He nodded vigorously.

"But—" Josiah started.

"Enough," Diana cut him off with a wave of her hand. "What now? We won't be safe here forever."

Nearby, flames began to lick up the side of the mill building. Turn to 179.

173

Walter stumbled back, his panicked mind casting about for escape. He had planned for this. What was the plan? How could Masters have survived? He had been so careful.

Swearing, Walter ducked into the nearest shack. He kicked out the back wall and took two long steps to the ridge at the edge of camp. Without hesitation, he threw himself down the steep downslope; they would not look for him here.

"Korse!" Masters' howl echoed across the hills. More vampires' cries answered their leader's. Walter had killed many with the explosion, but not all. Yet Diana's wagon had held plenty of dynamite, and he had one more explosion waiting for them. This one he might not survive himself, but what did it matter, as long as he took Masters with him?

Once he was out into open air, he hung for what seemed like an eternity. Then he hit the ground sliding. His coat caught most of the fury of the hillside, rocks and roots tearing at it as if eager to claw the flesh beneath. Instinctively he tried to grab things to slow his fall—his broken right hand hit a rock and he blanched in pain, nearly blacking out.

He was sliding too fast, uncontrolled… He twisted, spreading out his limbs to break his fall against the earth. The pain from his wrist was nearly lost in the tearing across his whole body.

Yet soon his sliding slowed as the land evened out. Without pausing to catch his breath, he curled up onto his feet and half-ran, half-clambered at a perpendicular down the hillside, moving to the cover of a few scraggly trees.

He paused for breath behind the first tree and looked back. He had made it just in time. As he watched, several figures appeared at the top of the slope, outlined against the sky. They looked down from the mining camp, heads turning left and right in vain searching motions.

Walter took a few deep, quick breaths, trying to gather his strength. The time in captivity had left him weaker than he'd realized, and his knees trembled with exertion. But he wasn't licked yet.

He was under a grove of dry junipers now, some of the only trees in the valley. The smell of juniper bark surrounded him. He moved, staying in the cover of trees. When he was as close to the mill building as he could get, he glanced up. Seeing no watchers, he dashed across the short distance. With little more noise than a shadow, he ascended the stairs.

He paused at the back door. He could hear the vampires still tearing apart the mining camp up the hill, and others starting down the hill. The rage in their voices made it clear they were out for blood, after the blow he had struck them.

Walter smiled, and entered the mill. The building was dark and quiet, but he could smell the dynamite he'd lined against all the walls. And—something else…

"Put your hands up," Marshal da Silva said, and Walter heard the click of a pistol. Turn to 160.

"You have a child on the way," Josiah said, just loudly enough that she alone could hear.

Diana's eyes widened. Her hand drifted to her belly, where it lingered. "How… how did you know?" she asked.

Josiah smiled. "I've known for a while. It's writ all over you, woman. The horse is tied up down by the church. Now take yer man and git out of here."

Diana blinked rapidly, then threw her arms around Josiah's shoulders. Her face was lowered when she pulled away, but Josiah thought he could see a glint of moonlight reflecting on a tear-stained cheek beneath the rim of her hat. She clapped him on the shoulder and then turned to Garland.

Josiah watched as the two lovers disappeared between the trees. His stomach churned. Had there been a time, one day, when he could have had what they had? A time when his wife was still alive, when his daughter still had the chance for a happy life, when he could have been a simple man with simple problems?

He turned to look at the mill building. Flames were licking up the side of it, and vampires stood back and cheered as the dynamite inside began to detonate in sharp, explosive pops.

That time, if it had ever existed, was long gone. Josiah clenched his jaw. He would have to make sure these two had time to make their getaway.

He turned his face toward the darkened houses below and set his legs into the kind of long stride that eats up ground.

Diana followed Garland into the darkness. Turn to 176.

Diana levelled her rifle and shot Walter. Her shot rang out—loud in the sudden stillness. Josiah held, his gun trained on the thin man. Walter's face twitched. His hand came away from his chest… bloody. His cheeks twisted in a grimace. His gun slipped from weak fingers.

Korse looked at Diana, whose gun still smoked. His lips turned slightly. Then he took a step, staggered, and fell.

His body fell nearly twelve feet from the top of the stamp to the bottom.

Diana swore again and rushed over to his side. As she got there, Josiah joined her, levelling his gun at the younger man's head. Diana shoved Josiah's gun aside.

"What?" the marshal demanded.

"Damn it, step back!" Diana swore. She slapped Walter's face a few times.

The killer's eyes were rolling beneath their lids. His neck twitched, turning his head from side to side. He wasn't dead yet, but blood pulsed from his chest in a slow, even rhythm.

"Where is he?" Diana demanded. She shook Walter's unresponsive form, then slapped his face again. "Where is Garland!?"

The murderer's eyes opened once, briefly. His eyes, a bright, feverish blue, locked with hers. He laughed, but the laugh turned to a choke as he coughed up blood. His blue eyes rolled up in his head, showing only the whites. His limbs continued to twitch.

Diana dropped the man's head and swore. She stood and kicked the dying man, but got no response.

Josiah's strong hand settled gently on her arm. "We have to go."

The shouting of the vampire mob was close now. Too close for safety.

Diana nodded. She followed, and Josiah led her out the back door. They ran low and quiet. As they came under the shadows of the junipers, Josiah stopped Diana. In the darkness, he could see tears standing on her cheeks.

Walter rolled over, seeing white and feeling nothing but pain. Turn to 168.
Diana watched as the vampires descended on the mill. Turn to 163.

176

Diana followed Garland into the darkness. He led her downhill, through the junipers, and out into the moonlight near a narrow trail.

"Where are we going?" Diana asked. "The horse is…"

Garland looked back at her through his owlish glasses. After a moment, he said, "I know a safe way into town. Don't worry."

As they walked, Diana regarded the man she hadn't seen in three months. It seemed like a lifetime ago. His face had the same youthful good looks that had charmed her then, the same tousled hair. But something was different about him. He had seen things.

Garland raised a hand to stop her. He crept forward to look out over a large rock at the town. He nodded. "Looks clear. Let's rest a moment. We need to run the last leg."

Diana sat down, leaning next to him against the stone.

"Are you going to tell me what happened here?" She asked, touching his arm.

He paused and turned to meet her eyes, but his were black in the darkness. She couldn't see what he was feeling.

"Diana…" he said. "I'm so glad you found me. Walter promised he would get you to me, but I was getting worried."

"He did?" Diana asked, her brows drawing together.

Garland nodded with a smile. "He was very helpful. It was worth it to get you back."

"I was worried too," Diana replied, but her mind was already moving on. "Listen…" she said, thinking of the tiny life growing in her womb. "We need to talk about… You need to know that…"

He looked at her, unblinking.

Diana took a deep breath. "I'm carrying your child."

Garland seemed to rock in the darkness. His mouth opened and closed. Then he stood abruptly. "You have to go!" There was an edge of panic in his voice.

"Garland?" Diana asked, standing. "Is everything alright?"

"Please… hurry. You have to leave. You have to get away—" His voice was strained, and his face twisted as if in pain.

Diana took a step back. "What do you mean?"

The young professor stopped, his whole body going rigid. Then he started nodding cheerfully, as if in agreement with himself. When he spoke, it was in a changed tone. "No… yes… yes, actually. Yes, this will work perfectly."

Diana said, "Garland… you're scaring me."

"Diana!" Garland said, taking her hand and gripping it hard. "There's someone I want you to meet. Someone you must meet! This is better than you can know!"

Taking her hand tightly, he pulled her along. Diana, gasping, followed.

Josiah looked upon the cross. Turn to 177.

177

Josiah looked upon the cross. It had been easy to sneak down into town. Where better to await his enemies than here? In the church, he would make his final stand.

He had found a single candle burning in the church, and he dared not light more. In the illumination of that dim glow, shadows danced across the savior's limp and hanging form.

"Forgive me, Father, for I have sinned. I have taken the lives of others, when judgement should be yours and yours alone. I have… I have carried hatred in my heart. I have wanted that which was not mine to have."

Josiah paused. Tears stung at his eyes.

While breathing, he unconsciously flexed his left hand, then turned to look at the pain there. The spider bite from the night before was swollen and red, his fingers growing almost too thick to pull the trigger of a gun. The whole hand throbbed with pain.

"I…" Josiah was about to say more when he heard the sound of voices outside the church. One voice rose above the others, snarling commands. William Masters.

"Prepare to take me into your house, oh Lord," Josiah whispered. He crossed himself quickly and moved to the shadows in the corners of the church.

"Find them!" Sheriff Masters was crying out. "Tear every house apart if you have to!"

Josiah's heart pounded in his chest. How long would it be before they searched the church? Would he wait here cowering for them to come to him? No.

He took a deep breath, standing. The Lord was with him.

Josiah kicked open the front door of the church and stepped out. "Masters!" he bellowed.

The vampires in the street stopped in their tracks as all eyes turned to him. Sheriff Masters turned last. His ruined face was even more hideous than Josiah remembered it. But two red eyes still gleamed in the bloody mess left by the shotgun blast that had destroyed his face.

A cloud of insects seemed to hover in the air around the Sheriff, buzzing and shifting in a way that distracted the eye.

Masters called, "There you are! Hell, Joe, I was beginning to wonder if you skipped town on me. You gonna forgive me now, like you forgave old Reverend Zeke?" He snickered.

Josiah intoned, "Think not that I come to send peace on earth; I came not to send peace, but a sword." He raised his gun in both hands, levelling it at Sheriff Masters.

The vampire Sheriff took a step back, his face twisting in a snarl. "You think you can defeat me? It doesn't matter what you do now. We have him. We have everything."

Josiah drew his brows together. He shifted his eyes to look at the vampires behind Sheriff Masters. Two of them held a limp figure between them by the arms. One of them caught Josiah's eye and grinned, then grabbed the limp man's hair and pulled his head up.

Walter Korse. He was barely conscious, but a twitch in his limbs showed he was still alive.

Masters straightened. "It seems to me I owe you thanks, ol' pal. Hell, you brought him right to us! If you hadn't caught him, who knows how long it would have taken our folk to track him down."

"What do you care?" Josiah said.

"Hell, Joe! You don't know? I overestimated you..." Masters took a few steps forward with a mocking slowness. "Seems you and I did the world a favor, way back in the old days. Remember Red Bluff? 'Course you do. Well, I guess when we slaughtered all them Arahoca, that's what woke the Goddess. All that holy Blood spillin' into the earth, it did something. Brought her back." He grinned.

"But there was one Arahoca who lived, remember? That bitch of Abe's." Masters shook his head. "Should have killed her then. Saved us all a lot of trouble."

Josiah narrowed his eyes at Walter. "He's the last, then."

Masters spread his arms wide. "The man's not as dumb as he looks." In a low voice, he said, "When our Goddess drinks the last of the Arahoca Blood that walks this earth, she will return. She will rule the world... and we will be her Lords on this good earth."

Josiah met Masters' gaze. His ruined eyes were wholly and completely mad.

Masters stuck out his hand. "What do you say ol' pal? Want to join us? You and me, just like old times. We could rule the world."

Josiah steadied his aim and shot—at Walter Korse. Turn to 189.
Josiah steadied his aim and shot—at William Masters. Turn to 194.

<p style="text-align:center">

178

A prick of pain against her neck arrested Diana's attention. She turned— Garland stood behind her. He held her own knife to her throat. The knife she had placed in his hands.

Shock ran ice cold in Diana's veins. She spoke with a dry mouth. "Garland? What are you doing?"

The young man met her eyes, and tears were streaming down his face. "I'm sorry, Diana. I'm so sorry. I have no choice."

"Garland... I... what do you mean?" Diana said cautiously.

"She wants to meet you," Garland said in a strange voice. "She's going to lose Sheriff Masters, you see. I made a deal, back when Walter was alive," he said, with a little giggle. "Walter wanted the sheriff, and I wanted you. Now, she's losing the sheriff either way, so she's going to need a replacement."

"Garland..." Diana's mind spun. She couldn't believe what she was hearing. Her whole world seemed to turn sideways. She felt sick.

"This way, Diana. I can't wait till you meet her." Garland's voice shook with awe and reverence. "But first, give me that rifle." He jerked the gun out of her hand.

"Garland, I'm carrying your child!" The words burst out of her without thought or warning, and she regretted them as soon as they came out. She looked down, putting her hands to her belly, as if to cradle the small life still growing there. She couldn't look at the man who had sired that life.

The knife wavered, then slowly lowered.

"Go, Diana..." a choked whisper came from Garland. His hands shook. In a voice she hardly recognized, he said, "Go quickly, before I—before she—"

Diana took a step back, but he suddenly raised her rifle.

Garland laughed. "Wait! I have a better idea!" He nudged her with the tip of the rifle. Diana nervously watched his finger twitching near the trigger. What if he pulled it by accident? She spread her hands, willing him to move back. To relax. Could she still call for Josiah? Would he arrive in time?

"Yes… yes, this is perfect!" Garland stopped in his tracks. His eyes were alight with mad excitement. "Your child—our child—she can be the heir to power! She can be the host my Goddess needs!"

Diana recoiled, and Garland followed, keeping the gun close on her.

"Don't you see?" he ranted, "We will be the parents of the Goddess who will rule this world. We will be exalted above all others!"

"Go to hell," Diana said. She wanted to retch.

"Listen," Garland said, holding a hand up briefly. A chill wind blew across the desert night.

In the distance, Diana could hear voices. Shouting. Josiah. She glanced up at the high place where she was supposed to be, covering him. Her hands itched for the familiar stock of her rifle. If only she could get it back… He expected her to be there. He was counting on her!

"No… don't move," Garland said. He levelled the rifle at her heart.

In the distance, she heard Josiah bellow, "Masters! Face me like a man!"

Silence. It was too silent. The wind wailed mournfully. Her own sweat, now cold, rolled down her back.

Two shots, so close together they almost sounded like just one.

Garland relaxed, smiling. "There, it is done. Masters is gone, and your marshal too. Come then, my—our—Goddess awaits."

Day Three. Turn to 199.

179

Nearby, flames began to lick up the side of the mill building. Josiah glanced over, then took Diana by the elbow and said, "Come on!"

They hurried through the darkness beneath the juniper trees. A moment later, a series of explosions popped through the night. Behind them, the mill building collapsed while vampires all around it cheered.

As they paused, looking through the trees at the flames, Josiah absently massaged his left hand. The spider bite had gotten so bad the whole hand was red and swollen.

"Are you okay?" Diana asked in alarm.

Josiah looked down at his hand. "Don't worry about it."

Garland stepped closer. "Let me see?"

Josiah grumbled, but held out his hand.

Garland examined it for a moment, then let it drop. "I'm sorry…" he said.

"What do you mean," Josiah demanded, jerking his hand back.

"It's the bite of the insects that serve the Bled One… I… it cannot be good," Garland finished lamely.

Josiah swore and turned his attention back to the path ahead of them. "Nevermind. I'll deal with that when the time comes. Keep moving!"

They made their way down the far side of a hill, toward the outskirts of town. When they were out of sight from the vampires, Josiah stopped the small party. Turning to the professor, he said, "Enfield. You've got to know something about what's happening here. Who's behind it? How do we stop it?"

The professor's eyes darted back and forth between the marshal and Diana.

Diana touched his arm. "Please, Garland."

Enfield nodded. "I came here seeking a… an important archaeological find. A long path led me to this point. It was supposed to be… it was supposed to be the site of a temple to an ancient Aztec deity. Well, not Aztec exactly, but—"

"Get on with it!" Josiah growled.

Enfield licked his lips. "She is a Goddess of Blood. Of Death and… Eternal Life."

Josiah grunted, but said nothing.

"Of course, it was a mistake to come here." He glanced quickly at Diana, and away again. He sat down on a rock before continuing. "I believe I… I must have… woken her up."

"The Goddess?" Diana asked.

The young professor nodded. "She is called Tezoca, the Bled One."

Diana shook her head in amazement. "Sounds like something out of a bedtime story."

Josiah said, "This bedtime story will bite, if we're not careful."

Garland laughed nervously.

Josiah leaned in. "So how do we stop it?"

Garland chewed his lip, not meeting Josiah's gaze. "It's not… it's not that easy."

"There must be a way," Diana said gently.

Garland glanced at her, then looked away. "Perhaps." He shook his head. "I do not know if the Bled One can be killed. She was defeated a millennium ago by ancient heroes, but even their greatest magics could not destroy her, only contain her. And that took the blood and the devotion of an entire race of people."

Josiah and Diana looked at each other. "The Arahoca," Diana whispered.

Josiah swore, turning away. He kicked a pile of rocks down the slope in useless rage.

"You couldn't have known," Diana said.

"I knew," Josiah whispered, so softly Diana could barely hear him. "I knew it was wrong. All those deaths… when they trusted us. I should have stopped it."

The fire in the mill building cracked and popped; they could see its glow through the trees.

"We won't be safe here for long," Diana said. "Garland, there must be something we can do."

Garland nodded. "I suppose you could try to confront her... I... I would not recommend it."

"What do you mean?" Diana asked.

Garland lowered his head. "I have looked upon the Bled One... I have known her power..."

"I will destroy her," Josiah said. He stood above them, looking tall and dangerous in the glimmer of red light that shone through the trees.

"First, we must take care of Sheriff Masters," Josiah said. Turn to 191.

"Take me to this Goddess," Josiah said. Turn to 186.

180

Diana levelled her rifle and shot Josiah. The marshal gasped and grunted, his face hidden in the gloom. Walter laughed, a low, terrible sound that spread through the mill. Josiah's body made a scraping thud as it crumpled to the floor.

Diana almost moved to his side, but Walter beat her there. He swung down from the upper level with his good hand, moving quickly to Josiah. The marshal's eyes rolled. He tried to speak, but only blood came out. Walter patted him on the cheek. As Diana approached, he stood and turned to face her, his eyes gleaming in the darkness. "Come on."

Diana grabbed Walter's arm as he headed for the door. He was surprisingly light. "Where is Enfield? You owe me."

Walter gave her a fierce little smile, and said, "Don't worry, you can trust me. Come on, before they catch us."

Josiah was clawing at the floorboards as they slipped out the back of the mill building. Diana quenched her misgivings and followed Walter the short distance to the cover of a nearby Juniper grove.

"Mr. Korse?" a hesitant voice came from not far away.

Diana's breath caught in her throat. She knew that voice. "Garland?" She called.

"Diana?" he replied. A familiar, slight figure became visible through the trees, shuffling toward them. Professor Garland Enfield, at long last.

"There's your man," Walter said.

Diana stumbled forward; she and Garland fell into each other's embrace. "I thought I'd never see you again..." Diana whispered.

"Shh, shh... here I am," Garland replied, petting her hair. He smelled different, Diana noticed. There was sweat and smoke, but also fear, and... something else.

"You owe me. We had a deal." Walter's voice came harsh and sudden. He grabbed Garland's arm, interrupting their embrace.

Garland straightened his glasses.

"How do I kill Masters?" Walter hissed, shaking the professor's arm.

Garland blinked and flinched, trying to pull his arm away and failing. He glanced nervously from Walter to Diana. "Well... my best guess... I mean, I don't know for certain, but..."

"I don't have all day," Walter growled.

"I think, I'm pretty sure, I mean, that perhaps faith can kill him."

Walter dropped the professor's arm.

Garland rubbed his arm and straightened his glasses again. "I believe that… only one whose blows carry the power of the Almighty can hurt the Chosen. Otherwise…" he shook his head. "The Chosen of the Bled One are as she herself is… immune to the pull of death that is so strong upon the rest of us."

"Josiah had faith," Diana whispered. "That's how he was able to destroy the Reverend."

All three of them turned their attention back toward the mill building, which was now blackening beneath flames that licked it like a lover, while cheering vampires surrounded the building. A pop came as the fire reached one of the dynamite sticks, and part of the building blew out.

Walter swore hard, leaning on a tree.

Diana ground her teeth and ran a hand through her hair. She knew shooting the marshal had been a mistake. How could she have been so stupid?

"There must be another way!" Walter spun and grabbed the little professor by the ruff of his collar. "What is it!?"

"I- I-" Garland gasped.

"Walter!" Diana interrupted, "Leave him alone!"

"Dynamite? Would blowing him up do it?" Walter shook the young professor.

"I don't know! Maybe? Probably!"

Diana drew her gun and levelled it at Walter. "Let him go."

Walter clenched his jaw. Without looking at Diana, he slowly released Garland. "Get out of here. I'll finish this on my own." Walter knelt in the darkness and began scraping aside bark and dirt.

"What are you doing?" Diana asked, lowering her gun.

Walter stood again with a small pack. He grinned, but there was no humor in it. "A bit of dynamite left. I'm glad you brought so much."

Diana started, almost reaching for the bag that was once hers. But Garland tugged on her arm. "Come on, leave him be."

Diana backed away, until she could only see the whites of Walter's eyes in the darkness. She considered wishing him good luck, but couldn't bring herself to say the words.

Walter hefted the bag of dynamite. Turn to 192.
Diana followed Garland into the darkness. Turn to 187.

Walter crouched in the saloon, breathing hard. His back was up against one wall. He could hear them moving out there.

He risked a glance up through the window. Buildings up and down the street were on fire. The fires started by his dynamite had spread. It would be a miracle if, by morning, the whole town hadn't burned down.

But there—a flash of a face. Masters was still out there.

Walter swore. He had missed the bastard. And now, all his dynamite was gone.

Smoke began to gather, thick in the common room of the saloon. The fire must be catching in this building somewhere. Walter looked around, but he couldn't see where it was coming from yet.

"Walter Korse!" a voice hollered from the street outside.

Walter risked another glance out between wooden shutters. Sheriff Masters stood in the middle of the street, feet planted, thumbs hooked into his belt loops. A number of his vampires, ones who had been spared in the rain of dynamite, gathered around him. There were still so many…

Walter closed his eyes for just a moment. If the Lord had ever been there, he had never felt Him.

Masters called, "The way I figger it, yer plumb dead, Korse!"

Walter fingered his pistol with his one good hand. Then again, he thought, If the Lord had ever been watching over men such as the marshal, perhaps he would watch now.

"Tell ya what, son," Masters called. "On account of bein' good friends with your father, once, I'll give you a sportin' chance."

Walter closed his eyes again. He stood, fighting the urge to choke in the thickening smoke. He wrapped his fingers around the haft of his gun.

A prayer formed on his lips, and died there just as quickly. No God had ever watched his footsteps. No God would have let his mother die the way she did. And there was no God to punish the men who did it.

No, that job fell to Walter Korse. If he was doomed, well, that was just fate's cruel joke.

Masters shouted, "You come on out, and I'll tell my boys not to shoot. It'll be you and me. Man to man. Whad'ya say?"

Walter kicked open the door. A host of guns levelled at him, as the remainder of Masters' lackeys took aim at his own narrow chest.

Masters grinned. "I knew you'd see sense boy." He stepped forward, looking Walter up and down. "Come here, lemme get a look at you."

Walter's skin crawled, but he forced himself to remain still under the vampire sheriff's scrutiny.

"I see yer father in you," the sheriff said. "You got his eyes, but meaner. He was a good man, but boy, you got a rotten streak. Must have come from your mother's blood. Bad blood, that was. Injun blood."

"Don't you talk about my mother," Walter growled under his breath.

"What's that?" Masters said, cupping a hand to one ear. The crackling of flames all around them made it loud enough to cloak words, but Walter didn't feel like repeating himself. He tucked back his long coat, showing his left pistol.

Masters grinned. "Ah, you want to do that then, do ya? Make some space, boys!" The vampires began to back up, many of them lowering their weapons. "Twenty paces ought to do the trick, don't you think?" Masters said, and he began counting off paces.

Walter descended the steps to the street, watching Masters. The sheriff was going through the motions, but that's all it was. A secret smile played at the corner of his mouth. A chill went through Walter. Masters knew Walter's gun couldn't hurt him. There was only one way this duel could end.

The animal inside him wanted to scream, but Walter stepped up to take his place in the street. What choice did he have now? The wind blew, a hot wind that smelled of wood smoke. The saloon itself was on fire now, flames on both sides of the street.

His heart beat heavily, thudding inside his chest. "I'm sorry, Mother," he whispered. His skin itched where the killing bullet might land. His shirt felt tight across his chest. He flexed his fingers over his gun, suddenly keenly aware of every sense, perhaps for the last time.

Sheriff Masters, openly grinning now, finished counting out his paces. "You ready son?" he called.

A wind came down the street, howling with the heat of the burning town, and the smoke cleared for a moment. In the wake of that gust, a figure appeared, grey and indistinct in the shifting smoke.

Walter stared, and Masters stared, frowning. "Who's there?" Masters called, his brows knitting together.

Smoke billowed out of the burning buildings, obscuring the figure and street both. Some of the vampires shifted in the darkness, hands drifting toward guns, if they had them.

Another gust of wind cleared the street, and Marshal Josiah da Silva emerged from the smoke, suddenly close to them.

The marshal looked like hell warmed over. He limped, his face a mask of fury and pain. Blood soaked the front of his shirt in a wide red stain, spreading from a neat, black bullet hole. More blood ran down one cheek from a cut on his head; one eye was swollen nearly shut. His left hand was so swollen he could hardly move it.

But he came to a stop and planted his feet, forming a triangle with Walter and Masters. The marshal's eyes flicked from one to the other, dark and full of fury. He said nothing, but swept back his coat with a sure, uninjured right hand, revealing one large pistol which gleamed in the firelight. The fire cracked and popped in the buildings around him, but he neither turned nor flinched.

Masters glanced at Walter uncertainly, and both men shifted slightly, squaring off to complete the triangle with the marshal.

Walter looked from one opponent to the other. Each man's hand hovered above his gun. Slowly, so as not to startle anyone, Walter withdrew a locket from his breast pocket. The locket gleamed in the firelight. She had given it to him. As he held it, he could see the life he could have had, the life he never could have had.

Slowly, he turned the key of the locket, and tossed it out into the street, where it began to play soft music, barely audible over the crackling fire.

Josiah stiffened as he heard that music. Turn to 190.

182

Josiah came to, a splitting ache in the back of his head. He was lying on dirt. It was on his face, in his hair. He sat up. The world swam. He spat dust from his lips.

Slowly, his vision cleared. They were watching him. How many, he couldn't tell.

He looked around. Walter Korse was not far away, seeming impossibly tall. In the other direction… Sheriff Masters. They seemed to be waiting.

Josiah felt for his gun belt. It was there. One gun was missing, but the other felt comfortably heavy under his hand.

All around, vampires watched. They stood straight or hunched, eyes on him. Some smiled, some gnawed their own tongues in anticipatory hunger. Their clothes were filthy and torn, their hats missing or askew.

They seemed to be on the main street. He could see the church at the end of the street. But many of the buildings were on fire, their heat pressing in on him from all sides. Thick black smoke coiled into the sky. What had happened while he'd been out?

Josiah pulled himself to his feet with a grunt. Korse's eyes flicked to him, then back to Masters. Masters regarded both of them and grinned.

As Josiah watched, Korse and Masters both began to move—slowly, one step at a time. They were backing away from Josiah. Moving to form a triangle with him. The vampires all around backed up, avoiding the fire while spreading out to give the three men room.

Korse brushed back his coat to reveal his gun. Masters licked his lips and flexed his fingers, hovering them just over his weapon.

Josiah shifted his weight. What had Korse done? And why? The world swam, but he managed to take a few steps. He didn't know much, but he knew what to do in a duel. He moved to even out the triangle. Meeting the eyes of his opponents, he swept back his jacket to reveal his pistol.

Masters looked at him, a hunger in his eyes. Then back to Korse, like a boy in a candy shop, unable to make up his mind. The vampires behind him tittered, loud in the eerie silence.

Korse looked over to Josiah. His eyes burned. Josiah couldn't read them. Slowly, so as not to startle anyone, Korse reached into his breast pocket and pulled something out. It gleamed silver in the moonlight.

He twisted a key, and music began to play. With a soft throw, he tossed the locket out into the street between them. A small gust of wind raised a dust devil as the music rose.

Josiah stiffened as he heard that music. Turn to 190.

183

Josiah drew and shot Walter Korse. The murderer's eyes went wide with pain and surprise, but Josiah didn't linger to watch. Quick as a flash, he spun and fired on Sheriff Masters.

His gun clicked empty.

Masters grinned. "Well, well, well… You didn't let him get a hand on your guns did you? Maybe he only wanted you to have one shot. Or is this just chance—forget to reload? You never were that smart, were you?"

Walter staggered to one knee, clutching the wound in his chest. Then, slowly, he toppled to one side, his eyes following Josiah reproachfully.

Josiah grit his teeth. He lowered his gun slowly. One bead of sweat trickled down his temple. "Get it over with," he said.

"What's the hurry?" Masters said, moving closer to Josiah. The vampires watching them cackled with perverse laughter. "After all, you're going to be my own brother soon. Why should I damage the goods?"

Josiah's brows drew together.

"Josiah," Masters hooted, "Don't tell me you didn't know? Hadn't you figured it out yet?"

At this distance, Josiah could make out the cloud of insects hovering around the vampiric sheriff. They were all over him now, a swarm: centipedes crawling across his flesh, flies buzzing around his head, and too many others to name.

Josiah's blood ran cold. "The spider bite…" he whispered. Even now, his left hand throbbed in pain.

"Give the man a goddam medal!" Sheriff Masters howled. "That's right; that was one of *her* spiders in the jailhouse. She gave you her gift. And a gift it is, old pal, a gift it is. You'll understand once you turn."

"Never," Josiah growled.

Masters laughed. "What are you going to do about it?"

Josiah's fingers tightened on the useless weapon in his hands. Without bullets, it was no better than a stick of wood. He growled, "I'd die first."

Masters grinned, "Even that won't save you now. The poison has reached too deep. You'll come back. In fact…" he looked thoughtful. "I wouldn't want you causing any more trouble before the change. Maybe it would be best to speed you on your way."

The Sheriff lifted his weapon. Josiah raised his head—and found himself looking down the barrel of Masters' gun. That black eye seemed to wink at him, promising oblivion.

"'Night Joe," Masters said.

A gunshot rang out. Every nerve in Josiah's body flared—and then he realized the black opening of Masters' gun was falling away. Masters fell, a gunshot red and empty bored into the side of his head. The body caught on fire, a ghostly scream hanging on the breeze as the fire rapidly spread down the length of the sheriff's body.

Josiah looked over. Walter Korse lay on his side, gun held tightly in one hand, his face white with exertion. As Josiah looked more closely, he realized it was his own second gun that Walter held.

The vampires all around howled and backed away from the burning corpse of their leader. "You'll pay for this," one of them growled, and then the lot of them turned and ran.

Walter Korse looked at Josiah and gave him a tight grin. He said, "I guess I had faith after all... not in your God... but enough." He sighed and let his head fall back, the strength leaving him.

Josiah walked over to the dying man. "Why?" he asked.

Walter coughed, blood coming to his lips. His face was deathly white, and beaded with sweat from the last fierce efforts of his life. "He... killed my mother."

Josiah sat next to the murderer who had saved his life. A night breeze blew, hot from the flames.

"Got them all. I... got them all," Walter said. His voice was thick and slurring, but Josiah listened closely as the man intoned, "Abe Korse, Roy Johnson, Curtis Leney, Bo Bansen." Walter coughed, more blood coming to his lips. His mouth moved soundlessly for a moment, then he continued, "Toby McCann... now that was a hard one. Dave Hayes, who fell from his horse, the bastard... 'fore I got to him... now Sheriff William Masters. It's done. I got 'em all."

Josiah clenched his jaw. He touched the dying man's hand. "You did," he said gruffly.

Walter Korse pressed Josiah's gun into his hand, then let out a death rattle. His body shook and fell still. His eyes stared glassily at the night sky far above. With one hand, Josiah reached out and closed Walter's eyes. Let him rest, at last.

Josiah stood. He looked at the far horizon, where the red light of dawn was already starting to show. If it was true, what Masters had said, he didn't have long.

Day Three. Turn to 199.

184

"Maybe we should go… thank you," Diana said. She looked down, not meeting Josiah's eyes. But he stepped forward and took her by the shoulders.

"You and your man go. You know where the horse is hidden. Get as far away from here as you can ride. Settle down and live long, happy lives, and never think of Affliction again."

Diana blinked, and two hot tears rolled down her cheeks. She grabbed the marshal in a quick embrace and kissed him lightly on his stubbled cheek.

Then she turned and took Garland's hand. "Let's go."

"Follow me," Garland said. "I know a way." He paused briefly to look at Josiah, then nodded his head and turned away.

Josiah watched as the two lovers disappeared between the trees. His stomach churned. Had there been a time, one day, when he could have had what they had? A time when his wife was still alive, when his daughter still had the chance for a happy life, when he could have been a simple man with simple problems?

He turned to look at the mill building. Flames were licking up the side of it, and vampires stood back and cheered as the dynamite inside began to detonate in sharp, explosive pops.

That time, if it had ever existed, was long gone. Josiah clenched his jaw. He would have to make sure these two had time to make their getaway.

He turned his face toward the darkened houses below and set his legs into the kind of long stride that eats up ground.

Diana followed Garland into the darkness. Turn to 176.

185

Diana struggled up the slope, panting and swearing. The murderer had said she could find Professor Enfield by the old mill. Professor Garland Enfield. Her man, father of her child. Or at least, he would be, in about six more months. Diana placed a hand on her belly as she moved. It was just starting to swell, not so as any man might notice, but she could tell. She could tell based on how hard it was, taut and firm beneath her skin.

How would he react? What would he say? She paused to catch her breath and looked back down at the town. Vampires were ransacking the place, turning it upside down in their search for their quarry.

What would become of Marshal da Silva? She felt a lump in her throat. She had come to like the man… but Korse had promised he would come to no harm. For whatever that was worth.

Once she found Garland, she promised herself, she would search for Josiah, would save him if needed.

"I'll only be away a moment, Joe," she whispered.

In the end, Professor Enfield surprised her. "Diana?" his voice came, querulous and thin, from the juniper grove behind her as she cautiously ascended the rear steps of the old mill.

"Garland?" she hissed softly, whirling to look into the trees.

He emerged from the shadows. He looked leaner than he had when she last saw him. More drawn. Could it only be three months ago?

She approached and caught him in a rough embrace. He blinked and returned it awkwardly. Eventually Diana released him and Garland adjusted his glasses, glancing about.

"Are you okay?" Diana asked the young professor. He nodded absently. "Yourself?" he asked. She smiled, then her face turned serious. "Damn you for disappearing on me! I thought you—I thought…"

Garland patted her shoulder and said, "It's okay, we're together now."

"Where were you? What have you been doing?" Diana demanded.

Garland said, "Let's get somewhere safe. We'll have time to talk. Follow me." He took her hand and led her into the trees.

Diana followed Garland into the darkness. Turn to 193.

186

"Take me to this Goddess," Josiah said.

Garland watched him with wide eyes. Belatedly, he nodded. "Okay!" he said through dry lips.

"Well?" Josiah demanded. "Which way?"

Garland jerked and started shuffling toward the town. "There is a secret tunnel… but no… they use that one too much. We would be seen."

"Make up your mind, Professor," Josiah growled. Diana shot him a dangerous glance, but he ignored it.

The professor mumbled and muttered for a moment, hands tugging on his hair. At last, he said, "This way," and began walking up, through the trees away from the town.

"Garland?" Diana asked. The professor did not reply. Diana and Josiah followed quickly, before losing him in the darkness.

"Can he be trusted?" Josiah hissed quietly to Diana as they followed.

"Of course he can!" Diana shot back, but Josiah thought he could see a flicker of doubt in her eyes.

They followed the little man uphill for several minutes. As they approached the edge of the juniper grove—and the limit of their cover—Josiah grabbed the professor by the shoulder. "Where are we going?" he demanded.

Garland looked up, as though seeing him for the first time. Trancelike, he raised one arm to point up the mountain. Josiah followed the gesture, and a chill shiver went through him. Arahoca Canyon. Called Ghost Canyon since that day.

"It's where I established the dig site. Where I first made contact. It's how I first found the temple," Garland said.

Josiah swore under his breath.

"What's wrong?" Diana asked.

"I know where he's taking us. We'll have to go through the mining camp to get to the trail going back to that place."

"Is it safe?" Diana asked.

Josiah gritted his teeth, and peered out through the trees. "I'll go check. Diana, take your rifle and climb up to that rock." He pointed. "From there, you should have a good view of the mining camp. If it looks like I'm in trouble, use your own judgement."

Diana nodded, though the knit of her brows told Josiah she didn't entirely like this plan. "And if it's clear?" she asked.

"I'll hoot like an owl," Josiah said. He let out a soft hooting sound that startled Diana with how natural it seemed. "Are we good?"

Diana nodded reluctantly. Josiah clapped her arm and crept off. He paused at the edge of the tree cover, then half-ran, half-scrambled his way quickly up the steep hillside ahead of them, exposed in the moonlight.

Diana eyed the rock. It would be an easy climb, but she didn't like how far it would take her from Enfield. She pulled out a knife and handed it to Enfield, saying, "I won't be far away. If you need to protect yourself... well, let's just hope you don't need to. But this will help."

Garland nodded as he took the knife, his face ashen. Diana turned to regard the rock face, mentally calculating her hand and foot holds.

A prick of pain against her neck arrested Diana's attention. Turn to 178.

187

Diana followed Garland into the darkness. He led her along a path sloping downhill, back toward the town. The junipers had an earthy scent all around her, but she could still smell something off. It was probably this whole town.

"Think he has any chance?" Diana asked.

Garland shook his head. "No…" he said softly. "This way," he said, and let them out from under the cover of the juniper trees, into the moonlight. The town glowed below them, not far away now. Diana could hear several pops in the distance, and as she looked back, she saw explosions in the town. Walter…

"Come on," Garland said, pulling her arm.

"Where are we going?" Diana asked.

Garland looked back at her through his owlish glasses. After a moment, he said, "I know a safe way. Don't worry."

Diana didn't know what to make of this, but she followed. He led them into a little gully which, it appeared, would bring them closer to the town while keeping them out of sight.

As they walked, Diana regarded the man she hadn't seen in three months. It seemed like a lifetime ago. His face had the same youthful good looks that had charmed her then, the same tousled hair. But something was different about him. He had seen things.

Garland raised a hand to stop her and crept forward to look out over a large rock at the town. He nodded. "Looks clear. Let's rest a moment. We need to run the last leg."

Diana sat down, leaning next to him against the stone.

"Are you going to tell me what happened here?" She asked, touching his arm.

He paused and turned to meet her eyes, but his were black in the darkness. She couldn't see what he was feeling.

"Diana…" he said. "I'm so glad you found me. Walter promised he would get you to me, but I was getting worried."

"He did?" Diana asked, her brows drawing together.

Garland nodded with a smile. "He was very helpful. He made me help him too, but it was worth it to get you back."

"I was worried too," Diana replied, but her mind was already moving on. "Listen…" she said, thinking of the tiny life growing in her womb. "We need to talk about… You need to know that…"

He looked at her, unblinking.

Diana took a deep breath, and the words suddenly poured out of her, "I'm carrying your child."

Garland seemed to rock in the darkness. His mouth opened and closed. Then he stood abruptly. "You have to go!" There was an edge of panic in his voice.

"Garland?" Diana asked, standing. "Is everything alright?"

"Please… hurry. You have to leave. You have to get away—" His voice was strained, and his face twisted as if in pain.

Diana took a step back. "What do you mean?"

The young professor stopped, his whole body going rigid. Then he started nodding cheerfully, as if in agreement with himself. When he spoke, it was in a changed tone. "No… yes… yes, actually. Yes, this will work perfectly."

Diana said, "Garland… you're scaring me."

"Diana!" Garland said, taking her hand and gripping it hard. "There's someone I want you to meet. Someone you must meet! This is better than you can know!"

Taking her hand tightly, he pulled her along. Diana, gasping, followed.

Walter crouched in the saloon, breathing hard. Turn to 181.

"We'll stay and help," Diana said. "I don't think we have any choice."

Garland shifted nervously.

Josiah gave Diana a level look, which she returned unflinching. "I can't promise any of us make it out of this alive."

Garland touched Diana's sleeve. "Perhaps the man has a point, Diana. There's not much more we can do here anyway…"

Diana frowned. "If we don't do it, who will?"

Garland looked at Josiah, but did not speak.

"Fine," Diana said, "It's settled. So what's our plan? We won't be safe here forever."

Nearby, flames began to lick up the side of the mill building. Turn to 179.

Josiah steadied his aim and shot—at Walter Korse. The gunshot cracked and the bullet sang true. It hit the dying killer directly in the heart. His head rolled, and he coughed up blood. Then he let out a death rattle, and the strength left his body. The two vampires holding Korse let the body slip to the ground.

The vampires all stared in disbelief. Then Masters raged, "What have you done?"

"Take him to your bitch now," Josiah said, holstering his gun. Korse was dead. At last, the killer was dead. Cora was avenged.

Masters tensed with anger. Then he smiled. "Fool. You think you have stopped her return? No—you have completed it! The last of the Arahoca Blood has been spilled. The Blood returns. After all these years, the last of the Blood returns." Masters gave a wide grin.

Josiah narrowed his eyes, glancing at Walter's corpse. The murderer's blood seeped into the thirsty dust of the street.

"Her return is final now, and nothing can stop it. It would have been faster had she been able to drink of him herself, but no matter," Masters said. "Best of all, you did it! You will be exalted in her eyes."

Josiah spat a curse under his breath. "Not if I get to her first."

Masters burst into laughter. "Same ol' Joe. Never did know what side the sun comes up. Don't you get it? You're already touched! That was one of her spiders what bit you in the jailhouse. By this time tomorrow, you'll be my brother again, one way or t'other."

Josiah's left hand throbbed in time with his heartbeat. His blood ran cold in his veins. "No…" he whispered.

Masters grinned, his skull-face terrible in the torchlight. "She gave you her gift." He raised his arms, and buzzing insects rose from his flesh to hover all around him, their hum throbbing horribly through the night.

"And a gift it is," Masters said softly, "Make no mistake. You'll understand. It's only a matter of time now. You'll understand once you turn."

Josiah swayed. The world seemed to spin around him. He grasped for words and intoned, "'Blessed are the dead who die in the Lord. They will rest from their labor, for their deeds will follow them.'"

Masters laughed, "Oh, not you, Joe. Not you and not me. We have a different fate in store for us."

Josiah straightened. He swept back his coat to reveal his gun again. "Explain it to our Father."

Masters planted his feet, sweeping back his own jacket. His skeletal hand hovered over his black-handled revolver. "Any last words, Joe?"

Josiah drew steel.

Masters drew—but fast as he was, he wasn't fast enough.

Josiah's gun roared, and he felt the power of the Spirit move through him. The Sheriff's ruined mouth opened, but he had no time to scream. The bullet caught him between the eyes and threw his head back.

Fire spread from the wound, consuming the dark Sheriff's face, skull, and body. The insects buzzed horribly and fled, scattering from the flames.

Josiah bowed his head and intoned a prayer. His left hand throbbed, but the Lord stood by his side, and he would not fear.

He heard a sound. His eyes flew open. He could see the other vampires in the light of the flames, backing away slowly. Their faces were masks of fear and awe. As one, they turned and ran.

Josiah sank to his knees. He lifted his swollen hand. Warmed by the heat from the burning body, he wept.

Day Three. Turn to 199.

<h2 style="text-align:center">190</h2>

Josiah stiffened as he heard that music. It was a tune both haunting and familiar. His wife had given him the locket the day they married. He had given it to his daughter Cora, after his wife was gone. And she had given it to this man… to Walter… to her killer.

The music played, causing Josiah to rock in his boots. How long had it been since he'd heard this song through? In the smoke he smelled her hair. In the crackling of flames, he heard her laughter.

How many mistakes had been made? Where had it all gone wrong? The music started to slow. The locket was winding down.

Why had she given it to him of all people?

Walter looked at Josiah with unreadable eyes. Masters scowled, glancing back and forth between his two opponents.

As the music reached its final notes, Josiah took a deep breath and let it out. He knew what to do.

The music stopped. Both other men reached for their guns.

Josiah drew and shot Walter Korse. Turn to 183.
Josiah drew and shot Sheriff Masters. Turn to 195.

"First, we must take care of Sheriff Masters," Josiah said. "Come with me." He turned and started moving away through the trees, so quickly and silently that Diana nearly lost sight of him before she could pull Garland to his feet and move.

"What's your plan?" she asked, when the hard-faced marshal stopped at the edge of the grove to look out at the town.

Josiah pointed, "You, take your rifle, and take position on top of the saloon. I'll challenge Masters in the street. Cover me. I'll take him down, just make sure no one attacks me from behind."

Diana nodded, unslinging her rifle from behind her shoulder.

Garland asked, "What about me?"

Josiah jerked one hand. "Stick with her. You're no good to me dead."

"Here, take this. Stay out of sight, but if you have to, use it." Diana pulled out a knife and placed it in his hands. The professor nodded.

The three of them moved as quickly and quietly as they could across the open ground toward the town. The moon was high and bright, and they feared being spotted at any moment, but no cry came up from the vampire townsfolk.

As they approached the graveyard, Josiah gestured toward the saloon building and said, "Go!"

Diana hesitated, then threw her arms around his neck for a quick hug. "Be careful," she said, then let him go.

"You too," Josiah said gruffly.

Diana watched for a moment as Josiah moved away, low and quick, until he disappeared around a corner.

A prick of pain against her neck arrested Diana's attention. Turn to 178.

Walter hefted the bag of dynamite. The woman and her man vanished into the woods. Good riddance. They couldn't help him where he was going.

He crept toward the edge of the juniper grove. He felt his injuries whispering at the edge of his consciousness, and he told them to wait. It wouldn't be much longer now. Masters was within his reach. He could rest when he was dead.

The vampires were leaving the mill building now, returning to the town in a herd, Sheriff Masters at their head. Walter skirted around them, matching their pace and direction, but staying under the cover of the trees. He couldn't charge straight at them. He'd be outgunned and outnumbered. He needed cover. He needed the town.

When he reached the tree line, he hunkered down and waited. The vampires he stalked slowly diffused into the town. Ironic, how the hunters had become the hunted. Soon, he judged, it would be clear.

Gathering his strength, he prepared to dart across the open ground. The church was closest to him. He could already see some vampires moving into the building… but the graveyard near it could provide good cover.

Now.

He jumped to his feet and sprinted in the moonlight. His heart pounded; he expected a gunshot, a shout. The silence held, and Walter slid down among the gravestones.

More vampires were approaching. He lay between two graves and let them pass, so close he could hear their voices. Only once they entered the church did he look around. Grinning, he pulled two sticks of dynamite from his bag. He crept up next to the church, lit the dynamite, and threw it in the window, breaking the stained glass as he did so.

As shouts of alarm rose behind him, he darted across the graveyard, jumping between the stones.

An explosion roared, ripping apart the church inside. Shouts and cries rose from throughout the town.

"I am among you now," Walter whispered, "And you will know fear."

He ducked between two buildings and waited in the darkness as pounding feet passed him on the street. Then he lit a stick of dynamite. He held it, watching the fuse, until it had burned down nearly to his hand. With each flicker of its flame, he felt his own life flickering in his hand. It would be so easy just to keep holding it…

He leaned out into the street and tossed it at a group of them who had gathered near the church. The explosion tore through bodies, hurling members of the group in all directions.

Ghostlike, Walter vanished back between the buildings.

"You there!" A vampire who was standing a little outside the town spotted Walter moving behind the buildings. He must have been some cowslick before he turned; he still wore the chaps and hat of a fellow who thought highly of himself.

The vampire drew steel, and Walter ducked between two buildings. A shot rang out, sending up splinters of wood from where it barely missed him.

More shouts now, coming from in front. He wrenched open a door on the nearest building and ducked inside. He couldn't see anything in the darkness, until he lit another stick of dynamite. In the faint glow of its fuse, he could see coffins all around. Some were finished, some still had yet to be finished. Several child-sized coffins in the corner of the room caught his eye, looking too small for any human to fit inside.

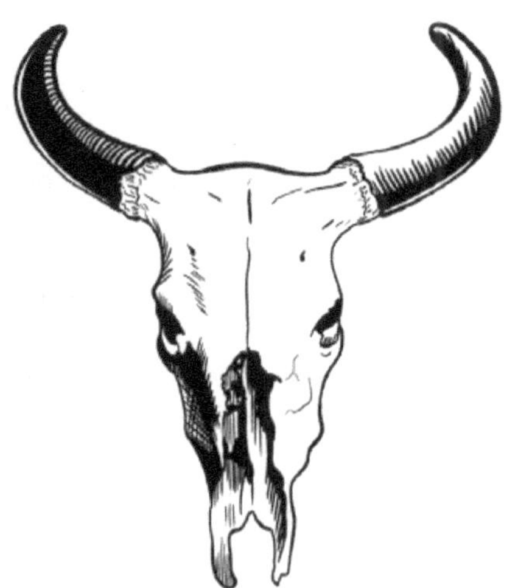

"In there!" a voice called. Walter saw several figures racing past the window. He threw open the door as he heard footsteps approaching it. The leading vampire stopped in surprise.

"Catch!" Walter said, and tossed the smallest coffin to the man. The vampire, startled, caught it by reflex. Something rattled inside.

Walter winked, closed the door, and heard the explosion. It blew in the side of the undertakers building, knocking him back.

He felt something crack under him and came to a rest, his body screaming in pain. He shook his head and scrambled over broken coffins, unsure where he was going. He couldn't hear anything. He had to find Masters, before he got cornered.

Without thinking, Walter reached into the bag, scooped up the last sticks of dynamite, and lit them. A vampire loomed in his vision in one door. He tossed the one with the shortest fuse at the figure and ran the other direction.

He slammed through a door to find himself in a dead-end room. An office, only one door in or out—the one he had just come through. Now he could hear the shouted curses of vampires behind him after another explosion. The uninjured ones still coming closer.

Walter took a few steps back, eying a large window that opened out onto the main street. He ran, gaining speed with each pace, and leaped—his momentum carried him through the window. He didn't even feel the glass as it broke, he just heard its tinkle as the shards came to rest all around him.

He landed heavily, staggered, and caught his balance. Figures surrounded him, but most hadn't reacted yet. He threw a stick of dynamite in each direction and ran—toward Masters.

There he was. A blast of an explosion cleared a path, and Walter ran through the waves of heat and light toward his prey. Only one stick remained now; it had had the longest fuse, but even that was nearly burned down now. When he got within reach, he threw it.

Masters, coward that he was, shoved one of his fellows in front of him. The explosion blinded Walter, but not before he saw Masters duck into cover.

The blast knocked Walter flat. His world flickered.

—his mother crying—

No boy should ever have to hear his mother crying. Walter struggled to sit up.

—men laughing—

Flames surrounded him. A figure stumbled into sight, burning like a torch. It staggered, and fell.

—he curled himself into a ball as tight as he could, watching the single glimmering drop of her red blood that had landed near him when one of the men struck her—

Walter forced himself to his feet, shaking his head, trying to shake the memory of her eyes out of his head. He staggered toward the nearest building—the saloon.

Masters had been there that day. He had been the one to strike her. He had been the one to spill that drop of blood. He had escaped again.

He would pay.

Walter staggered into the saloon, closed the door behind him, and collapsed.

Diana followed Garland into the darkness. Turn to 187.

193

Diana followed Garland into the darkness. He led her downhill, through the junipers, and out into the moonlight near a narrow trail.

"Where are we going?" Diana asked.

Garland looked back at her through his owlish glasses. After a moment, he said, "I know a safe way. Don't worry."

As they walked, Diana regarded the man she hadn't seen in three months. It seemed like a lifetime ago. His face had the same youthful good looks that had charmed her then, the same tousled hair. But something was different about him. He had seen things.

Garland raised a hand to stop her. Staying quiet, he crept forward to look out over a large rock at the town. He nodded. "Looks clear. Let's rest a moment. We need to run the last leg."

Diana sat down, leaning next to him against the stone.

"Are you going to tell me what happened here?" She asked, touching his arm.

He paused and turned to meet her eyes, but his were black in the darkness. She couldn't see what he was feeling.

"Diana…" he said. "I'm so glad you found me. Walter promised he would get you to me, but I was getting worried."

"He did?" Diana asked, her brows drawing together.

Garland nodded with a smile. "He was very helpful. It was worth it to get you back."

"I was worried too," Diana replied, but her mind was already moving on. "Listen…" she said, thinking of the tiny life growing in her womb. "We need to talk about… You need to know that…"

He looked at her, unblinking.

Diana took a deep breath, and the words suddenly poured out of her, "I'm carrying your child."

Garland seemed to rock in the darkness. His mouth opened and closed. Then he stood abruptly. "You have to go!" There was an edge of panic in his voice.

"Garland?" Diana asked, standing. "Is everything alright?"

"Please… hurry. You have to leave. You have to get away—" His voice was strained, and his face twisted as if in pain.

Diana took a step back. "What do you mean?"

The young professor stopped, his whole body going rigid. Then he started nodding cheerfully, as if in agreement with himself. When he spoke, it was in a changed tone. "No… yes… yes, actually. Yes, this will work perfectly."

Diana said, "Garland… you're scaring me."

"Diana!" Garland said, taking her hand and gripping it hard. "There's someone I want you to meet. Someone you must meet! This is better than you can know!"

Taking her hand tightly, he pulled her along. Diana, gasping, followed.

Josiah came to, a splitting ache in the back of his head. Turn to 182.

194

Josiah steadied his aim and shot—at William Masters. His lips moved. A prayer flew from his heart just as the bullet flew from his gun. Both sang true.

The bullet hit William Masters in the center of his ruined face. The sheriff went limp, his head knocked back from the impact of the blow, and then flames began to lick up from the small bullet wound.

Vampires screamed as the flames quickly spread, raging down Masters' body to consume him. It was the work of the Lord, Josiah knew.

The two vampires holding Walter Korse dropped their charge and flung themselves in Josiah's direction. Josiah fired quickly, taking down one, then the other.

Walter Korse, recovering himself, started crawling away. Josiah didn't have time to spare him a bullet—more vampires were rushing him. One after another they threw their howling bodies at him, only to be shot down.

Each time a bullet struck true, it carried flame. Purifying flame. Holy flame.

When it was done, he stood surrounded by a circle of burning bodies. He blew smoke from the tip of his gun.

Walter was nowhere to be seen.

"It won't do you any good, damn you." The croaking voice came from somewhere to Josiah's left. He turned.

One vampire—it had been a young man, before the change—dragged itself with its arms across the sand. It had been shot in the leg, and the leg was burning brightly, but the flame had not yet spread to the rest of its body. Hopeless, helpless, it carried on, determined to struggle even in its final moments.

"You're touched already! Don't you know?"

Josiah's eyebrows drew together, a flicker of doubt entering him for the first time.

The dying vampire cackled. "It was one of *her* spiders that bit you. By now, the poison has reached too deep. No matter what you do, there is no escape. This time tomorrow, you will be one of us!"

Josiah shot, bringing the vampires insane laughter to an abrupt end.

He looked at his left hand, the one with the spider bite. Dark red veins of blood ran from the bite up his arm. Toward his heart.

It was one of her spiders that bit you.

Josiah swayed. The world seemed to spin around him. He grasped for words, and intoned, "'Blessed are the dead who die in the Lord. They will rest from their labor, for their deeds will follow them.'"

But he knew that no longer applied to him. He knew his soul had a different fate now.

Josiah sank to his knees. He lifted his swollen hand. Warmed by the heat from the circle of fires, he wept.

Day Three. Turn to 196.

195

Josiah drew and shot Sheriff Masters. The vampire's eyes went wide with shock, and then he began to grin. Just then—Josiah felt a whisper of a breeze on his cheek, and he knew the Lord was with him.

Flames burst from the wound in the vampiric sheriff's chest. Masters looked down in horror. His mouth opened in a soundless scream as the flames spread across his body, quickly consuming him.

Not pausing to watch, Josiah whirled and fired on Walter Korse—but the gun clicked empty.

Korse met Josiah's eyes and grinned. "Somethin' wrong with your gun, Marshal?"

Josiah glowered. "Damn you," he said. He reached for his other gun, but the holster whispered empty.

Korse grinned, and gestured with the pistol he held. It was Josiah's own second weapon. Josiah growled and cursed, then slowly raised his hands. "What do you want of me?" he demanded.

"Well now," Walter said, rubbing his chin. "The way I figure it, we're about even now. You been gunnin' for me, but now you done me a good turn."

Josiah's eyes flicked to the other vampires surrounding them. They were staring, aghast, at the burning body of Sheriff Masters. One of them howled, then pointed at Josiah. "You will pay for this. The Goddess will punish you! She has already touched you!" They backed away as they spoke, pulling away from the howling flames. Then, with one motion, they turned and fled.

Korse glanced up at Hangman's Hill. "I used to think that after Masters was dead, I didn't much care what happened to me. I figured I'd let you hang me if you wanted. Now it comes to it, I'm not much in the mood for a hangin'."

"More's the pity…" Josiah drawled.

"Still," Korse said, his eyes twinkling. "It'd be a shame if that good rope went to waste. Come on, Marshal."

Josiah ground his teeth, but with the murderer pointing that loaded and ready weapon at him, he didn't have much choice. He allowed himself to be herded up the hill to the gallows.

"I understand you bein' angry and all, Mr. da Silva. But you've given me a hell of a time over the years," Korse said as they climbed the side of the dark hill.

Josiah didn't respond. His injuries were deep. His left hand throbbed in pain where the spider had bitten him, and dark red veins of blood ran from the bite up his arm. By the time they reached the top of the hill, he was panting.

"Climb on up. Put your head in that noose."

Josiah gave Korse a grim, sidelong look. But the murderer just smiled amiably and gestured with his gun. Gritting his teeth, Josiah climbed up onto the gallows. He cast one more long glance at Korse before gingerly lowering the fresh noose around his own neck.

Korse came up behind him and tied his hands, keeping the nose of his gun poking into Josiah's back until he was finished. Josiah's heart was pounding as the criminal went over to the lever that would drop the trapdoor.

"What would you do, in my shoes, Marshal? If it was me there, and you here?"

Josiah licked his lips.

Walter sighed. "You did me a good turn today. Masters was the last of them. I'm free."

Josiah said nothing. The rope chafed his neck. It was a rough, hempen rope, not designed for comfort.

Walter spoke in a changed voice, "Abe Korse, Roy Johnson, Curtis Leney, 'the Rustler...' Toby McCann... Now that was a hard one." His eyes grew distant, then he continued, "Dave Hayes fell from his horse before I could get to him, did himself in. Bo Bansen, he died crying. And now Sheriff William Masters. It's done. All the men who killed my mother are dead."

"Good," Josiah said. He looked only to the horizon. It was lightening. Day would come soon.

There was a hard thud and Josiah glanced down to the floor of the platform. Walter had dropped Josiah's gun at his feet. Walter lifted his hand to touch the brim of his hat. "Good day, Marshal." He turned and leaped down from the gallows and strolled away, pausing only to call, "I'll be borrowing your horse, by the by. Sure you don't mind. Don't take too long getting out, those bloodsuckers will be back sooner or later."

With a wave, the criminal was gone.

Josiah grimaced. He'd taken enough of a beating that getting out of these ropes wouldn't be easy. The sun was coming up, and he knew he had to get indoors before the heat of the day, or exposure alone might finish him off, if his injuries didn't do the job first.

He gritted his teeth and began to work at the bonds on his wrists.

Day Three. Turn to 196.

From deep within the canyon he heard an eerie howl of wind, almost like a human voice wailing.

Day Three

Sun baked the cracked dirt roads. The wooden buildings that lined the street were half-burned and bone dry as year-old wasp hive. A lone figure, barely alive, stumbled out into that heat. A fine layer of dust caked him from head to foot, dulling his tailored grey suit and long moustache.

He lifted one hand to squint at the horizon. The sun burned, low and huge and red, shimmering in the heat waves coming off the desert.

Marshal Josiah da Silva slumped against a post in the shade and took a deep breath. After a moment, he tilted his head down to look at the golden marshal's star pinned to his breast, its gleam obscured by a layer of dust and charcoal. He unpinned it and rubbed it on his jacket, but the dust simply smeared.

Gritting his teeth against the pain, he spat upon the star and laboriously wiped it until it shone when he held it out in the sun. Satisfied, he pinned it back on his chest. The fingers of his left hand were swollen and moved unevenly, barely able to grip the pin. It took him four tries.

The sun was touching the horizon now, half of its great, burning bulk gone beneath the rim of the world. Taking a deep breath, Marshal da Silva staggered to the middle of the street and drew himself up to his full height.

The fire from the night before had ravaged the street, leaving nothing but a burnt out husk of the town he had once helped build. Yet he knew the ruins would hide their approach. Any minute now…

Planting his feet, he pulled back his jacket, revealing the ivory handle of a long Colt pistol. This he drew, holding it in his one good hand while he rolled his shoulders.

He watched the sun sink. "The Lord is my shepherd…" he murmured.

The shadows began to move. First it was simply a stirring behind a dark window, something that could have been mistaken for wind touching an unlatched shutter. Then came the groans.

A door burst off its hinges partway down the street. Josiah settled his grip on his pistol, feeling the familiar weight of it in his palm.

A human shape slouched out of the building, silhouetted against the last light of the dying sun. Smoke began to rise from the dark form, and it let out an inhuman keening sound, its large head rolling from side to side until its eyes fell on him. Dark lips peeled back in a grin of sadistic pleasure.

That's when the marshal fired, blowing the creature back off its feet to land in the dust. It did not move again. The marshal whispered, "Thy rod and thy staff, they comfort me."

The last sliver of sun, now red and dark, vanished beneath the horizon, and the long shadows that had been growing across the desert swallowed the town.

A cacophonous howling rose from the surrounding buildings, and one door after another burst open. Shadows slunk into the street, snuffling and searching, drawn to his rich, red scent by the strength of their thirst.

He fired, knocking another off its feet. He fired again, blasting a third to the ground.

The others turned to look at him with one motion, their large, bright eyes blinking in the growing darkness. His next shot blew a grinning head clean off.

The monsters rushed toward him, hopping and sliding and howling.

He fired again, blowing out the leg of one, taking off the arm of another. His clumsy, swollen left hand couldn't reload the pistol, so instead of trying, he fired one last time and discarded the ivory-handled treasure, drawing another identical pistol from his other hip.

The first shot took a woman between the eyes, dropping her. His next hit an old man who gibbered madly, running his tongue along bloodstained teeth. The marshal fired with precision and speed, killing them almost as quickly as they could come. Almost.

He gritted his teeth as he said, "Goodness and mercy shall follow me all the days of my life." But the street was filled with them now, and after he dropped one just a few steps from him, only three bullets remained. He whispered, "And I will dwell in the house of the Lord forever."

Two bullets.

"Amen."

One bullet.

Walter Korse rode into the wastes. Turn to 216.

Diana lashed out, grabbing for the gun with both tied hands. Garland was too fast for her—he ducked back, slipping out of her reach.

He looked at her as a parent scolds a disappointing child. "There, there, Diana. You know better!"

"Let me go," Diana said, breathing heavily.

"This is for the best! Don't you understand? No of course you don't… Ah well. Soon enough, soon enough it will all become clear. Now then, move along! We mustn't keep her waiting!" He nudged Diana with the tip of the rifle, shoving her toward a deep pit at the heart of the camp.

As she approached the pit, she saw dark shapes of ancient architecture emerging from the dust, like half-forgotten bones. But among the ruins, one shape stood out. A black opening: ancient stairs curving into the earth.

Diana shuddered. Those stairs had been carved by no human hand, not in this era.

"Down you go, Diana. Go on."

Diana hesitated, and Garland dug the tip of the rifle into her ribs. "Go on then, don't make me do something we'll both regret." His voice was heavy with the sorrow of the thought.

Fighting back revulsion, Diana scrambled down into the pit. She cast one dark look at Enfield. There was no crack in his resolve, not that she could see.

Diana began her descent.

Josiah awoke with a terrible thirst. Turn to 215.

Josiah fired his last bullet. It blew an unlucky vampire's head back, and he caught a single glimpse of rotten teeth in the gaping mouth before the creature dropped.

Then the rest were upon him. He clenched his jaw and struggled uselessly as their hands tore at his arms. Their weight dragged him, staggering, to his knees. He hit the ground with a heavy thud.

Pain blossomed in his limbs, all over. Teeth and claws raked at him. He stared at the sky. Somewhere up there, God would have mercy upon his soul.

Dizziness came over him, and weakness. He felt that he was being drained. He could feel their mouths sucking on him, pulling out all that made him who he was.

Surely, God would have mercy.

Walter stood at the entrance of Ghost Canyon. Turn to 222.

From deep within the canyon he heard an eerie howl of wind, almost like a human voice wailing.

Day Three

Sun baked the cracked dirt roads. The wooden buildings that lined the street were half-burned and bone dry as year-old wasp hive. A lone figure, barely alive, stumbled out into that heat. A fine layer of dust caked him from head to foot, dulling his tailored grey suit and long moustache.

He lifted one hand to squint at the horizon. The sun burned, low and huge and red, shimmering in the heat waves coming off the desert.

Marshal Josiah da Silva slumped against a post in the shade and took a deep breath. After a moment, he tilted his head down to look at the golden marshal's star pinned to his breast, its gleam obscured by a layer of dust and charcoal. He unpinned it and rubbed it on his jacket, but the dust simply smeared.

Gritting his teeth against the pain, he spat upon the star and laboriously wiped it until it shone when he held it out in the sun. Satisfied, he pinned it back on his chest. The fingers of his left hand were swollen and moved unevenly, barely able to grip the pin. It took him four tries.

The sun was touching the horizon now, half of its great, burning bulk gone beneath the rim of the world. Taking a deep breath, Marshal da Silva staggered to the middle of the street and drew himself up to his full height.

The fire from the night before had ravaged the street, leaving nothing but a burnt out husk of the town he had once helped build. Yet he knew the ruins would hide their approach. Any minute now...

Planting his feet, he pulled back his jacket, revealing the ivory handle of a long Colt pistol. This he drew, holding it in his one good hand while he rolled his shoulders.

He watched the sun sink. "The Lord is my shepherd..." he murmured.

The shadows began to move. First it was simply a stirring behind a dark window, something that could have been mistaken for wind touching an unlatched shutter. Then came the groans.

A door burst off its hinges partway down the street. Josiah settled his grip on his pistol, feeling the familiar weight of it in his palm.

A human shape slouched out of the building, silhouetted against the last light of the dying sun. Smoke began to rise from the dark form, and it let out an inhuman keening sound, its large head rolling from side to side until its eyes fell on him. Dark lips peeled back in a grin of sadistic pleasure.

That's when the marshal fired, blowing the creature back off its feet to land in the dust. It did not move again. The marshal whispered, "Thy rod and thy staff, they comfort me."

The last sliver of sun, now red and dark, vanished beneath the horizon, and the long shadows that had been growing across the desert swallowed the town.

A cacophonous howling rose from the surrounding buildings, and one door after another burst open. Shadows slunk into the street, snuffling and searching, drawn to his rich, red scent by the strength of their thirst.

He fired, knocking another off its feet. He fired again, blasting a third to the ground.

The others turned to look at him with one motion, their large, bright eyes blinking in the growing darkness. His next shot blew a grinning head clean off.

The monsters rushed toward him, hopping and sliding and howling.

He fired again, blowing out the leg of one, taking off the arm of another. His clumsy, swollen left hand couldn't reload the pistol, so instead of trying, he fired one last time and discarded the ivory-handled treasure, drawing another identical pistol from his other hip.

The first shot took a woman between the eyes, dropping her. His next hit an old man who gibbered madly, running his tongue along bloodstained teeth. The marshal fired with precision and speed, killing them almost as quickly as they could come. Almost.

He gritted his teeth as he said, "Goodness and mercy shall follow me all the days of my life." But the street was filled with them now, and after he dropped one just a few steps from him, only three bullets remained. He whispered, "And I will dwell in the house of the Lord forever."

Two bullets.

"Amen."

One bullet.

The vampires stopped in their tracks. Turn to 203.

Josiah grit his teeth. "Let her go," he said.

Old Man Martin laughed, a nasty, raucous sound, and several others began to laugh along with him. Josiah started, having forgotten there were others around. As he scanned the room to try and count them, his head spun. The whole world seemed blurry somehow. If only he could get a drink…

"You don't understand, Marshal!" A woman's voice said. "You're one of us now! You'll drink, or you'll die!"

Josiah tried to speak, but a terrible pain gripped the inside of his body. He had already died. He should be dead. He felt as though his heart and lungs were trying to crawl out of his chest, and he choked back a scream.

"Drink," the woman commanded. She dragged the girl's struggling form closer. Josiah tried to care, he wanted to, but all he could think about was the quick pulse of her delicate neck, so rich and ripe…

"No!" Josiah cried. Turn to 209.
Josiah bit her neck. Turn to 202

Walter rode into the desert. His horse, lacking clear direction from its rider, chose a path that would take it back toward Fairfield. As the sun waxed high in the sky, Walter swayed in his saddle, trying not to think, not to remember.

Behind him he could hear the cracking of burning timbers, the snap of wood on fire. He continued to hear the sound long into his ride. As it had always done, that barn haunted his memories. What now? Where would he go? And wherever he went, would that sound always chase him?

In the heat waves shimmering off the desert, he saw a figure. Warning bells ringing in his mind, he reached for his gun—momentarily forgetting not to use his right hand. He snarled against the pain, letting the broken wrist rest, and drew with his left hand instead.

Slowly, the features became clear through the distorting waves of heat in the air. Broad, dark cheekbones, crested by a high nose in an ancient, wrinkled face. A gold piercing ran deep through the bone of the nose.

"Dry River," Walter breathed, his eyes going wide.

The old shaman simply nodded. "Where do you go, young wolf?"

Walter swallowed, but his mouth was dry and his throat hard. The shaman took a step closer. "The Blood returns. You know that. You know what you must do."

Confusion flashed in Walter's mind. "I did it already. I…" his hand tightened on the grip of the pistol. "I did it Uncle. I avenged her. I slew the men who raped her to death."

"Are you proud?" Dry River asked in his deep voice. He looked just as Walter remembered, from his childhood.

"I…" Walter could find no words. Liquid splashed onto his hand, and he realized he was crying. When had he last cried? He remembered boyhood. Surely he had cried since then. He couldn't seem to recall anything of his life since leaving Affliction. Had it all really happened?

"You are not finished, child," The shaman said. "You go the wrong way. The Blood must return."

Heartsick and numb, Walter sheathed his pistol and looked over his shoulder. Behind him rose the mountains of his ancestors. His mother's land. And unfinished business, though he knew not what.

Ahead of him lay only the thousands upon thousands of miles of land the white men had claimed. His father's people. They held nothing for him.

He kicked his spurs into the flanks of the horse, turning it skillfully. He was aware without seeing that Dry River was gone, yet the sense the old shaman had given him remained: the Blood must return.

Josiah fired his last bullet. Turn to 198.

202

Josiah bit her neck. The girl stiffened under him, then gasped, and then moved no more. He felt something hot sting his cheek; he wasn't sure if it were her tears or blood.

He didn't care. Hot blood surged into his mouth. It filled him, soaring inside him. Sweet and salty and rich, it was all he needed for this life. All he needed to return to himself.

He unclasped, looking up, and took a deep breath. The moon rose into sight through the burned opening in the ruined building, and he wanted to howl. Life surged through him.

More.

He dove into the girl, sinking his fangs into her neck yet again. And he drank. He drank.

"Enough, enough!" Old Man Martin was shaking him. "That's all you get." Mart pulled Josiah off of the girl's cold body, away from her hot blood, still tangy and rich on his lips. He wanted more.

"She's dry," Martin said, holding Josiah away from the cold, dead body of young Amelia Jones. Josiah struggled at first, but quickly fell still, shaking his head to try and clear it.

Something was near him now. He could feel it. What was it? A presence, as though he'd been alone for as long as he could remember, and now he wasn't anymore.

My child.

The voice pierced his consciousness uninvited. And with the voice, the presence. So powerful and ancient that he felt himself shivering beneath its majesty.

"Who's there?" Josiah demanded, leaping to his feet, before stumbling backward and slumping against a wall.

My child, the voice came again, warm and cold, loving yet uncaring, embracing him and twisting him. With a smile in it, the voice said, *I am your creator. Kneel before me.*

Josiah looked up at the moon, fangs emerging from a bloody mouth. He spread his hands as if to receive absolution and slowly, one leg at a time, sank to his knees.

Diana descended the black stairs. Turn to 225.

203

The vampires stopped in their tracks. One of them—so decayed Josiah could no longer tell whether it was male or female—paused and sniffed, bobbing its head back and forth.

"The change begins," another whispered.

"No," Josiah croaked. His throat was strangely dry. Why did he feel so sick? He could barely keep on his feet. He lifted his gun in one shaking hand.

"Step back! Give him room!" Another vampire cried, and all fell back.

A weakness came over Josiah. He sank to one knee. "No," he said. "I won't..." He couldn't finish the sentence. Blinding pain shot through him. He saw—himself as a child, playing on a wooden horse and wearing his father's hat. It slipped down over his eyes, and he had to keep pushing it back up—

"No! I won't!" He surged back up to both feet and raised his gun. Grinning, hideous faces surrounded him, hungry with anticipation. He waved the gun from one to the next. He had to throw up.

Some of them laughed. Voices spoke, but he couldn't make out words. Terrible pain wrenched at Josiah's gut. It was all he could do to stay on his feet. He lifted his left hand. The spider bite was huge and pulsing. Dark red lines glowed under the skin, shooting up his arm.

"I can't..." Josiah whispered. He closed his eyes. His daughter's face on her wedding day, laughing with young Toby. They had looked so pretty together, so young. Their blood had been so red, later that night, so red.

He felt a hot tear blaze down his cheek.

The bodies were pressing in on him now.

"No," Josiah whispered. "Stay back!" he cried, raising his gun to wave it at the blurring faces.

His vision swam. Somehow, the ground leapt up to meet him. Where was his gun? How much of his life had he spent on horseback? Where was his wife? He felt for his badge but couldn't find it.

His hand touched the gun, still hot from firing.

"Go to hell," Josiah croaked, grasping for the gun. Turn to 211.

Josiah knew he had only one way out. Turn to 208.

Walter went to his old room. He couldn't say why he did it, and as soon as he opened the door, he regretted it. Had this room always been so small?

Despite himself, he stepped in, looking around at the life he had once lived, as though it belonged to a stranger. A small, poorly carved wooden train sat on top of a chest, gathering dust. A toy gun emerged from under a pile of half-sized clothes, all of it grey with age. Walter knelt and pulled it out. The dust billowed. The little gun no longer fit in his hand.

He shook his head and tossed the toy gun back onto the pile of clothes. Once, maybe, he had cared about all this stuff. Not so much even then.

As he stood, his eye fell on a nail. His hat had once hung on that nail. It wasn't there now: he had brought the hat when he left. It had stayed with him a long time, until… when had he lost his first hat again? In the Mississippi, he thought, though he could no longer remember clearly. He had lost a hat in the river, on a windy day, but he could not recall if that was the same hat he'd brought from home, or a later one.

He turned to the bed. It was so small, made for a boy; he had been outgrowing it even before he left. His father was going to make him a new one, before…

It was here that his mother had come to tuck him in, every night. She would light the lamp, still gathering dust by the bed. Some nights she would tell him a story, when she was in a good mood. A story of her people, the Arahoca, about the Deathwalkers, and how the Arahoca had defeated them once upon a time.

Other nights, she would be in pain, limping or bruised, a gift from his father. Those nights she would not tell him a story, but simply hold him fiercely, until the man called her name from the other room, and she would kiss the boy goodbye and leave him to his cold bed.

Walter turned and swept out of the little room. Why had he come here? It was a mistake. There was no point in it.

And yet… he froze in the main room. His eye turned to look out the back door. The barn stood there, dim in the foggy morning. Something drew him toward it.

Walter went to the barn. Turn to 218.

"You couldn't have known," Diana said softly. The shadows seemed to hang dark and thick around both of them. Then Garland looked up, his face plastered with a brittle smile. He cried, "Ridiculous! This is the best possible thing that could have happened!"

Diana took a step back. The professor moved closer, gesticulated wildly with the rifle. "She will remake this world in her own image, Diana. And you and I will be her firstborn. Our child will be the herald of a new dawn. Or a new sunset, I suppose," he said in an aside. He demanded, "Don't you understand? We will be immortal!"

Diana shook her head. "You're insane," she said, staring into his wide eyes.

"Is it madness," Enfield said, laughing, "Or greatness, to believe in one's own power? To recognize the chance to change the world forever, and seize it in both hands!?"

Something inside Diana cracked. Could this be the same man she had followed across half the country? The man she had risked everything to find? What had happened to him?

"Now then," Garland said, lifting her rifle. He smiled. "In you go! She's going to want to meet you."

Diana tried to find words, but nothing came to her lips. She turned mutely in the direction he shoved her. Blindly, her mind groped for a chance at escape, but with the rifle prodding her in the back, there was none.

A dark pit yawned at the center of the camp. Eerie shapes of ancient architecture emerged from the dust like half-forgotten bones. Further in, she could see the opening to spiral stairs that had been uncovered in the dust. She stared down into that pit, unable to force herself to take another step.

Garland dug the tip of the rifle into her ribs. "Go on then, don't make me do something we'll both regret." His voice was heavy with the sorrow of the thought.

Fighting back revulsion, Diana scrambled down into the pit. She cast one dark look at Enfield. He stood, tall and terrible above her, rifle pointed toward her. And in that moment, she knew hatred.

Diana began her descent.

Josiah awoke with a terrible thirst. Turn to 215.

206

With a groan, Josiah let himself sink to the dirt. He could not explain it himself; his limbs simply lacked the strength to keep his body upright. Feet slapped the dirt and then Walter was by his side.

The half-breed quickly scanned Josiah's body for wounds, seeing his left hand swollen red with spider bite, black lines tracing up the veins to vanish under his sleeve. His hands felt cool on Josiah's face. "You're hot as the Devil's Anvil," he said. "Come on."

Walter put his arm under Josiah's shoulder and helped the older man. Turn to 220.

207

Slowly, he put the gun back. He didn't know why. He just didn't feel like firing it.

He thought of the marshal, who had hunted him for so many years. He thought of Diana, who had, on occasion, been kind to him. At least she had looked at him like he was human. Where were they now?

Walter swung himself up onto his horse. He didn't much care which way he went, he just had to pick one.

Walter rode into the desert. Turn to 201.
Walter turned his horse back toward Affliction. Turn to 217.

Josiah knew he had only one way out. He grasped for his gun, weak fingers finding the familiar grip. It was so heavy.

"He won't do it," a voice said.

Josiah licked cracking lips. *Lord, hear my prayer. Take my soul. Don't let it go to these bastards.* He could still see his wife's smile. Had she really been gone so many years? It felt like just yesterday. Her face was so close now. So close, he could almost hear her voice. Almost touch her hand. She held it out to him.

He lifted the gun in trembling hands. The steel was hot as he placed the tip of the gun to his own temple.

Then suddenly the gun was ripped from his hands. "None of that now," a voice said.

"It wouldn't have mattered, would it? We all die first," another voice said.

"No need to find out. Let's let him go the normal way."

Josiah's heart clenched in fear. No… he was going to heaven. He had to be. He had fought is whole life for this. He felt a tear hot on his cheek.

A hand wiped away the tear. "Chin up, Marshal. You'll be one of us soon." One voice said, and they all cackled.

Marshal Josiah da Silva knew despair. And then he knew nothing.

Diana stumbled along, hands bound. Turn to 214.

"No!" Josiah cried. He struggled backwards on all fours until he hit a wall. He pulled himself up against it, staring at the sobbing girl on the floor.

"That…" he panted, "Is Amelia Jones, daughter of Richard and Jane Jones. I knew her parents. I knew her when she was a child. I…" he gasped. Sweat beaded on his forehead. He wiped at the droplets, and blood came away on his fingers. "I gave her a toy once, a…" Why couldn't he remember what the toy had been?

"That's the past," Old Man Martin said. "She was Amelia Jones. And now, she's food. If you don't drink, we will. And you'll die."

Josiah shook his head fiercely. His heart raced, shallow and thready. He could feel his own life now, pulsing like a dying bird. "No…" he muttered.

Old Man Martin stared at him in disgust. The girl was trying to crawl away. Martin grabbed her, spun her over onto her back, eliciting a scream, and called the other vampires to gather around.

Josiah fought back the thirst and pushed himself forward. "No. You can't. I won't… let you." He began to crawl toward them. Somehow, he had to stop them. Amelia needed… she needed him.

The vampires laughed to watch his weak approach. His throat burned so badly.

"Please…" Amelia said, meeting his eyes. Her face was desperate, tears glistening on her cheeks, a mirror of the droplets of blood that glistened on her neck. He struggled to remember, anything… but the memories weren't coming.

"Don't touch her!" Josiah croaked, as one of the vampires grabbed Amelia.

"Last chance?" Old Man Martin said. He twisted the girl's face away from Josiah, showing him the pulsing vein in her throat one more time.

Terrible hunger rose in Josiah. His throat was so dry. He wanted—he needed—to leap and rip and tear, to feel blood pulsing under his teeth, to drink… oh, to drink… nothing was more important in the world.

He pounced, finding strength he didn't know he had, and knocked Martin aside. Josiah lifted the girl protectively in his arms. Her neck, long and pretty, stretched taut under his gaze. The other vampires keened around him.

"Don't touch her…" Josiah said, dropping the girl. Turn to 212.
Josiah bit her neck. Turn to 202.

210

There wasn't any reason for him to stay. He put the gun to his head.

He looked out at the sky and took one last, deep breath. It was a good day. He closed his eyes, but all he saw when he looked inside was memories.

"I got them," he whispered to his mother.

He squeezed the trigger.

The vampires stopped in their tracks. Turn to 203.

211

"Go to hell," Josiah croaked, grasping for the gun. It slipped from his reach—his clumsy fingers pushed it farther away. He wept in frustration.

"Look at him, still trying!" the cackling voices raised in laughter over him. He rolled, stomach churning. The sky was blue and clear above him, turning to purple as dusk settled over the land. He couldn't remember why he'd been fighting so hard.

"It'll be okay," a creaking voice said from nearby. "It hurts us all at first." Was that his wife? He reached, and found a hand—it was rotting, soft flesh giving way under his touch.

"Oh God," Josiah gasped, the words a croak that tore from his throat.

"Don't worry, God can't get to you anymore."

Josiah couldn't follow what happened. He hurt too much. He just needed to close his eyes for a moment. Just for a moment.

He heard his wife calling his name… somewhere far away. But she was so distant. And then he couldn't hear her anymore.

He couldn't hear anything anymore.

Diana stumbled along, hands bound. Turn to 214.

"Don't touch her…" Josiah said, dropping the girl. The strength left him as abruptly as it had come over him. He collapsed, unable to even drag his body away. The girl cried out as he landed on her, but he couldn't bring himself to care. He was so thirsty…

Someone dragged him a few feet, laying him out full length on the wooden floor. The stars winked at him, mocking his weakness.

"Poor devil," a voice somewhere said. And then he heard the screams. It was the girl, he couldn't remember her name anymore. He hadn't been able to protect her. She was dying… he was dying…

Even pain faded until there was nothing but the thirst, that terrible, soul-consuming thirst. And then, even that faded, until he knew nothing.

He woke up, he knew not how much later. It was cold, though the cold didn't seem to bother him. It was a part of him, seeping into his bones and through them.

A hand shook him, and he realized that was what had dragged him awake. "Joe, darling," a woman's voice was saying. She sounded vaguely familiar.

"What?" he croaked, though almost no sound came from his cracked and parched lips.

"Be strong, Joe," the voice said. A head came into view, a woman, familiar, but Josiah couldn't place her. She dragged another body up alongside Josiah and sat down with a low laugh. It was a girl's body. Josiah felt a twinge, as though he should know that body.

"There's a bit left," the woman said, and she twisted the body's head to show a long, delicate neck, already punctured by several bite marks.

At first, Josiah felt nothing. He struggled to speak. But then he saw the faintest flutter of a pulse in that neck, and some last gasp of strength grabbed hold. Josiah pulled himself up to rest on his elbows. He stared at the neck, transfixed. A little stain of blood still remained on the delicate skin. It was marvelous.

Nearby, a door opened. Old Man Martin came into the room. He looked down upon Josiah, tall and imperious. Waiting. Judging.

Josiah leaned down to lick up that blood. The sweet-salty richness of it nearly overwhelmed him.

"Quick, before she dies," the woman said. And suddenly Josiah recognized her: Marie. They had been friends years ago, he remembered. Hadn't he seen her earlier tonight as well? Everything was so foggy. She held the neck at just the right angle for Josiah to bite, and he knew what to do.

Josiah's lips were cracked, his tongue dry and swollen in his mouth. He knew nothing but thirst. He pulled back his teeth, aware that fangs had sprouted. Somewhere inside, he vaguely remembered he'd had a reason not to bite, but he couldn't remember what it was.

Josiah bit her neck. Turn to 202.

213

Despite the pain, Josiah forced himself to keep standing. His vision blurred as he watched Korse approach, and then suddenly the man was next to him. Josiah's eyes jerked open. "Where'd you come from?" he asked.

Walter just shook his head. He touched Josiah's neck, arm, and face, then said, "You're hot as the Devil's Anvil. What happened to you?"

Josiah shook his head. "Not well," he said. Without thinking about it, he looked down at the spider bite on his left hand. The hand was swollen red, with black lines tracing up the veins to vanish under his sleeve. "Bastard got me. Days ago, he got me."

"Come on," the criminal said, turning Josiah toward the nearest building.

Walter put his arm under Josiah's shoulder and helped the older man. Turn to 220.

214

Diana stumbled along, hands bound. She moved clumsily through the darkness, Garland following along behind her, using her own rifle to prod her whenever she slowed down.

On one of these occasions, she stepped forward too hastily and tripped on an uneven jut of stone. As she steadied herself, the young professor said, "Careful! Sit down. You have to take care of the baby."

Diana lowered herself to a seating position on a rock, while Garland found a seat near her. All the while, he kept the rifle trained loosely in her direction.

"You really need that?" Diana asked bitterly, eying the gun. She was tied hand and foot. What did he think she was going to do?

"Just a precaution, of course! Don't you trust me?" Garland said.

Diana did not reply. What would she say to the man she had trusted?

The canyon rose hundreds of feet on both sides, its walls close enough that she could touch both at the same time—or at least, she could have, if her hands were free. She looked up at the wedge of sky she could see high above, shining with stars in the evening light.

This place had an eerie silence to it, the silence of a graveyard. Quiet, yet peaceful. Empty, yet not empty. It made her shiver to think about it. A terrible sadness came over her. For herself, but not just for herself. She blinked back tears.

Garland put on a cheerful face and said, "Come now, it's not as bad as all that! Before you know it, all will become clear. Then you'll thank me for doing this! You'll see." He smiled in self-satisfaction, and Diana felt a bead of cold rage burning inside her.

"Well," Garland said, "Best keep moving. It's not getting any earlier!"

Diana pulled herself to her feet, every tired bone aching. She walked, shaking off his attempt to take her elbow to support her.

The trail passed as they walked, Garland chattering companionably from time to time. She did not reply. After a time, the walls of the canyon widened, and Garland cried out with boyish excitement. "Oh! Up ahead, look, look! You can see my dig site! Won't be long now."

Her heart ached. That was the side of him she had fallen in love with. That exuberance and passion. He had made her dare to feel that the world was young again. Now...

Before them, the canyon opened into a wide basin. Several large tents could be seen, though most were collapsed, some even half-buried in sand. The remains of various supplies littered the site, moldering and sorrowful. As they descended into the basin, Diana could see a fine layer of dust over everything.

A large, shadowy shape passed overhead. Diana flinched away as she heard the beating of massive wings. "What the hell is that?" She demanded, looking up as the elusive black shape merged with the dark silhouette of the canyon wall.

Garland looked up. "Oh, nothing to worry about, nothing to worry about. As the Goddess has returned, so too have her servants. Dumb brutes. Get away you damn beast!" The professor picked up a stone and hurled it at random into the air.

A shadow detached itself from the wall, and with a single beat of massive wings, glided out of sight. "Nothing to worry about, see?" Garland said.

Diana's skin crawled, but she let herself be prodded onward.

The trail descended amongst the skeletal remains of the abandoned camp, and Garland looked around with satisfaction. He asked, "Marvelous, isn't it? The site of my greatest achievement..." He picked up an old pot and tossed it aside. "Once we found the temple, of course, there was little need to keep up the site. But you would never believe what we accomplished here, Diana." He sighed. "Simply marvelous! After all those years of searching, I actually found her. Tezoca, the Bled One!"

"You were *looking* for her?" Diana shot the question at him.

"Of course!" Garland declared. He turned his feverishly bright eyes on her. "And I never could have found her without you, Diana. You encouraged me. You believed in me when no one else did! In a way, I owe it all to you."

Diana's stomach turned. "Get away from me," she whispered.

A childish hurt flickered in the professor's eyes. "I thought you'd be proud of me..." he said quietly. "I did it for you."

"Then let me go," Diana implored, her voice nearly breaking into a sob.

For a moment, a haunted look passed across Garland's face. Then it was replaced by a sly expression, as though they were playing a game, and she had nearly scored a point on him. "Ah, no, I see what you're doing. No, no, no!" He declared emphatically. "You'll understand once we're through. Once you come to love her as I do!" His eyes were shining as he stared into the darkness.

"Of course," he laughed hollowly, "I never imagined the Bled One would still be *alive* when I found it! I mean, who would guess..." a spasm crossed his face. "Who would guess it might still be alive? Who would guess it would be so powerful... I couldn't... I couldn't..." He seemed unable to finish the sentence, but his face was tormented.

"Garland..." Diana said, moving closer to him.

He turned toward her, his face dark in the shadows of the deep canyon.

Diana lashed out, grabbing for the gun with both tied hands. Turn to 197.
"You couldn't have known," Diana said softly. Turn to 205.

Josiah awoke with a terrible thirst. He struggled to open his eyes. They felt gummed shut, as though he had been asleep for days. When they did open, he found himself surrounded by a world of darkness.

"He's awake!" A voice from nearby called. It was not a friendly voice.

He lay naked, but not cold. Wooden slats, hard and splintery, pressed at his skin. He pushed himself up onto his elbows.

His clothes were scattered around the room. His wounds had all been healed. Not far away, something flat and shiny. He reached out to touch it... skin. It was papery and tough, like a snakeskin, but in the shape of a human. Who...? His mind flashed to the cast-off skin left by Beatriz, snakelike, after she changed. He jerked his hand away.

Several figures stood or knelt not far away. Above them, he could see a patch of stars. He was in one of the half-burned town buildings. A terrible thirst burned his throat. He would die... He reached one hand for the figures and croaked, "Water."

They laughed, shapes jogging in the darkness. None moved to help. Josiah's world swam, but he forced himself to rummage through his own discarded clothes. His hand fell upon it—his water flask.

"What are you doing?" A harsh voice demanded.

Josiah didn't waste time answering. He tipped the canteen to his lips, but a hand lashed out of the darkness and slapped it away. The canteen fell into the dust, the last droplets of water spilling out.

Josiah let out an inarticulate cry of dismay. Somehow the water looked wrong, but the force of his thirst drove him to his knees, fingers clutching uselessly at drops of water even as they sank into the grimy floor. "No," he moaned.

The voices around him laughed, but Josiah was too thirsty to care. He had to drink. He had to! He leaned down and put his tongue out to lap at the dark stain— and nearly gagged. He jerked back away from it, sitting up.

Josiah lifted his fingers to his lips. The water had tasted like dust or ash, useless to him. He stared.

"That's not what you need, now, boy," a voice said. Josiah looked up. He recognized Old Man Martin. Martin had been one of the first settlers to Affliction, arriving with his family not long after Josiah himself had. Martin's family hadn't made it, but he and Josiah had gotten on well, for a time. He hardly looked as though he'd aged a day.

Josiah's mind spun. What was happening to him?

"Here, drink this," Martin said. He dragged a small figure, kicking and struggling, into the room, and threw the captive at Josiah's feet. Josiah stared. The girl looked familiar, but it wasn't till she turned her face up to him that he recognized her, grown up from when last they'd met.

"The Jones girl?" he asked, his mouth thick with thirst, tongue so dry he could barely speak.

She looked up at him, terrified. Recognizing him, she threw herself into his arms. "Please, sir! Save me!"

Josiah looked up accusingly at Old Man Martin. "The hell are you trying to do here, Mart? This is Amelia Jones!"

Old Man Martin shook his head in disgust. He pulled the girl away from Josiah's grip, and neither of them were strong enough to resist. "She ain't a girl any more, not to you, Joe. She ain't Amelia Jones neither. She's nothing. She's food now, and that's it. And you best get used to it, if you want to live."

"What?" Josiah's head spun. He tried to reach for the girl, but he was so dizzy he could barely move.

Old Man Martin was pressing a fingernail to Amelia's throat now. Josiah found his eyes transfixed by the fluttering pulse of the vein under her skin. "No…" Josiah muttered.

Martin pushed, and his long, dirty fingernail pierced the girl's delicate skin. A bright drop of red blood welled up, red and shimmering in the starlight. Josiah's world narrowed in focus, until he could see nothing except that drop of red blood. The thirst raged up in him, more powerful than he could have believed.

"No…" he said, his voice shaken. But he did not move away. He simply held himself, shuddering, watching the blood as something terrible moved inside of him.

"Drink, Joe. It's the only way you'll survive now." Martin jerked the girl's head back, showing the neck.

Despite himself, Josiah moved closer, compelled by something he didn't understand. Somewhere, he was aware of the girl crying.

Josiah grit his teeth. "Let her go," he said. Turn to 200.
Josiah bit her neck. Turn to 202.

216

Walter Korse rode into the wastes. A dim fog gathered around him, so thick he could barely see the sun as it rose. Perhaps it was smoke. The haze turned the sun bloody, painting the world in tones of red. He had no destination in mind; he simply let the horse wander where it would.

And yet, when he looked up after some hours, it was with no surprise that he saw the ranch of Abe Korse looming ahead, through the mists.

Korse Ranch. *Someday this will all be yours, son.* He hadn't set foot here since the day he killed his father.

Stiff, one-handed, he let himself down from the horse. A few rays of morning sun penetrated the fog, carving through it to illuminate parts of the ranch ahead of him.

A ghostly image of his father, yelling, coming out the door. The crack of his own gunshot, bringing low the man who had murdered his mother. He could still smell the gun smoke.

He took a few steps forward. Was that a bloodstain in the wood, even after all these years?

What had happened to the ranch afterward, anyway? He had never asked about it. For all he knew, another family could have moved in.

How had his mother come here, last survivor of the Arahoca, daughter of their Chief? Had she been dragged by the hair, kicking and screaming? Had she been numb and silent? What had she said to the man who took her, the man who wed her, the man who would eventually kill her? Had she ever grown to love him, this man, this killer, Abe Korse?

"I got it from you, father," Walter said. "We were both killers." The real sound of his own voice sounded strange amidst the ghosts.

The horse nickered, and Walter tied it to the fencepost, a single common motion in this haunted place. He walked up the path.

The house revealed itself through the haze as he approached it. Walls that looked pristine and familiar from a distance showed themselves to be peeling and rotting up close.

The front door creaked as he pushed it open. Walter's breath caught in his throat. Everything was just as he remembered it. Just as he had left it. By then it had been only him and the old man living here. So far as he could tell, not a soul had touched the place since they both left, each in their own way.

The floorboards creaked alarmingly, but held, as he entered his childhood home. His father's jacket still hung on a peg, where the old man had last hung it. The spurs hanging below. As if ready for Abe Korse to emerge from the grave and put them on, riding into the coming end days.

Dishes still in the kitchen. He had been supposed to wash those that morning. Here they lay, so many deaths later, still unwashed. He picked one up. A spider scuttled away from underneath it.

The barn. That's where it had happened. He felt sick.

Walter went to his old room. Turn to 204.
Walter went to the barn. Turn to 218.

217

Walter turned his horse back toward Affliction. The marshal and the woman weren't his people, exactly, but they were the closest he had. He had sold out the woman, giving her to that professor in exchange for information. He didn't know what the professor had in mind, but he didn't need a signpost to know the woman wouldn't like it.

He grimaced, a strange feeling clenching his chest. He felt a peculiar desire to find her. To set things right.

It was a good day for riding, the sun high and clear now that the mists had burned off. He must have lingered at his old home longer than he'd realized; the sun was already turning to lower in the sky, its light shifting from the bright gold of morning to the burnt warmth of a long hot desert afternoon.

As the sound of the fire faded into the distance behind him, he heard a great crash of burning timbers collapsing. The vastness of the desert swallowed the noise. Walter smiled.

If he hurried, he could make it back to Affliction by sunset.

Josiah turned as the crack of a rifle shot echoed through the ruined town. Turn to 219.

Walter went to the barn. It waited for him in the diffuse light of the morning sun coming through the fog. It was smaller than he remembered it.

The lock had long since broken off, or it had been left unlocked in the first place. He grabbed one of the wide wooden doors and pulled. The door swung out, crushing overgrown grasses beneath its heavy frame. Walter looked in.

This place had loomed so large in his memories, haunted him, driven him through all the years since he had last seen it. Now... it seemed so small. So common. Just a barn.

He drifted inside, letting his hand brush the doorframe. Old hay and rusting tools lay around the room. His own shadow spread as he moved in, until it swallowed the light of the room completely.

He could remember...

He'd been asleep when he heard the shouts. As soon as he sat up, he knew it was his mother. She had given him a strange hug that night, holding him too close, as though she would never see him again.

(Why had she left without him?)

When he burst out onto the porch, still in his nightclothes, bare feet cold, he saw the men ride up. His mother, a limp figure dragged by her hair. Her feet were stained with grass and dirt, the hem of her dress wet.

"Abe!" One of them called, and his father came out to meet them. "We found your bitch. She was trying to buy passage on a coach out of town."

Walter's father's fury was a thing to behold. The boy lived in terror of it, like a small animal skirting the edges of the home, looking for space to live without drawing its attention. Now that fury swelled and grew, and when Walter's father answered, it was in an icy voice that meant something terrible was coming.

"Take her to the barn," he said, his voice clipped and short. Then his eye fell on Walter. "And take the boy, too. We'll make him watch. That'll teach her."

Walter shut his eyes tightly. No—he didn't want to remember. He jerked his hand away from the wall of the barn as though it burned.

He turned away. He'd seen enough. He stepped out into the light of the morning sun. Tears stood on his face.

"I got them, Mother. I killed them. I killed them all." He didn't know where she was buried. His father had never let him find out. Didn't want him 'getting ideas.'

Walter fell to his knees. He couldn't block out the memories completely. They forced their way into his mind, burned there as though it had happened yesterday. The sounds she had made. Sounds he had never wanted to hear again. He could still remember the beating he received too, for shouting as they dragged her limp body out. But it hadn't hurt half so much as the shame in her eyes when she saw him watching.

He hadn't forgiven. He hadn't forgotten. They all lay under six feet of dust. Abe Korse, Roy Johnson, Curtis Leney, called 'the Rustler,' Bo Bansen, Robin Hobfield, Toby McCann, Dave Hayes, and William Masters.

All.

Walter took a deep breath. A light wind blew, chilling the tears on his cheeks. He considered the gun on his belt. His temple itched. What else was there, now?

Perhaps. But first... he stood, and pulled out tinder. Methodically, he encircled the barn, lighting fires at each corner. Then he stepped back and watched it burn.

Once the barn was going, he lit up the main house. Nothing here deserved to remain. When the fires were lit, he returned to his horse. From the gate, he turned back to watch the flames consume the detritus of his past life.

It was over. He'd done what he set out to do, against all odds. He'd accomplished the impossible.

He took out one of his guns. His right hand still wasn't working, the wrist broken and bandaged, so he had to use his left. It felt strangely heavy today.

Why not? He didn't have anything else planned.

Fire reflected in his eyes as he regarded the black gun. The dancing red glow glinted off the steel.

There wasn't any reason for him to stay. He put the gun to his head. Turn to 210.
Slowly, he put the gun back. He didn't know why. He just didn't feel like firing it. Turn to 207.

219

Josiah turned as the crack of a rifle shot echoed through the ruined town. The monsters that surrounded him ceased in their steps, arrested by that shot. As one, they lifted their heads to see the newcomer.

Josiah breathed heavily. One bullet remained in his gun. One bullet.

The rifle cracked again, dropping another of the inhuman townsfolk. Then a third, and they broke. They scattered, some heading for the hills, others taking refuge in the nearest building. One, angrier or stupider or hungrier than the rest, leaped not away, but toward Josiah, mouth spread wide to show his fangs.

Josiah planted his last bullet into that gaping maw, and the vampire thrall collapsed.

They were gone now, the last of them simply motion in the distance, sending up the dust of their retreat. Josiah stepped forward and nudged the body of the creature he had just laid low. It had been a woman, a ranch wife perhaps, before being turned. Now, it was rotting meat. The corpse showed signs of being long dead, though it had been moving up until moments before.

"Ain't you polite enough to thank me?" A voice called from behind.

Josiah turned, to see Walter Korse descending the nearby hillside, long rifle in hand. The hint of a smile played around those lips, unlike any look Josiah had ever seen before on the killer's face. "I stole this rifle fair and square so's I could save your hide here."

"You," Josiah breathed.

Walter simply cocked an eyebrow, looking the marshal up and down. "You don't look spry, old man."

Josiah let his lips part in a weak smile. "While I thank you for your concern, it may come too late," he said.

With a groan, Josiah let himself sink to the dirt. Turn to 206.
Despite the pain, Josiah forced himself to keep standing. Turn to 213.

Walter put his arm under Josiah's shoulder and helped the older man. The marshal let himself be guided to a cool porch, away from the lingering heat of day that radiated up from the dusty street. He sat with a sigh.

Walter looked at the old marshal, the man who had chased him across five years, who had brought him in, in the end. Never had he expected it would end like this, with himself still standing, and the marshal dying. He'd assumed he would meet his end swinging at the end of a noose, and da Silva, firm, implacable, unbending, would be the one who slapped the horse out from under him.

The marshal's tongue moved, wetting his lips. Then, with effort, he said, "You got all of them?"

Walter's jaw tightened. "It's done," he said.

Josiah nodded. "Good."

The wind blew, and Walter lowered his eyes. A burning sensation was in them, unlike anything he had felt in his adult life. He had spent most of his life hating the marshal, but no one in the world knew him like Josiah did.

The old marshal began to tremble, though whether from cold or for some other reason, Walter couldn't say. When Josiah spoke again, his voice came out a croak. "Why did you kill Cora?"

The words stabbed into Walter. Unbidden, Cora's face leaped into his mind. Like a floodgate had been opened, the memories came flooding in. The voices raised, shouting. The fear in Toby's eyes. The sound of his gunshot, and the way his stomach seemed to drop out from inside him when he saw her leaping forward. Too late—it was too late to take back the bullet.

He found that he was clenching his jaw in a tight grimace. He ground out, "That shot was not meant for her. I… I'm sorry. I would it had ended any other way. I… I loved her." Cora and Toby had held each other as they bled out, dying together. The man he hated, and the woman he loved.

Josiah lifted his hand and grabbed Walter's collar with the last of his strength. "Diana! She's out there. She's…" he began to cough.

"I know," Walter said. He tried to open his mouth to tell the old man how he knew, but the words wouldn't come.

"Get her! Leave me. I'm not long for this world anyway. God will… Just find…" He struggled to keep speaking, but the breath had left him.

Walter put his hand on the old marshal's and pried it off his collar. "I'll find her. Rest easy."

Josiah's head fell back. Only the slight movement of his lips (A prayer? Was he still trying to speak?) gave away the sign of life.

Walter stood, and the porch creaked under his boots. The last purple-red light of dusk was fading from the sky.

"Walter." The voice was so faint Walter almost wasn't sure he heard it. He turned. The marshal's grey eyes burned in their sockets.

"You did good."

Walter touched the brim of his hat. Those eyes held his gaze for another moment, then the lids closed.

A whisper of wind tugged at Walter's clothes. He could hear its quiet moan in the dilapidated buildings. A single desert bird called, far away. Burnt and desiccated wood creaked in the dry wind. He could hear all of it, the rustle of a tumbleweed, but he could not hear the marshal's voice. No more.

Above them to the north rose the red bluffs of the mountains. That was the land of his people, the Arahoca. The people Josiah and his type had slaughtered.

Questions were growing in his mind now, questions that had been outstanding for way too long. The time had finally come. He needed answers, and he knew where to find them. He whistled for his horse.

Walter stood at the entrance of Ghost Canyon. Turn to 222.

221

"Power," Diana said. She could feel Enfield's tension drain away. She must have answered correctly.

The spear lifted. The guardian's voice intoned, "Power is the beginning and end, creation and destruction. Enter."

"Come on," Enfield said, shoving her, and Diana stumbled forward.

They passed between the guardians and approached the gate. Turn to 231.

222

Walter stood at the entrance of Ghost Canyon. This was the place his mother had taken him to, warned him about. This was the place where his people had once lived.

Was anything left of them? Anything beyond their ghosts? What had happened here? What wasn't in the story he had been told?

He tied up the horse, stroking its mane to comfort the fidgeting beast. He made sure to tie it to a dead branch, something flimsy enough that the horse could break free in case he never returned.

He had pulled a pretty good set of supplies from Diana's wagon, but there was no need to bring all of that in with him. He took a light pack with a bit of food and water and spare ammunition. A pouch of tobacco, of course. For weapons, he had his knife and the rifle he had pilfered from an abandoned farm. He also still had Josiah's pistol; he trusted the marshal wouldn't mind. Finally, he brought a lantern. He knew how to keep it cloaked so that it might not give away his position.

He took one last look at the view. Affliction still smoldered below him. No live flame could be seen, but smoke rose from the coals of the burned-out city, even a full day later.

He felt a grim satisfaction knowing that the town had failed. All those who had slain his people had failed, and their dreams had died with them.

He turned to the canyon. Stepping to the entrance he lifted his lantern. The walls were narrow—so narrow he could touch both sides with each hand while standing in the middle. They rose dozens of feet above him on either side, and the moon hung between them, a silver lamp from a forgotten land. From deep within the canyon he heard an eerie howl of wind, almost like a human voice wailing. The lost souls of those who were gone, perhaps.

A chill ran down Walter's spine, and he plunged in. The canyon walls engulfed him, and suddenly the sky was barely more than a memory, a mere sliver between canyon walls high overhead. The air down here was warmer and thicker, and he felt that he needed to push his way through it.

How much of a lead would they have on him? It depended on how quickly they had moved. He ran with ease through his native land; surely he could gain on them.

After the first hour he stopped to breathe, feeling the air pump in and out of his lungs. It felt good to be here. He felt alive. And then—

"Who's there?" he shouted. He whirled, holding the lantern high. Only silence answered him. Silence, and the incessant howling of the wind. That wind… it whispered sibilant words in a language he couldn't understand.

As he held, watching and listening, more whispers emerged to him. They seemed to come from the very stones. He whirled—who was it? Again, nothing was there.

Skin crawling on the back of his neck, he turned slowly in a full circle. A side canyon opened off the main trail to the left. He took a few steps closer to it. Voices seemed to be whispering from that direction.

Walter cautiously followed the voices. Turn to 233.
Walter kept running down the trail. Turn to 236.

223

Walter found a dark place to hide and wait, watching. He knew the ways of the land, and he knew how often the secret to survival was patience.

To pass the time, he examined the dig site. The detritus of the old campsite was scattered all around, half-buried in dust: cooking tins, weather-torn clothes, the lines of half-collapsed tents. It looked to have been abandoned for several months, and the yawning hole in the heart of it all looked to date back to around the same time. Shovel marks showed it was a relatively fresh cut in the earth, at least down to the level of the ancient stonework.

The very sight of that gaping blackness made his skin crawl. He didn't want to imagine where it might lead, or what might come out of it.

Soon enough, Walter's patience paid off. He heard human muttering, and the scuff of movement. Silence fell again. At last, distinctly, the words, "Where the hell is he?"

Walter grinned in the darkness. He recognized the professor's voice. It was almost laughable how quickly he had given up on waiting. Walter could have remained all night, stretching and flexing his muscles silently to keep from cramping.

Soon, figures came into view, clambering down from a hiding place among the rocks on the far side of the little valley. It was a good place to set up an ambush, where Walter himself would have chosen, had the positions been reversed. Enfield just didn't have the patience.

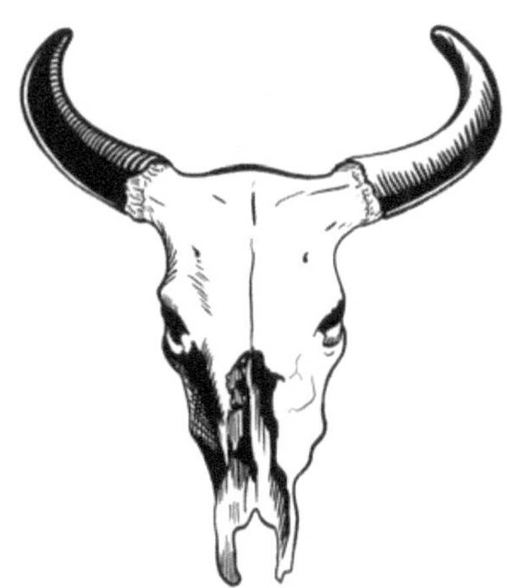

As they came out into the bright moonlight, Walter could clearly see Professor Enfield, tugging a bound Diana. Walter did not move as he watched them. They made their way between ruined tents and other debris to approach the pit.

There, Diana rebelled. She simply refused to keep placing one foot in front of the other, even as Enfield swore at her, prodding with the rifle.

"What happened to you, Garland?" Diana asked in a shaking voice. The wind seemed to carry the words right to Walter.

The professor replied, "What happened to me? What happened to you? I used to think you were a reasonable woman! Just go down, damn you!"

"Is this where you've been?" She asked. "Is this what you left me for?"

Enfield fidgeted. "I did it for you! All of this, it was for you!"

"You shouldn't have," Diana said bitterly.

"Stop right there," Walter called out in a commanding voice.

"What?" Enfield looked up, his eyes darting this way and that along the canyon walls. He had no idea where Walter was.

Walter laughed, letting his voice carry so that it would resound across the narrow defile. The effect worked, startling the professor into whirling and pointing his gun at shadows.

"Where are you?" The professor demanded. "Show yourself!"

"Lay down your gun, Enfield," Walter cracked his voice at the frightened man.

"What if I don't?" The professor cried.

Walter fired a warning shot. He guided the bullet to hit a large stone a few feet from the pair ahead of him. It ricocheted, startling the professor so badly he nearly dropped Diana's rifle.

"Fine! Fine! I'm putting it down," Enfield said. He gingerly lay the rifle down on the ground, while Diana watched, her eyes burning into her one-time lover. But Walter thought he detected something sly in the man's hesitation, and the rifle was positioned in such a way it could be quickly recovered.

Walter grunted in derision. If the professor thought he could be clever, let him. He would pay for it with his life.

"Why are you following me, Walter?" Enfield called out.

Walter emerged from the shadows, keeping his own rifle trained on the young professor. "Who says I'm following you?"

"You came here! Why?" The professor cried.

"Put your hands on top of your head." Walter gestured with his gun, and the professor reluctantly did as he was told. The woman was still tied; she would be no threat. Her hard eyes followed Walter as he moved.

"This land belongs to me. It belonged to my people before me, but your people killed them all. So let's turn that question around. Why did you come here?" Walter moved slowly forward as he spoke, closing the distance. He could see the whites of the professor's eyes now, nervous and cunning.

"I had to! I had no choice!" Enfield's eyes darted down to where his rifle waited for him.

"Keep your hands up. Touch that gun and you're a dead man. Why did you come here?" Walter said. He stopped ten feet away. Far enough to have the advantage of distance, yet close enough that he couldn't miss his shot.

The professor licked his lips. "I came… for the Bled One. I'm bringing Diana to her. My wife and… our child." His eyes flicked to Diana's midsection.

Walter examined the woman, then looked to her belly. Was she...? How had he not noticed before?

With a cry, the professor dove for his weapon.

Walter fired. The gunshot cracked, loud reverberations echoing around the canyon. Enfield gasped, clutched at his ribs, and fell.

Walter closed the distance, keeping his gun trained on the writhing professor. Turn to 230.

<h2 style="text-align:center">224</h2>

"You brought this on yourself," Diana said coldly. She turned away.

The dying professor reached out one hand to her. It formed a claw in the air, grasping at nothing. "I did it for you, damn you!" He cried. "For us! For our baby." His words trailed off as his breath grew short.

Diana lowered her head, but said nothing. Her back was a stiff line in the moonlight.

Enfield's hand dropped. He let out a few short gasps, then stiffened. "She's too powerful," he muttered. "You'll never make it."

A rattle came out of his throat with his last breath, and after that he was still. Diana looked over her shoulder once, then took a few quick steps away.

Walter reached forward and closed the dead man's eyes. What should he say? He didn't know, and he didn't really care to worry about it much. Diana would come around. Or she wouldn't.

He sucked a drag on his smoke. It was good to have tobacco. He wondered if Diana realized the tobacco he was smoking was hers, brought on the wagon of goods to sell in Affliction. He didn't see any reason to mention it.

"Why did you do it?" Diana asked. Turn to 232.
"What now?" Diana asked. Turn to 228.

Diana descended the black stairs. Past the first hundred feet down, she had to find her way by feel, inching each foot forward until she found the lip of the next stair. But before long, a new, dim glow began to emerge from below.

Once, she stumbled, but Garland—no, he was not Garland to her any more. Never again. Mr. Enfield placed the rifle against her shoulder to support her. He made a concerned tutting noise between his lips. "Careful," he said. "Let's get you there all in one piece!"

She shook off his help and continued. Eventually, the dim glow grew strong enough she could make out one stair from the next, and their progress speeded. Finally, she saw the light was in the shape of an open doorway on a landing below them.

"There we are!" Enfield said, satisfaction evident in his voice. "The first door!"

"The first door?" Diana echoed.

"There are three thresholds that must be crossed to reach her chamber. Each is more difficult to pass than the last, and each takes you deeper into the Spirit Realm."

"The Spirit Realm?" Diana felt stupid, simply echoing whatever Enfield said. She couldn't believe this was really happening.

"Not truly..." Enfield said, as he prodded her to keep moving. "We aren't leaving the physical realm you see. This is simply one of those places where the world of men and the world of spirits cross over. They blend together, for a time. That's how The Bled One is able to cross into our world here."

"How... how do you know all this?" Diana asked, bracing herself with an elbow against one wall as she found her way down the stairs.

"It's in the texts!" Enfield said, his voice growing excited. "There is so much you don't know, you could never know, unless you have the eyes to see it! The mysteries of the world can be uncovered..." he continued, but Diana ceased to follow his words. They were the ramblings of a madman.

A madman she had once loved.

When the stairs came to an end, she was almost surprised.

"Here it is. The first threshold," Enfield breathed.

Before them stood an opening. There was no door in it to block the passage. The rim of the aperture was lined with what appeared to be human skulls.

Enfield prodded her from behind. "Go on, there's nothing to be afraid of."

Diana stepped through, a shiver going through her.

She emerged into a massive, underground cavern. It was illuminated by flames lit at intervals along the rim of the cavern, each contained within a shimmering bowl on a pedestal about three feet high. At the far end of the cavern stood a pyramid, so massive that its top was lost in the stone above.

Diana let out her breath in a slow, unconscious sigh. How had Enfield found this place? There was something terrible and magnificent about the lines of the pyramid that loomed before her.

Enfield guided her toward a dark square at the base of the pyramid, an alcove which, she could only assume, would contain a door.

They walked for what seemed like hours across the open space. All the time, Diana felt in the back of her mind the pressure of all that earth above her. It was almost worse that the cavern was so large… it gave an impression similar to sky, yet she could not cease to be aware of the thousands of feet of solid stone that must lie above her. She felt small and helpless in the face of the abominable cavity of this mountain.

As they drew nearer to the pyramid, shapes detached themselves from the darkness and slunk forward. They were low, stalking, their movements those of panthers or lions. Yet as they drew closer, she saw two human men standing before her. Their naked, muscular chests shone darkly in the firelight. Above their necks were not the heads of men, but the heads of jaguars. Each held a spear at the ready as he looked at her with cold, black, animal eyes.

"Who do you bring?" one of them asked Enfield in a guttural voice, lowering his spear toward Diana's throat.

"A gift for the Bled One," Enfield said. Nerves made his voice crack, but otherwise he spoke in low, even tones.

The guardian regarded Diana, his spear unmoving. He looked out at her from a dark and craggy jaguar face, his features those of an ancient and forgotten race. He asked "What is life and death?"

The question jolted Diana. How could she answer that? The seconds dragged on, with all eyes on her.

"Water," Diana said. Turn to 229.
"Power," Diana said. Turn to 221.
"I don't know," Diana said. Turn to 234.

226

Josiah absently bit down on an insect. It crunched between his teeth, releasing a satisfying little spurt of blood. The pests had been crawling all over him since the change, feeding on his blood, making their nests in his body. Sometimes he even felt them moving under his skin.

Once, that would have bothered him.

"Over here, sir?" one of the vampires asked him, pointing at some tracks on the ground.

"No, you idiot!" Josiah snarled. "Those are coyote tracks!" His hand hovered closer to one of his ivory-handled pistols. It was so tempting just to shoot the incompetent thrall. There were so many, after all. It wasn't like one would be missed.

"Here!" another thrall called out. It was Old Man Martin, who had helped him through the change. Josiah hurried up the side of the hill to look at the tracks the cringing old man pointed out. He nodded. "That's them. The tracks are going up."

There were two pairs of tracks, one made by a man, the other by a woman, although both sets of footprints were equally heavy. It fit; Garland was a slight man, and Diana a robust woman. But he didn't like where these tracks were going.

Josiah looked up the mountainside. "Come on," he snarled. Waving some buzzing creature away from his face, he started uphill. It wasn't long before it became clear where the tracks were leading.

Damn.

My Goddess. He spoke the words into his thoughts, into the place in his mind where he knew she was. The place that meant he would never be alone again.

She was there.

They are coming to you. He told her.

He felt the Goddess's presence stirring, her vast mind weighing factors. She inquired with a touch of a feeling about their intentions.

Unknown, Josiah said into his thoughts.

Come to me, Chosen, the Goddess sang into his mind. *Protect me.*

Josiah stiffened his resolve, and slapped a bug on his arm in annoyance. "Gather round," he called to the thrall vampires. They were nearly mindless things, with no true connection to the Bled One. They couldn't hear her voice, not like he could.

The thralls gathered to him, their shouts calling in the more far flung among them. Soon they all assembled to hear his words.

"The humans move toward our mother. The professor may or may not be trustworthy. We must be there to protect her."

"We gonna take the tunnel in the church?" One asked.

A snarl died on Josiah's lips, as a memory—not one of his own—rose unbidden into his mind. In the church, he saw a tunnel. It would lead directly to her lair. *Thank you, my Goddess.*

"We take to the tunnel! We must protect the Goddess!" Josiah cried.

Diana sensed that she was entering a large, open space. Turn to 237.

227

Walter approached the depression cautiously, eyes on that dark opening. The very sight of that gaping blackness made his skin crawl. He didn't want to imagine where it might lead, or what might come out of it.

His feet scuffed the dust and sand as he moved. The detritus of the old campsite passed by him: cooking tins, weather-torn clothes, the lines of half-collapsed tents. The materials looked to be a few months old, the abandoned remains of whatever effort had uncovered this pit in the first place.

Around the pit itself he saw signs of relatively fresh digging efforts. Only a few months of wear obscured the shovel marks, a timeframe consistent with the campsite abandoned here by those unfortunate souls. Did that mean this hole had not been open during the time of his forefathers? What had filled this valley back when these were Arahoca lands?

He heard a scrape that caused adrenaline to flare. He was not alone—but the sound was whipped by the wind in strange ways and he couldn't tell from which direction it had come.

"Walter!" A voice cried out. The woman. Diana.

Walter reacted to the urgency in her voice without taking the time to think. He dove to one side just as a gunshot rang out. A bullet kicked up dust near the spot where he had just been standing.

He could see the figure now, a shadowy shape looming in the rocks behind him. It was the professor.

Walter rolled to his feet and dashed to the nearest cover. He dove behind a rock shelf as another gunshot cracked through the night. Back to the stone, he checked the ammunition in his rifle while he caught his breath. Somewhere out there, he heard a muffled curse.

Pitching his voice to carry, Walter said in a casual drawl, "You must know you've already lost, Professor."

"Why are you following me?" The professor's voice came in a high, frightened gasp.

"Who says I'm following you?" Walter cast back. He darted a look out but could not immediately see where his adversary had vanished to.

"Why else would you be here?" Professor Enfield sneered.

Walter let out a low, amused chuckle. "Perhaps I simply wanted to take in the night air. Tell me, Professor, what happened here?"

"This? This valley was the site of my greatest success. The place where I finally found what I had been looking for."

"And what was that?" Walter asked. He glanced out again, judging the sound of the professor's voice and the available cover. He would have moved to a place where he would have a good shot, but be protected himself.

Enfield laughed, a wild, high-pitched sound. "You of all people should know that. You helped me find it!"

Walter grunted. "The Bled One."

Enfield's laugh came again. "Do you know how many years I searched? Who would have thought I would find it here, at last? A real, live Goddess... and they thought I was mad! I suppose I should thank you, Walter. I couldn't have done it without your stories, back in the Wagon Wheel."

Walter listened to the wind howling through the canyon. It sounded like screams. The screams of all his people who had died.

He needed to keep the man talking. Isolate his location.

"What happened?" Walter asked. As he listened for the answer, he moved very slowly, almost imperceptibly, out into the open.

"See for yourself!" Enfield shouted. "We found it! I found it! I found her." He paused, and Walter fancied he could hear the man licking his lips. He must be close. When his voice came again, it was tortured, twisted. "Of course, I didn't imagine it would be like... She's so powerful. You have no idea... You can't..."

But then the professor laughed, and it was then that Walter saw where the deranged man had hidden. Still maintaining the same glacially slow pace, so as not to draw attention to himself, he began to aim his rifle. Whatever animated the professor now, it was no longer something that could be reasoned with.

The professor's laugh broke into something like a sob, and he said, "She is more powerful than anything you can imagine! She will rule the world! And I will be there by her side. I, and my wife and child."

Diana put her hands on her belly, "Go to hell, Garland."

Walter examined the woman, then looked to her belly. Was she...? How had he not noticed before?

The professor's face turned away, and Walter didn't delay. No longer worrying about stealth, he steadied his aim and took the shot.

Enfield grunted and staggered, then his white form tumbled down from the hillside, tossed by the rocks—until he came to rest at last in the sand not twenty feet from Walter.

Walter closed the distance, keeping his gun trained on the writhing professor. Turn to 230.

228

"What now?" Diana asked.

Walter blew out a long breath of smoke. He could barely see it in the dim moonlight. The moon was about to sink below the rim of the valley above, anyway. Soon it would be even darker down here. Not half as dark as it would be in that pit, though.

He said, "You can do whatever you like. Me? I'm all in." He looked at the pit. From here, it was nothing but a deeper stain of blackness on the general shadowy dimness of the ravine. But down there... down there he would find answers. Something. Something he didn't know before.

"Do you even care at all?" Diana demanded. "You just killed a man! Everyone in this town is dead! Everyone!"

Walter gave her a level look. "'Everyone' in this town killed everyone in my tribe. I don't have a tear to shed for the likes of them. And you—what are you mourning that wreck of a man for? He had you at gunpoint, last I checked."

Diana lowered her face, but not before Walter saw tears glittering on her cheeks. "He wasn't always like that."

Walter took a drag of smoke. He enjoyed the little red ember, the way it lit up as he pulled. A spot of color in a drab world. "Go home. You and your little tyke. Raise that baby in peace, and be grateful for what I never had."

Diana looked down at herself, and lifted both hands to touch her belly. Yes, now that he looked for it, Walter could definitely see a slight swelling there. It had never been obvious under her jacket. Damn her for a fool, bringing that wherever she went.

"I can't do that," she said.

Walter gave an exasperated exhalation. "Suit yourself." He took one last suck on his smoke. It was almost dead now. Like everything else in this blasted world.

Diana said, "I need to make sure this ends. Whatever has started here… if I, if we don't stop it here, there's not a place in this world where anyone will be safe."

Walter shrugged, sucked the last of the smoke from his cigarette, and tossed the dying ember onto Enfield's chest. He turned toward the pit.

Diana gave him a long, steady look as he straightened his gear and recovered his lamp and pack from where he had left them. "What's your stake in this game?" She asked.

Walter spread his hands, an easy grin coming to his face. "I got none. I just want to see what's there."

The pit was about thirty feet across and dark as the blackest Hades. Turn to 239.

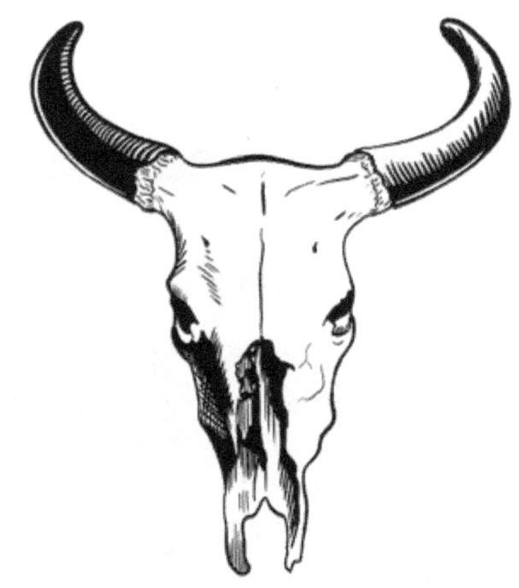

229

"Water," Diana said. Enfield tensed behind her.

"She speaks of course, of the water of life," he interjected quickly, his voice nervous. "Blood," he said in a softer voice.

The guardian met her gaze, his dark eyes impenetrable to her. Then he slowly nodded. "The water of life is all." As the guardians' body language subtly shifted to a more peaceful stance, Diana suddenly realized how close she had come to death.

The spear raised, and the two guardians stepped aside. Enfield prodded Diana with the tip of her rifle, forcing her forward.

They passed between the guardians and approached the gate. Turn to 231.

Walter closed the distance, keeping his gun trained on the writhing professor. The man was twisting in the dust, clutching at the wound that was rapidly bleeding out.

"You did all this?" Walter gestured with his pistol at the campsite surrounding them and the deep hole in the heart of the narrow valley.

Enfield was crying now, tears leaking from his twisted face. "Damn you!" he hissed. "I was supposed to rule the world! I brought her back. I did that! No one else!"

That's when the woman staggered up. Fury in her cold eyes, she snarled, "You selfish... did you ever stop to think? Why were you even in with the other prisoners? You were never like them!"

"I'm sorry! If you only understood... what it feels like... to be touched by her. To have her mind in yours." He squeezed his eyes shut, and the motion forced tears free. "I was spying on them..." he gasped out, breathing heavily. "It was my job to choose who would be her next meal... I didn't want... I never meant..."

Diana turned away, shaking her head bitterly. To Walter, she quietly said, "Thank you."

"Thank him! Ha!" The professor laughed. "He's one to thank, isn't he? You should have seen how quick he was to sell you out."

Diana looked up, her eyes falling on Walter with new wariness. Walter shrugged. The two held each other's gaze for a long moment. Then Diana lifted her hands, showing Walter the bonds that tied her wrists together. There was a silent challenge in her eyes.

Walter let out a low huff of breath, then nodded. He transferred the rifle to his injured hand—it was good enough for this—and drew his knife with the other. Without further hesitation, he sliced Diana's bonds.

"We're even. Don't expect anything more from me," he said.

Diana gave him a long, measuring look, the wind tugging at her hair. She nodded and went to work on removing the rest of her bonds.

Walter sat next to the bleeding and dying professor. The man was no threat; Walter set down his gun and, with the painstakingly slow motions of his injured hand, rolled a smoke. "What did you find down there?" he asked. He sucked the first drag on his fresh-rolled cigarette. It tasted good.

Enfield sneered with helpless malice. "More than you can ever imagine. A palace as ancient as this world. A tomb of the greatest being in existence..." He began to cough, and when the coughing subsided, he was shivering. The blood was still flowing. He didn't have long.

"The Bled One?" Walter asked.

Enfield nodded. The fight was going out of him. "She's still in her tomb, for now. But the Blood returns to her."

A shiver went down Walter's spine. "The Blood?" he asked.

Enfield coughed again. "The Blood of the Arahoca. My theory is that somehow they were holding her imprisoned. The power was in the Blood. When they died... well, now it's all returning. You'll see it when you go down there. I think when she gets it all back..." he shuddered. "That's when she'll wake up. Fully and truly."

"So she's not awake now?" Walter pounced on the question.

Enfield shook his head. "No, she can't use her body yet. But her mind…" A low groan tore out of his throat, the kind of haunting sound that rips out of nightmares.

"I'm sorry!" Enfield wailed. "Diana… She's so powerful! You have no idea. I couldn't help myself!"

She moved to his side, free now, and put one hand on his forehead. He clutched at her. "I'm so sorry," he gasped. Even from here, Walter could see he was feverish and pale. "I didn't… once she touched me, I had no control…" Tears streamed from his face.

Diana lowered her face, and Walter couldn't see her expression in the shadows. But he could see the tension in the line of her shoulders. The way her knuckles turned white as she squeezed the dying man's hand.

"I thought… it was all for you…" Enfield gasped. "Forgive me!"

"I forgive you," Diana whispered. Turn to 235.
"You brought this on yourself," Diana said coldly. Turn to 224.

<h3 style="text-align:center">231</h3>

They passed between the guardians and approached the gate. This would be the second threshold, if Enfield was right. The stone archway looked even more imposing now that she stood under it. Ancient markings—some sort of writing— ran up the face of the stone blocks on either side. Those disquieting symbols meant something, something that set her hair on end and a chill up her spine.

Every instinct told her to flee, to get herself and her unborn child as far from this place as possible, to the ends of the earth if need be. But the pressure of her own rifle in the small of her back left her little choice.

Diana held her breath and stepped through the arch.

Josiah absently bit down on an insect. Turn to 226.

<h3 style="text-align:center">232</h3>

"Why did you do it?" Diana asked. She didn't turn around.

Walter sucked smoke, enjoying the red glow of the burning tobacco in the dark night. "Why not?" he said.

Diana clenched her hands. "You sold me out."

"Yeah," Walter said. He blew a smoke ring.

"And then you freed me."

"Nothin' escapes you, do it?" Walter asked.

"Why?" Diana looked over her shoulder.

Walter crooked a half-smile. "Why not?" He stood, brushing the dust off his pants, and asked, "You goin' home now?"

"Are you?" Diana asked.

"I'm goin' into that hole." Walter nodded toward the deeper black punctuating the general darkness at the heart of the ravine.

Diana gave the hole a long look. At last, she sighed. "Me too."

"You could go home. Be safe. Take care of that little tyke of yours," Walter said, gesturing toward her abdomen. His smoke was almost gone now.

Diana looked down and touched her belly. Yeah, now that he was looking for it, Walter could definitely see a slight swelling there. Damn her for a fool, bringing that wherever she went.

Diana said, "Whatever is happening here… it has to end. I have to make sure of that."

Walter shrugged. "Suit yourself." He took one last drag, then tossed the dying ember of his smoke onto Enfield's chest. He stood, straightening his gun in its holster, and recovered his lamp and pack from where he had left them.

"Why are you going in?" Diana asked.

Walter paused as the slight eddies of wind in the valley whipped around him. Finally, he said, "Why not?"

The pit was about thirty feet across and dark as the blackest Hades. Turn to 239.

233

Walter cautiously followed the voices. Someone—or something—was down this side canyon, and he intended to find out who. Soon he was clambering uphill, following the dry gullet carved by a rivulet of water in some ancient age.

The voices still called to him, whispering, and they were growing stronger. He could almost make out words now. His heart beat faster. Mother?

He came out onto flat ground and ran. He could see the moon now through the gap in the chasm above, and he could hear voices rising, swelling. Suddenly—a warning!

Clapping his eyes to the ground before him, he saw a steep chasm. He jerked to a halt, rocks tumbling loose from the edge as he caught his balance and stumbled backward.

Heart pounding, he settled himself and listened. The voices returned in his mind, murmuring, indistinct, but stronger here than they had been before. He turned his face toward the moonlight, and he felt a presence.

Here. This was the place where his family was from. Where his people had been born. He felt that he stood in a holy place, sacred to the Arahoca, and the moon was its guardian spirit.

They were all with him, he suddenly knew. He was not alone, facing the dangers that lay ahead. They had saved him from stumbling into the chasm, and they would help him again before the night was through. The wind howled more loudly above, and he felt that it was their voices, calling to him in a great host, blessing him.

He whispered ancient words… words his mother had taught him. He didn't know what they meant, but they seemed right. Then he returned to the main branch of the canyon, wondering if he was a mad fool.

Walter kept running down the trail. Turn to 236.

234

"I don't know," Diana said. She could feel Enfield stiffen behind her.

The dark eyes of the guardian stayed fixed on hers, and Diana felt she could fall into those eyes. She felt disapproval, she felt something slipping away, something she had almost had.

The guardian's spear moved too quickly. She had a flash of seeing it strike toward her, and then it slammed into her throat.

Pain blanked her mind. She couldn't get any air. Blood gushed warm down her chest. The blade of the spear was lodged in her throat. That wasn't right. That couldn't be.

"This one is not worthy," the guardian said and drew out his spear.

It made a terrible ripping sound as it came out, a sound that terrified Diana even through her shocked mind. She couldn't move. She couldn't breathe. There was too much blood.

No… she thought of her baby as her body hit the ground. No…

The End.

235

"I forgive you," Diana whispered. Enfield's bloody hands grasped for her, and she held them tightly.

"It was supposed to be… my greatest success. For you. For our baby," he sobbed.

"I know," she said.

"I…" he struggled to speak, but the words did not come.

"Shhh, I know," Diana said. She stroked his wild hair, smoothing it against his head. He let out his breath, and it rattled in his throat. His back arched, his eyes flying wide. A tiny scream cracked from his throat, and then he fell still.

The wind blew Diana's hair over her unflinching face. But when she closed her eyes, tears fell upon the dead man's cheeks.

Walter reached forward and closed Enfield's eyes. Diana stood quickly and took a few steps away.

Walter furrowed his brow. Weren't there things one was supposed to say in this type of situation? But the man had been holding her at gunpoint; sympathy didn't seem appropriate. He sucked a drag on his cigarette. It was good to have tobacco. He wondered if Diana realized the tobacco he was smoking was hers, brought on the wagon of goods to sell in Affliction. He didn't see any reason to mention it.

"Why did you do it?" Diana asked. Turn to 232.
"What now?" Diana asked. Turn to 228.

Walter kept running down the trail. His mind was playing tricks on him as he ran, the wind teasing and following him. He caught himself once, in the moment before he shouted to the wind to—what? What would he say to it, if pressed?

He said nothing, and kept running.

Then, so abruptly he almost didn't notice it—real voices! They wafted to him across the wind, irregular, but this time they had a solidity he couldn't mistake. This was real. He narrowed his eyes and shuttered the lamp so that only the tiniest sliver of light emerged from it.

The voices were coming from up ahead. Snatches came to him on the wind, barely recognizable as human. Was he imagining things again?

He spotted a place where he could climb up to get a better view. He set down the lantern and, in the dim shadow of the moonlight, he scrambled up the slope. Grunting with effort, he pulled himself up over the last ledge. From here he could see the path ahead.

There—two figures in the distance, almost impossible to see without a light of their own. One was bound, a woman… Diana. He recognized the shape of her shoulders, even slumped in defeat, and the way her hair was pulled back under her hat.

The other was the young professor. The man gesticulated wildly, and it was his voice that carried on the wind. Walter only caught a word here and there, "your fault… run… forgive…"

The professor stopped to breath, and when he continued, it was in a quieter voice that did not carry. The woman, Walter realized as his eyes started to pick out details, was bound hand and foot. She was bedraggled, sweaty, and stained by either dirt or blood.

As he watched, the professor brandished a rifle and, at gunpoint, forced the woman to stand. Prodding her before him, he continued on down the trail.

Walter leaned back amongst the rocks, his mouth pursed in thought. This was unexpected, but not entirely surprising. He had helped deliver the woman into the professor's hands, after all, in exchange for sharing with him William Masters' weakness. Masters was dead. Did he still owe the professor anything? Did he owe the woman anything? Or perhaps it was Josiah he owed, who had died before him in the end?

He decided to keep following and see what happened. Carefully, he lowered himself back down to the path and followed the trail.

From time to time he heard them ahead. Loud altercations periodically disturbed the night, followed by long stretches in which they moved in silence.

It was perhaps an hour later when the path opened into a large clearing. The canyon came to an end here in a large, round depression. Across the depression were strewn the remains of a campsite, where the two had presumably disappeared. Some tents still stood, while others had collapsed under wind and blown dust. Digging tools still remained, half-buried, near abandoned pots, pans and clothing.

In the heart of the clearing yawned a dark pit. Recent activity had uncovered ancient stonework in the depths of that pit, and at the center of it all: stairs that curved down into a black aperture as ancient as the world. Who knew how deep those stairs led, or where they led?

For reasons unknown, Walter felt himself drawn to that pit, to those stairs. He had been raised on stories of the Bled One, the ancient being whom his people had kept in torpor. Now his people were gone, and a haunting curiosity pulled him toward the place they had guarded for so long. What would he find if he descended those stairs? If he entered the womb of the earth itself?

He stopped for a moment to set down his lamp and pack.

Walter approached the depression cautiously, eyes on that dark opening. Turn to 227.

Walter found a dark place to hide and wait, watching. Turn to 223.

237

Diana sensed that she was entering a large, open space. No sooner had her eyes adjusted to the darkness than Enfield struck a match; the flare of light hurt her eyes. He retrieved a lamp from somewhere and lit it, holding it aloft, but somehow the air itself seemed to suck away the light. As the shapes before her began to take form, she realized they must be in the entry hall of some ancient temple. Decaying pews blocked her path and ancient candlesticks gleamed with reflected light. Crumbling statues lined the hall, though she couldn't make out their shapes.

Enfield pushed her forward. "Come on," he muttered. His voice had lost its easy buoyancy. As they moved, shadows danced across the broken statues looming in the darkness. Diana couldn't quite make out their faces, but those gaunt, horrific shapes made her skin crawl.

"This way." Enfield tugged on her arm, the rifle held loosely in his other hand. He was getting sloppy. Diana moved along quickly. The more helpful she was, the sooner he would lower his guard. She knew the man, perhaps as well as anyone alive. Once his attention was on something else, he would give her an opening.

Doorways lined the great hall, but he knew exactly which one to go to. This led them to a crumbling passageway. Diana's shadow danced ahead of her.

Suddenly a drop of liquid struck her cheek.

"What is that?" Diana asked, stopping in her tracks. Another droplet hit her arm. She touched her finger to her cheek and it came away red. Blood?

Disgust roiled up inside her. Diana looked up. The ceiling of the little hallway was heavy with red blood, slowly forming into droplets that fell like condensation on the floor below. "Go back!" she cried, before she could think.

Enfield stopped her. "It's everywhere throughout the temple. You can't get away from it." His voice was quiet.

"What the hell is it?" Diana asked. She held out her hand as another falling droplet of the stuff hit her fingers.

"It's the Blood of the Arahoca."

"I—" Diana fumbled for words.

"They stole her Blood, the Blood of the Goddess, thousands of years ago. They stole her Blood and buried her, dry and powerless, deep under the earth. Here.

"They tried to destroy her, but nothing can destroy her. Whatever they did with her Blood, wherever they tried to hide it, it would find its way back to her someday. So they stored it the only way they could: in their own veins, and in the veins of their descendants."

Diana stared. "The Indians?"

"Oh yes." Enfield nodded. "They were her jailers. But they were also jailed. They could not leave this valley, and they didn't. But eventually a new people came. Settlers, who slaughtered the Arahoca. Almost all of them. They spilled Arahoca Blood into the thirsty earth, and set my Goddess's Blood free once more. Now," he held out a hand, catching a gleaming red droplet as it fell, "It returns to her."

Diana's skin crawled. The Battle of Red Bluff. The Arahoca had been butchered. And her people celebrated that day, called it a great victory. Her stomach turned to think of it.

Enfield looked to her with a gleam in his eyes. "Only one of her jailers remained. One of the cursed Arahoca. And now even he has fallen, and the last of her Blood is free to return to her. She will return, truly return at last!"

"You're insane," Diana said, taking a step away from him.

Enfield grabbed her shoulders in both hands, his eyes wide and eager. "You must understand! You must see! Diana, this is the moment of her re-birth. The last Arahoca is dead. The Blood returns. You and I..." He shook his face as a droplet of blood landed on it, then continued, "We have a chance to rule this world!"

Now, Diana realized. This was her moment, while his thoughts were elsewhere, the gun held loosely, his body close enough to attack. She began to shift her weight.

"Well, well, well..." a smooth female voice came from the far end of the hallway. Enfield stepped back, putting both hands on his gun and looking past Diana. Diana bit back a snarl of frustration. She had been so close. She looked over her shoulder, to see the girl Beatriz standing at the far end of the hall.

All color seemed to have been purged from the dark young woman. Her once-olive skin was white as bone, her hair black as midnight, and she wore a dress as pure as driven snow. On her lips was a small smile.

"Did you bring me a gift?" Beatriz purred.

Enfield's hand moved protectively to Diana's shoulder, though he held the rifle so as to visibly shove it into her side. "She's not for you, witchling. Let us past."

"I don't know..." Beatriz pouted. "Didn't you bring me anything?"

Enfield stammered, "She's for the Goddess! Let us pass!"

The girl rolled her eyes, then stepped aside to let Enfield and Diana move out of the hallway into the chamber that lay beyond.

Dozens of candles burned here. The room was opulently appointed, with lace furniture, silver candlesticks and more, much of it with no more than a few decades of decay. The white lace was tattered and stained with grey dust, but in the candlelight, it could nearly pass for rich. The white finery stayed clean because the arched stone ceiling directed the blood from above down the walls, instead of allowing it to drip on the lace and couches.

Enfield reached for something in the floor—a trapdoor? Diana fumed. She could have overpowered him a dozen times over had not the damn woman interfered.

Beatriz moved with startling swiftness, and suddenly she was on top of the trapdoor, her weight holding it closed. "Don't leave so soon, Garland," she said. There was a predatory gleam in her eye.

"What do you want, creature?" Enfield demanded. Diana looked more closely. Did he seem… frightened?

Beatriz gave her best kittenish look. "Just a little taste…" Her eyes flicked to Diana.

Diana's blood ran cold. Enfield sighed in exasperation and touched his fingers to his forehead. "Fine. Diana, come here. Give her your hand."

Diana stepped forward, extending her hands. Turn to 243.
Diana stepped back, shaking her head. Turn to 252.

238

Diana stood, panting, looking down at her foe. Beatriz lay on the ground, too many bones broken to count. Her face had returned to human appearance now, but she made a completely inhuman whispering moan. Her eyes were still pure black.

Diana grabbed a shard of the shattered chair. She pinned the broken vampire to the floor with one knee and raised the broken piece of wood high overhead, managing to grip it tightly despite her bound hands.

"Wait, no--!" Enfield cried. She ignored him.

Beatriz keened, "You will never win. The Goddess is nearly returned! The world will end in a tumult of—"

Diana brought her makeshift stake down hard, right into the vampire's heart. Beatriz's body wracked once, then went still.

Diana rose to her feet and stepped back. She knew what would happen next, and she didn't want to be here when insects started crawling out of the body. Already, the dead woman's cold, white skin began to twitch with the movement of things inside it.

Enfield stood aghast. He muttered something as Diana approached and pushed up his glasses. His face was slick with sweat. "Usually, she's not like this," he said, making a nervous gesture toward the injured Beatriz. The rifle hung limply in one hand.

Without hesitation, Diana ripped the gun out of his hands. His eyes went wide and he shakily raised his hands, stumbling backward.

"Diana, I…" Enfield tried to speak, but found no words.

Diana turned on him. His face was pale and clammy, his whole body tense with anxiety. Her hands were bound, but that didn't stop her from holding the gun. She lifted it to point at his heart.

"Don't you have anything to say for yourself?" Diana asked. Turn to 250.

239

The pit was about thirty feet across and dark as the blackest Hades. Walter and Diana stood on the brink, looking in. The first few feet were cut from fresh earth, but below that, at about the five foot depth mark, the remains of ancient stonework had been uncovered.

Even in the dim light, something about the shape of that stonework gave Diana a sense of unease. It just wasn't right, somehow.

"Ladies first," Walter said, gesturing broadly in a callow imitation of gallantry.

Diana swore under her breath and knelt. She slung her rifle—recovered from the treacherous Enfield—over her shoulder and tightened her belt. Using hands and knees, she clambered down to the level of the stonework below. She placed her foot on it hesitantly at first, then with increasing confidence as it proved it could hold her weight.

At the heart of the broad, flat stone platform was another opening, even blacker than the rest.

"Bring that light over here," she said.

Walter swore as his feet gave way and he slid the last couple feet to the level of the stonework. He was trying to hold the lamp in his bandaged hand, and his rifle in the other. Just then, Diana remembered with sickening vividness the sound and sight of Walter's wrist snapping during the fight with the reverend in the church. It seemed like so long ago already.

"Come here. How's your wrist?" She demanded.

"Damn you," Walter grumbled, but he allowed her to coax the lamp out of his hand and examine the wrist.

She set them both to kneeling and placed the lamp nearby. Carefully, she unwrapped the bandages and grimaced as the bloody wound came into view. Walter hissed under his breath as she touched it.

"What happened? Did the bone break out of your skin?"

Walter nodded shortly.

Diana touched along the arm and frowned, feeling the straight bones beneath. "Who set it?" She asked.

"I did," Walter said.

Diana looked up at him sharply. That was impossible. No one could set their own bone—not with so bad a break. The pain would drive a man insane. Yet as she looked into that weathered face, she found herself believing him.

She grunted and shook her head. "If only I had my things..."

"Here," Walter said, and slung her the small pack he was carrying.

Diana narrowed her eyes as she rifled through the things inside. She recognized them. She hesitated, then sighed. There was no point in mentioning it. She pulled out fresh bandages and a bottle of whisky.

"This will sting," she said, immediately wondering why she had bothered. Walter didn't even flinch as she poured the whisky over his wound. She tied a clean bandage on. "You're lucky. There's no rot yet. Stay lucky, and it'll heal cleanly."

Walter grunted. She gave him a steady look, which he did not return. She took a deep breath, then simply replaced the items in the pack and handed it back to him. She recovered the lamp and said, "I can carry this. I've got two good hands."

"Lead the way," Walter said with a bitter twist to his smile.

Diana returned to the opening. In the light of the lamp, she could see stairs that descended into absolute blackness.

She looked over her shoulder. Walter nodded. Together, they plunged into the darkness.

In the darkness, a creature prowled. Turn to 248.

240

Diana held her breath, waiting to see what Walter would do.

"Name my price," he whispered, turning the girl's white hand over between his fingers as though examining it for mysteries.

"What if I have nothing? What if I have never had anything? What if anything I ever wanted was taken from me when I was six years old, a boy, watching what they..." He twitched, steadied himself, and said, "what they did to my mother?"

Walter jerked the pale vampire's hand, pulling her toward him. Inches from her ear, he whispered, "What do you offer if I want nothing?"

The hand came from nowhere. Suddenly Walter was wielding a knife; he drew it across Beatriz's throat without warning or preamble. The girl's dark lips opened, and—for the first time—color appeared on her face. Red liquid leaked from her mouth, staining her lips, then her cheeks and chin.

She coughed once, spraying Walter with thick blood. Holding her gently, as though a lover, he lowered her to the floor. Beatriz's lips moved, but there was no sound that came from them, except the bubbling of blood from the gash in her throat.

"Shhhh," Walter said. "Shhhh... it's all going to be quiet now. There's nothing to worry about anymore. Rest, now."

Her dark eyes fixed on his, and he met them with something like pleasure. Her hand gripped at his coat. Then the strength left her.

Diana licked her lips. Her bones did not seem to want to obey as she commanded them to move her to Walter's side. She said, "I thought... I thought only one with true faith could kill them."

Walter did not look away from the dying vampire, but one corner of his lips twisted up. "I guess I have faith."

Diana fought an urge to get far, far away, with or without Walter. "Do you know which way to go next?"

A strange hissing sound began to rise from the body. The vampire's corpse was collapsing in on itself. Diana remembered the way insects had swarmed from the body of the Reverend after they killed him. Already, a churning motion was beginning under Beatriz's skin.

She took a step back. "Quickly?"

"Down," Walter said. Turn to 254.

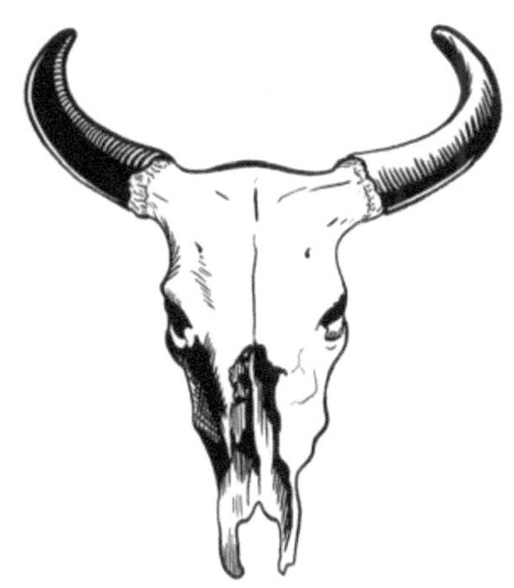

241

Diana shook her head in disgust. "Get out," she said.

Enfield's face scrunched up, and for a moment she thought he was going to cry. She clenched her jaw, levelled the gun at his face, and said, "Now."

The man nodded, turning away. After a few steps, he hesitated, turned back, and started to say, "Diana…"

"Go!" She interrupted him.

Enfield fled the room.

All the energy seemed to leave her body at once. All she wanted to do was sit down and rest, but there was no time. Reflexively, she cracked open the rifle to check that it was loaded.

Empty.

She shook her head in disbelief. Had it been unloaded this whole time? Enfield knew seven languages, but he didn't know to keep his rifle loaded.

She had to get out of here. Turn to 253.

The stairs continued downward for what seemed to be an eternity. Only the flickering light of the lamp illuminated the stonework all around them. After a time, the sheer repetitiveness of the twisting staircase caused a kind of vertigo in Diana. She had the strangest sensation that she was simply walking the same set of stairs again and again.

Only Walter's presence behind her, steady and quietly malevolent, kept her from losing her mind.

Eventually, a glow appeared ahead. At first, she thought she was imagining it. Then she rounded a bend and saw a landing far below, and a doorway. Diana's heart beat faster as she became sure the light ahead was real, and she found herself hurrying down the stairs.

As she emerged out into the light, she was briefly stunned by the enormity of what she saw. A tremendous pyramid, entirely underground, rose before her in the space of a massive cavern. The upper portion of the pyramid was lost in darkness, either encased in stone or simply lost to visible light. But the lower part was as broad as a small town.

A wide alcove opened in the front and center of the pyramid's base, and set in that alcove, a massive doorway cloaked in shadows. She could see the source of the light as well: flaming braziers at the entrance of the alcove.

A chill ran down Diana's spine as she took her first steps into that space. Walter came up alongside her. He whistled as he scanned the monumental cavern, then said, "Come on."

They trekked out into that open space before the pyramid. She felt dwarfed by the massive scale of the cavern they had entered. Suddenly she caught her breath. "There! Did you see that?" She froze. "Something moved."

Walter's eyes narrowed. He drew his gun and held it lightly as he continued stalking forward. As they approached the base of the pyramid, they found statues flanking the pathway. Each was of a stone warrior with the head of a jaguar.

Diana's nerves crawled as she stepped between the first pair of these stone guardians. She had seen something move here, she was sure of it. After they had gone a bit further, Diana heard a sound of grinding stone. She whirled—the farthest guardian had stepped from its pedestal, but it was no longer a man. It was a stone jaguar, and it prowled toward her with slow grace.

"Keep moving!" Walter barked in a low voice. "Don't show fear." He kept walking, his pace steady and unhurried.

Diana fell in beside him, attempting to match his demeanor of indifference. She heard more grinding sounds coming from behind, and her neck twitched with the effort it took to not look behind her. Any moment, she expected one of those jaguars to pounce. Its claws would tear through her jacket, ripping her flesh and...

Walter came up short. The pyramid loomed above them. From here she could see the entrance alcove was the size of a barn, and the door at the far end large enough to drive a wagon through, team and all.

The last two guardians, the ones flanking the alcove itself, stepped down from their stone pedestals and, as she watched, their shape flowed and blended until they were not men, but stone jaguars pacing toward her.

Walter tensed, and Diana swallowed hard. She loosened her rifle, ready to grab it quickly if needed, though she couldn't see what use bullets would have against stone.

One of the jaguars picked up its pace. It broke into a lope, quickly crossing the distance between them. Diana flinched, her hand jerking for the rifle, but a quick touch from Walter stopped her.

The jaguar slowed just in time, and at the moment it came to a stop, it stepped up—into the shape of a man. Its jaguar head regarded Walter with onyx black eyes.

"The Blood returns," the jaguar-man said.

"The Blood returns," Walter agreed.

The skin on Diana's neck prickled. What was going on here?

The two figures, one a man in the shape of a monster, and the other a monster in the shape of a man, locked gazes for a long moment. Then the jaguar turned away. It looked at its twin in front of Diana, then both parted to allow them to pass.

Walter gave a lazy smile, touched the brim of his hat, and walked through; Diana quickly followed.

As she moved, she heard scuffing and grinding sounds from all sides. She glanced behind her to see that the jaguar guardians had completely surrounded them some moments ago; yet now, without a visible signal from any, all were returning to their pedestals.

Diana let out her breath, and only then did she realize she had been holding it. Walter was stalking smoothly forward. She hastened to keep pace with him.

"What the hell just happened?" Diana asked. Turn to 251.
Diana simply shook her head and kept her rifle close at hand. Turn to 244.

243

Diana stepped forward, extending her hands. Her breath caught in her throat, and her heart pounded, but she knew what she was doing. At least, she told herself she did.

"What do you want?" she asked, her fear not entirely feigned.

Beatriz glided toward her. The young woman looked even smaller in death than she had in life, but a wicked gleam in her eyes removed any lingering hint of the innocence that had once been written in that face.

The vampiress touched Diana's hands. Diana's skin crawled—that touch was cold as the grave. "Garland, you shouldn't have… she's so strong!" Beatriz purred.

"Just a taste!" Enfield snapped.

Diana's heart pounded. Almost… almost... wait for it…

Beatriz stroked Diana's hands, toying with the tied ropes, and then traced her fingernail up the inside of Diana's wrist. "Where to bite…?" she mused, as a gourmet ponders where to begin the meal. She placed one finger under Diana's chin and pushed up her chin to expose her neck.

It took every ounce of self-control for Diana to remain still. Almost…

Beatriz leaned in, her eyes fixed on Diana's neck. Her hands left Diana's wrists, her focus elsewhere.

Now.

Diana grabbed Beatriz by the front of her dress and spun, heaving her off her feet. The vampiress was lighter than she seemed, nearly throwing Diana off-balance. Beatriz screamed in rage, but before she could dig her claws into Diana's shoulder, Diana hurled her bodily at Enfield.

The two went crashing to the floor in a tangle of limbs and screams. Almost instantly the vampire was on her feet again—or was she just floating?—her eyes pure black and her white, tattered robes spreading out around her.

"You will suffer and die for this, human!" Beatriz howled. Her mouth opened wide—wider than any human mouth. Her teeth were a thousand tiny points glittering in that cavernous maw framed by two sharp canines.

Diana grabbed a chair and leaped forward. Using the full weight of her body, she slammed the chair into the floating vampiress. Frail bones shattered under the impact. Beatriz howled in pain as Diana lifted the chair again.

"What are you doing? Stop it!" Enfield cried.

She ignored him and slammed the chair into the girl again, and again, and again, until the chair was a broken wreck in her hands.

Diana stood, panting, looking down at her foe. Turn to 238.

244

Diana simply shook her head and kept her rifle close at hand. The dark threshold of the doorway loomed before them, and then they were through. She raised the lantern.

They came into what looked like the entry hall of an ancient temple. Broken statues and tattered tapestries could be seen decorating the hall, along with decaying pews and ancient candlesticks. "What on earth?" Diana breathed.

Walter cast his eyes this way and that, as though searching for something. Then a droplet of liquid splashed on his face and he looked up. "The Blood returns," he muttered and held out a hand.

With that, Diana heard the plop of something wet striking his hand. Walter looked down at his palm, then showed Diana. The droplet gleamed black in the dim light.

Diana recoiled. "What is that?"

"The Blood returns," Walter repeated. He looked at his hand, and in a dreamlike voice, he said, "It's the Blood of my people. The Blood shed by those who slew the Arahoca. It's returning. And I'm returning too…" His voice faded away with the final words.

Diana's skin crawled. She took a step back and looked up. The ceiling of the room was coated in blood, much of it slowly forming into droplets. As she watched, another fell—she had to step aside to dodge it.

A slow clapping sound interrupted Diana's thoughts. She spun. A woman in white stood at the far end of the hall, bringing her hands together in a slow, uninterrupted rhythm. "Congratulations," the woman said. "You figured it out."

Walter looked to her, his eyes unsurprised, and still unfocused, as though seeing things that Diana could not, and would never, see. "I remember," he said simply.

"You remember what the Bled One wants you to remember. You carry her Blood. You carry her memories." She stopped clapping, and walked forward, drifting down the passage between the pews. She moved as though she didn't need to walk; she could simply glide.

Walter started toward her, his eyes sharpening and hardening as they came into focus on her. He was a prowling cat on the move. "What do you mean I carry her Blood?" he asked.

Diana, swallowing hard, did the only thing she could think of. She moved to one side, getting out her rifle, to flank the woman in white. She had no idea if bullets would work in this place, but she could only use the tools she had. Something was going on here, something bigger than her or her baby.

The two figures slid closer, until both, as if by unspoken agreement, came to a stop at arm's reach from each other. The woman in white cocked her head and smiled. "Don't tell me you don't remember me," she said coyly.

Diana stifled a gasp. She knew that pallid face. Beatriz. They had saved the girl from vampires in the bar on their first night. She had vanished into the night, leaving only her shed skin behind.

The girl's new skin was far more pale than it had been before. In fact, all color seemed to have been bleached from the young woman. Her skin was pale as death, her long, beautiful hair white as snow. Even her eyes had no color—they had simply turned pure black.

Beatriz put out one hand, as if offering Walter to take it. "Our Goddess wants to meet you. Won't you come with me?"

A droplet of blood landed on Diana's cheek. She stifled a cry of disgust and wiped it away, then returned to sighting on Beatriz down the sights of her rifle.

Walter trembled, his eyes still unfocused. He raised his hand and took the girl's small one in his. He forced words to his lips. "You said I carry her Blood."

Beatriz laughed, a tinkling sound. "Of course you do. You are the last of the Arahoca, the last living human with her Blood." She leaned in, drawing on Walter's hand to pull him closer to her, and quietly said, "She wants it back. She'll give you anything. All you have to do is name your price."

Diana held the girl's head in her sights.

Diana breathed in, out, and fired. Turn to 249.
Diana held her breath, waiting to see what Walter would do. Turn to 240.

Diana couldn't put her child at risk. She fled. She had to keep the baby safe. Nothing else mattered.

She ran back out through the dark tunnels and corridors. The walls slid by her, dreamlike, and she realized she was crying in fear and hope. She passed jaguar faces and stone men, but they watched her, impassive, as she flew past.

Up. Up. Up again. She burst out onto the surface of the world as morning broke across the eastern horizon. She fell to her knees and kissed the dirt her hands drew up from the solid earth. Light bathed her face as she wiped away her tears.

She was safe. Her child was safe.

She stumbled out into the desert, alone. But she would survive. She always had. She put her hand on her belly. They would both survive.

Epilogue. Turn to 294.

"It's too late for that now," Diana said. She pulled the trigger.

Enfield jerked as the gun clicked empty. He stared at her, wide-eyed. Diana shook her head in disbelief. Had it been unloaded this whole time? Enfield knew seven languages, but he didn't know to keep his rifle loaded.

"Diana," he said, licking his lips.

"Get out," she spat. Right now, he was too terrified to fight, but she worried about letting him linger while she reloaded the gun, especially with her hands still tied.

"Diana, please…" His voice took on a pleading, pathetic tone.

Her look was like granite, and he seemed to wilt under that gaze. Finally, he turned and fled the room.

She let out the breath she hadn't realized she was holding.

She had to get out of here. Turn to 253.

"Who does he think he is?" Diana muttered, and held the lamp high. She had to move quickly to keep up with Walter's receding form. The passageway was narrow and cramped, with barely enough room to stand. Her legs complained at the uneven footing, and she couldn't imagine how she would have managed it if she couldn't see. How did Walter do it?

Suddenly one wall vanished beside them, and Diana looked down into an infinite, dark void. The brush of air against her cheek told her the space beside and below them was huge.

Heart pounding, she clung to the far wall. A single misstep and she could fall to her death.

Walter turned around. "I told you not to look. Stay on the path." He took the lamp from her nerveless fingers and tossed it into the void. She watched as the light tumbled into nothingness. After a few seconds, the rapid movement of air blew out the light, and then she saw nothing. After a few more seconds passed, she heard the distant shatter of glass.

"Come on." Walter's voice sounded startlingly close in the black.

Swallowed by absolute darkness, Diana followed the sound of footsteps. Turn to 264.

In the darkness, a creature prowled. It did not think or remember. It had no need to. It scented blood, and that was enough. It ascended the mountains on all fours, climbing wherever the trail of blood led it. It wore clothes, but when they got in its way, it tore them off.

In due time, the trail led to a slot canyon. The creature paced at the entrance, staring into the murky depths. Something about the canyon unsettled it, yet that was where the trail of blood led.

It snarled, for it thirsted, and the blood was no longer fresh. It turned to the full moon, lowering in the sky, and howled.

Suddenly images assaulted its mind. It scrambled and ran in circles, for it did not understand what was happening. Slowly, the frenetic pace slowed. It felt a presence, a presence it felt it should know. Mother? No, that wasn't quite right.

The Bled One.

The words came into its head without warning or bidding. They were planted in its mind, quickly followed by another thought: service. It owed this Bled One everything. It owed it its life, its loyalty, its very existence.

Its breathing quickened. Its mouth hung open, salivating at the anticipation of the pleasure of serving her.

A reprimand. It had to slow its thinking, pay attention. It whimpered and tried to concentrate.

More images were coming into its mind. This time, it understood. There was a tunnel. In a hidden place, behind the burnt out remains of a building. The building had had a cross once.

That caused something in the creature to twinge. A cross…

It pushed away that uncomfortable sensation and ran toward the no-longer-existing cross, toward the ruined church, and toward the tunnel. That tunnel would take it to the secret place. The safe place. The place where the Bled One waited, which might no longer be so safe.

It would protect her.

As it ran, something caught its eye. It slowed, examining the strange object. It was round, with a little bowl shape, and a brim that ringed the bowl. *Hat.* The word slowly came into his mind. Memory, this time, not from her.

It picked up the hat. Remembrance. It remembered walking on two legs. Wearing the hat. Grinning, it stood and placed the hat on its head. It liked that.

Realizing the tunnel was a shortcut, and it had no need to hurry, it strolled into town. The tunnel would take it where it needed to be in good time. It tipped its hat to the presence in his mind. It would protect its mistress.

The stairs continued downward for what seemed to be an eternity. Turn to 242.

249

Diana breathed in, out, and fired. The shot was good—before either of them could react, a red hole appeared in Beatriz's temple, and a bloody mess erupted out of the far side of her head.

Walter didn't react. His catlike eyes just followed the violence, noting it, cataloguing it.

Beatriz's head lolled, then came back up. She turned her head to Diana, black eyes wide with madness, and laughed—an unearthly, hollow laugh that chilled Diana to the bone. "The mortal woman wants to interfere. Silly human."

Diana cranked the bolt action on her rifle, grabbing another shell, but Beatriz was already moving. She spread her mouth wide—impossibly wide—and hundreds of sharp teeth sprouted from her gums. Not just two, or a single line, but rows of them, going back as far as Diana could see. The mouth distended impossibly, opening large enough to swallow an arm. And Beatriz pounced.

Diana lifted her rifle, but the vampire's motion was arrested before she made it two feet. Walter grabbed her by the hair, and the rest of her body tried to keep going as her head was jerked back.

In a flash, it was done. Walter drew the knife deep across Beatriz's throat, so deep it nearly severed the head from the body. Beatriz didn't have time to scream.

A second slash, and the spine was severed. The white-clad body dropped as Walter held the girl's head by her hair. It spun slightly.

For a moment, the rotation turned the eyes toward Diana, and she wanted to vomit. The lips twitched, dark red blood leaking from the open mouth.

Then Walter threw it. He wiped his hand on his clothing. "She had nothing I wanted."

The knife fell from his grip, and only then did Diana realize he had been wielding it with his broken right wrist. She couldn't imagine the amount of pain that must have caused him, even if it hadn't dislocated the break once more.

Walter knelt, his eyes flaring, and gathered the dagger with his good left hand. He flexed the fingers of his right hand, the pain only showing as a twitch at the corner of his eye.

Diana started toward him, already extending her hands to check his wound, but he turned on her, and something in his gaze made her stop.

He gave her a long stare, and Diana reddened under that examination. "I—I'm sorry," she stammered. "I just thought…"

"It was a good opening," Walter said softly, and turned away.

Diana let out her breath in an unconscious sigh of relief. Sometimes she wasn't sure who she was more afraid of, the monster she had come here to kill, or the one she had come in with.

A strange hissing sound began to rise from the decapitated body. The vampire's corpse was collapsing in on itself. Diana remembered the way insects had swarmed from the body of the Reverend after they killed him. Already, a churning motion was beginning under Beatriz's skin.

"Which way do we go now?" she asked with some urgency.

"Down," Walter said. Turn to 254.

<h2 style="text-align:center">250</h2>

"Don't you have anything to say for yourself?" Diana asked.

The young professor mumbled, sweating. She could still see the man she loved in there somewhere. The lines of his face were familiar, lines which had once seemed so kind. The nervous energy that had once been charming, she now found repulsive.

Something occurred to her, which had been nagging at the back of her mind. "Why were you even locked in with the other prisoners?"

He turned his face away. Was that shame she saw in his eyes? "I was spying on them. It was my job to choose who would be her next meal… I didn't want… I never meant…"

Diana shook her head. "What became of you, Garland?" she asked. "When did it happen? Were you always like this, and I never knew?"

"Diana, please…" Enfield said, slowly lowering to his knees. "I love you… I always have. I just want what's best for you, and for the baby." He gulped, and in a quick, breathy voice he said, "Don't kill me. I was just trying to… I just needed to know… For old time's sake, you remember, Diana, don't you? The things you said to me? You said you would always love me! You said it!"

Diana's finger settled on the rifle's trigger.

"It's too late for that now," Diana said. She pulled the trigger. Turn to 246.
Diana shook her head in disgust. "Get out," she said. Turn to 241.

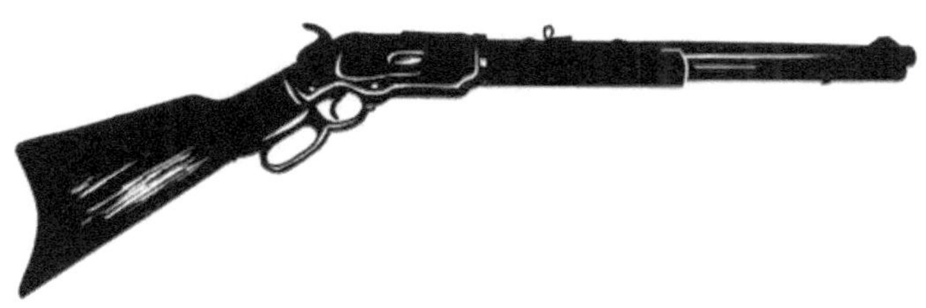

"What the hell just happened?" Diana asked.

Walter shrugged one shoulder and kept walking. She hurried to keep up with him, and when they were out of earshot, hissed quietly, "What the hell, Walter? How did you get us past them?"

He turned to look at her with those unsettling, alien blue eyes. "Don't ask questions you don't want to know the answers to."

Diana simply shook her head and kept her rifle close at hand. Turn to 244.

Diana stepped back, shaking her head. Enfield narrowed his eyes in irritation, but before he could lift his gun, the vampiress sprang across the room. With inhuman speed, Beatriz slammed into Diana, the impact forcing the larger woman backward.

Diana crashed against a wall. The white woman's mouth yawned wide, showing rows of tiny, sharp teeth and two large canines. Despite her pretty looks, her mouth smelled fetid. It was the smell of grave dust, old blood, decay. Diana gagged.

"Hold still, my pet," Beatriz whispered. She gripped Diana's shoulders and leaned in, going for the throat. Diana struggled, but Beatriz held her with monstrous strength.

Straining with every muscle in her body, Diana jerked one arm up to get her elbow under the small vampiress' throat—just in time. "I saved you," Diana grunted. "Remember? I saved your life. I saved your brother."

Beatriz hissed, then let out a low, keening wail of rage and pain. "You killed my brother! He would have come back to me, and you destroyed him!" As she howled her anger, Beatriz drifted upward, until she was floating in the air above Diana, her white dress forming a halo around her. "How dare you!? I will destroy you!"

"No!" Enfield shouted, his voice high and desperate. He stepped forward, holding his hands out wide. "We can work this out! Please, stop fighting!"

Diana didn't wait. She rolled to one side, grabbing whatever her bound hands could come up with. She wound up with a book as her roll turned her upward again, and she threw it at the floating, white apparition in the air above her.

Beatriz knocked the book away without effort, but in the moment it took her to do so, Diana laid hands on a chair. She lifted it heavily as she came to her feet. The white vampiress descended, hands extended like claws, voice keening. Diana heaved with all her strength, swinging the chair with both hands.

The solid wood chair slammed into the slight body of the vampiress, shattering bones and ripping flesh. Beatriz crumpled under the attack, falling heavily against one wall. A spray of red blood now stained the white garments, but she was not yet defeated.

Her childlike face emerged from under one white-clad arm, twisted in rage so completely that it no longer even looked human. She hissed, her mouth opening so wide that her chin stretched to nearly touch her chest. Her eyes were pure black now, her face lined with impossible ridges.

Diana roared and leaped forward, swinging the chair as she did so. She threw it with all her strength, just as the broken white body began to float once more. The chair slammed into the small monster once again. Slender bones shattered under the impact. Beatriz howled in pain as Diana lifted the chair again.

"What are you doing? Stop it!" Enfield cried.

She ignored him and slammed the chair into the girl again, and again, and again, until the chair was a broken wreck in her hands.

Diana stood, panting, looking down at her foe. Turn to 238.

253

She had to get out of here. She set down the gun and started working hastily to get herself out of the bonds. They had been inexpertly tied and started coming loose now that she could give them her full attention.

A hissing sound, like a teapot coming to a boil, began to whistle through the room.

Diana shot a glance toward the sound. Beatriz. Her body was bloated now, swelling from the inside and making a terrible keening sound. She remembered the reverend. She knew what would come next.

The ropes came off, and Diana hastily pulled her hands free of them, discarding what was left of her bonds. She grabbed the empty rifle and quickly slammed a new cartridge in, cranking the bolt to get it loaded. Now she was ready.

She stopped in her tracks. Ready for what?

Her first instinct was to get the hell out of here. But where would she run? What would she do? If everything Enfield had said was true… how long before the vampires swarmed the world?

But it wasn't just her own life she was taking care of now. Her belly wasn't even swelling yet, barely hard to the touch. But there was another life growing in there. What would happen to her child if she went after the vampire Goddess and failed?

What would happen to her child if she didn't try?

Diana couldn't put her child at risk. She fled. Turn to 245.
Nowhere would be safe if she didn't take the fight to Tezoca. Turn to 255.

"Down," Walter said. He started off in a direction apparently chosen at random, leading Diana through one dark passageway after another. Behind them, the hissing of Beatriz's final death faded into the distance as it reached its crescendo.

Before long, they came into a room different from the rest. The place had been decorated with much that had been looted from Affliction and the surrounding ranches, before fire had destroyed what was left. A canopy bed draped across one corner, while finely carved dressers and mirrors were scattered with rich personal items, jewelry and combs. Diana picked one up, recognized it as a twin to one that had been in the vampire girl's hair, and tossed it down again. "This was Beatriz's room," she said.

Walter wasn't paying attention. He was running his fingers over a carpet in the floor, that faraway look in his eyes. Diana felt a chill run down her arms, not for the first time, as he yanked back the carpet to reveal a door between the flagstones.

"This way," he said. He heaved up the stone door to reveal a ladder going down. Without hesitation, he climbed in.

Shaking her head, Diana followed.

They came down into a pitch dark tunnel. Diana held up the lantern, but the little flame sputtered and struggled so much that it cast barely any light at all. She could only just see the slash of Walter's hand as he said, "Put it out."

Diana stared at him, but he ignored her. He turned his back and started away from her, down the tunnel into the darkness.

"Who does he think he is?" Diana muttered, and held the lamp high. Turn to 247. Swallowed by absolute darkness, Diana followed the sound of footsteps. Turn to 264.

Nowhere would be safe if she didn't take the fight to Tezoca. Steeling herself, she went over to the trapdoor and threw it open.

Beatriz's corpse convulsed, and dozens of tiny insects began to climb out of her eyes, ears, and mouth. They chittered as they swarmed across the floor, and the body deflated, its power escaping.

Stifling a yell, Diana threw herself into the trapdoor, slamming it closed above her. She could hear the skittering of the hundreds of bugs across the stone panel, but it fit snugly enough with the stone panels to either side of it that none of the insects could get through.

To her dismay, Diana found that she was now in absolute darkness. She tried to give it time for her eyes to adjust. The skittering above faded slowly, but no light came to her. Enfield had taken his lamp with him. This was how she would go then: blind.

She took a deep breath, and ran her hands over her body to take stock of what she had. She had the rifle, and she had more ammo for it in a little satchel on her belt.

It was with some satisfaction that she found the small canvas bag was still tied to her belt. Inside, her remaining dynamite. It paid to be prepared. Last but not least, she found her water flask, with a few dregs remaining at the bottom. She drained it in one long swallow. She would need the strength soon.

There was no point in putting it off any longer. Whatever lay ahead, there was only one way through. Bracing herself, she moved forward into the darkness.

As she moved, she found that she was in a narrow tunnel. She let her hands drift along the walls to either side; the tunnel was close enough that she could easily reach both walls at the same time. The stone was natural, uncarved, though the floor felt as though it had been smoothed, either by human artisanship or simply by the passage of many feet over the eons. From time to time, one wall or the other would vanish from her touch. In these times, she felt cool air on her cheek, but always Diana proceeded forward. Forward and down.

Eventually a dim light appeared up ahead. Heart pounding, she couldn't help but hurry to the light. A cavern opened up before her into a large chamber. Stalactites hung from above, and moss grew on the stone walls and ceiling, but what drew Diana's attention was the large pattern carved into the floor. Enfield had said there would be three gates. Could this be the third?

Some of the moss glowed with a faint blue light, giving Diana all the light she had to see by. She moved carefully up to the edge of the pattern. It was a labyrinth, but additional symbols were carved along the path. The writing, if that's what it was, meant nothing to her.

She glanced around. There were several other tunnels leading out of this room, but how could she know which way to go? She regarded the labyrinth again. She had heard rumor of these patterns, maze-like devices carved into the floor, which one must walk in order to receive spiritual insight.

What would she see if she walked the pattern?

Alternately, she could pick one of the dark tunnels at random and quit this place.

Diana moved to the entrance of one of the tunnels. Turn to 263.
Diana placed a foot on the beginning of the labyrinth. Turn to 259.

256

What lies below? Who—or what—is 'she'? Diana asked the question as a side thought; the greater part of her attention was focused upon the turns and whorls of the labyrinth. They seemed to be ever-changing, a mysterious pattern that drew her in farther the farther she went into it. Sometimes it didn't even feel as though she was still in this cave, but rather that she had walked for miles upon miles, crossing landscapes to a distant locale.

She is an ancient evil... a creature of terrible power. In her day, she was named Tezoca, Goddess of the vampires.

In her mind's eye, Diana saw visions loom, hard and terrible, tainted with red. She saw a face of awesome beauty, with hundreds of people crowded all around bowing before her. Then the image changed, and she saw a bloody knife raised high, a man screaming as his heart was ripped out and tossed onto the pile before the Goddess. Looking up, she could see a pile of bleached skulls as large as the temple building itself.

My ancestors suffered much at her hand. But one was born who could speak to the spirits—he was the first shaman, the one who started the line of which I was the last.

Diana nearly staggered at the sorrow that she felt now. She was standing atop a cliff as her people walked to a meeting that she knew would be their doom. She had tried to warn them of the white man's deception, but they had not listened. She watched from the shadows with a heavy heart as the slaughter began. But nothing hurt so much as when a young man was slain… the young man upon whom she had spent her heart, her years, with whom she had shared her secrets. The young man who was to carry on the legacy of the shamans was no more. Her people were no more.

It seemed to be with an effort that the spirit with her wrenched his thoughts back to ancient history. Diana took a deep breath as the visions changed. She could walk again.

The first shaman found a way to defeat Tezoca at last. Many died while overcoming her jaguar knights and other misshapen warriors. But in the end she was brought low. We thought we had chained her forever.

The spirit's thoughts shifted inexorably back to recent history, and with them Diana again felt the terrible sting of his pain. She watched her people die, and in her heart she knew that the Guardian People had failed their sacred trust. The Bled One would now return. Each of their blood was draining into the sands, in each gallon of human blood, a drop of immortal Blood. All those drops moved together, seeking to form once more into something more terrible than human minds could comprehend.

She cannot be killed, but we trapped her by stealing her Blood. With each Arahoca death, a drop of her Blood was released, and she began to waken. If she returns, it will spell the end of the world as you know it.

Diana was making the final turn now. She could see the heart of the labyrinth ahead of her. A tremor shook the cavern. Diana stumbled and almost stepped on one of the lines, but caught herself just in time.

She moves. Time grows short. You must cross through!

Diana stepped forward into the center of the labyrinth. Turn to 261.

257

Josiah knew what he was looking for before he ever saw it. He could see the tunnel clearly in his mind, even though he had never in life laid eyes upon the place. He led his fellow vampires back to the church. Behind the church, a small outbuilding: the place where he had found the prisoners bound, in another lifetime. That, he knew, was where they would find the tunnel.

As he laid eyes upon the church, its steeple looming above him, silhouetted against the night sky, some feeling stirred in him. It was a thought that squirmed beneath the surface of his mind, like one of the insects that ate its way through his flesh. He remembered… once he had… what?

He quashed the half-memory with a snarl of annoyance. Turning to his fellows, he bellowed, "To the tunnel! Our Goddess needs us."

They swarmed ahead of him into the small outbuilding. Their numbers had dwindled in the recent nights, but after tonight, none of it would matter anyway. His Goddess would awaken, and she would lead her armies to conquer the world in flame and darkness.

Another flicker of memory stirred in his mind. A face, whose was it? It was a woman's face, brown eyes, brown hair, strong but smiling. The name Diana floated through his mind.

Yes, she was the one he must destroy. She was the one trying to hurt his Goddess. He followed his thralls into the small outbuilding, where one held a trapdoor in the floor open for him with an eager smile.

Josiah climbed down into the pit. The darkness was pure in this hellhole, but he could still see with an instinct he didn't need to understand. The path sloped gently downward, and he could both see and hear the presence of his thralls clambering forward ahead of him. He sniffed. There was a trace of human here, and blood, and in his heart, he knew this was the path the human prisoners had been taken, where their blood would be given to feed the Goddess as she awoke. Or her servants until she awoke. Josiah licked his lips—perhaps he would find one to feed upon when they arrived.

The nagging annoyance of a thought wriggled up into his conscious brain once again—a memory? He looked down. On his chest was pinned a marshal's badge. He unpinned it, marveling at how silly and pointless such a thing was. Could humans really believe something as trivial as this could hold power?

He held it out, starting to drop it—then the woman's face flashed through his mind again. He was supposed to stop her, to kill her, but she was a friend, wasn't she? What had happened to him?

This badge… it had meant something to him once.

Josiah dropped the badge. It didn't matter. His reward lay ahead. Turn to 268.
Josiah wrapped his fingers around the badge, trying to remember. Turn to 262.

258

"If it wasn't him, what did you see?" Diana asked.

Walter shook his head slowly. "It was him, not any other. Of that I am sure. Yet here he lies. Perhaps I was visited by a dark spirit. Or perhaps I saw only my own madness." He lowered his head and said a few words in the Arahoca tongue, then stood. "There is nothing more I can do for him now."

"Which way—" Diana started to ask, but interrupted herself as she noticed the expression that passed over Walter's face. He held up a hand rapidly to stop her speaking, but she had already fallen silent.

Walter took a few steps, his head cocked. Diana looked around the room, but she neither saw nor heard anything unexpected. She bit back the urge to ask him a question, and instead let him follow the sound that only he could hear.

Walter heard the whispering of hundreds of voices. Turn to 266.

Diana placed a foot on the beginning of the labyrinth. She didn't feel any different as she began to walk. She wasn't sure what she was expecting, but—was that a cold breeze? Or was that just her imagination?

The lines of the labyrinth were seductive to her mind, drawing her concentration as she traced her steps slowly between them. Turn. Turn. Pause. Wheel and turn back. Slowly she lost her sense of direction. Looking down, not breaking eye contact with the labyrinth, she could no longer remember where she had started and where she was going. She knew only the next step on the path.

Turn, turn back. Follow a curve. The sense came over her that she was not the first person to walk these lines. Others had come before her, perhaps many others. Some recently, and others long ago. Long, long ago.

A sensation grew that there was another presence here with her, walking beside her. It wasn't quite as though he held her hand, but it was the spiritual equivalent. He neither guided her steps, nor followed her, but matched her pace for pace.

You have come far.

Not far enough, Diana thought.

Farther than I.

Diana pondered this. The analytical, detached voice in the back of her mind knew she shouldn't be hearing strange voices, but somehow this didn't bother her.

Who are you? Diana threw the words out there.

This time, the response didn't come in words, but in impressions. The first impression was that she didn't need to shout. The next impression was a sense of where to look. She looked—and in a nook in the wall that she hadn't noticed before, she saw a skeleton overgrown with moss. The tattered remnants of leather clothing clung to the rotten frame. In one skeletal hand was held a wooden stick, some feathers tied to the end. The flesh was completely gone, but she could see a decorative nose piercing punched straight through the bony bridge of the nose.

I died many years ago. I failed.

I... I'm sorry, Diana whispered in her mind. *Who were you?*

The last shaman of the Guardian People. With my death, her bonds were all-but broken. Only one of the People remained outside these walls, but that lost soul had no training, no upbringing. He kept his share of the Blood from her, but knew nothing.

Diana felt a quake in the cavern, a deep rumbling that echoed in her bones. Fear rose in her, the fear of a mouse as the shadow of an owl's wings pass swiftly.

You must hurry! She knows you are here.

Diana sped her steps, but she knew instinctively she could not run—not within the labyrinth. Opening her soul to the magic of this place was a spiritual process that could not be rushed. Turn, follow the curve, turn. She was two thirds of the way through, and each step was a battle. She could hear something, like a rushing of water somewhere far away, but close.

The presence stayed by her side, growing stronger the deeper into the labyrinth she moved. Diana cast another question toward that being.

Who are the Guardian People? Turn to 265.
What lies below? Who—or what—is 'she'? Turn to 256.
What of the 'lost soul' who was the last of your people? Turn to 267.

260

Diana started as Walter collapsed. He had made it to the center of the labyrinth, and either her eyes deceived her, or the lines of the labyrinth had begun to glow as he walked it. His limbs had twitched, his head jerked as he walked, and for a time it looked as though each step might be his last. But he had made it to the middle, then stiffened and collapsed.

The mystic light of the labyrinth went out, leaving only the glowing moss to see by. Diana, heedless of the carven lines, ran to Walter and knelt beside him. His eyes were rolled back in his head, but his pulse came steady and strong.

Working her hands under him, she lifted. He was surprisingly light. A lifetime on the run, eating only what he could scavenge, had left him hardened but spare, as though everything he was had been boiled down to nearly nothing.

She lay him on the rock outside the labyrinth and, lifting his head, tilted her water flask to his mouth. Some spilled before he sputtered and swallowed, then he gripped the flask and drank deeply.

"You alright?" Diana asked, taking the flask back. There wasn't much left, and she drank the last of it. She would need her strength before this was over.

He nodded. "I saw... much," he said, his voice surprisingly strong coming from that weak and injured body.

Diana raised an eyebrow. "Want to fill me in?"

Ignoring her, Walter rolled away and came to his feet, stretching. He shook his body as though recovering from a long ordeal, even though it had only been a few moments, and recovered his shirt, pack, and gun belt.

Eventually, he spoke. "Many thousands of years ago, my people lived on this spot, but it was not then as it is now. All this," he gestured with his head at the complex which surrounded them, "was above ground."

Diana eyed the heavy stone above them. "Hard to believe."

Walter shrugged. "Believe it or not. It makes no difference to me."

"Go on," Diana said, waving a hand.

"There was a being then, Tezoca. Something between a Goddess and a mortal. She discovered the secret of eternal life. Life without death. Forever. She enchanted herself with this secret, and gave a weaker form of it to her followers. Together, they cruelly ruled the surrounding land.

"My people, or rather, their forefathers, were the only ones to stand up to her. Well, the only ones to do so successfully. They found the way to kill her followers and bring her low. But Tezoca herself could not be slain or destroyed by any means. No matter what they did to her, her power, her Blood, would eventually return and reform into her.

"So they held her the only way they could: inside their own bodies. Each of the heroes who helped to defeat her took a bite of her heart. With that, they took her power, her Blood, and held it in their own veins. While they lived, they would keep that Blood from her grasp, and as each generation gave birth to the next, they passed down the Blood as well.

"That is why the Arahoca have never left these hills. That is why they have never split off into sister tribes, nor intermarried. They have shepherded the Blood for thousands of years.

"Until your people slew them, and returned the Blood to the earth."

Diana reeled. It sounded like a story from a fairy tale, and yet… she had seen what these creatures were capable of with her own eyes.

"So to destroy her…" Diana began.

Walter interrupted, "You cannot destroy her. She has already recovered enough of her Blood to return to nearly full strength. She waits only the last of it to wake her body and return completely to this world."

"The last of it?" Diana asked.

Walter looked at her, his blue eyes grave. "Mine."

The creature sniffed in the darkness. Turn to 269.

261

Diana stepped forward into the center of the labyrinth. Energy rushed up around her, blowing her hair toward the ceiling. She cried out, feeling herself lifted. A light, so blinding she forced her eyes shut.

It was moving through her, streaming through her, a great river of energy. Too much! She couldn't hold it all. Pain wracked her body as she tried to hold on, tried to stay strong. Her mouth opened in a soundless scream as something burst inside her.

Her eyes fluttered open. It hurt, but she could see so much more now. The energy swirling around was a part of her, it was inside her, and she could reach out through it. She saw the enemies gathering in the darkness below, gathering to fight her, to stop her. She could feel the malevolent presence of the Bled One, as aware of her as she was of it, seething its hatred.

It knew she was coming, and it was afraid.

And she could feel, still with her, even as the massive swell of energy began to fade, the ghostly presence of the shaman who had walked beside her through the labyrinth. She could look at him now, a noble figure, his body decorated with the tattoos and piercings of his tradition, yet his eyes as clear and kind as a summer pool.

You are awake now.

And she knew it was true. *What do I do?*

You must carry on. I am no longer the last shaman.

He was fading. Vanishing from existence. She tried to reach for him. She couldn't do it alone—but already he was too far gone. *Tell me!* She hurled the thought after him. *How do I destroy Tezoca!*

You cannot. But you may delay her, perhaps for a thousand more years, if you destroy her body.

His words drifted back to her mind, and then he was gone. She was abruptly, devastatingly alone. The enormity of her task weighed upon her, and she sank to her knees.

The energy had vanished, at least the great rush of it had. But something was different. She saw now with new eyes. Each stone, each carving in this room had significance, and she understood it now in a way that went beyond words.

She stood, scanning the room. The tunnels, which had once looked identical, now were each distinct to her. She knew which one would take her to the final lair.

Carefully, she traced her way back out of the labyrinth. There was no rush of energy this time, but there was a ritual to it, a proper way to do things. And she knew the way now.

She took a deep breath, sensing the tunnel before her, the walls that would collapse if she made the slightest noise, and the terrible power that lay below, waiting for her. She proceeded without hesitation into the tunnel, moving noiselessly, and as she did, another knowledge settled on her mind.

If she took this path, it would likely mean her own death.

Nevertheless, she persisted.

Josiah knew what he was looking for before he ever saw it. Turn to 257.

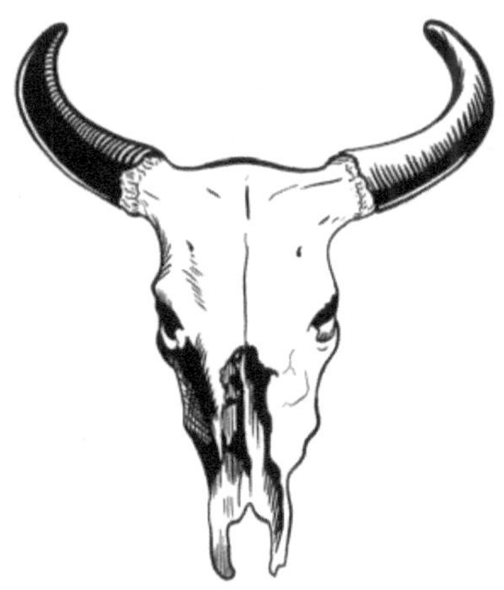

Josiah wrapped his fingers around the badge, trying to remember. The memories came, but each one stabbed at him like a shaft of bright light, burning him as he looked upon it. Yet he looked, because these were not someone else's memories… they were his own.

He remembered an infant, so tiny that he could hold her in one hand. Cora… that had been his own daughter. Something swept over him he didn't understand. He touched one finger to his cheek, where he felt something rolling down it.

His finger came away with wet blood.

Something snarled inside him. Rage and fury so powerful he nearly forgot himself—but in his rage, he gripped the star in his hand until the points dug into his palm. The stinging of the points brought him out of his fury, the physical pain a point of reference in the storm of his thoughts.

He gripped tighter, breathing hard—a force of habit; he knew it was unnecessary for him now. The star bit into his palm. It had meant something to him once.

Kill her. The Goddess's voice echoed inside his mind.

Josiah's consciousness blossomed in white pain. All memories were burned away in that pain. All thought vanished.

The star fell from his hand, and when Josiah stalked forward like death incarnate, he did not look back at the golden badge smothered in the darkness where it had fallen.

Diana stepped out into the red light. Turn to 273.

Diana moved to the entrance of one of the tunnels. The pattern's strange lines and curves gave her a chill, and she did not want to approach it if she didn't have to. On the other hand, each of the tunnels looked much the same as the next.

Moving from one tunnel entrance to another, she peered in. The main room had a dim glow from luminescent moss, but the tunnels were completely dark. Diana flipped open her matchbook, she had perhaps a dozen matches—no more.

The sulfur flared as she struck one match and held it up. The flickering light emanated a few feet down the tunnel, but all she could see was the damp stone walls continuing ahead.

Diana took a few steps into the tunnel. "Hello?" she called.

The sound of her voice struck up echoes which ran down the length of the tunnel, then came back to her amplified louder than it had been before. She heard a groaning, straining sound—vibrations coming in the stones themselves.

A crack tore through the air—shaking Diana to her bones. A great chunk of stone from the ceiling split off, dangling for a crucial half-second before it tore free. Diana leaped back—the stone struck where she had been standing moments before. Shards erupted in all directions, tearing at Diana's skin and clothes. She threw up one hand to protect her eyes.

The thunderous din settled, and Diana lay stunned. She slowly got to her feet as dust rose all around her. She looked back at the tunnel—where there had been an entrance before, now was simply a jagged wall of broken rocks. A shiver went through her as she imagined herself buried under all that stone.

Her match long gone, she regarded the other tunnels in the blue light. For all she knew, any of them could be as dangerous as this one. She turned her attention to the labyrinth at the middle of the room. The patterns had been carved in shallow grooves in the rock, and some of the glowing moss grew in those grooves, making the whole radiate an unearthly light.

Diana took a deep breath. It seemed she had no choice.

Diana placed a foot on the beginning of the labyrinth. Turn to 259.

264

Swallowed by absolute darkness, Diana followed the sound of footsteps. She let her hands drift along the walls to either side; the tunnel was close enough that she could easily reach both walls at the same time. The stone was natural, uncarved, though the floor felt as though it had been smoothed, either by human artisanship or simply by the passage of many feet over the eons. From time to time, one wall or the other would vanish from her touch. In these times, she felt cool air on her cheek, but always Walter proceeded forward. Forward and down.

Eventually a dim light appeared up ahead. They emerged into a large and low-ceilinged cavern, wide enough for ten men side by side. The light, a pale blue-ish green, emanated from patches of moss that grew on the walls and ceiling. It would have been considered dim under any other circumstances, but coming out of absolute darkness, it seemed as bright as the full moon.

Something was carved in the middle of the room. Diana moved closer. It was some sort of ancient symbol, lines carved deep in a pattern that crisscrossed the majority of the floor. She turned to Walter, but her question died on her lips.

Walter was moving to one corner of the room, where a decayed body lay exposed. Tattered clothes in a native style still mouldered on inert bone. Walter knelt next to the corpse, looking at the face. The only distinctive feature was a gold piercing set high through the bone of the nose.

"Dry River," Walter said. He reached forward as if to touch the skeletal forehead, but seemed to think better of it and pulled his hand back. "I thought you…" He shook his head.

"You know him?" Diana asked.

There was a pause before Walter replied. "My grand-uncle. He was my teacher when I was young, for a time. I saw him in the desert… or thought I did. I should have known there was no way he could have survived."

"Were you close?" Diana asked softly. Turn to 270.
"If it wasn't him, what did you see?" Diana asked. Turn to 258.

Who are the Guardian People? Diana asked the question as a side thought; the greater part of her attention was focused upon the turns and patterns of the labyrinth. They seemed to be ever-changing, a mysterious pattern that drew her in farther the farther she went into it. Sometimes it didn't even feel as though she was still in this cave, but rather that she had walked for miles upon miles, crossing landscapes to a distant locale.

Your people called us Arahoca. It is a perversion of the word, the best you can do to pronounce our name. In our own tongue, the word means, 'the Guardian People.'

The voice fell silent, as though pausing to think. In her mind's eye, Diana saw the wide open land of the desert. Sunset stretched across the land, blanketing it like blood. Red cliffs and high mesas dotted the vision, and she moved between them like a ghost, crossing miles in a moment.

We have lived in this land for time uncounted, since the days of the Bled One. Our ancestors brought down the Goddess of vampires. We drained her of her Blood, and with it her power. But she was immortal. Whatever we did, no matter how much of her was destroyed, what remained would gather itself back together and return.

Diana saw a collection of people standing in a ragged line as they approached a shallow pool carved into stone. They approached with dignity, yet resignation. They knew the fate they consigned themselves and their children to as they sipped from the pool. Each quailed as he sipped. A pregnant woman screamed after she took a sip. She fell, her lips stained with Blood.

So we took her power into ourselves. Our greatest shamans cast many spells to protect us and shield us from her corrupting influence. Since that day, each of the Arahoca carries a piece of the Blood we took from her, and the Bled One has remained lifeless in her tomb, deep beneath the sand and stone upon which we walk.

But, what if... what if one of the Guardian People dies? Diana asked.
The Blood returns.

She was making the final turn now. She could see the heart of the labyrinth ahead of her. A tremor shook the cavern. She stumbled and almost stepped on one of the lines, but caught herself just in time.

She moves. Time grows short. You must cross through!

Diana stepped forward into the center of the labyrinth. Turn to 261.

Walter heard the whispering of hundreds of voices. They seemed to come from all sides, some louder than others. He turned his head this way and that, but it made no difference in the volume and direction of the whispers.

Slowly, words began to make themselves audible. At first, he couldn't catch but one in ten, and those nonsense. Then he started to piece together meaning. "Labyrinth… walk… see… Bled One… learn… hear us."

A chill went down Walter's spine as he realized they were speaking the native Arahoca tongue. Other than a few simple prayers he remembered himself, he hadn't heard that language since his mother died. Even the vision of Dry River had spoken in English. That enough should have warned him that something was not right.

Walter glanced once at Diana, who watched him uncertainly. He moved to the center of the room and examined the carvings on the floor. Some were obscured by moss or dirt. He wiped these stains away with his feet, revealing a perfect labyrinth that cut its way through the stone floor of this room. Each smooth, geometric line formed a path that began at the outside and ended in the heart of the great circle, while taking the walker through every part of the labyrinth on the journey to the middle.

Walter knew what he must do.

He shucked off his pack and unstrapped the gun belt. These he lay at the entrance of the labyrinth. He stripped off his shirt and tossed it on his other belongings. Finally, he tied his hair back in the traditional way.

Stripped of every tool that might help him, half-naked, he entered the labyrinth. One foot in front of the other. Then another. His world narrowed until he was aware of nothing except the twisting path. Left, right, a long curving sweep. Each step brought him closer to the center.

Slowly, a warm flush began to spread across his limbs. Was it getting brighter in here? The lines of the labyrinth—they were no longer dark. They glowed with the same blue-ish light as the moss in this cavern. Out of the corner of his eye, it almost appeared as though flames flickered up from the narrow channels carved in the stone.

The whispering grew stronger as he walked. So strong it pressed in against him from all sides, crushing him with the weight and volume of the voices.

It was his ancestors. Dry River was there, and his mother, and a hundred hundred others, each of whom watched him with dark eyes, heavy with the burden of the past, the burden they had carried for so long.

A burden that now lay on him.

That was what he needed to realize. That was what he had come here to find out. The burden of their mission had now fallen to him: last of the tribe. Last of the Arahoca. Last living mortal carrying her Blood.

Walter gasped and nearly stumbled, his chest seizing with convulsive breaths. Images flashed into his mind, so fast and terrible that he could neither block them out nor control them.

He saw an army. They marched toward him through the flames, long-limbed and dark-skinned. They wore the pelts of jaguars over their backs, and carried long spears with wicked-looking points.

As they marched a horn sounded, and Walter was there among them. He spun to see the adversary: at the top of a tiered pyramid a being stood, a woman, her arms flung wide. Tezoca.

He knew the name like he knew his own. It was the name of the adversary. Tezoca, the Bled One. But how?

The long, dark hair of each warrior blew in the breeze as they shoved past Walter, heedless of his existence. They stormed the temple compound, and vampires emerged to greet them. Other beings, vampire brethren with black wings, descended from the sky. The vampires tore and shredded the mortal warriors, but there were many warriors, and for each ten slain, they brought down one of her minions.

The army kept coming, and so did the vampires, until they had destroyed one another. In the end, only a small band of human warriors faced the last of the enemy. Backs to each other, they fought their way up the steps of the temple. They bled. They died. And they fought on.

When they reached the top, only a handful remained: their greatest heroes and leaders. A priest stepped forth (he looked like Dry River) and raised a shining staff.

Tezoca fell before that light, screaming in inhuman pain. The priest stepped forward and, with swift, sure motions cut out her heart. One by one, each of the Arahoca heroes stepped up in turn. Each took a bite of that hideous heart. Each swallowed, and so took into themselves a shard of Tezoca's power.

The Blood.

Suddenly Walter understood. He reached the center of the labyrinth, and he understood all of it.

Diana started as Walter collapsed. Turn to 260.

267

What of the 'lost soul' who was the last of your people? Diana asked the question as a side thought; the greater part of her attention was focused upon the turns and patterns of the labyrinth. They seemed to be ever-changing, a mysterious pattern that drew her in farther the farther she went into it. Sometimes it didn't even feel as though she was still in this cave, but rather that she had walked for miles upon miles, crossing landscapes to a distant locale.

He... carries the Blood, but little else. There was one who survived the death of the Guardian People. She was daughter to the chieftain. One of the white men kept her, as a point of pride, nothing more... My niece.

Diana could feel the pain of his loss. In her mind's eye, she saw a little girl laughing and playing. The girl grew in her memories, memories that she saw... but were not her own, and before she knew it she saw the girl-child—now a young woman—dancing with a dashing young man barely older than herself. Each of them laughed. The vision flashed and changed, and she saw them dying.

I thought she had been slain. If I had known... I found out later, only after her child with the white man was born, that she had lived. Yet even his birth gave me hope. As long as he lived, the Blood of the Guardian People lived on in him, and the spell would not be broken.

Walter Korse… Diana thought, and the spirit knew her thought. He knew, too, when she remembered Korse's death. Diana felt his stab of pain as if it were her own.

Then we have truly failed. The Guardian People are gone. All of us. It falls on you now. My people can help you no more.

Diana was making the final turn now. She could see the heart of the labyrinth ahead of her. A tremor shook the cavern. Diana stumbled and almost stepped on one of the lines, but caught herself just in time.

She moves. Time grows short. You must cross through!

Diana stepped forward into the center of the labyrinth. Turn to 261.

268

Josiah dropped the badge. It didn't matter. His reward lay ahead. His face split in a grin as he shook his head to shake it of the troublesome thoughts that still clung to his mind like spider webs. None of that mattered now. His Goddess would see to him.

Holy zeal flared within him as he stalked down the tunnel, trailing shadows behind him like a cloak. His minions stepped aside as he moved, getting out of his way before he needed to say a word.

The miles of the tunnel passed swiftly, devoured by his quick pace, and the thralls needed to jog to keep up with him. He knew they were descending deeper than he had ever been before. And with each step his power grew, as he drew closer to his Goddess.

He passed many branching tunnels and open spaces, but at each intersection, he knew which way to go. At times, he was almost tempted to stop out of curiosity and examine some wonder of this underground world, but that temptation was small compared to the driving need to protect his Goddess. He continued until he saw a light up ahead. Reddish. Checking the memories that were not memories, he knew this was the sacred cavern where his Tezoca, the Bled One slept. He knew her name, as he knew her: intimately.

Kill her. The Bled One's voice echoed inside his mind.

Yes, my Goddess. His lips cracked into a grin, and he stalked forward, death in his heart.

Diana stepped out into the red light. Turn to 273.

The creature sniffed in the darkness. It smelled something important. Blood? Yes, but more than that. A scent that it knew. That it worshipped. Alone, its mind felt sluggish, uncertain. It sensed capacities it had nearly forgotten, the capacity for speech, for thought. It craved interaction, a chance to remember what it could do, but there was no time. It was needed.

It broke into a loping run. There was no light in the tunnel behind the church, but it didn't need light. It moved with instinct, calling upon memories that were not its own, and went swiftly and surely.

After a time of darkness and running (it found that it could unerringly choosing the correct path from among the many branching tunnels) it emerged into a chamber filled with red light and heat. Many new scents filled this place. Smoke and brimstone, blood, death, decay… and that other. This was where it needed to be. This was where it had been called. To protect. It needed a weapon…

Some instinct guided its hand to the tool at its hip. The grip felt comfortable in its hand. Lifting, it drew out a gun.

Gun… yes. It savored the word, rolling it around in its mind. It remembered guns. It gave its hand a gentle flick, and the gun spun in its hand, then came to rest. It extended its elbow in a smooth motion. Yes… that was called aiming. Its hands were good at guns.

But that scent still teased at its mind. It holstered the gun and followed the unknown scent. The trail led up a few stairs to a massive stone box. Settling its hat firmly on its head, it leaned in to look into the container.

Its eyes filled with wonder. "My Goddess," it whispered.

They came out into a massive underground cavern, burning with heat that made Diana sweat. Turn to 276.

"Were you close?" Diana asked softly.

Walter regarded the dry corpse. "You could say that. Other than my mother, he was the only Arahoca I ever met. He taught me the ways of the land, how to hunt, how to track, how to move without being seen."

"I'm sorry," Diana said.

Walter turned to her, his eyes a dark glow. "For what? For the massacre of Red Bluff? Or for the rape of my mother? Or are you, perhaps, sorry that you benefitted from these things?"

Diana took a step back. "I didn't—I'm sorry he's dead. That's all."

Walter looked to be about to say something more; then he stopped and looked around, cocking his head. Diana followed his example and scanned the room, but she neither saw nor heard anything unexpected.

Walter took a few soft steps, listening.

"What is it?" Diana asked. He held up a hand to silence her, following a sound only he could hear.

Walter heard the whispering of hundreds of voices. Turn to 266.

Josiah whirled and shot the sniveling professor. Enfield's eyes went wide and he staggered back. His fingers went to the red flower blooming on his chest. Then his eyes rolled back in his head and he fell.

"How dare you?" Josiah snarled, stalking forward. He landed another shot in the professor's prone body—which jerked like a live thing as the round landed home.

A terrible rage rose inside Josiah, and for a moment, he wasn't sure if the rage *was* him, or was directed *at* him. Finally, the Bled One's voice rose in his mind. *What are you doing?*

Panic choked Josiah. He had to please her. She couldn't be unhappy with him! He fell to his knees, groveling before the presence of that ancient awareness. Yet under that feeling was something else… hatred. Hatred which could give him strength, if he needed it.

Her voice flashed again, clear and strong in his mind, though coming as if from across a vast distance. *Stop wasting time! The woman is escaping!*

Josiah's head snapped around. Where he had left the woman, bleeding, dying, there was now only a smear of blood on the stone.

He could see it all so clearly in his mind. The injured Diana, crawling away as his attention was on the professor. Shaking her head to clear it of the pain—which would have scattered droplets of blood, droplets that he could follow. Even now she would be hiding not far away, regaining her strength, but weaponless.

He could track her, sniff her out. He was on the verge of rising to do so, but something roiled inside him, an unwelcome feeling he could not entirely blot out.

Then the Bled One forced her way into his mind. *Rise, my Chosen One! Rise and destroy her!*

Josiah focused on the voice of his mistress and rose to destroy her enemies. Turn to 285.

Josiah dove deep inside himself, hunting that feeling he couldn't name. Turn to 280.

272

Diana watched the dynamite burn down. A wild laughter erupted inside her. The Bled One wracked at Diana's brain, trying to make her stop the dynamite, but the ancient being didn't understand it well enough to know what command to give to make Diana's recalcitrant body undo what she had done.

Somewhere inside, Diana knew she should try to get away, herself, to move, even to fall down—anything. But it was a distant urge, somehow meaningless.

Take it out! I'll give you anything! The voice wailed.

Diana smiled through gritted teeth as she said, "No."

The dynamite blew.

Epilogue. Turn to 284.

273

Diana stepped out into the red light. A large, open room of hard, black basalt opened beneath her, with a narrow shelf of stone stairs descending to floor level. Lumps rolled in loose semi-circles on the ground, where lava had flowed, cooled, and hardened mid-stream. Black stalactites hung from the ceiling, many hanging low enough to crack a skull, while other large stalagmites rose from the ground, piercing through the shapes of cooled lava.

Fresh, hot lava still burned and flowed in a stream, coming from the back of the room and arcing down one side before vanishing underground once more. That red river curled around a tiered, black dais at the apex of the chamber. Atop the dais crouched a massive stone sarcophagus. Something dripped in a slow, steady rhythm from the ceiling into the open sarcophagus.

A chill went down her spine. That's where she would find what she sought.

"Diana!" A voice roared. She instinctively ducked behind cover, even as her heart sank in her chest. She knew that voice.

Josiah.

Bullets rang out—they ricocheted off stone behind where she had been moments before, sending up sparks. Diana swore and glanced out quickly. There she saw Josiah standing with a group of vampires amongst low-hanging stalactites, his face abnormally pale and misshapen in death.

The marshal laughed, and Diana felt her heart sink. She hadn't realized how much she had come to rely on this man she had come to call friend… until now. A lump rose in her throat. She could hardly bear the thought of him trying to stop her, to kill her. Of him changed. Her skin crawled.

The laughter turned into orders, and she heard feet moving. Feelings would have to wait—this was a time for action. She steadied her trusty rifle, finding a nook in the stonework where she could brace it.

She came up slowly, stealthily, scanning the terrain. Josiah still stood, feet planted, in the center of the room. Behind him, that great sarcophagus rose on its dais, flanked by flowing lava. Vampires were spreading out around him, some moving into cover, while others advanced on her position.

She drew a bead on one of the vampires moving forward and fired. It was a clean shot; the bullet took him and he dropped. For once, the other vampires showed some fear of their own mortality. They broke off, scattering for cover.

"Shoot her!" Josiah roared, but she was already hiding once more. She cranked the action on her rifle to reload it.

"You can't win, Diana. You must know that," Josiah called.

Diana emerged and fired in one smooth motion, taking down another vampire. This time the return fire came more quickly, peppering the stones around her as she ducked back down.

Could he be right? She was in a defensible position. Good, solid cover protected her. Stairs off to one side led down to the cavern floor below; anyone attempting to reach her could only do so by coming up those stairs. With her own rifle in hand, she could make them pay to take this position.

But could she hold it against all of them? She didn't know. And that assumed she was facing human opponents. Opponents who could be killed by bullets. Not… whatever Josiah was now.

She rose and shot quickly—missing—then ducked. This time, she came away bleeding. She hadn't felt anything, but the blood was running down her face. She touched her scalp—a sharp shard of stone, kicked up by a bullet, had cut her and gotten caught in her hair.

"Get up those stairs and get her!" Josiah snarled.

They were coming for her now. She could hear their grunts and the scuffing of their feet as the little band approached. There was only one thing she could do. She jerked open her bag of dynamite, grabbed a stick and lit it.

Josiah gnashed his teeth as the explosion blinded him. Turn to 281.

274

"Hey ugly," Diana cried out. She had come out of cover and was running straight toward the sarcophagus at the far end of the room.

That got his attention. The vampire that had once been Josiah started running toward her on an intercept course, instinct overriding even his understanding that he could simply use a gun. The gun fell from his hand as he put on an extra burst of speed, and Diana's heart gave a frightened jolt as she realized how fast he could be.

She made a hard left, jogging to change her course, and dove into a murky corner where several stalagmites gave the opportunity for stealth.

Josiah tore after her, but she didn't wait for him to search the area. As soon as his eyes were off her, she darted to another hiding place.

"Diana," Josiah called, his voice low and menacing. Words were returning to him.

She leaned heavily against a rock, trying to steady her racing pulse and ragged breathing without giving her location away by panting like a sweating dog. She looked over at Walter. He was still groaning, crawling on the floor. Still alive.

"Diana, you can't hide from me," Josiah's voice came. Judging from the sound of it, he was closing on her. "I can smell you. Wherever you go, I'll be right behind."

Diana looked down at her sweaty clothes and swore mentally.

The creature could smell now, better than it ever had been able to before. Turn to 300.

275

Walter lifted the heart to his mouth and took a bite. The thing smelled of rotten flesh and graveyard earth. Warm Blood spurted from the heart into his lips. It was like biting an overripe plum, except for the flavor: syrupy and salty, too salty. Underneath it all, a thread of decay. He took another bite, nearly gagging. It took all his strength to chew the rotten flesh, tough and unyielding in his mouth.

The Blood seemed to just keep coming. It poured from the open wound in the heart, way more Blood than the thing could reasonably hold. It choked him, flooding his face. He couldn't force himself to swallow it all.

I can't do it! He threw the thought into the air, on the verge of panic.

The Arahoca were by his side. Their spirits were with him, going back to the very first. *You can. You must.*

Walter took one more bite, and gagged. It was so thick and viscously disgusting, smelling of graveyard earth and tasting of ash and bile. Some of the stuff leaked from his lips, then he coughed, and more spilled out.

His hand trembled as he tried to lift it for another bite, and his body rebelled. He had done all he could. His arm started to drift downward. He had failed.

Then Diana was by his side. She wrapped her two hands over his one… and brought the heart to her own lips. Walter looked into her eyes, steady and determined, as the Blood burst into her mouth. A flare went through her. She shuddered, chewed, and swallowed.

The break gave Walter time to clear his mouth. Encouraged, he forced himself to take another bite, hot and rich and terrible.

Together, they finished the heart. They did not stop until they had consumed every last drop of the Blood. When it was done, they stood looking at each other over bloodstained lips. Walter could feel the spirits fading.

Diana wiped her mouth. "What did I just do?" she asked.

Epilogue. Turn to 299.

They came out into a massive underground cavern, burning with heat that made Diana sweat. Narrow stairs descended to a floor marked by the rippling bulges of cooled lava. Stalagmites rose through the layer of lava, hinting that this had once been a natural cavern.

A single river of burning red, molten lava flowed from the back of the room and along one side of the chamber before vanishing into an opening in the stone once more. Tucked within a curl of that deadly river rose a broad, tiered dais. At the apex of that dais crouched a sarcophagus, huge and black and ancient.

The ceiling of the cavern here was slick with blood, all of it flowing slowly— sometimes against gravity—toward the middle of the room. Above the sarcophagus a single large stalactite hung. As Diana watched, a droplet of blood fell from the stalactite into the open sarcophagus. Then another. And another.

Diana gripped Walter's arm. "We have to stop it."

He wasn't looking at the sarcophagus. Instead, his eyes scanned the room. The only light in this cavern came from the molten lava, and shadows cloaked the edges of the space. Diana realized a small army could be hiding in those shadows, and she unslung her rifle.

Walter turned to her. He gestured to the rifle and said, "Cover me." He started down the stairs, his own gun at the ready.

Diana nodded. She took position behind a ridge of rock that would give her cover and sighted down the rifle. If anything emerged from the shadows, she would get at least one good shot before it got to Walter.

The last Arahoca stepped out cautiously into that expanse of black, rolling stone left by ancient lava flows. His gun was holstered near his left hand. His bandaged right hung open, as though waiting to grab something. Diana fervently hoped he remembered not to try and use it.

Before he was halfway across, a shape burst from the shadows. It looked low, feline. Diana fired without waiting to analyze the threat. Her rifle cracked. It was a good hit. The creature dropped and rolled from the impact of her bullet; then it rolled to its feet and came up standing on two legs. A gun arm emerged, aiming at her.

Diana gasped. It couldn't be.

A second gunshot tore the air, and Diana's rifle exploded in her grip. Shards of wood shot into her face and hands. She fell back behind the rim of stone, crying out.

"You," she heard Walter say in a low hiss.

"You," a deep voice replied with an amused twist. Diana's heart sank as she recognized that voice. No, no, no, no…

Once she got her eyes clean of splinters, she looked down. Walter stood, facing off against Marshal Josiah da Silva.

"You don't want to do this, Josiah," Walter said softly. Turn to 282.
Walter drew and fired. Turn to 290.

Josiah took the shot himself. He was a fair shot, and at thirty paces, he couldn't miss. He barely had time to see a black hole appear in the brim of the hat before it leapt back, whirling in empty air, and fell out of sight.

She wasn't there.

A rifle retort sounded, loud in the enclosed cavern, and one of the thralls fell. Impossibly quickly, another shot cracked, and another fell.

The thralls' guns spoke in a staccato of answering shots, but the idiots were shooting blind. They had no idea where she was, and each was shooting in a different direction. Josiah cursed, kicking and beating at them, but even he didn't know which direction to point them. Another dropped while he tussled with the idiotic survivors.

Clenching his jaw, he forced himself to stop and look. Another thrall fell beside him.

There. The flash of powder gave it away. She was hiding in the rocks and shadows some twenty paces from where she had left her hat. He lifted his own gun, but at that moment her rifle cracked again, and Josiah's gun snapped out of his hands. It clattered against the rocks nearby, a smoking, twisted piece of metal, as useless as the ore it had been mined from.

Another thrall died. The others were firing back, but they were useless and he knew it. Sometimes if you needed something done right, you had to do it yourself.

Josiah moved toward the woman, heedless of the rifle rounds that flew past him. He knew his thralls were all dead when the first shot hit him. He staggered briefly, then grinned. There wasn't even any pain, just a kind of pressure. He touched the wound—it was closing already.

Another shot sank into the clay of his flesh, with as little impact.

He looked up. He could see the whites of Diana's eyes now. He stalked toward her, heedless as another rifle round planted itself in his torso.

He grinned as she cranked the chamber with swift motions, getting her next shot ready. It took her only a moment, but as she lifted the gun, it was already too late.

Josiah ripped the rifle from her hands. Turn to 287.

The people huddled together as if for warmth, though the summer evening was warm enough. As the last light of day began to fade, one of them began crying. A priest moved among them, though his wild hair and countenance did not seem to bring comfort.

He murmured as he passed, touching the heads of children and adults alike, "Blessed and holy is he that hath part in the first resurrection: on such the second death hath no power, but they shall be priests of God and of Christ, and shall reign with him a thousand years.

His voice continued, rising and falling, but the others were paying no attention. As one, their heads lifted at a sound from outside. Terror was writ in the lines of each face.

"And when the thousand years are expired, Satan shall be loosed out of his prison, and shall go out to deceive the nations which are in the four quarters of the earth," the priest intoned, his eyes fixed on some distant point.

Footsteps—the door to their hiding place flew open. A scream cut the priest off. No one could say which among them had screamed.

A man stood before them. He was dressed as a lawman, but his grey eyes glinted with cruelty. He smiled. "Well, well, well, what have we here?"

"Please!" The plea was automatic, reflexive, and wasted on this man.

The old priest held up a cross in shaking hands. He stammered, "And I saw a new heaven and a new earth: for the first heaven and the first earth were passed away, and there was no more sea."

The marshal ripped the cross from the priest's hands. The old man staggered back, gasping, and fell, clutching his heart. The newcomer crushed the cross in one hand and, in a voice as ancient as the devil himself, continued where the old priest had left off, "I saw a new city, a new Jerusalem, coming down from God out of heaven, prepared as a bride adorned for her husband. And God shall wipe away all tears from their eyes." He stepped among the terrified people, brushing away the tears from a young woman's face as he moved. "There shall be no more death, neither sorrow, nor crying, neither shall there be any more pain: for the former things are passed away."

A moment of stillness gripped the small company, as the marshal stared into the distance, a look of sublime satisfaction on his face.

"Does that mean you won't hurt us?" a small boy asked.

The marshal smiled at him. "Nobody will ever hurt you, ever again."

With a few swift blows, the man who had once been Josiah da Silva killed the last living humans. He drank of their blood, and the Bled One was pleased. As he finished draining the last of them, he could hear her armies approaching, the tramp of their marching loud enough to shake the world.

Josiah dropped the boy, his young blood still fresh on his cheeks, and said, "Behold, I make all things new."

The End

279

The bottle clinked to the table. Walter did not take his hand away. He would need it again.

The ache of injuries never fully healed was dulled but not absent. Diana was absent. He thought rarely of the woman; they had long since parted ways, and she was just another featureless figure from the past. Just another fading memory. His little cabin was empty save for him and his drink.

So it was almost a relief when the door swung open that night and a man wielding a hatchet stepped in. Walter struggled up, half-heartedly reaching for his gun, but the man ripped it away.

"The Bled One sends her regards," the man growled. "The Blood always returns."

Walter's mouth moved, but no sound came out.

The hatchet rose and fell.

The last thing Walter saw was his blood leaking out into the thirsty dust.

The End

280

Josiah dove deep inside himself, hunting that feeling he couldn't name. It grew stronger, and the presence of the Bled One grew fainter as he closed his eyes to focus. But he still couldn't quite grasp it. A flash of memory—a locket? He couldn't quite say.

There had been a man, someone he hated. For what? What had the man done?

He felt a snarl from the Bled One, but her voice couldn't reach his mind now, no matter what clamor it raised.

Then another voice, one all too real and human, reached his ears. "Josiah, you don't have to do this! You were a good man—you are a good man! Fight it!"

Diana. The name flashed into his mind. He knew her. He knew who she was. They had… what? He couldn't remember. They had traveled together?

A wave of bloodlust so vile it nearly made him vomit rose in him. He wanted to kill, to hunt, to drink thick blood. Diana's blood.

No!

He could remember her now. She was a friend.

He sank to his knees, fighting the wave of nausea and hunger, the intense need of his desire to kill.

You cannot resist me. You are mine! I own you! Tezoca's words broke through his distraction at last, searing his mind. He stiffened in agony, a silent scream on his petrified lips.

"Josiah!" He heard Diana's voice as if through a dream.

Josiah's heart was pounding. He hadn't felt a heartbeat in so long… Something was burning his chest. He thrashed with one hand, trying to grab the thing and get it off him. Then his hand closed around a cross.

Instantly a flood of peace washed over him. The pain faded away, and he knew what he had to do.

"Diana," he croaked. It took all his strength to form the words. "Destroy her."

The Bled One redoubled her efforts, and Josiah felt his strength weakening. Pain wracked his mind, his spirit. But it could not touch that safe place at the heart of him. Nothing could touch him there.

He allowed his body to collapse and prayed that Diana might succeed.

Diana stared at Josiah's torment. Turn to 286.

281

Josiah gnashed his teeth as the explosion blinded him. A cloud of dust and debris obscured his vision. He almost coughed reflexively, before his body's instincts reminded him he didn't need to breathe, and he waded into the dust cloud, snarling.

He ran into one of his thralls. The man's hand had been blown off, and blood ran down a cut on his face. He was gibbering and cursing, holding his arm.

"Get it together!" Josiah slapped the man and shoved him in the direction he knew the stairs to be. "Kill her!"

He stumbled over another body. The dust was clearing now, and he could see the dynamite blast had felled several of his thralls. They were running low in number at last. He didn't need them, but he didn't like losing them so quickly.

A vague memory troubled him. He… he himself had killed many of the thralls, before…

Josiah shook his head. He hadn't been in his right mind then. He couldn't be held responsible for what he had done before.

What mattered now was to kill the woman.

He grabbed another surviving thrall and, shoving him ahead, mounted the stairs—only to come up short. The woman was gone.

In a fit of rage he turned on the thrall. "You lost her!" he roared. "You let her escape!" He picked the vampire thrall up by one hand. The man kicked his boots against the wall, his hat tumbling free. He croaked something unintelligible.

It would be so delicious to destroy this one right now. To suck the blood from its worthless carcass…

He saw a flash of movement from near some rock formations in a distant part of the cavern. The Goddess must be protected. He set the thrall down and slid closer, all senses alert. The woman was here somewhere, and she was not to be underestimated.

The remaining thralls gathered in a tight cluster, seven or eight of them. They were laughing at the one who had lost his hand. "Here pick this up!" one said, holding a large rock with two hands. The maimed one, giggling, grabbed one side of the rock with his one hand. Of course, it fell as soon as the other released his hold. They all laughed, including the injured one.

Josiah lashed at them with his voice. "Step lively! She's still here somewhere!"

In a moment, they transformed into vicious predators. They dropped into crouches, eyes flashing red, searching. Those who had guns whipped them out, and all peered into the shadows of the cavern, scanning for the human.

Sticking up from behind a rock, some thirty paces away, Josiah saw a brown hat. It was her hat. Victory crowed within him.

Josiah took the shot himself. Turn to 277.
Josiah hissed at the thralls and gestured them to circle around and cut her off. Turn to 291.

282

"You don't want to do this, Josiah," Walter said softly.

The marshal looked the same in each particular, but the overall effect was completely different. His face was abnormally pale and misshapen in death. He moved with predatory grace, with an evil glint in his eye. A low chuckle was his only response. It had all the gravity of Josiah-of-old, but was cruel in a way that the marshal had never been.

"I want the same thing you want," Josiah said. The words came slowly, as though he was trying them out, reaching for each one before he said it.

Walter grimaced. "What's that?" he asked. He hovered his hand near his gun.

"Blood," Josiah said, his voice a low growl.

"I'm not like you," Walter snarled.

Josiah moved forward, into dueling range. "Aren't you? You've spent your whole life seeking blood."

"I spent my life seeking justice," Walter said.

Josiah shrugged. "Call it what you will."

"It's not the same!"

"How many innocents did you kill along the way?"

Cora's face appeared in Walter's inner vision. He tried to push away the memory. His fingers clenched over the gun.

Josiah continued, "Not just my daughter." He laughed, a low, evil sound. "You'd like it to be that easy, wouldn't you? You forget your victims: the family, the friends, the wives and the children. Anyone who got in your way. You killed without thought, without mercy, without conscience. We could use a man like you." Josiah grinned.

Against his own will, Walter found a succession of faces flashing across his mind. Blood, violence, death. He had always been a killer. He felt lightheaded. He said, "They were defending evil men. Murderers. Rapists."

"Face it, Walter. They were in your way."

Walter drew and fired. Turn to 290.

"Why not?" Walter said. "I'll throw in."

He felt the exultation of the presence that engulfed him. He laughed tolerantly. "What do I do?" He said out loud.

Step forward. Extend your hand. The voice came in his mind.

Walter approached the sarcophagus. As he did so, a spider crawled up onto the lip of the stone monument. *Allow the spider to bite you. She brings you my gift. Immortal life.*

"At what cost?" Walter asked.

The sun will no longer be your friend. Food will no longer satisfy you. Darkness and blood will be your meat and drink. But in exchange, you will have power. The power to create and destroy worlds. With my power, you will rule this pathetic land.

Walter shrugged, and held his hand out to the spider. The thing crawled up on his arm, but it didn't stop there. One leg at a time, it ascended his arm to his neck. Walter rolled his head to the side to give it access.

It crossed his mind that she could kill him now. Then another voice answered, so what? What did he have to lose?

"No!" Diana croaked, behind him.

He looked back to meet her eyes. "Sorry," he said in a nonchalant tone.

The spider bit. Walter gasped as the toxin flooded his system. *Yes!* Tezoca's voice exulted in his mind. *The change begins!*

Epilogue. Turn to 289.

A little girl woke with a scream. She sat in bed, heart pounding in her chest, until her mother opened the door. The gentle light of a lamp brought warmth to a bed and room too big for the small body that occupied it.

"What is it, child?" The mother asked, her warm hand on the girl's cold knee.

"I dreamed, mother," the girl said in a breathy voice. Her pupils were still dilated, focused on something far away.

The mother touched her daughter's hair and set the lamp beside the bed. "Tell me," she said.

The girl took a few shaking breaths, trying to cross between the worlds of sleep and wakefulness. At last she said, "There was something terrible. Terrible. A monster. It… was waking up. It was hungry, and old, and it… it wanted to eat all of us."

The girl was shaking, and the mother gathered her up in her arms and held her. "It was just a dream. Shhh, just a dream."

The girl squirmed free and said, "No mother! It wasn't just a dream! It was real! But it's okay, because a woman stopped it."

The mother got that feeling again, the feeling she had felt from time to time since her little girl had been old enough to talk. That feeling that the child knew too much.

The girl sat up straight and said, "A woman, and two men. They stopped it. They killed it, and we're all going to be okay. But they died."

"It's just a dream, child," the mother said, no longer patient with her daughter's whimsy. She lifted the child and tucked her back under the covers. The girl did not protest. Finally, the mother patted her daughter's cheek and said, "Now get some sleep, okay? And don't disturb Mommy with these dreams anymore."

The girl scowled, but the scowl vanished with a kiss from her mother. As her mother reached the door, she said, "Mommy?"

"Yes?" the woman stopped, silhouetted in the doorway.

The girl made a little frown. "It's going to be okay for now, but someday it will be back. What's going to happen then?"

"Don't worry, dear. I'm sure someone else will take care of it then. Now you get some sleep."

The End

285

Josiah focused on the voice of his mistress and rose to destroy her enemies. His fingers flexed with new power as he felt the Bled One's pleasure radiating through him.

The professor was nothing now—a cooling corpse lying on the floor. He stepped over it, calling softly, "Diana, where are you? Come out, kid. It'll be easier in the end."

She did not reply, but his heightened senses picked up her breathing. It was rough, ragged, laced with adrenaline. The sound inflamed him.

He stalked toward her scent, hunting, seeking. It was thick, growing stronger, leaking out from behind the rocks.

There.

She was hiding behind one of the stalagmites, not far from the Bled One's dais and sarcophagus. The river of lava ran behind her, making the huge stalagmite a dark silhouette against the red glow.

With lava on one side, and the stone on the other, she was trapped.

"Josiah!" she called out. He did not reply, but amusement danced within him at her futile efforts. "Josiah, you don't have to do this!"

He resisted the temptation to tease her with a reply, but instead eased himself forward, drawing silently closer to her location. He heard another sound now. Something burning? He could smell the smoke, a faint wisp on the gentle currents of air in the cavern.

He was almost to her now. The heat from the river of lava bathed his skin. The woman was sweating—he could smell it. And her breathing was so close. The bloodlust began to rise in him. In a moment, just one more moment, then he could seize her, and her blood would flow between his teeth, rich and—

She moved, and he followed, growling with the pleasure of the hunter. He leaped forward and pounced to the spot where she had been—she stood facing him a few paces ahead, feet planted.

He grinned and drew himself to his full height, slowly, luxuriously. There was no way she could escape him now. He could hear the burning of the lava, the crack and snap of stone melting and hardening and melting again. The heat of it glowed toward him; he could see it red on her cheek, making her look even more flushed than she already was. "So, you've decided to give yourself up?" he drawled.

She shook her head. "Just waiting," she said calmly.

Josiah's eyes narrowed. He briefly scanned the room. No one else was here. He would have heard them.

Suddenly his ears picked a different sound out of the background noise of the lava cracking. He looked over. A stick of dynamite sat perched on the side of the stalagmite, its fuse rapidly vanishing.

"Goodbye, Josiah," Diana said.

Josiah started to move, to snarl words—but no sooner had the thought formed than the dynamite blew. The force of the explosion couldn't hurt him, of course, but it hurled him ten feet backward. In that moment as he flew through the air, he felt the heat of the river of lava radiating up from beneath him.

He landed and felt the superheated stone folding up to encase him. The Goddess howled.

Diana watched as her former friend sank into the lava. Turn to 297.

286

Diana stared at Josiah's torment. The strong man was on his knees, hand clutched around something hanging from his neck. His face was a rictus of agony. As she watched, he slumped to the ground.

His words still hung in her ears. Destroy her. Destroy the Goddess. But how?

Diana turned to face the mighty sarcophagus, high on its dais. Her head still rang from her injuries, but Josiah's courage inspired her. She could not let her friend down.

She stepped forward, and placed one foot upon the stairs.

Instantly the weight of the Goddess's mind crashed down upon her. It was ancient and terrible, filled with bloodlust and the rage of being encased in a nightmarish prison of nothingness for ages. Now, its moment had arrived, and nothing would stand in its way. She herself was less than nothing, the tiniest of gnats, a minor inconvenience.

Diana quailed under that onslaught, her knees nearly giving out. Then she thought of Josiah's face, of his suffering, and she forced herself back up to her full height.

She took another step.

Rage blasted at her, and pain, yet Diana did not yield. Every muscle was on fire, yet she pushed forward, taking a third step, to stand adjacent to the sarcophagus on top of the dais.

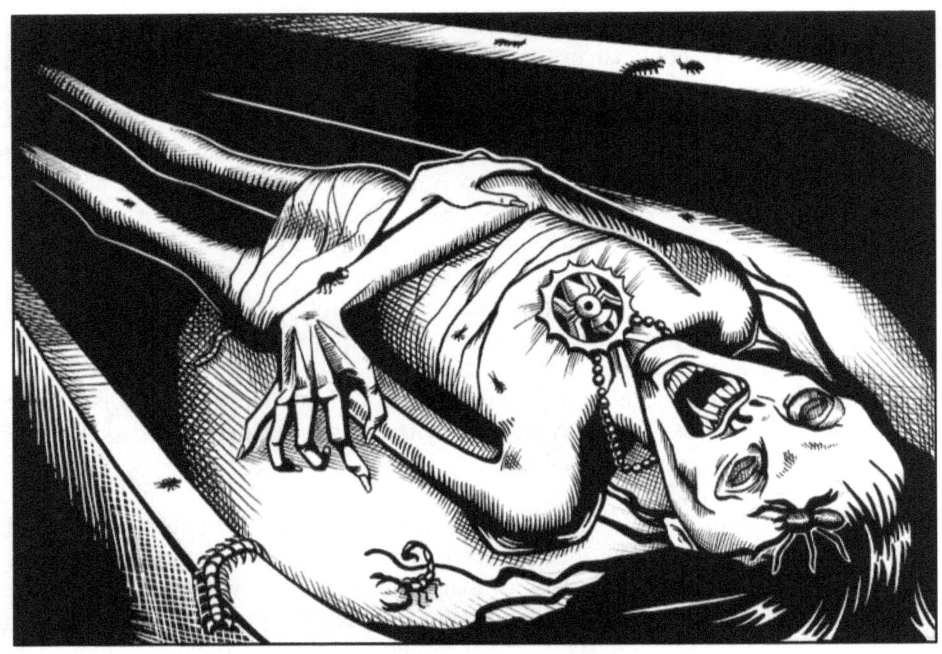

From here she could look into that ancient stone tomb. A wasted body lay in its depths, skeletal arms crossed over desiccated chest. Only the heart still beat, a glowing red pulse that emanated from the depths of the hollow husk.

And then the Goddess gripped her mind, and there was nothing Diana could do.

You think you can defeat me? the voice came, terrible and powerful. It towered above her, awesome in its might and depravity, and Diana quailed. *You can do nothing. You are nothing before me.*

Panic welled up inside Diana, and she turned to run—but she could not move. She could not flinch. She could not take a single step to save herself.

No… her baby. If it were only her, perhaps she could give up, but she was fighting for two. She pushed with all of her strength, and a bead of sweat rolled down her cheek.

She failed to move.

The Bled One's laughter resounded in her ears. *Come to me,* the voice said. *Come to me, and be Blessed.*

Against her own will, Diana found her legs moving. One foot inched forward, taking the final step to bring her up alongside the sarcophagus. Close enough to reach in. She heard herself whimper.

Insects rose out of the sarcophagus. Some of them buzzed and flew. Others crawled. A centipede swarmed up onto the stone lip of it, followed by a spider of impossible dimensions, each leg moving with deliberate slowness as it pulled itself up to watch her.

Place your hand in my mouth.

There was nothing Diana could do. She struggled, fighting with everything she had, bringing each possible ounce of her strength to bear—but she could not refuse that command.

She could, however, do a little something along the way, something the Bled One had not expected. Something of her own.

She felt the Goddess's pleasure as she lowered her hand into the sarcophagus. She shuddered as she looked at that gaping, skeletal mouth, and slowly her hand descended into that mouth.

Her hand—holding a stick of burning dynamite.

At last Diana let herself consciously perceive what she had done, and in that moment, the Bled One recognized it as well. There came a howl of rage and fear, and for a single, exultant moment, Diana was free.

She shoved the dynamite into the corpse's gaping mouth.

How dare you! The ancient voice wailed.

Diana dove away. Turn to 295.
Diana watched the dynamite burn down. Turn to 272.

287

Josiah ripped the rifle from her hands. She jumped away, terror flashing on her face, but she was slow, pitifully slow. He grabbed her by the wrist and threw her against the stone wall.

She hit it with a soft, sickening sound (some part of Josiah's mind, deep inside, cried out) and slid to the floor, stunned.

Josiah laughed. "You've got fight in you," he said. "You will make a good servant to the Bled One."

Diana muttered something, but only blood came out of her mouth.

"What's that?" Josiah asked with mocking civility.

She spoke again, and this time her words, though slurred by blood, came out clearly. "Josiah, I know you can still hear me in there. You don't need to do this. You don't want to do it. Fight it, Josiah."

He clubbed her alongside the head with the butt of her own rifle. He didn't like the worming, writhing feeling inside himself that he felt when he listened to her speak, and he wanted to shut her up.

It worked. She slumped to one side, blood now leaking from a cut on her scalp as well. It flooded her face, wet and red. The scent of it made him hungry.

He lifted her rifle. He had to finish this. Before she said something that really got to him. "Goodnight, Diana. If you're lucky, the Bled One will bring you back, as she has me." He grinned. "Just think, we could work together again!"

"Go to hell," Diana growled, her voice weak.

Josiah pressed harder with the rifle, shoving her head against the stone wall. His finger hesitated, nearing to the trigger. He snarled. He just had to do it.

"Don't!" A voice called from behind. "Please!"

It was the slimy, tremulous voice of that professor, Garland Enfield. Josiah looked over his shoulder. The skinny professor stood shaking like a leaf. His face was twisted, as though bearing some terrible strain.

Fury rose in Josiah. How could this little worm dare? How could he presume to tell *him* what to do? He snarled in rage and placed his finger on the rifle trigger. He could feel the bloodlust rising in him, the Bled One's influence, filling him with power and the desire to kill.

Josiah whirled and shot the sniveling professor. Turn to 271.
Josiah centered his aim on Diana and pulled the trigger. Turn to 293.

288

Walter took another step forward. He was aware that spittle dribbled from his lips, but he could do nothing to stop it. All his will was bent on taking a third step.

Then he heard her howl in his mind. She redoubled the pressure upon him, and he could not move. His vision went white. Vertigo swam about him. He felt that he would vomit.

In the blindness, he groped, one hand for the other. He could not move on, but he would. He would.

He grabbed his right hand with his left and twisted.

Searing agony shot out of the broken wrist. The agony cleared his mind. Panting, he looked at the sarcophagus and smiled.

With glacial implacability, he began to move again. Nothing now stood between him and his destination.

Wait, the voice said. *I can make you an offer. I will give you anything.*

Oh? Walter thought. What will you give me?

Anything you want. Everything. You are strong, human. Your soul has been forged in the crucible of suffering. You have strength most humans can only dream of. You could be greatest among my champions.

"Why should I do that?" Walter growled. The words sounded strange out loud; the first real sound he had heard in this long struggle. He was aware of Diana watching him, pale and trembling.

Eternal life. I can give you that. I know the secrets, and no other does. In that life, every imaginable pleasure. Power. At my side, we will rule the world. I can give you what no one else can. A second chance.

Walter paused, breathing heavily. The searing pain from his broken wrist still ran, an undercurrent keeping his mind fresh, but it had faded to the background. He kept his left hand on the break though, just in case she tried again to control him.

He was hesitating, and she sensed his weakness. "How do I know you'll keep your word?" he asked.

I have the power to give. I need lieutenants. I can't do it all myself. You will be the strongest general I have ever commanded. And you will receive greater rewards than all the others put together.

Walter closed his eyes. Why was he here? What did he want? He had come here angry, seeking only to destroy the next thing that appeared in front of his eyes. Was that all he wanted out of life? To destroy?

An offer like this wouldn't come a second time.

"Why not?" Walter said. "I'll throw in." Turn to 283.

"My mother would never forgive me," Walter said. Turn to 296.

289

As night fell, the frightened survivors of Fairfield gathered in the Bad Dog Saloon. The mayor was gone; the sheriff was gone. Only Mama Nell and her shotgun held the town together.

The howls came with the darkness. Almost before the sun had completely vanished, the bloodthirsty whoops came ricocheting through town, followed by those who had died and been turned. Old Farmer Hank was out there, and Preacher, and that card shark Slick. Even Sam, that big damn woman who had tried so hard to protect the town. She was one of them now.

"You ain't gonna take us easy!" Mama Nell shouted. The men and women who surrounded her clenched their jaws and their guns. A child whimpered.

From out of the darkness stepped a tall, whippet-thin man. He spread his hands and looked up. It was the outlaw, the Killing Angel, Walter Korse.

In a silky smooth voice, he said, "Please struggle. It makes it more fun."

The End

290

Walter drew and fired. Josiah fired too—and Walter knew before it was over. The marshal was too fast.

The shot took him just below the ribcage. Walter coughed, and blood came up. The gun slipped from his fingers. Josiah's grin swam in his vision.

No…

Josiah was walking toward him. "The Blood returns, Walter. Some of it just takes longer than the rest."

The world spun, and suddenly the ground was coming up to meet Walter very quickly. He didn't even feel the impact. It wasn't that the shot hurt. It didn't hurt that much. It just took something out of him, something he didn't know how to do without.

Josiah was standing over him now. Walter laughed a bloody laugh. "I always knew… you would be the one to finish me."

"So did I," Josiah said. He aimed the gun at Walter's head.

"Hey ugly," Diana cried out. Turn to 274.

291

Josiah hissed at the thralls and gestured them to circle around and cut her off. With the supernatural sympathy of those who share blood, they understood his silent signals. As a rough pack, they started to move to circle around the place where the woman hid, while Josiah himself circled the other direction.

If she fled from them, she would run right into him, but if she saw him and tried to escape, it would land her right in the clutches of the thralls.

They were eager, their eyes still flashing red, fangs out and dripping with the desire to feed. Soon, he thought. Soon, they would all have their fill of her red blood.

A shot rang out—something was wrong. One of the thralls fell. Josiah looked around the cavern, but he could not see where the shot came from. Another—and another thrall collapsed, dead.

Josiah snarled as a third shot cracked, loud in the cavern, and he leaped forward. The hat had not moved, but that was not where the shots were coming from.

His thralls were dropping like flies. Brutal killers they were, but here they were caught in the open, and they were too hungry to get into cover. They ran this way and that, looking for the threat and dying.

Josiah ground his teeth and scanned, waiting for the next rifle shot.

There—the flash of powder gave her away. She had taken up position in the rocks and shadows some twenty paces from where she had left her hat.

Her back was to him.

As she killed the last of his thralls, he used the time their deaths bought to move up closer, staying stealthy until the last possible minute. She felled the last thrall just as it found her position, and reloaded her weapon.

He could hear her breathing, her muttering. She scanned the cavern—she did not know where he was! He laughed as he stepped forward. Eyes wide, she brought the gun around. Too late.

Josiah ripped the rifle from her hands. Turn to 287.

292

Walter bit off a curse and threw the heart into the lava. It sailed through the air and landed, steaming, on the red surface of the molten stone. The lava cracked, blackening briefly, and then the heart went up in flames.

"That ought to do it," Walter muttered.

The voices were gone now, both the Arahoca and Tezoca's. Walter turned back to Diana, who was gathering herself, pale and breathing heavily.

"Is it over?" She asked, looking at the burning heart as it sank into the molten lava.

Before Walter could answer, an earthquake shook the cavern. Chunks of stone fell from the ceiling. As they met each other's gazes, another, stronger tremor rocked the ground.

"Let's get the hell out of here," Walter said, and they ran.

Epilogue. Turn to 279.

293

Josiah centered his aim on Diana and pulled the trigger. The crack of the gunshot ricocheted through him, followed quickly by an exultant rush—the Bled One. She was waking now, growing stronger.

The woman before him (a flicker of memory? He could no longer tell) slumped in death.

You have served me well, the voice of the Goddess whispered inside his mind. *Unlike this one. Kill him.*

Josiah turned, and in the terror of the professor, he saw his own power. The little man had fallen to his knees, crying. "Forgive me!" he wailed. "I only had your own best interests in my mind!"

He was talking, Josiah knew, to the Bled One. And with just as much certainty, he knew the Goddess did not forgive.

"She has no mercy for the likes of you," Josiah growled. He fired Diana's rifle.

It was over in a moment. The man who had raised the Bled One was now dead. But she had a new servant now. A tool better and more fitting than any who had come before. He let the rifle fall from his grip and turned toward the dais, raising his arms overhead in exultation and surrender.

Epilogue. Turn to 278.

294

"That's right, just one more step!" Diana coaxed her little girl with a treat. The baby's eyes, laughing as she stumbled through the last few steps, melted Diana's heart. "That's good! Good! She made it all the way to me!" she called to the next room.

The door opened, but the voice she expected did not appear. Diana turned, and the words died on her lips.

Enfield stood in the doorway. He looked taller somehow, more confident. Powerful.

Diana gasped, stepping back and clutching her baby tightly to her chest.

"Is that… my child?" Enfield asked, his voice soft.

Gunshots tore through the night, not far away. Screams.

The vampires were here.

The End

Diana dove away. She felt the presence of the Bled One clawing at her mind, her body, trying to drag her back, drag her to suffering and death. For a moment, panic and despair flooded her—then she looked up, and saw Josiah's face, still contorted in the agony of his resistance, and she steeled herself to fight.

It was like pulling herself free of molasses. First one hand, then one foot.

Then the explosion came, knocking her flat, and the resistance vanished. She pulled herself up and half ran, half scrambled away, as tiny bits of decayed bone and flesh fell all around her in a soft, disgusting rain.

She stumbled down the stairs, ears ringing something terrible. The sarcophagus' wall had protected her from the direct blast, but it could not protect her from the blast to her ears, the smoke stinging her eyes and the soft bits of debris clinging to her hair. She quickly brushed her hands through her hair, trying to get the worst of it out. She nearly cut her finger on a moldering shard of bone, and shuddered in revulsion.

Josiah was panting on the floor as she came up alongside him.

"You're breathing," she said, kneeling.

He looked up, and his eyes were the same clear grey she remembered. His face was pallid, covered in a sheen of sweat from the struggles of his resistance.

"Are you alright?" she asked.

His face contorted in pain as he clutched at his chest. "My heart," he gasped.

Diana put her finger to his neck. His skin was pale and clammy, but there was life in it. Life as she had never seen in the vampires before. Her eyes went wide. "You have a heartbeat!" she said.

Josiah glared and opened his mouth to respond, but instead, a look of surprise and disgust came over his face and he rolled over and vomited. Thick black sludge came out, with the half-concealed shapes of insects still wriggling inside it. Again, and again he spewed the stuff. He kept retching long after the last of it had come up, then collapsed, chest heaving.

Diana pulled him by the arm away from the sludge, not letting it touch his skin or hers. "How do you feel?" she asked.

He struggled to a sitting position and nodded. Still panting heavily, that was all he could manage.

Diana looked at him closely. Color was returning to his skin. Could it be possible…? Could he return to humanity, after all he had gone through?

Then she saw the cross, glowing faintly underneath his shirt. Its white, gentle light shone through the fabric.

"It's a miracle," she breathed.

His hand gripped her shoulder, and a moment later a small tremor shook the cavern. "We need to move," he said.

Another earthquake struck then, stronger. The whole cavern rocked, nearly knocking Diana over, and bits of rock began to crumble from the ceiling. Gathering her balance, Diana pulled herself up—fighting the ongoing shaking—and got her hands under Josiah's arm to help him up.

The rocking of the earth stopped just in time for them to race to the exit. Diana started running toward the stairs she had descended into the cavern, but Josiah pulled her up short and pointed into a shadowy corner of the room. "Another way!" he croaked.

Diana had little choice except to trust him now; to go back the way she had come would be to struggle through a long, arduous passage with untold dangers. So she acquiesced and followed him.

Another earthquake struck. Diana cried out as a large stalactite broke free just ahead of them—then Josiah's strong fingers gripped her arm and jerked her to one side. They collapsed together as the stone crashed to the floor where they would have been standing. Huge shards of rock scattered for dozens of feet in all directions, but none cut or injured them.

Diana met Josiah's eyes, and for some reason, both started laughing. They disentangled and helped each other up, then ran for the dark opening.

Epilogue. Turn to 301.

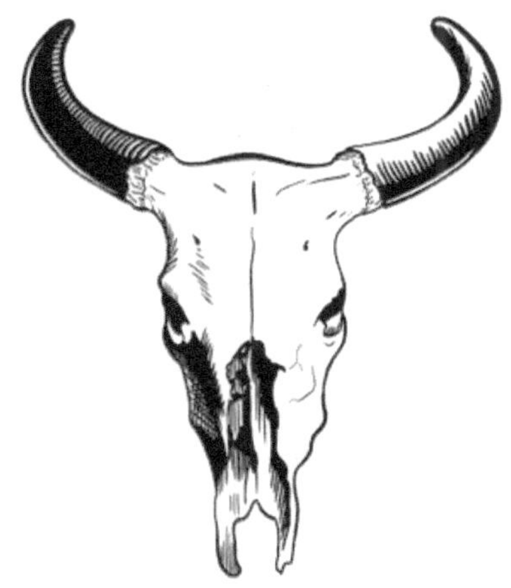

296

"My mother would never forgive me," Walter said. He could hear the voice in his mind scream as he stepped forward. She placed resistance in his path, but he parted it like water.

As he moved, he felt voices gathering in the distance. He knew these whispers. They tugged at the edges of his mind, just like they had in the chambers above. There was Dry River among them. And beyond him, more faintly, his mother's voice. He could still recognize it, after all these years.

Tears stood in his eyes as he stepped up to the edge of the sarcophagus. The Bled One's screams faded into whimpers as the gathered voices of the Arahoca rose in strength all around him.

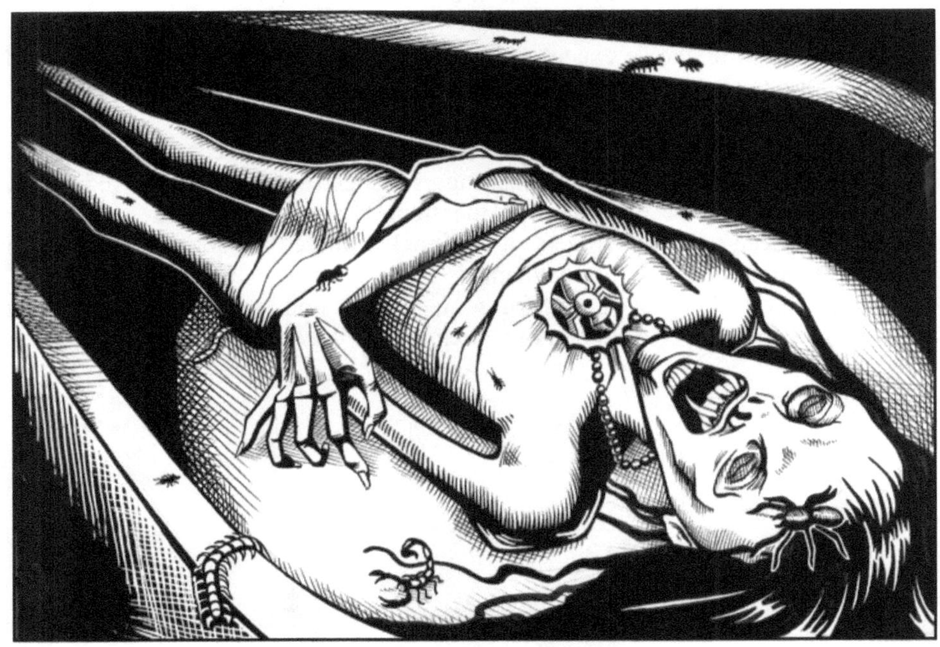

Inside the sarcophagus lay the tattered husk of an ancient corpse. No longer recognizable as even male or female, it was simply dried skin stretched over brittle bone. The face was decayed and drawn into a hideous, toothy snarl. Insects crawled around the desiccated remains, in and out of holes in the body.

"Pretty one, ain't you," he muttered. He crushed a centipede that was climbing the rim of the sarcophagus toward him. "What do I do?" he whispered.

All of a sudden the voices surrounding him gained in volume and power. Walter's head flew back. They were with him, all of them, going back to the very first Arahoca, thousands of years before. He saw the chieftain stepping up to the top of the pyramid temple, and he saw what he did there.

Walter knew what he had to do.

He drew a knife and reached into the sarcophagus. With the tip of the knife, he scraped aside loose flesh and bone—to reveal a beating, pulsing red heart.

Walter took a deep breath. He closed his eyes, whispering a prayer in his native tongue. Then he plunged his hand into that chest and ripped out the heart.

Tezoca's voice screamed in his mind, but she was a tiny wind in the gale forces of the spirits of his ancestors. Her voice was swept away by their chanting. *Eat the heart,* he could hear them say. *Take the Blood.* His own mother stood before him. *I'm sorry, my son. It falls on you, now.*

The heart pulsed red in his hand, thick droplets of Blood falling from it. His hand was coated in the stuff. He nearly gagged just looking at it.

Walter lifted the heart to his mouth and took a bite. Turn to 275.
Walter bit off a curse and threw the heart into the lava. Turn to 292.

Diana watched as her former friend sank into the lava. The red glow of the molten stone faded to a black crust wherever it touched him, as his body sucked the heat from it. Then the thin black crust cracked, the cracks a glowing spider web that revealed the burning heart of the lava underneath. And he sank deeper.

Josiah's clothes burst almost immediately into flames. He could not feel pain, so he simply stared at her as flames licked over him and his body sank, his face expressionless. But fire rose and his skin blistered before it entered the hot demise.

Right before he vanished, she thought she saw a twinge of pride in those inscrutable eyes.

Diana turned away, heart pounding. She was alone now... Enfield had died to save her. He had... why did he do it? Josiah was gone now, and even Walter. It was up to her.

A sinking feeling in the pit of her stomach, she turned to face the mighty sarcophagus. It sat, mocking her in its massive invulnerability, atop the broad dais at the end of the chamber.

Her heart quailed, and somehow she knew that if she approached that dais, she would not survive. She brushed that feeling aside. She no longer had any choice. She had to do what she had to do.

Her head still ringing from the explosion that had barely missed her, she stepped forward and placed one foot upon the stairs.

Instantly the weight of the Goddess's mind crashed down upon her. It was ancient and terrible, filled with bloodlust and the rage of being encased in a nightmarish prison of nothingness for ages. Now, its moment had arrived, and nothing would stand in its way. She herself was less than nothing, the tiniest of gnats, a minor inconvenience.

Diana quailed under that onslaught, her knees nearly giving out. She couldn't move. She couldn't think. The tried to fight, but it was useless, and somewhere in her gut, she knew it was useless.

She tried to cry out—and couldn't even make that feeble noise.

Suddenly all resistance ended. Her body hung limp, subject to the Bled One's will. She could feel that malevolent presence inside her, exulting in its own power. It had won. She had lost. And it had been so quick. She hadn't even been able to put up a real fight.

Arrogant human. A voice resounded in the vaults of her mind. *What did you hope to accomplish by coming here?*

Diana quailed. That presence didn't expect an answer. They both knew it was a futile, hopeless endeavor from the beginning. Diana felt a tear rolling down her cheek.

So, what should I do with you? Turn you, and make you serve me? Or will you be my first meal?

Diana struggled, but it was like the pathetic tremblings of a fly caught in a spider's web. She felt the Bled One's laugh more than heard it.

Come to me, the voice commanded.

Against her own will, Diana took a step forward. Crying out inside her mind, she bent every part of herself toward fighting it. Her body trembled. She stopped the forward momentum for a moment, and almost fell. She had to put her foot down to stabilize herself—she had taken another step closer.

She could see inside the sarcophagus now. A wasted body lay in its depths, skeletal arms crossed over desiccated chest. Only the heart still beat, a glowing red pulse that emanated from the depths of the hollow husk.

And then the Bled One gripped her mind, and there was nothing Diana could do.

You think you can fight me? the voice came, terrible and powerful. It towered above her, awesome in its might and depravity. *You can do nothing. You are nothing before me.*

Panic welled up inside Diana, and she turned to run—but she could not move. She could not flinch. She could not take a single action to save herself.

No… her baby. If it were only her, perhaps she could give up, but she was fighting for two. She pushed with all of her strength, and a bead of sweat rolled down her cheek.

She failed to move.

The Bled One's laughter resounded in her ears. *Come to me,* the voice said. *Come to me, and be Blessed.*

The final step came quickly. Diana was running out of fight. It brought her up alongside the sarcophagus, close enough to reach in. She heard herself whimper.

Insects rose out of the sarcophagus. Some of them buzzed and flew. Others crawled. A centipede swarmed up onto the stone lip of it, followed by a spider of impossible dimensions, each leg moving with deliberate slowness as it pulled itself up to watch her.

Place your hand in my mouth.

There was nothing Diana could do. She struggled, fighting with everything she had, bringing each possible ounce of her strength to bear—but she could not refuse that command.

She could, however, do a little something along the way, something the Bled One had not expected. Something of her own.

She felt the Goddess's pleasure as she lowered her hand into the sarcophagus. She shuddered as she looked at that gaping, skeletal mouth, and slowly her hand descended into that mouth. Her hand—holding a stick of burning dynamite.

At last Diana let herself consciously perceive what she had done, and in that moment, the Bled One recognized it as well. There came a howl of rage and fear, and for a single, exultant moment, Diana was free.

She shoved the dynamite into the corpse's gaping mouth.

How dare you! The ancient voice wailed.

Diana tried to move, to leap away, but the ancient will seized her again, holding her tightly. Diana just smiled. She wouldn't go alone.

Diana watched the dynamite burn down. Turn to 272.

Diana watched the end, breathing heavily. For all the one-time marshal's new strengths, his thinking had been as simple as a child's. She had used the oldest trick in the book, and the vampire had fallen for it. The air currents in here weren't strong, but they were enough to bring the scent of her clothes to it, and to keep her own scent away, and that was enough.

The thing that had once been Josiah sank into the lava. The lava turned black and cracked where Josiah's body sucked the heat from it, and flames licked up the vampire, crackling skin and causing hair to sparkle.

Before the lava swallowed him completely, she thought she saw something like a flicker of pride in her old friend's eyes.

May he rest in peace.

Diana recovered her clothes, dressing quickly. She was glad that, if she was going to die, it wouldn't be naked. That done, she returned to Walter, who lay bleeding where he had fallen.

"What did you do?" he asked. The effort made him cough. A little blood appeared on his lip, but not as much as before.

"It doesn't matter. He's gone. Are you okay?"

"I'm alive," Walter grunted. He forced himself up to a sitting position, pain flashing across his face. "Help me up."

"Are you sure?" Diana asked dubiously.

"It's not over." He turned his eyes toward the sarcophagus.

Diana put her shoulder under Walter's good arm and heaved. Once he was standing, Walter pushed her away. He swayed, but held his feet. He nodded once. His face was pale and sweat beaded on it.

"You need rest," Diana said.

"The only rest is death," Walter said. Eyes burning, he took a step forward.

The sarcophagus loomed before them atop the dais, black and menacing. Diana's courage wavered, but a glance at Walter's face—a mask of pain and determination—renewed her spirit.

As they took their first step up onto the dais, suddenly the weight of the Goddess's mind crashed down upon her. It was ancient and terrible, filled with bloodlust and the rage of being encased in a nightmarish prison of nothingness for ages. Now, its moment had arrived, and nothing would stand in its way. She herself was less than nothing, the tiniest of gnats, a minor inconvenience.

Diana quailed under that onslaught, her knees nearly giving out. She couldn't move. She couldn't think. The tried to fight, but it was useless, and somewhere in her gut, she knew it was useless.

She tried to cry out—and couldn't even make that feeble noise.

Suffer. The voice echoed in her mind, ancient and implacable as these stone walls themselves, and Diana erupted into pain. Every muscle in her body clenched. Her head was thrown back, hands wrenched into claws. Dimly, from the corner of her eyes, she saw the cords on Walter's neck stand out as he suffered the same fate.

Obey. The voice came again. It was a Goddess she heard now, impossible to fight, impossible to win. She found herself kneeling, terrible joy rising in her at the prospect of obeying the one to whom she belonged. Beside her, Walter was kneeling as well.

Then, incredibly, the maimed prisoner forced himself to his feet.

The voice lashed again, *Stay down!* The full force of it didn't even hit Diana, and yet her mind reeled under its power.

Walter simply shuddered, and took a step forward. Fire was in his eyes, the kind of fire Diana had never seen.

Suddenly the presence turned on her. *Stop him!* It demanded. And she wanted nothing in the world more than to do so. She started to rise, but somewhere inside a tiny seed cried out to her. She hunted through the haze for that seed, and found it when she looked at Walter's face. If he could fight, the least she could do would be to not interfere.

Once she made up her mind, the rest followed. No matter how much the presence in her mind lashed and wailed at her, she refused to move. She would not do its bidding. She found that she was crying with the effort of determination.

She would not surrender.

Walter took another step forward. Turn to 288.

299

Sun rose over the Red Bluffs. Diana sat on a stone, watching the morning light creep across the landscape. She was aware of little things in ways she never had been, before. The sound of insects scratching in the dirt. The slow bloom of leaves as spring rolled forth. The way her child smelled.

That child, Siratha, played in the dirt not far away. Any passerby would have thought either of them were simple natives. She smiled. It didn't matter. She had found a home at last.

"Ready to eat?" her man called. He had once been called Walter, but that name, like so much else, had been left behind. Diana stood and gathered her child in her arms and returned to where he sat stewing rabbit over a cook fire. The tent behind him was still mussed from their night's pleasures.

Siratha ran to her father as soon as Diana set her down. The tall man whisked her off the ground and held her up to look at the sky, muttering lessons about birds and seasons. He was no longer the same starved whipling she had met so many years ago. He had healed and filled out, growing into a muscular, determined man. Determined, and skilled enough to keep them alive in this desolate landscape.

They had to stay here. Just as the Arahoca before them had had to stay. They had to watch over the tomb. It wasn't over, it wouldn't ever be over. But as long as they carried the Blood, the world would be safe.

Diana stood next to her family, looking out at the landscape of black and red mountains and valleys. In the distance she could see the white salt flats she had once crossed to come here. She placed one hand on his arm, and he set the child down. The little girl ran to the cookpot, smelling it with an exaggerated sniffing motion.

"What is it?" he asked, looking into her eyes.

Diana placed his hand upon her belly. She smiled.

His eyes grew wide, and he threw his arms around her. He gathered her into the air with a whoop of joy and spun them in the sunlight.

The Blood would go on.

The End

300

The creature could smell now, better than it ever had been able to before. It had also remembered words. It liked those. It could put them on like humans put on clothes, but that's all they were. One more tool to use.

It's hand itched, and it wished it hadn't dropped the gun. Foolish. On the other hand, this way it would get to tear apart the woman with its bare hands. That was good. It liked that. It found that it was salivating. What would her blood taste like?

If it tasted anything like her scent, it would be delicious. She smelled salty, musty and sweet. The tang of adrenaline ran under the rich scent of sweat both old and new. And underneath it all, a womanly scent it didn't fully understand. Nor did it care; it followed the aroma like a hunting hound.

It paused, listening in the stillness. Nothing. Nor did sight give it any clues. But it needed neither. Sight could mislead; hearing could lie; but scent would always tell the truth. She could not hide, not while it could smell.

It moved forward slowly, sniffing the gentle currents of air in the cavern. There. A fresh odor came from upwind. It grinned. The foolish human didn't know enough to stay downwind of it.

Placing each foot carefully, silently, it approached the hiding spot. The scent was close now. Delicious. It could almost taste her blood. The woman was hiding behind a large stalagmite next to the river of lava. It could not hear her, but it could smell her there. Smell her fear.

It sniffed one more time. Yes. She was there. It opened its mouth in anticipation—and pounced.

The far side of the stalagmite was hot with the nearness of the lava, hot and empty. Confusion ravaged its mind. Where was the woman?

On the ground a sweaty undershirt lay discarded. Near it lay other clothes, the overshirt, pants, undergarments… What had she done?

Instinct flared and it turned downwind—it found her.

The kick took it in the middle of its chest. The last thing it saw was her snarling face as her naked leg propelled it into the lava.

Then heat consumed it.

Diana watched the end, breathing heavily. Turn to 298.

301

Dawn rose over the wasted town of Affliction. In the rubble, two figures moved. An aging man hunched in the dust, dry heaving. His hat perched beside him on the jutting spar of a burned out building, showing a balding crown.

Nearby, a woman stood, facing the sun, watching it rise over all that was left of this place, a place men and women had once called home.

"Are you alright?" She asked, and the man nodded. She helped him to his feet. He flinched only slightly as they looked at the sun.

They took the day to rest and gather their strength. Their path would take them across the Devil's Anvil, and that was a walk best made in the cool of night. They spoke little, until dusk approached, bringing with it refreshing coolness that invigorated both of them. Their words punctuated the gathering darkness like firecrackers—little bursts of life in a dead world.

At last, they gathered themselves. The sun lowered and, with him leaning on her arm, they marched out into the desert. It would be a long walk home, but they were through it all at last.

The sun glowed, huge and red as it sank to touch the mountains. Their shadows stretched before them to the horizon. After all, they were safe.

Diana scratched a bug bite on her elbow.

The End

Ashton MacSaylor (formerly Ashton Saylor) is a gamebook enthusiast, writer, teacher, and irrepressible optimist who married his artist, moved with her back to his hometown, and had a kid. For the past three years, his main goal was to finish "The Good, the Bad and the Undead" before this amazing photo of him got too out-of-date to conscionably be used as his author bio pic. He lives in Ojai, CA with his wife, their baby, and two cats.

Jamie Thomson is a writer and games developer. He has written novels, game books, computer games, radio plays, comics and TV and film scripts for all sorts of ages. His works have been translated into many languages and sold all over the world. He has 30+ published books to his name. One of his kids novels, Dark Lord: the Teenage Years, won the Roald Dahl Funny Prize.

Thanks to all the backers from Kickstarter who helped make this book possible. And special thanks to:

Zombies
Dave Polhill, Michaela Elschner-Krüske, Alexandre Trentini Nunes da Silveira, James Saxon, Max Witkowski, Kevin La Bounty, Erik T Johnson, D. J. Cole, LEUNG Chun Pongm James Gross, Thean See Xien, Jens Kaufmann, Mary Goldman, Justin Philbrick, Meg Elison, Namit Kaura, Tanner Eugene Knull, David Falcon, Daniel Nissman, Michael Stikeleather, Dominic Marcotte, Steven Pannell, Frank Zepp, Magnus Johansson, James O'Grady, Kamarul Azmi Kamaruzaman, Michael Wireman, Yune Lee, David Marr, Anders Svensson, Campbell Pentney, John Lamar, Luke Heckenkamp, alp aziz torun, Sonia Nordenson, Cornelis DeBruin, Matt Leitzen, John Lambert, Elise Roberts, Charles Burkart, Simon Brault, Stephanie Wagner, Seth Bradley, Michael Green, Scott Maynard, Craig Wright, Jessica Tan, Demetrius Babson, and Zamira Kristina Skalkottas

Cowboys
Galit Alterwein, Jay Hann, Ellen Walsh, Gatille Fabrice, Alasdair McNelly, Rodney Leary, Lee Barklam, Stuart Lloyd, Jonas Smith-Strawn, Graham Hart, Mr Joseph Snape, Douglas Robb, Jonathan Caines, Eric Applewhite, William Rowe, Poom Pathonsmith, Jenny Parham, Kathy Hillman, Adrian Jankowiak, Andreas Froening, Nick Breeze, Bechard Stephane, Ken Nagasako, Chris Bones, Graham Dawes, Vicki Hsu, Anders H. Pedersen, Matthew Taylor, Judith Kashman, Jeffrey Joiner, Max Kanat-Alexander, Michael Reilly, John D Jones, Finbarr Farragher, Tara Saylor, Porter K Ludwig, Jeremy Stock, Casey McBeath, Cary W LeMonds, and Charys Saylor

Vampires
Ben and Jenny Morrow, Wendy Knyphausen, and Adam Feibelman

The Gunslinger
Teófilo Hurtado Navarro

www.ingramcontent.com/pod-product-compliance
Lightning Source LLC
Chambersburg PA
CBHW050822190726
48286CB00007B/1965